First Traitor

America is on the verge of World War III and the vice president of the United States is a traitor bent upon world domination. His plot to conspire with America's enemies and bring the world to its knees seems foolproof. The conspirators have planned for everything - everything but Lieutenant Commander Jake Gregory of SEAL Team 5.

As the plot unfolds, Russia sorties her entire pacific submarine fleet, placing her nuclear ballistic missile boats dangerously close to America's West Coast. The President of the United States orders two battlegroups to intercept the enemy threat. A major war at sea ensues, thrusting the world to the brink of a nuclear holocaust.

Just when it seems things couldn't get worse for America, it is discovered that Russia has secretly traded nuclear missiles to Iran, missiles the Iranians intend to use against the United States and her allies. American bombers are launched for a pre-emptive nuclear strike and only LCDR Jake Gregory can turn them back.

D1429792

FIRST TRAITOR

JEFF WADE
LIEUTENANT COMMANDER, UNITED STATES NAVY (RET.)

BULLET BOOKS

Chula Vista, CA

Copyright © 2003 by Jeff Wade

BULLET BOOKS ® and colophon are registered trademarks of Bullet Books.

ISBN: 0-9747955-0-X

Library of Congress Control Number: 2003115441

Cover Design by Jeff Wade and Doug Brandenburg
Back Cover Photo by Scott Wright

Manufactured and printed in the United States of America

10   9   8   7   6   5   4   3   2   1

To the brave men and women of the Armed Forces of
the United States of America

Acknowledgements

A few people were instrumental in getting this book into print. Some offered constant encouragement and some provided much needed technical expertise. Special thanks go to my mother Jean and my wife Mary for their belief in this project. They rallied my spirits all along the trail. Don Roy is a dear friend and ensured the aviation related scenes were as close to the real world as is possible in the fictional account you are about to read. Doug Brandenburg created the graphics and typeset the manuscript. His technical expertise in graphics and the printing industry are largely responsible for turning my manuscript into a book. Lastly, I'd like to thank Cathy Purdy of Bookmasters for guiding me through the publication and distribution process.

Prologue

January 23, 1968, Moscow

NIKKI MAKAROV SLIPPED on the deserted icy street and fell forward onto her hands and knees sending her camera skittering across the frozen pavement. She hardly felt her bleeding knees through the numbing cold of the wintry Moscow night as she slid to a stop in the middle of the tiny side street. Seconds ticked away as she remained motionless on her hands and knees trying to decide if she should surrender or keep running.

Her pale blue eyes darted from side to side as she frantically looked for someplace to hide. She saw nothing but walls and sidewalk and there was no one in sight to ask for help. The few streetlights that were still working cast eerie looking cones of light onto the pavement and illuminated the blowing sleet as it swept mercilessly in her direction. A few windows in the apartments above the empty shops lining the street were lit, which helped the feeble streetlights break the darkness' hold on the night. In spite of the late hour Nikki could see a block in each direction.

Nikki knew that physically she was nearing the end of her endurance. She wouldn't be able to outrun the secret police. She felt trapped. She'd never before been in such a jam.

At five feet eight inches tall and one hundred twenty pounds the twenty-two year old agent was the kind of woman who made men stop and stare. Auburn hair curled softly around her angelic face in the popular western pageboy haircut. Usually, the men around her melted in her presence and she got her way without having to rely too heavily upon her near-genius IQ. That was not going to be the case today. These men were intent upon killing her.

Slowly, she struggled to her feet and ran to the other curb where her camera had come to rest. Dressed only in her skimpy waitress outfit, the cruel arctic wind slashed into her nearly naked body like a million angry needles. To make matters worse she was barefooted. Her high heels weren't made for running, so she had shed them in the bar as she bolted out the back door. Her feet had been so cold at first that she had cried. But now she couldn't even feel them.

Shivering uncontrollably she crossed her arms across her chest for warmth and gripped the camera tightly to her chest. She ran to the corner of a building and tried to get out of the wind. Looking back the way she had come she squinted her eyes against the sting of the blowing sleet. Maybe she had lost them! God, please, let them be gone, she prayed.

A bullet smashed into the wall inches from her head sending fiery fragments of cinderblock into her face. She wiped the blood from her eyes in time to see two secret police cross to her side of the street on a dead run less than a block behind her.

She clutched the camera tightly to her chest and took off down the alley determined to keep the film from the KGB. If they were going to such great lengths to get it away from her there must be a reason. Nikki was going to get the film to her superiors in the Mossad.

Nikki was a realist. She knew that her prospects of living through the night weren't very good. In her condition she'd be lucky if she lived long enough to see her next meal much less complete her mission. Nevertheless, she wasn't about to hand over the camera. Not as long as she was still breathing!

Reflecting back, perhaps she had made a tactical error by taking the picture with so many people watching. It seemed logical at the time. After all, the tavern's management had hired her to take pictures and sell them to customers.

The run down soldier's bar didn't seem like much but it was the perfect cover for a pretty young Mossad agent. Admittedly, she wasn't very excited the first time she entered the crowded, smoke filled, little bar. The smell of urine, cigarettes, beer, and body odor was so overpowering it penetrated the senses of even the most intoxicated patrons. But she soon learned that the place was an intelligence gold mine.

She'd collected an unbelievable amount of valuable information by flirting with the off duty conscripts. It was amazing what a little liquor and a pretty girl could get a man to say. Her senior agent was looking forward to bigger things in the future. But that was all lost. Her cover was blown and she'd have to go back to Israel – that is, of course, if she lived.

What was so special about the last three men she'd photographed? One of them was an American. That was obvious from more than the fact that he spoke English. His expensive clothes were a dead give away. He was in his early twenties, and, although he was seated, Nikki estimated his height to be at least six feet four inches. His athletic build, strong chin, and sparkling blue eyes made him look like an American movie star.

Sitting next to the American was a middle-aged Arab. He was short, probably no more than five feet two inches tall and one hundred and ten pounds. Set above an enormous nose, his dark brown pupils were surrounded by a malevolent yellowish tint where the whites of his eyes should have been. His cheap suit hung awkwardly from his thin frame and made him look like an evil gnome.

Judging from the reaction of the third man when she took the picture he must've been KGB. To be honest, he was quite attractive and not at all like the stereotypical knuckle-dragging, dim-witted, Russian thug she'd pictured KGB spies to be. He was about the same size and age as the American and at least as good looking. However, one thing didn't seem to fit. His eyes - they were a cold gray and seemed out of place on the smiling, handsome face.

She remembered smiling her best smile as she snapped the picture of the three men around the small table. The Russian jumped up and slapped her across the face and grabbed for the camera. Instinct saved her life. She ran for the back door just as he pulled a pistol out of his jacket and fired a shot at her. Two other men seated in the far corner threw over their table and chased after her.

That was over an hour ago and they were still behind her. She had been running through the dark streets and alleyways of Moscow's red light district in the freezing ice and sleet trying to elude her persistent pursuers. She'd lost them for a few minutes twice but they always managed to find her.

Her escape and evasion training had been extensive and she was in excellent physical condition, but the cold was just too brutal. She was near the end of her rope and the warmly dressed KGB agents would soon catch her if she didn't catch a lucky break.

Three shots rang out as bullets whizzed by her ear. Nikki picked up her pace and rounded the corner into the next street. She was looking over her shoulder to see how close the secret police were getting when she inadvertently ran into the path of a slow moving delivery truck.

The startled driver slammed on his brakes and fought to keep from losing control on the icy road. His truck fishtailed wildly to the right and almost started to spin out of control. Years of experience driving in Russia's merciless winter conditions were all that saved him. He corrected by steering in the direction of the slide. When his front wheels got traction he slowly steered himself back into a straight line of travel. He'd barely slowed down at all during the entire harrowing ordeal. He hadn't been going very fast so he had time to correct the slide before his truck slammed into anything.

Fortunately, there was only one other truck on the road and it was already past him traveling in the opposite direction when the girl ran into his path. He looked in his rearview mirror and didn't see anybody lying in the road. He shrugged and kept driving.

Nikki peered out from under the canvass tarp covering the cargo and watched the two secret police standing dejectedly in the middle of the road. A thin smile crossed her lips as she drifted off to sleep.

Thirty-five years later, outside Washington, D.C.

GENERAL MARSHALL FREEMAN, the fifty-three year old Director of the CIA, slowed his 1992 Jeep Cherokee and turned into the gated driveway leading to Vice President Donald Braxton's private twelve-acre estate. Short and thin with gray thinning hair, General Freeman didn't have many friends in Washington. Too many years of smoking, drinking, and carousing had taken their toll, and he looked more like sixty-three than fifty-three. His lifeless brown eyes took up space on a badly wrinkled face that was permanently locked in an ugly scowl.

Freeman liked to dress like he had more money than he really did.

Tonight, he wore a gray Armani designer suit with a black silk shirt. His *Gucci* shoes were like polished black mirrors. He wore his *Rolex Oyster Perpetual* and diamond ring conspicuously for all the world to see. He liked everyone to know how important he was.

The word was that he was the Vice President's boy and he hated him for that. Freeman didn't picture himself as anybody's boy. The general was seething inside and struggling hard to get himself under control. The Vice-President was a powerful man – and it paid to be nice to powerful people. He was too smart to let personal feelings get in the way of what someone like Braxton could do for his career.

BRAXTON REPRESENTED EVERYTHING Freeman detested. The house was just one example of Braxton's pampered lifestyle that infuriated him. Located forty minutes outside of Washington, D.C. in the rolling Virginia foothills, Braxton's nineteenth century mansion was the picture of old money and everything it represented. It had been in his family since his grandfather purchased it shortly after being elected to Congress in 1948. It reminded General Freeman how much he resented Braxton for his extravagant, pompous life-style and inherited wealth.

Freeman had scratched and clawed his way to the top while people like Braxton looked down their aristocratic noses at people like him. "People born with money always think they're so much better than those who have to earn it," thought Freeman as he stared at the white colonial pillars of Braxton's home.

As he stopped the Jeep at the guard shack his mind raced ahead wildly to the meeting awaiting him in the house. What possible reason could Braxton have for summoning him to his residence at 10:00 p.m. on a Thursday evening? He recalled Braxton's words from the short telephone message, "General, I need you at my residence right away. It's time to return the favor." That was all the Vice President had said. Waves of fear crashed through his mind as he tried and failed to silence his wild imagination.

There was no doubt that he owed the Vice President a favor. Months earlier, at a black-tie dinner in Washington, D.C. just before he was confirmed as the Director of the CIA, Braxton had taken him aside and let him know that he'd discovered his most tightly held secret. General Freeman had been taking money from the KGB in exchange for information. Freeman didn't consider himself to be a traitor, but after getting served a crushing defeat in divorce court, he'd been strapped for money and wasn't willing to be humiliated publicly by having to dramatically lower his somewhat lavish standard of living. Taking the money was nothing more than a pragmatic solution to an unpleasant situation. Having served as Chairman of the Senate Foreign Intelligence Committee before being selected as President Carpenter's running mate, Braxton had access to untold numbers of intelligence sources. Which intelligence agency had discovered the connection between him and the former KGB was still a mystery.

The strange thing was that Braxton didn't have him arrested, turn him over to the Justice Department, or even inform the Army of his indiscretions. To the contrary, he'd taken a personal interest in his career, recommending him to the President to serve as Director of the Central Intelligence Agency. How ironic it seemed at the time that Braxton had recommended him, a known spy, to be Director of the CIA. He'd watched in bemusement as the Vice President lobbied and coerced the powers that be until he had landed the nomination. Braxton did all that without ever mentioning to anyone else the fact that he was selling national secrets to the Russians.

General Freeman remembered the sleepless nights he'd suffered as the CIA and FBI ran security investigations during the nomination process. He remembered lying awake at night wondering if at any moment the FBI would come crashing through his door to arrest him. But, that never happened. He was given the highest recommendation for the posting. Somehow they didn't find out. If they didn't know then how did Braxton find out?

For whatever reason Braxton had never mentioned his Russian connection since the first encounter several months earlier. He had a nagging suspicion that all of that was about to change in the next few minutes.

Freeman showed his ID to the private security guard at the gate and slowly drove down the winding driveway toward the estate's front entrance. The general glanced out his window at the extravagant landscaping. Somebody had spent a lot of money on special lighting and the effect was overpowering. A large circular flower garden with a fountain was illuminated with colored lights and sat in the middle of the driveway near the entrance. Spotlights were focused on four white, two-story columns rising majestically from a marbled portico. It made Freeman think of the White House.

The general parked where a secret service agent indicated and shook his head in disgust at the overt display of opulence. The agent opened the car door for him and said, "Good evening, General. I'll have Mr. Braxton's chauffeur park your vehicle. Give me a heads up when you're ready to leave and I'll have it waiting."

Freeman nodded assent without even looking at the agent. To him people like the secret service agent were nothing more than mindless minions. They served a purpose but weren't worth wasting time with.

The door opened before he reached it and an elderly uniformed black maid greeted him politely, "Good evening, sir. Right this way please." The maid made a sweeping motion with one arm, turned, and started off down the highly polished marbled hallway without looking back.

The two oversized cherry wood doors leading to the expansive study were already open and General Freeman could see the Vice President sitting in a wing-backed chair by the roaring fire reading through an overstuffed manila folder. He looked young for fifty-seven with the hair of a twenty-year-old and bright blue eyes — another reason to hate him.

Braxton never seemed to age. Dressed in a sweater and jeans, the Vice President looked more like a middle-aged computer company executive than the number two man in the most powerful nation on the face of the earth. Freeman tried not to think about Braxton's inappropriate casualness. The man didn't even have the decency to show him enough respect to dress for the meeting.

Before the maid could announce his arrival Braxton smiled warmly and said, "Ah, General. I'm glad you could make it on such short notice. Please, have a seat."

Freeman made his way to the seat the Vice President indicated and smiled wanly.

"Thank you, Margaret. That will be all for now. Please close the doors on your way out," ordered Braxton.

"GENERAL, I NEED your help on a project that I'm sure you will find most interesting. Not to be quaint, but I'm going to make you an offer you can't refuse. You are no doubt acutely aware of all that I have done for your career in maneuvering you into your present posting with the CIA. You're also aware that I have detailed knowledge concerning your past dealings with the Soviet KGB. I've not made an issue of this matter for reasons that I'm sure you have never understood. I've risked my own political career to help you and keep you out of prison. Tonight, I am going to give you a chance to repay the favor."

The Vice President stared off into space as if he was in the room alone, apparently deep in thought considering his last comment. Several minutes of awkward silence elapsed. Freeman, not accustomed to being on the hot seat, felt the need to break the silence. "I've gotta admit I owe you a lot. What is it you'd like from me?"

The Vice President's hawk-like eyes snapped out of their fixation on the corner of the ceiling and riveted on General Freeman. The newly appointed Director of the CIA felt goosebumps rising under his jacket despite the glowing warmth emanating from the fireplace.

"General, do you believe that throughout history certain men are born to change the course of world events?"

"Well, gotta admit, I've never given it much thought," said Freeman.

"Perhaps you should, General. I'm offering you an opportunity to be one of those men."

"Look, let's cut to the chase. I don't need you to blow smoke and wax eloquent on my behalf. What do you want from me? You and I both know I don't have any choice but to cooperate, so spit it out! You want me to kill somebody, or what?" asked General Freeman.

"General, that's only part of what I want from you. I'll try to make this simple. I know you are accustomed to linear thinking so I'll get right to the point. I'm giving you an opportunity to make a choice between gaining incredible wealth and power by assisting me in forging the greatest alliance the world has ever known or a bullet in the back of your head before the night is over. Is that clear enough, General?"

To his credit, General Freeman responded as if they were discussing the score from last Sunday's Washington Red Skins football game. "Crystal clear, sir. Please go on. I'm all ears."

"You and I don't share much philosophically in the way of politics, but I think even you can appreciate that the current state of affairs in the world leaves much to be desired. Countries with enormous natural resources are unable to feed their own people. Wars are raging out of control across the globe. Economies are collapsing, famine and pestilence are killing women and children by the millions; while a few rich nations stand by and watch doing little more than giving lip service to the plight of the helpless. The industrialized nations of the world are polluting the earth and poisoning the air we breathe and the water we drink. I think it's time someone had the moral courage to stop the cycle," Braxton said.

"Excuse me for interrupting," spat General Freeman gruffly, "but I didn't earn my stars in the *Salvation Army*. The way I see it, all those third-world countries you're so concerned about have gotten what they deserve. The stuff you're talking about is nothing more than nature's way of ridding itself of the weak. And don't start on me with that environmental line of trash. I don't buy it for a second. Anyway, what do you think I can do about any of it?"

The Vice President made a placating gesture with both hands and said, "Oh, you are quite certainly going to play a very large role in these affairs. Frankly, I don't care about your lack of concern for the earth or her people. You'll help me for your own reasons. If I understand you as well as I think I do, you'll help me for two reasons: first, because you are greedy, and secondly, to save your own neck. Whatever your motivation, I'm only concerned about the bottom line."

This seemed to satisfy the general. He nodded, unsmiling, and said, "OK, Mr. Vice President. What's the plan?"

Braxton pursed his lips as he looked down at his feet and adjusted his socks before answering. He stood up and walked over to the fireplace and poked at the fire. Turning to face Freeman, he said, "Before I tell you the specifics, let me give you a little background that will help you to understand the dynamics of the situation."

Braxton replaced the poker in its holder, intertwined his fingers behind his back, and began slowly pacing in front of Braxton's chair. "While I was pursuing my formal education as a young man I went abroad and studied as a Rhodes Scholar. As you may be aware, that was during the height of the Vietnam War. I was passionately opposed to America's immoral and senseless involvement in the war. For that reason I traveled to Moscow to participate in a rally for peace.

"While there I met two men who shared my passion for peace and we discovered a common desire to see a world system of government where people would not make war on each other and kill innocent men, women, and children in their lust for power and wealth. We became fast friends and allies and have surreptitiously kept in contact through the years. As fate would have it, we have all risen to the highest levels of our respective governments," said Braxton.

He sat down in his chair and crossed his legs. Reaching to his right, he picked up a tumbler of Tennessee sour mash whiskey off of the chair-side table, took a long sip, and placed the drink back on the table.

General Freeman crossed his arms across his chest and asked, "So, who are these two men you're talking about? Anyone I know?"

The Vice President smiled showing all of his perfect teeth as he said almost triumphantly, "The one most responsible for your presence here tonight is Alexi Yanochev."

"Yanochev?" blurted Freeman as he bolted to his feet. "You mean the Director of the Russian Foreign Intelligence Service?"

"Yes, of course. He was the one who informed me about your involvement with the KGB. Now calm down and have a seat," Braxton said, motioning with both hands like he was trying to train a puppy to sit.

"So, that's why I wasn't discovered," Freeman said more to himself than to Braxton as he fell back heavily into his chair.

Braxton tented his fingers under his nose and said, "Indeed. I immediately recognized the opportunity this presented and began laboring to place you in the office that you now hold. You see, General, I need you as much as you need me."

"How's that? I mean, I can see how my position can help in providing you with intelligence, but you have plenty of contacts other than me that can do the same thing. So, why me?" asked Freeman.

The Vice President dropped his hands to the arms of his chair and stared intently at General Freeman. "General, I'm more interested in your using the CIA to debunk the intelligence assessments of NSA and DIA than any intelligence you may provide. I imagine I'll need you to pass information along to the Russians from time to time as well.

However, it's not intelligence alone that I require. But that can wait. Let me go on," Braxton said.

"After the demise of the Soviet Union my friend Alexi recognized a unique opportunity to usher in a New World Order. I am not referring to vain attempts to reform the corrupt governments in Europe and America that are sucking the life out of their people and driving the less fortunate of the world further into poverty and hopelessness. I'm talking about a totally new system of government. A government that will bring peace to the entire planet! A government that will guarantee the basic necessities of life to all and at the same time halt the reckless destruction of our environment."

"Forgive me for saying so, but are you serious?" asked Freeman. "Do you expect me to sit hear and listen to this malarkey? I think you're out of your mind!"

"I think you should hear me out before you jump to any conclusions, General. What I am talking about is no fairy tale. After you listen to what I have to say, I'll welcome any criticism you may have. However, I doubt that you'll be able to discover any flaws in the plan. Alexi and I have been formulating and testing this concept for months. I'm confident the plan is foolproof."

"If you say so. Unfortunately, I don't see that I have much choice but to help you with your harebrained idea. Let's hear the rest of it," Freeman huffed impatiently.

"As I was saying, Alexi Yanochev developed the basic concept for this New World Order and asked me to be a part of his plan. I have to admit that I was skeptical at first, but after closely examining its merits, for the first time in my life I saw that it was within my grasp to live in the kind of world that in the past I'd only dreamed to be possible."

"How do you and Yanochev plan to pull this off? Don't you think a few of the governments you plan on replacing might have something to say about all of this?" asked Freeman.

"I imagine they will be quite put out indeed. However, the beauty of it is that they will have no choice but to concede power."

General Freeman shifted in his chair and asked, "And just what makes you so sure?"

"My confidence is built upon the fact that world leaders will have no recourse other than to do as we ask. That leads me to the second friend I made while in Moscow. He is none other than Ayatollah Ali Bakr Rafalgemii of Iran. He is the third party in what will be the planet's ruling triumvirate." Braxton paused to let the general grasp what he had just said.

When Freeman didn't react he continued. "Let me briefly outline how we three will bring the world to its knees and convince reticent countries to see things our way. First, Alexi will stage a coup in Russia. Once in power, he will join forces with Ali Bakr and seize all of the Persian Gulf oil fields. They will, of course, create a diversion that'll ensure no one understands what's happening until the invasion of the Arabian Peninsula is underway. After they have secured the world's richest oil reserves the industrialized countries of the world will be denied oil unless they concede to our demands. We've calculated that most leading nations will deplete their oil reserves in less than ninety days. Some European countries will last longer. Without oil to fuel their power plants, factories, and automobiles, their economies will collapse. Then they should be willing to reconsider our offer," said Braxton confidently.

General Freeman stood to his feet and poured himself a drink from the decanter beside his chair. "Before you go on I have just a couple of questions," interrupted Freeman.

"Certainly, Marshall. What is it you don't follow?"

"Oh, I follow you pretty well. I just wanted to throw out a few considerations you might want to explain to me before we get too far along," Freeman said, swirling the ice in his drink absent mindedly.

"And what might those be?"

Pointing at the Vice President with his glass, he said, "Well, for starters, what makes you think the Free World is going to stand by and let you take control of the Arabian oil fields? Don't you think Europe might intervene? For that matter, what about President Carpenter? You know that he's an old war-horse like me. He'd have half the U.S. Navy tossing Tomahawk missiles at the Russians before they captured twenty percent of the oil fields; not to mention what the U.S. Air Force would do."

Braxton smiled and said, "Believe me, General, we've taken all of that into consideration. In the first place, Europe will be unable to come to a consensus or form a credible threat to our armies in sufficient time to do anything about it. They will be too concerned about how they will fare if we are successful. They will most likely sit back and hope America intervenes.

"Secondly, should they attempt military intervention Alexi will annihilate them with his still formidable arsenal of nuclear missiles. Believe me, General, he has the resolve to do this."

"And what makes you think America will sit on her hands and let this happen?" Freeman again interrupted, gesturing wildly with his free hand.

"That's where you come in, General. You're going to kill President Carpenter before he has the chance to stop us! Then, when I'm sworn in as the President, I'll demand that America exercise the same restraint as Europe," exclaimed the Vice President.

Freeman slammed his drink down onto the table and glared at the Vice President. "Are you crazy?" he shouted. "If you think I'm going to assassinate the President of the United States just to keep myself out of prison, you're nuts!"

"Sit down, Marshall. You will indeed eliminate President Carpenter, but not merely to stay out of prison. You have much more to gain than that. I'm offering you wealth beyond the limits of your imagination."

General Freeman bit his lower lip as he considered the Vice President's words for a few seconds. He was clearly interested in the money. "And how do you plan on doing that. I have a pretty big imagination."

"Simple. I need someone to administer the control and distribution of oil to the North and South American continents. That man is you, General. Of course, you'll receive a percentage of the profits for your troubles. We are talking billions of dollars. I think that should be sufficient motivation to convince you to consider my proposal."

"What are you talking about? What's all this business about controlling oil?" asked Freeman.

"Very simple, really. We'll ration oil to nations according to need. They in turn will pay a tribute of twenty percent of their national revenues to our ruling triumvirate. They will not need to worry about diverting revenues to national defense because we'll demand the elimination of all weapons and standing armed forces. We will provide protection to the world through our own peacekeeping forces.

"An additional requirement for receiving oil will be compliance with our directives requiring all industrialized nations to provide food and shelter to the less fortunate nations. We've run financial models and determined that by controlling assets, food production, and allocation of natural resources on a world-wide basis and removing the economic impact of war, the world will attain a much higher level of prosperity than is possible under the current economic system."

"You still haven't told me what my cut is from all of this," blurted Freeman.

"Well, how would you like to get one percent of all oil payments on the American continent? That's what I'm willing to compensate you for your services. I need President Carpenter dead for this to work. I must be President before America has time to mount a credible defense of the Arabian Peninsula."

"And when is the invasion going to take place?" asked General Freeman.

"Soon, General, very soon! Can you keep your end of the bargain?"

"Count on it, Mr. Vice President. I'll stake my life on it," said Freeman.

"You will, indeed!" said Braxton. "You will indeed!"

1

The Present, Ethiopia

LIEUTENANT COMMANDER JAKE Gregory thought the worst was over as he lay silently under an uprooted palm tree trying his best to conceal his six foot four inch, two hundred twenty pound frame in a depression barely large enough for a man half his size. Fortunately, his camouflaged gila suit made it impossible to recognize the shape lying under the tree as human. Too bad insects are smarter than people. Three black camel flies were snacking on the back of his neck through the netting of his gila suit. Focusing his binoculars down the small hill that was now his forward observation post he noticed movement amid the rubble of what had until recently been the American Consulate.

There was no mistaking the identity of whom he saw stumbling out of the smoking ruins. Ambassador Theodore McClintock was alive. The patrician looking ambassador's survival probably would've made Jake feel much better had it not been for what he saw approaching from the north less than one thousand yards away. Approximately sixty-five partially uniformed members of the National Islamic Peoples Liberation Army of Ethiopia were leisurely making their way toward the consulate compound.

Twenty-four hours earlier Jake and his elite team of Navy SEALs had traded jokes about the rag-tag army they'd nicknamed NIPPLE. The U.S. military was forever creating acronyms for everything and since the first letters of this particular third-world rebel army were N.I.P.L.A.E., it required only a very small imagination to make the leap to NIPPLE. He wasn't laughing now.

Just after midnight last night the other four members of his team left his position to conduct a routine reconnaissance of the NIPPLE troop concentrations in the immediate area. They'd done the same thing under much more trying circumstances numerous times so they weren't overly concerned about the danger involved in their mission.

They were now dead, victims of a surprisingly sophisticated ambush carried out by these supposedly untrained, bush-league soldiers. Jake went to investigate when he heard the noise of the firefight. He arrived just in time to watch the rebels stripping the bodies of his team. It was all he could do to restrain himself from emptying his rifle into the group of shouting, dancing savages who'd killed his men, but professionalism prevailed. It wouldn't help them now anyway.

Alone and vastly outnumbered, Jake would now have to complete the dangerous mission by himself. A lesser man would've scrubbed the mission and called it quits. But there was no quit in Jake Gregory. No, having an observer near the consulate, "eyes on the ground", as the admiral called it, was critical to the planned consulate evacuation and he couldn't let his people down. He'd see this mission through. Once he took on a mission there was no turning back regardless of the consequences.

At least, those were his thoughts last night. The NIPPLE bombardment of the American Consulate commenced less than thirty minutes before three CH-53 helicopters and four AH-1A *Cobra* helicopter gunships were to have landed outside the compound. It was frustrating to realize that all of the detailed planning that had gone into this mission was now for naught.

Jake had been on the radio constantly with the Afloat Command Center aboard *USS Tarawa* and was receiving continuous reports on the inbound helicopter positions. Just as he was making preparations to leave his observation post to help with the evacuation the first rounds began impacting the consulate.

Immediately, he reported the attack to Rear Admiral Jeffrey Taylor aboard *Tarawa*. Jake was devastated by the next words he heard on the radio net. "ABORT! ABORT! All birds return to home plate," the aircraft controllers ordered.

Jake was forced to helplessly sit and watch the devastation unfold before his eyes. Thunderous explosions propelled tons of earth skyward as each artillery shell impacted the consulate. The overpressure from the nearby barrage nearly deafened him in his shallow foxhole. He could only imagine how terrible it must be for the poor souls trying in vain to find refuge inside the shattered remains of the consulate.

He knew Americans were dying. How could anyone survive the ferocity of the attack? He'd seen several Marines in the compound over the last few days as well as a number of civilians.

The noise of war stopped without warning, replaced by stark silence as tremendous dust clouds settled back to earth. There was very little left of the buildings he'd been so carefully observing for two days. Jake knew in his heart that the sustained artillery attack was thorough enough to kill everyone trapped inside the consulate when the shells began to fall.

Yet, there was Ambassador McClintock standing out in the open dusting himself off. Hazel eyes burned from behind the cracked lenses of his sixties style wire rimmed glasses. He didn't look scared to Jake. No, the feisty old man was just plain mad. His dignified looking close-cropped gray hair was still neatly combed and there were no apparent holes in his thin frame despite the badly soiled and tattered linen suit he was wearing. The ambassador straightened himself to his full height of five foot eight inches. Jake didn't know how the old man had managed to keep from getting himself killed but if his eyes weren't lying to him he was indeed a survivor. However, if he didn't do something fast that was all going to change. The ambassador was completely unaware NIPPLE soldiers were within minutes of capturing him.

Awarded two Silver Stars for gallantry in action, Ambassador McClintock had earned quite a reputation from the early days of the Vietnam War as a hard-nosed, brave soldier. But that was forty-years ago. Jake had no illusions about how the ambassador would fare as a prisoner of the NIPPLE forces. They'd made a point of publicly desecrating the bodies of dead American soldiers on CNN. They'd even gone so far as to release an audiotape of the torture of an unfortunate French UN observer. Terror was their favorite weapon.

Jake made the choice subconsciously without giving his next action serious consideration. There was no way under heaven he could allow the ambassador to fall into enemy hands. He lifted his semi-automatic Pausa sniper rifle and centered the sights on the chest of the pistol waving NIPPLE major nearest the front of the column. A small grin spread silently across his face. There were no words to express how gratifying it felt to finally be able to strike back at those who'd killed his men.

Squeezing the trigger unleashed a punishing recoil against Jake's shoulder as the heavy .50 caliber projectile rocketed out of the barrel, but he figured it didn't hurt him nearly as bad as it did the other guy. He quickly dropped two more rebels near the front of the advancing militia, laid the weapon aside, and stripped out of his camouflage "fuzzies." He was out of time. McClintock was standing up in the middle of a war zone unaware of the advancing NIPPLEs. Jake had to go get him or the rebels would get their hands on him.

Jake wasn't going to let that happen. He picked up his rifle and LST-5 radio and ran as fast as his thirty-four year old legs could carry him to where the still dazed ambassador had crouched after hearing the shots.

THE REBELS WERE panic-stricken and shooting their weapons in every direction. Gunsmoke wafted lazily through the frantic soldiers as the sound of gunfire thundered in their ears. Men were screaming as they were hit and propelled awkwardly to the ground. The smell of cordite and fear stung at their nostrils.

Ten rebel militiamen were killed in the ensuing melee. Who could possibly be shooting at them? After subjecting the American Consulate to forty-five minutes of merciless mortar, artillery, and rocket fire, they were sure they'd cleansed their sacred land of the American devils.

The cowardly United Nations Peacekeeping Forces had withdrawn from their sector of the country days earlier. Having executed the last members of the ruling party's small tribe hours before they unleashed the bombardment on the American Compound and now after having killed all the Americans in the area with their bombardment they were sure they'd eliminated all opposition.

As if by some demonic hand, Major Mafusu Ahmed Bin Nagali, the newly self-appointed President-for-life's oldest son, lay dead with most of his back missing. He was their leader. Trained in Syria in military and guerrilla warfare tactics, he was the only one in the group capable of leading them into battle.

The rebel fire slowly began to dissipate. What was once a cacophony of automatic weapons and small arms fire for nearly five minutes was now only an occasional rifle shot. The discouraged militia retreated into the city as fast as their feet would carry them, pursued by some imaginary satanic army of devils.

A MBASSADOR McCLINTOCK TRIED to clear his head as he stumbled out of the smoking ruins of his makeshift consulate. It hadn't been a very fancy building. Six months earlier the compound was nothing more than an abandoned summer estate once owned by a British exporter.

The late president of Ethiopia had decided only seven months earlier that it was in his best interest to establish diplomatic relations with the United States. It had taken nearly a month just to clean the trash out of the empty shell of a building and then another two months to repair the walls and patch the roof. The ambassador had begun conducting consulate business a short ninety days prior to today's attack.

However, the site did have a number of advantages that made it appealing to the ambassador. Located near the outskirts of the city, the entire compound was surrounded by a wall seven feet high and eighteen inches thick. The storage building next to the main house was one of the few structures in the entire city constructed of steel reinforced concrete. Particularly conducive to his selection of the old estate was the fact that it had its own well.

Now, in less than forty-five minutes, all his hard work had been violently destroyed. The only building left standing was the old storage building that he'd recently converted into an armory for the Marine Diplomatic Security Detachment. The small armory had saved his life. The young lieutenant in charge of diplomatic security had pushed him into the armory as soon as the shells started raining down upon the compound.

His head was still ringing from the noise and concussions of the attack when he heard three quick shots. Out of the corner of his eye he saw a large, camouflage-clad soldier running straight for him. The soldier's bright green eyes blazed malevolently as he loped in his direction. He was carrying an enormous looking rifle with both hands pointing it menacingly to the north and sweeping it from side to side as he ran.

McClintock immediately recognized the man's desert cammies as that of an American soldier. This soldier was big. It was hard to believe a man that large could move so fast and possess such amazing agility.

"Where did you come from?" the ambassador asked with relief. He knew he wasn't part of the Marine Security Detachment and as far as he knew there were no other American forces in the area.

"I've been watching the compound from that knoll over there for the past two days," Jake replied, pointing to the west. "But there's no time to talk. I've just taken out a couple bad guys and the NIPPLEs aren't going to be too happy about it. I've stirred up a hornet's nest and they'll be swarming this place any minute." The ambassador almost laughed out loud when he heard Jake's heavy Appalachian accent. "What idiot sent this hillbilly to rescue me?" he thought to himself.

Jake knew he had to get the ambassador out of hostile territory, *Indian Country* in SEAL-speak, as quickly as possible. Fortunately, the batteries in his radio were still good after two days of what was supposed to be nothing more than a reconnaissance mission. It took only seconds to raise the amphibious task group stationed just over the horizon. Five minutes later Jake was informed that four *Cobra* gunships and a CH-46 Combat Search and Rescue helicopter were airborne. All he had to do was find a place to hide the sixty-seven year old ambassador until the helos could make the forty-five minute flight to his position.

Jake watched the ambassador's countenance change. The old man regained his composure and began to vent his anger. "Where have you guys been. I've been under attack for forty-five minutes and the entire United States Navy has been sitting out there on their nice safe ships drinking coffee. I thought I was supposed to be evacuated hours ago. I'm going to have that incompetent admiral's stars for this. He's responsible for the deaths of seven brave men. Look around. I want you to remember what you see. Those dead Marines are your fault!"

"The old guy must think the danger is over," Jake thought as he surveyed the compound. There were indeed seven brave Marines lying in the rubble and it was readily apparent they were quite dead. The ambassador had failed to mention two civilians who'd also given their country the ultimate sacrifice. They were no doubt the resident CIA agents, or rather were, until a mortar round had spread their bodies over a twenty-foot area. Jake put them out of his mind. If he didn't want to join them he'd have to locate to a defensible hiding place within the next few minutes. He was running out of time. What a way to start the New Year.

He scanned what was left of the compound and noticed that the storage building was still in relatively good shape. As was customary in this part of the world the roof had a parapet about three feet high that went all the way around the structure. Without a conscious thought Jake was running for the building pulling the ambassador along by the scruff of his neck.

"Get on the roof!" Jake shouted. The ambassador, obviously embarrassed by his outburst and ashamed that he had temporarily overlooked the seriousness of their situation, complied without any further complaint. Noticing how easily the ambassador climbed to the roof Jake mentally noted that the old guy was in pretty good shape for an aging diplomat. He would have been surprised to discover the ambassador could still run ten kilometers in less than fifty minutes. Old was a matter of perspective.

Jake leapt and pulled himself up onto the roof in one fluid motion. The roof had suffered a direct hit by a mortar round. The only reason the building hadn't been demolished was that the roof was constructed of eighteen inches of steel reinforced concrete. All the mortar round had done was blow a hole large enough to pass a fifty-five gallon drum through. Jake was impressed. This was a good place to wait on the helos.

Jake began to do the mental calculations ingrained in him by twelve years of Special Forces training. Forty-five minutes until the helos could be overhead; that was too long. The NIPPLEs would surely regroup and investigate what had caused the deaths of three of their clan. The hair on the nape of his neck began to stand up as it did when he sensed imminent danger. This wasn't going to be a clean extraction. He didn't know how prophetic that thought would prove to be.

ABOARD *USS TARAWA*, Jake's radio call elicited an excited response from the SEAL Team. When they learned of his situation Commander Kevin Lewis, the Commanding Officer of SEAL Team Five, cornered Rear Admiral Taylor and begged him to add a little surprise to the rescue package the admiral had ordered.

The SEAL commanding officer was a stark contrast to the fifty-year-old admiral. Commander Lewis, hard looking at thirty-seven, was five feet eleven inches of twisted steel. His neck muscles started at his ears and formed one long bulge down to his massive shoulders. His face was chiseled granite with two cold gray eyes set over a nose that had been broken years before in a long forgotten fight.

Admiral Taylor on the other hand looked more like a long distance runner. He was six feet of bridled energy who always seemed to be struggling to slow himself down so that others could keep up. His dark brown eyes burned holes through whomever he focused upon and had the effect of coercing people to get right to the point when they spoke to him.

The admiral wasn't in any mood to be trifled with by a commander but he had to admire the man's guts. This guy wasn't just asking the admiral's permission; he was telling him they were going and wanting to know if the admiral was going to help.

With most admirals the commander's actions would've been tantamount to mutiny, but not with Admiral Taylor. He deeply respected men who were willing to put themselves in harm's way for a comrade-in-arms. Well, why not, he thought. He could certainly understand Commander Lewis' sentiment and it never hurt to add a margin of safety.

Taylor picked up the handset to his Secure Tactical Termination (TACTERM) satellite radio and contacted Vice Admiral Benjamin Pierce, Commander of United States Naval Forces Central Command, at his command center in Bahrain.

"Admiral, this is Jeff."

"Admiral Taylor, this is Commander Skip Bowers, Staff Watch Officer. Please hold while I call Admiral Pierce."

TWO MINUTES LATER Admiral Taylor heard the radio come to life. "Jeff, this is Ben. Sorry for the wait. I was on the STU-III with Central Command in Tampa about your situation. What can I do for you?"

"Roger, sir; we've got a sticky situation here as you know. The rescue mission for Ambassador McClintock is underway. I feel we need to increase the mission package and give ourselves a little more insurance," Admiral Taylor said. "If you don't mind sir, I'd like to have the Air Force AC-130's out of Mombassa we launched earlier in the day remain on station just out of visual range. Additionally, I intend to launch a package of two CH-53's. One helo will carry five members of SEAL Team Five to secure the ambassador's position and the second helo will carry a Marine rifle company. How copy, sir?"

"Copy all, Jeff. The plan appears sound to me. I'll make the call to the "blue-suiters" in DC and let them know the plan. I'll take care of sending the message chopping operational control of the AC-130's as well. We'll take care of the Execute Orders and all the paper work from this end. You go get the ambassador. Over."

"Roger, sir; thanks for the support."

"No problem, Jeff. That's what we're here for. God bless you. Pierce, out."

Admiral Taylor turned to Commander Lewis and said, "Mister, you have your mission. Bring'em back alive!"

"Yes, sir! Thank you," Commander Lewis said as he quickly pivoted and left the command center.

"Battle Watch Officer, contact Air Ops and delete the Combat Search and Rescue helo. We'll be replacing it with two CH-53's," ordered Taylor.

"Aye, aye, sir;" replied the BWO.

Rebel Command Center, Ethiopia

LIEUTENANT FRANCIS SALLE stood rigidly at attention in front of his commanding officer's desk. The gaunt looking soldier had short, curly black hair and huge black eyes. His overly long arms were trembling as he stared at a spot on the wall behind the man seated in front of him.

The man responsible for his trembling sat behind a small wooden desk littered with maps, radios, and various reports. A swagger stick rested menacingly on the right hand corner. The man was dressed in a dessert camouflage uniform with the oversized rank insignia of a full colonel. His eyes blazed at the frightened lieutenant.

The small office was stifling hot and sparsely furnished. The only furnishings in the room were a desk, two rickety wooden chairs, and an ancient filing cabinet. A picture of President Nagali hung on one wall.

The colonel rose from his chair, picked up his swagger stick and stormed around the desk and stood inches from Lieutenant Salle's right ear. "You stupid coward," shouted Colonel Benjamin Mohammed Isa. "You run like a frightened child when three shots are fired?"

"Yes, Colonel; but Major Nagali was killed before my eyes," answered Lieutenant Salle. "I saw his flesh torn off his body as if by the hand of Satan. Men began dying all around him. It is only by the grace of Allah that I myself survived. Then our brave freedom fighters were attacked from every side. Many more were killed. I knew we must either withdraw or be annihilated."

"You fool! You killed more of your own men than did your unseen enemy!"

"No, sir; I only acted to save the lives of my men!"

Colonel Isa was not impressed with the caliber of the local fighting men. In times like these men were promoted due solely to the amount of cruelty they displayed when they eliminated President Nagali's enemies. Men who'd once been nothing more than psychotic thugs were now granted commissions in the National Islamic Peoples Liberation Army of Ethiopia. Well, the Colonel knew how to handle these "soldiers." Fear made these people obey. Fear ensured they would accomplish his desires. He'd long ago discovered that those who thrived on the suffering of others were the biggest cowards of all.

"Lieutenant, assemble the officers in the street in front of my office."

The lieutenant complied immediately, obviously eager to escape the colonel's wrath. Once the officers were assembled Colonel Isa swaggered to the center of the street to address the slightly cowering troops. He knew that by now they'd all heard about Lieutenant Salle's shameful performance in the face of such insignificant resistance. He imagined what was going through their pitiful little minds, "they think this will be just another withering reprimand for their incompetence. Well, I'll show them!"

"Fifteen minutes ago Lieutenant Salle's troops returned from a reconnaissance in force mission." Colonel Isa loved to display his command of military sounding terms around his officers. "This was a simple mission to search the American Consulate for survivors and to bring them back to my command center," he stated as he moved toward Lieutenant Salle. "I placed sixty-five brave soldiers under the command of our President's son, Major Mufusu Nagali. Lieutenant Salle was his second-in-command. Upon the death of Major Nagali it was his responsibility to take command and complete the mission."

Colonel Isa was now standing less than two feet from Lieutenant Salle. "Due to his incompetence and cowardly actions thirteen of our soldiers have been killed. Their blood cries from the ground for revenge."

Colonel Isa was now motioning wildly with his pistol. The assembled officers shifted nervously from one foot to another. They visibly cringed each time the colonel loudly emphasized a point. As terrified as they looked they didn't appear nearly as frightened as did Lieutenant Salle. His legs began to tremble.

"Blood requires blood," Isa shouted as he continued to wave the pistol. "All those who are responsible for the deaths of our men must die. Let it begin now!" With that, Colonel Isa leveled the pistol and fired two rounds into Lieutenant Salle's face.

Colonel Isa now had the complete, undivided attention of the twenty-three "officers" who stood before him. Unbridled fear was evident on every face. *Good, now they know who is in charge.* He was now relatively sure his orders would be carried out. *It was his firm conviction that it was good for the troops to be more afraid of failing him than of facing the enemy.*

"Now that I have your attention I want you to listen very carefully. You are all as of this moment directly responsible for completing Lieutenant Salle's mission." Colonel Isa explained the tactics and disposition of forces they were to use for the mission in quick, concise words. "Unless you desire to enter Paradise with Lieutenant Salle this very instant I advise you to assemble your troops and obey your orders. May Allah be with you. You are dismissed!" Just for added theatrics Colonel Isa fired three rounds into the air.

The officers almost trampled each other in their haste to assemble their troops. The terrified junior officers accomplished one of the most impressive displays of military skill the colonel had ever seen. They managed to assemble two hundred and thirty NIPPLE soldiers in less than twelve minutes and were now hurrying toward the American Consulate in what resembled an organized military formation. Four "technical" vehicles sped off ahead of the troops eager to be on the scene first. "Technical" was the name given to old pick-up trucks with crew-served automatic weapons mounted in the back. It was the poor man's version of an armored vehicle.

2

THE FIELD OF view from the top of the storage building was excellent. Jake could see several hundred yards in all directions. He turned to the ambassador and said, "This is a good spot to hole up until the helo's get here. I only wish I had something besides my rifle to keep us company. I'd give my first-born son for something large caliber with the word 'automatic' in its nomenclature."

"Maybe I can help," the ambassador said smiling. "I failed to mention that we're sitting on top of my armory."

"Why didn't you say so before?" Jake shouted as he threw himself through the hole in the roof. Once inside the armory Jake was ecstatic to find most of the weapons in good shape. The mortar round that had blown a hole in the roof had done little damage to the contents of the armory.

Jake felt like a little boy at Christmas. There were two M-60 machine guns, a 40mm grenade launcher, four boxes of hand grenades, and much to his surprise six "stinger" missiles. The stinger missiles may have been designed to shoot down aircraft but their heat seeking guidance system would also home in on the heat from a truck engine.

"Ambassador, give me a hand," Jake shouted as he stuck an M-60 through the hole in the roof.

The two men worked in silence as they loaded weapons and ammunition onto the roof. There was no need for words. They both knew their only hope of survival lay in the preparations they were now making. Once they had emptied everything out of the armory Jake thought would be useful he climbed back onto the roof and began preparing for the attack that was sure to come.

It took twenty-five minutes to load the roof with the weapons Jake thought they'd need. They pre-positioned weapons all around the roof and stacked several boxes of ammunition and grenades by each weapon. The exercise had winded them both and they were ready to take a breather. When they finished with the weapons the area around the consulate was clear of rebels so it seemed safe to sit and catch their breath for a moment.

Jake was keeping the airwaves busy as he rested, exchanging messages with the Afloat Command Center. They were informed that things were not going well in the rest of Ethiopia. The rebel forces had just completed their capture of Addis Ababa, the capital of Ethiopia. General Mohammed Bin Nagali was reported to be standing on the balcony of the Presidential Palace declaring victory in their war of liberation to thousands of cheering supporters.

The United Nations Security Council was in emergency session at this very moment and it was rumored they were ready to concede defeat.

It had been leaked to the media that they didn't see any way to diffuse the situation without an all out invasion and thought that the former President of this small African country wasn't worth the lives of thousands of United Nations troops. Television commentators were saying that most representatives on the Security Council didn't see a lot of difference between the former President and Nagali. In their opinion they were both egotistical despots. The only noticeable difference between the two was that one favored taking money from the United States and Iran was funding the other.

"Well, if that wouldn't make a preacher cuss," Jake drawled. "I've been eating dirt for two days, the American Consulate is blown to high heavens, we've lost thirteen men to these animals in the last twenty-four hours, and now we're going to pull-out! People died for this?" Jake said in disgust.

"Commander, just thank the Lord that we're getting out of this alive. Some of our men haven't been so fortunate," McClintock commented soberly.

"Yeah, well, it really burns me that I lost four good men in this jerk-weed country for nothing!" Jake turned and brought his binoculars to his eyes scanning the road in the direction the retreating rebels had taken thirty minutes earlier. "Ambassador, right about now I wouldn't be making too may bets on us getting out of here alive. Look!"

The ambassador's heart skipped a beat when he looked over the top of the parapet that hid them from open view. Four trucks were speeding toward them. Even without the aide of the binoculars that Jake now offered to him he saw about three hundred rebel soldiers approaching.

Jake looked the ambassador directly in the eyes. It was a look that sent chills down the spine of the senior diplomat. "Ambassador, listen carefully. I don't know much about protocol but if you want to live you're to do exactly as I say."

The ambassador didn't argue. The last time he'd seen eyes like

Jake's had been forty years earlier in Vietnam. His position was about to be overrun and the eyes had belonged to his executive officer. The XO was a tough captain who'd earned a battlefield commission in the last war. Then only a first lieutenant, McClintock knew instantly his only hope of survival lay in the skill of that experienced combat veteran. He saw the same hard, determined look in Jake's eyes now. Yes, he'd trust his life to this young man.

"Soldier, I'm getting too old for this business," McClintock said to Jake.

"Well sir, something tells me we aren't going to get a whole lot older if we don't get some help real soon!" Jake picked up the radio and raised the Flag Command Center. "L4N, this is Haboo...Over".

"Haboo, this is L4N. Roger...Over."

"L4, we've got about three hundred rebels making approach to our position. EOB (Enemy Order of Battle) includes four *Technicals*...Over."

"Roger, Haboo. *Cobras* now ten minutes out. Be advised, AC-130's making approach from north. ETA fifteen minutes... Over."

"Roger, L4. Will activate beacon. Happy hunting...Out." Jake switched his LST-5 radio to the beacon mode. This would allow the airborne assets to locate his position and hopefully prevent any overly ambitious pilot from attacking him by mistake.

"Sir, I don't need to tell you how much trouble we're in. Those NIPPLE's aren't going to wait for the helos to get here before they attack," Jake explained. "I don't know what our chances are but live or die I figure I owe those creeps out there some grief. They butchered four men very close to me. I intend to dispatch as many of them to hell as I can."

"I'm with you, son. I was completely helpless during the artillery attack but now I've got a gun in my hands and plenty of targets in front of me. I'm not very current on combat tactics but I can still shoot fairly well," the ambassador said resolutely. "You can deal me in. They killed a few of my men also."

"OK," Jake said, "the way I see it they'll do a fast scout with the *technicals* first. Then the troops will move in to search the compound. If we can take out a couple of the technicals maybe we can keep their heads down until the *Cobras* arrive."

Jake's team had been briefed stateside by the CIA. The *Agency* had assured them the rebels had no stomach for sustained combat. His recent experience earlier in the day seemed to confirm that estimate. It seemed plausible that they wouldn't press the attack once he started throwing some heavy stuff their way.

The four *technical* vehicles were now within one hundred yards of his position. Jake removed a stinger missile from its container and aimed it at the lead vehicle. The ambassador prepared the other missiles without waiting to be told. The next thing they heard was a loud "whoosh" as the first missile departed its launching tube.

The rebels in the *technical* vehicles raced toward the consulate at break-neck speed. Suddenly, the lead vehicle erupted into a white-hot fireball directly in the path of the onrushing second technical. It was too late! The second *technical* smashed into the first truck and careened out of control crashing into an abandoned house near the roadway. The soldiers serving the weapon in the back were killed instantly but the driver managed to crawl out of the wreckage and escape.

Trucks three and four slammed on their brakes and attempted to turn around on the narrow road that led to the consulate. Jake fired the second missile and was rewarded with a direct hit on the nearest truck. The driver of the surviving vehicle managed to get turned around and was now speeding away in the opposite direction.

"Yes!" shouted the ambassador. "That'll give them something to think about."

"Don't get too excited, sir. There're still a couple hundred bad guys out there," Jake replied calmly. Deep inside Jake was hoping this small victory would buy him some time but something told him he wouldn't be so lucky.

IT WAS UNFORTUNATE for the soldiers in the *technical* vehicles that the Americans had a few missiles, but it wasn't all bad news. Missiles were large enough to be seen with the naked eye. They could be observed from the time of launch all the way to their target. The rebel militia now knew where the enemy was hiding.

As Colonel Isa had explained to his men the Americans had shot at the first target that presented itself. It had been necessary to sacrifice a dozen men to pinpoint the exact location of the enemy, but what was that compared to the thousands who'd already given their lives in the holy war for liberation? Now that they knew where the enemy was hiding it was time to spring his deadly trap.

Jake was getting nervous. It'd taken only seconds to destroy the three *technicals*. He'd been much more successful than he'd hoped. What disturbed him was that three minutes had elapsed without a single shot being fired in his direction. He knew there were a couple hundred enemy troops out there. What were they doing and why weren't they shooting at him?

He didn't have to wonder for long. The NIPPLE militia did the unexpected. They moved as one man and came came charging out from where they'd taken cover. They were running straight at the consulate. It was out of character for them to conduct a frontal assault but if that was the way they wanted it Jake would play the game their way.

"Alright Ambassador, let 'em have it," Jake bellowed. Jake and the ambassador opened fire simultaneously. Rebels were falling like rows of corn mowed down by the devastating automatic weapons fire meted out by the two defenders.

Jake was sure they'd killed at least seventy or eighty men when the advance halted as quickly as it had started. The rebels were still directing heavy automatic weapons fire at the consulate but it was falling far short of their position. Something was wrong with the picture but Jake couldn't put his finger on it. The enemy had advanced to within seventy-five yards of the compound. Most of their rounds were now missing.

Jake looked at his watch desperately hoping it was time for the helicopters to arrive. Only five minutes had elapsed since the attack had started. They still had five minutes until the scheduled ETA of the choppers. That was too much time. He wasn't sure he could hold on that long.

Suddenly, the rebels stopped shooting. The stark silence concerned Jake more than the shooting. Then it came to him. Now he knew why they'd stopped shooting. Knowing he was already too late he spun around just as the first three infiltrators stepped onto the roof.

The ambassador saw motion out of the corner of his eye and turned to see death staring him in the face. The enemy nearest him had a pistol extended at arms length, hammer back, pointed straight at his head. Jake was a blur as he leapt into action. The ambassador couldn't remember seeing anything as frightening as what Jake did to the man who was pointing the gun at him. Sure, he'd seen martial arts demonstrations before but he'd always thought it was all hype. What Jake did to the enemy soldier definitely was not hype.

Jake killed like it was just another routine task. The ambassador watched as Jake stood slightly to the outside of his opponent's out-stretched arm, grabbed his gun hand, stepped into the elbow and yanked it toward his body. The man's arm made a loud popping noise as the forearm bone came tearing out a hole where the elbow should have been. Almost at the same instant Jake hooked his left arm around the man's neck with the inside of his arm against the man's throat. Dropping to one knee, he twisted the unfortunate soldier's neck and slammed the enemy's back across his knee, producing two more sickening pops.

The ambassador almost vomited when he realized what Jake had done. With no more effort than stepping on a bug, Jake broke the man's elbow, neck and back. This big country boy was indeed a dangerous man.

Still on one knee, Jake kicked another soldier attempting to tackle him, shattering his kneecap. As the man fell Jake jumped on top of him and drove his left thumb deep into his left eye. A split second later, he drove his right thumb under the man's Adam's apple, closed his fist around the now quivering cartilage, and ripped it out of his body.

He was too late as he went for the third man. The remaining enemy pulled the trigger on his AK-47 at the same instant the ambassador fired four rounds from his M-60 into the man's chest. The dying rebel's finger depressed the trigger as he fell backward, spraying Jake with steel jacketed bullets from the right thigh to the left shoulder. He was hit once in the leg, once in the stomach and two more times in the shoulder.

The ambassador jumped to the back of the armory and opened fire on thirty rebels who'd climbed the back fence under cover of the frontal assault. These guys weren't as ignorant as everyone thought. This had been a brilliant plan, but thanks to Jake's last minute understanding of the battle plan it hadn't worked.

Ambassador McClintock wasn't going to let anyone on the roof, not while he had an M-60 and several boxes of hand grenades. It was like old times for the ambassador. He sprayed the back courtyard with his M-60 while he lobbed hand grenades down upon the fleeing enemy. He pulled the grenade pins with his teeth just like he'd seen on television. In less than two minutes the courtyard was strewn with thirty dead rebel bodies. Seeing nothing living in the back courtyard he ran to the front of the roof. Nothing moving there either.

Crouching next to Jake he was surprised to see his eyes still open.

"How'd we do, sir?" asked Jake.

"Pretty good, soldier," the ambassador replied. "Try not to talk. I've got to take a look and see how bad you're hit."

"How long 'til the helo's get here?"

"I don't know. I think they should be here any moment," McClintock replied.

"I almost got you killed, sir; I should've figured out their game plan sooner."

"Nonsense, son; I owe my life to you. If you hadn't taken out that man with the pistol I'd be dead now."

The ambassador stripped Jake's uniform away from his wounds and was pleasantly surprised to see four small holes penetrating Jake's body. He'd seen this kind of wound in Vietnam. When a man is shot with a steel-jacketed bullet the projectile often passes through the body without making a hole any larger than the projectile itself. Whereas, lead bullets fragment, making a small penetration hole but a very large exit wound.

The leg injury was a clean flesh wound. The arm was going to take some fixing stateside. It appeared his shoulder blade was rearranged a bit. What concerned him the most was the bullet that had passed through Jake's abdomen slightly above and to the left of the navel. Jake was going to need emergency surgery if he was going to live.

The ambassador wasn't sure Jake could hold on long enough to get back to the *Tarawa's* operating room. As far as he could determine from the amount of blood that now drenched the fallen SEAL's uniform he would probably bleed to death in the next fifteen to twenty minutes.

Rebel Command Center

COLONEL ISA WAS pacing his office as a messenger burst in and informed him that the diversionary frontal attack and infiltration to the rear had failed. Isa was furious. He'd sent two hundred and thirty troops to capture a few Americans hiding in the American Consulate and they couldn't get the job done. Enough was enough! He'd personally take command of the embarrassing mission and make the

Americans sorry they'd ever invaded his sacred homeland. He still had another two hundred soldiers in reserve. He'd commit them to the battle and make a quick end of the Americans.

The enraged colonel quickly assembled his troops, loaded them into flat bed trucks, and ordered the drivers to drive as fast as possible on the winding city streets that led to the American Consulate.

Colonel Isa ordered the troops that had participated in the first attack to provide covering fire as he unloaded his militia on the enemy's left flank. He personally walked the line ensuring his men were in position and understood his orders. All was now ready. Colonel Benjamin Mohammed Isa was going to make history with this victory. The free people of Ethiopia would long remember the valiant charge that had destroyed the last remnants of the American aggressors. Surely, the new president would hear of his bravery and brilliant leadership. He could almost hear the words of praise he'd receive from the grateful president. Perhaps this victory would be the impetus that would propel him into the political arena.

Quickly surveying the deployment of his troops one more time he was confident he'd not overlooked anything. "Major Migandi, order the troops to charge the consulate!" he barked to his Chief Staff Officer.

American Consulate

THE AUTOMATIC WEAPONS fire that stopped when the infiltrators stepped onto the roof began again in earnest. The ambassador risked a quick look over the parapet of his makeshift fortification.

"Jake!" he shrieked. "The rebels are charging the compound!"

Jake lifted his head and peered over the protective wall of the rooftop parapet he was hiding behind. As the ambassador had said, the rebels were indeed charging. What he'd failed to notice was that they were approaching unabated from two directions.

"Sir, you take the group to the front. I'll try and do something with the ones on our left," Jake said in a weak voice.

The ambassador was having a hard time believing Jake was still alive much less still conscious and trying to fire a weapon. Jake was barely awake and drawing upon his last spark of life to kill a few more enemy soldiers. The wounded SEAL was propped up against the parapet and bleeding badly through his makeshift bandages. His eyes were starting to glaze over but he was fighting to remain conscious and do what he could to help. "This guy isn't going to be an easy kill. If the rebel thugs want to get their hands on him they're going to pay for the opportunity," thought the ambassador.

The ambassador was scared Jake would die and leave his flank exposed. He watched as Jake grabbed the top of the wall and tried to lift the M-60 into firing position and bring it to bear on the enemy. The gun dropped out of his grasp and clattered to the deck. He'd lost too much blood. But,the kid was a scrapper. McClintock saw him pick up the 40 mm grenade launcher. "Good move, Jake," he thought. "You're too bad off to fire an automatic weapon but you can handle the launcher quite well." The ambassador drew courage from Jake's losing struggle and found himself rooting for Jake, no longer fearing the onrushing rebels.

Holding the stock under his injured arm, Jake broke down the breach with his one good hand, loaded the cartridge type grenade, changed the weapon to his right hand, and fired with amazing accuracy. He managed to do this four times before he quietly slid down the wall lapsing into unconsciousness.

The ambassador was now certain he was only moments from death. Unable to hold off the attackers to his front he did his best to slow their approach. With Jake out of the equation he knew he didn't have much of a chance.

Suddenly, the ambassador saw the attacking soldiers to his front begin to disappear in a steady stream of blinding flashes. His ears where assaulted with the overwhelming concussions of numerous violent explosions and a strange "BRRRRRRRRP" sound. He saw *Cobra* gunships swooping over the attacking troops leaving a wide path of death and destruction in their wake.

The helicopters were crisscrossing the rebels and the pilots were using their helmet mounted laser sights to direct a devastating barrage of rockets and 20mm mini-cannon projectiles onto the confused and panic stricken attackers.

"Yeah! Give it to them," shouted the ambassador jubilantly. He jumped up and down on the rooftop oblivious to the inherent danger. The rebel soldiers were being decimated.

But suddenly, just as it seemed the helo's were about to completely annihilate the enemy, they flew away and disappeared over the horizon. The rebels were immediately on their feet and charging the consulate. The ambassador couldn't believe his eyes. Why did the *Cobras* leave? Why don't the rebels go away? Hasn't there been enough killing?

The ambassador saw the enemy approaching and knew he had to do something, but his body wouldn't move. He didn't feel scared. He didn't feel angry. In fact, he didn't feel anything. He was completely drained of all emotions. How could this be happening? Just when he thought he was about to be rescued the helicopters flew away.

McClintock was still lingering on that thought when he saw several solid streams of fire crisscrossing the enemy troops. The destruction was many times more devastating than the *Cobras* had inflicted on the first attack. Bullets were impacting every square inch of an area the size of two football fields. The ambassador vainly searched the sky for the gunships that were raining so much death upon the enemy. He saw nothing but tracer rounds resembling a continuous laser beam. There were four of these lasers dancing among the dead and dying, no doubt the work of the AC-130 gunships. Like the *Cobras*, these deadly "lasers" disappeared abruptly. Seconds later four *Cobra* gunships reappeared on the horizon escorting two enormous helicopters. One of the large helicopters approached flying barely above the ground. Suddenly, it flared up and hovered thirty feet overhead. The down wash from the five rotor blades finally caused him to move. He crouched low in one corner of the rooftop covering his head with his arms.

McClintock was hoping the helicopter would land and take him and Jake out of harms way. Instead, he saw five men dive out of the back holding onto ropes. Two feet before they impacted the deck the ropes went taut and the men simply released their hold and landed safely on the rooftop.

COLONEL ISA HEARD the approaching helicopters before he saw them. He was expecting the American Navy to send helicopters and had issued over twenty SA-5 shoulder launched missiles to his men. He had two separate fire teams deployed, one with each contingent of soldiers. However, expecting *Cobras* and knowing their full combat potential are two different things.

The rebel forces were cut to pieces by the airborne shrieking machines of death. Colonel Isa's men had no chance to shoulder their missiles before they were riddled with hot 20 mm cannon fire.

The rebel commander stood up to run for cover but before he took his first step he was violently propelled into the air. He landed ten feet from where he'd been standing. He tried to reach for his weapon which lay close-by but something was very wrong. He couldn't make his arm move. It was then that he noticed his arm was still attached to the pistol lying several feet away. A number of large holes appeared in his chest as he lay there calmly observing his severed limb.

It dawned upon him through his shock-clouded mind that this was unusual. The scenery around him began to grow dark. So, this was what death was like. He'd inflicted death upon more men than he could recall at the moment but he'd always thought that he'd somehow escape its grasp. His last thought before he departed this life was that there was no one who'd mourn his passing. He'd lived a solitary life always seeking more power and prestige. Too late he realized that his entire life had been wasted.

3

F IVE U.S. NAVY SEALs from Jake's' unit, SEAL Team Five, fast
roped onto the roof of the armory. Commander Lewis had received
permission to lead the rescue mission less than an hour ago and was now
standing on the rooftop looking down upon his severely wounded
Executive Officer. He quietly cursed himself for not confronting the
admiral sooner. "If I'd arrived ten minutes earlier I probably could've
saved my XO," he thought.

The SEAL team corpsman worked feverishly on Jake's unconscious
body. Blood was everywhere. The medic looked up at the CO and shook
his head leaving little doubt as to the seriousness of Jake's wounds.

"Skipper, we've got to get him out of here right now," the young
petty officer told his commanding officer. "He's lost so much blood. I've
done everything I can. I've stopped the bleeding in his shoulder and leg,
but the abdomen has me scared."

"Alright, son; we're doing everything we can," replied Lewis.

The SEAL team took up defensive positions on all four corners of the roof. They were loaded for bear and expecting trouble. Much to their dismay it looked like the Airedales (military jargon for those who fly aircraft) had done their work fairly well. There was nothing left alive among the scattered enemy bodies except a lone stray dog sniffing around the corpses.

Commander Lewis picked up his radio and informed the orbiting helicopters that it was safe to land. They immediately banked hard left and dropped into the compound, sending swirling clouds of dust in all directions.

The Marines disembarked from their helo and quickly checked the compound. Satisfied there was no longer any danger they posted several observation teams and sent the rest of the troops to carry stretchers. Several corpsman ran out from the back of the helo and checked the bodies that were strewn all over the compound. They found no survivors.

Gunnery Sergeant Mack Washington ordered a few of his men to load their fallen comrades onto the waiting helo. Marines always bring their heroes home, often going to great lengths to make sure their dead are honored. The lone bugler sounding taps, the rifle salutes, and the senior member of the funeral detail presenting the American flag to the widow "on behalf of a grateful nation," were deeply moving traditional rites that these men had earned. Gunny Washington was going to make sure they got what they deserved.

On the roof Commander Lewis and his SEAL team directed efforts to keep their wounded comrade alive. He watched as his men strapped Jake onto a stretcher and lowered him over the side of the armory. The waiting corpsmen quickly loaded the dying warrior onto the helo upon which the SEALs had arrived. Two young SEALs assisted Ambassador McClintock over the side. After all, he was an old man. The rest of the

SEALs jumped over the side and boarded the helo behind the ambassador. Jake's helo took off without waiting for the one that would evacuate the Marines a few moments later.

ONBOARD *TARAWA* the Senior Medical Officer was preparing his operating room for emergency surgery. Captain Nelson Rutherford Barnes Jr. was a third generation surgeon and son of Admiral Nelson Rutherford Barnes Sr., the former Chief of Naval Medicine from 1962-1964. Captain Barnes Jr. didn't let his pedigree interfere with his compassion for those whom he served. He was a first-class surgeon with years of experience in combat medicine.

The corpsmen aboard the helo briefed him over the radio on what to expect. Barnes decided to operate on the abdomen first. The other injuries could wait. His first problem was that he had to find a way to keep Jake alive long enough to operate on him. A forty-five minute return flight didn't do much for his chances of survival.

"L4N, this is S9K...Over." First Lieutenant Bob "Shorty" Crenshaw radioed.

"S9, L4, Roger...Over;" the Flag Command Center replied.

"I have a corpsman who wants to talk with Dr. Barnes... Over."

"Roger S9, wait...Out."

Moments later a tired voice came on the radio net, "S9, this is Dr. Barnes...Over."

"Roger, sir; this is Petty Officer Thomas. Commander Gregory's condition is worsening. His BP is 80 over 50. I think we're losing him, sir."

"Roger that. It doesn't look like the IV fluids are going to be enough. What blood type is the patient?"

"Wait one, sir;" the corpsman said as he grabbed Jake's dog tags. "'A' negative, sir."

"Does anyone on the aircraft have 'A' negative?" the doctor asked, not really expecting to be so lucky. "Uh, sir; this is 1st Lieutenant Crenshaw. I'm the HAC. I have 'A' negative," volunteered Shorty.

"OK Marine, is there anyone else up there who can fly that thing?" asked Captain Barnes.

"Yes, sir; I have a 2nd seater who can take it from here."

"Good, report to my corpsman. We just might be able to save your passenger."

Shorty looked at his copilot and shrugged. "You heard the man, Pete; you have the aircraft." Shorty unstrapped from his seat and reported to the corpman as requested.

"Well, "Doc; I guess you want to suck my blood," Shorty chuckled, but the feeble attempt at humor didn't work.

"Roll up your sleeve and lay down beside the commander, sir," the young medic said unceremoniously. Shorty heard the young medic's voice breaking as he said, "You just might be able to keep Mr. Gregory alive."

Shorty meekly complied, something Marine Corps officers didn't do very often. The SEALs had let everyone participating in the rescue know who it was they were going into harms way to pick up. A few stories of Jake's past exploits and heroism under fire went a long way to inspire the Marines to go the extra mile. Shorty's quick submission to the wishes of the corpsman was evidence the SEALs had been successful.

Thomas prepared Jake and Shorty for the transfusion. He was leaning over his severely wounded patient when Jake let out a gasp and stopped breathing. The medic froze. Shorty saw the fear in his eyes and reached over and squeezed his arm.

"It's OK, you can do this," said Shorty.

"What if I mess up?" cried he frantic corpsman.

"Look, if you don't do something he's going to die! Now snap out of it and do your stuff!" barked Shorty.

"God, help me," the desperate young man sobbed. "Don't let him die!"

Petty Officer Thomas pulled himself together and started doing what he was trained to do. He placed his fingers on Jake's jugular vein and felt for a pulse. "Good, there's a pulse. It's weak, but at least his heart hasn't stopped beating," said Thomas.

"OK, check the airway," the medic said to no one in particular. "Bingo!" he shouted. "The airway is blocked."

JAKE VOMITED. ROLLING his patient onto his side Thomas used his fingers to clear the airway. He rolled him onto his back, pinched his nose with his left hand, pulled his mouth open with the thumb of his right hand, and puffed three short breaths into Jake's mouth. Miraculously Jake started breathing.

"Alright!" shouted Thomas.

The emergency behind him, Thomas continued setting up for the transfusion. "Lieutenant Baker, let's do it," he said, holding up an enormous needle. "If we wait any longer his blood volume will be so low his heart will stop," the young corpsman explained.

Thomas worked silently. Shorty watched quietly as the young man skillfully went about his business. Petty Officer Thomas was merely nineteen years old yet he worked like a professional with twenty years of trauma experience.

Twenty minutes later HM3 Thomas was back on the radio to Captain Barnes. "Sir, I think the transfusion is working. His vitals are beginning to stabilize."

"Roger, keep up the good work. We're ready for him when you touch down."

Although alive, Jake hung precariously close to death. "Sir, if we don't get him into the OR he's not going to make it," he informed Shorty. "How much longer?"

"Just a couple of minutes. The pilot just reported over the intercom that he has the boat in sight."

The *Tarawa's* Air Boss cleared all air traffic from the skies around the ship and ordered Jake's helo to make a straight in approach. Captain Barnes and a stretcher team were waiting just inside the hatch closest to "Spot 2" where the helo was directed to land. The doctor had everybody in the OR "standing by".

"S9 on deck," a loudspeaker announced. Rotor blades still turning, two sailors in blue jerseys ran underneath the big helicopter and put chocks under each wheel. As they were connecting chains to several tie-down points four SEAL's emerged from the helo carrying Jake's stretcher trailed by HM3 Thomas holding an IV bag.

Doctor Barnes met the stretcher halfway across the flight deck and walked along beside the patient examining his wounds as they headed for the operating room. "This is going to be a tough one," said Barnes.

Before entering the OR Doctor Barnes directed the SEALs to place Jake on a gurney. Without a backward glance Doctor Barnes ordered all non-medical personnel out of the operating room. Commander Lewis didn't move. "Doc, this man and I have been through hell and back together. I'm not leaving him now!"

Captain Barnes spun around so fast that Lewis instinctively took a defensive stance. "Commander, if you're still here in thirty seconds I'll have the Master-at-Arms arrest you. I'll personally attend your court-martial and ensure that you spend the rest of your life in Leavenworth," Barnes snarled. "Mister, you're wasting my time and endangering this man's life. Now move!" Commander Lewis was convinced and meekly obeyed.

Doctor Barnes was not serious about the court-martial. He was a seasoned combat surgeon and over the years had used the same speech numerous times to keep a wounded sailor or marine's CO out of the OR. He understood the bond between men who routinely trust their lives to each other. He'd have allowed Lewis to stay with his friend if he could but obvious medical considerations and common sense precluded the practice.

ADMIRAL TAYLOR WAS sitting in the Flag Cabin when a Marine sentry escorted Ambassador McClintock into the room. "Ambassador, have a seat."

"Thank you, Admiral; please excuse my appearance. It's been a busy day," McClintock said chuckling.

"So I've heard. I understand the corpsman has checked you over and you're OK."

"Yes, sir; thank you for your concern. I'm tired and dirty, but besides that, I'm in pretty good shape."

"AMBASSADOR, I KNOW I need to let you get cleaned up and get some rest but I need a quick debrief of today's events. We're getting calls from the Secretary of Defense, Central Command in Tampa, and the State Department. Everyone is screaming to know what happened. We're preparing a press release and I'd like you to take a look at it before it's released," the admiral explained.

"Yes, sir; I understand. I'll be glad to fill in the details about what happened at the consulate, but first I've got a few pointed questions for you," retorted a now serious McClintock. The elation of being rescued was beginning to fade and he wanted to know why he hadn't been evacuated.

"Admiral, why didn't the Marines pick us up as planned?" the ambassador asked with fire in his eyes. "I lost nine men in that attack!"

"Sir, as I'm sure you remember, we had planned to evacuate you at first light. When you radioed and said you couldn't leave until your men completed shredding documents we delayed the mission for two hours.

Based upon late breaking intelligence provided by photo's from an AV-8 *Harrier* we decided to launch the mission at 0900 even though you still weren't ready," Taylor stated flatly.

It was apparent the admiral was starting to get angry. "As we reported to you at the time we saw the enemy making preparations to shell your compound. We couldn't take them out due to their close proximity to civilian housing areas. Central Command tasked the Air Force to provide two AC-130 gun ships out of Mombassa to provide overhead cover for the mission. We had our own *Cobra* gunships escorting CH-53's to make the pick-up."

Admiral Taylor was getting up a head of steam as he continued. "About thirty minutes out our man on the ground reported that you were under attack. Since the artillery pieces were located in a housing area our gunships were prevented from attacking due to the political ramifications of injuring civilians. We couldn't land while the rounds were impacting your position so we had to cancel the mission. You have my word that we did everything possible to get you out. So please, Ambassador, spare me the condescending attitude!"

McClintock was stunned. He couldn't remember the last time he'd received such a scalding reprimand. Ambassadors were normally accorded preferential treatment. Admiral Taylor must've missed that lecture at the Naval Academy.

"Admiral, forgive me. I have a way of losing my temper when things don't go my way," McClintock confessed. He now realized that he had no reason to feel betrayed. The Navy had indeed done everything possible to evacuate his men and had pulled off a brilliant rescue. As he thought about what had transpired he realized how dangerous the mission had been. Inserting troops and landing helicopters in the face of a vastly superior number of determined enemy soldiers is not what one would consider an easy task.

"Alright Ambassador, apology accepted. Now that you know what happened on our end let's hear your side of the story," the admiral said smiling benignly. McClintock quickly recounted everything he could remember.

Taylor listened quietly staring at his hands the whole time. His heart was stirred when he heard of the bravery of the two outnumbered defenders. His eyes watered as the ambassador told how Jake saved his life when the infiltrators gained access to the roof. McClintock described how the mortally wounded SEAL fired grenades and tried to protect him with his last dying breath. Admiral Taylor made a snap decision. "Ambassador, that young man is going to get a Navy Cross. I just hope it isn't posthumously."

"Admiral, if I've ever known a man who deserved a medal this one does. I owe my life to him," McClintock said.

Admiral Taylor reached out and gently placed his hand on the ambassador's shoulder. "Sir, now I owe you an apology. I misjudged you. What you did took great courage."

The two men sat quietly staring at each other, a new feeling of mutual respect passing between them. They both knew they'd established a bond between them that would remain long after they retired from public service. Their new friendship was something only men who've shared the brutality of combat could understand.

DOCTOR BARNES AND his surgical team worked feverishly on Lieutenant Commander Gregory. The abdominal injury was serious. He removed Jake's shirt and was momentarily nauseated. He'd never grown accustomed to seeing a man's intestines protruding from his stomach. Medically, the protruding intestines really weren't all that serious of a problem. He pushed them aside and made his incision six inches above and below the gaping stomach wound.

Although Jake had been hit with a steel jacket bullet, which striking him anywhere else would've resulted in a much smaller wound, the abdomen had a special set of rules. Stomach muscles have a tendency to pull apart when the abdomen is punctured. Originally, the stomach wound had a diameter approximating that of a pencil. Now, the entry hole was the size of a fifty-cent piece. Compounding matters further, fast moving projectiles create an overpressure in the body when passing through soft tissue. A vacuum is created behind the bullet which destroys much more tissue than does the projectile itself. This resulted in a large gapping wound in Jake's back and untold shock damage to his internal organs.

Retracting the tissue around the incision Doctor Barnes gingerly investigated the extent of the injury. Jake had been fortunate. Miraculously, no major arteries had been severed. The profuse loss of blood he'd suffered was the result of a nick in his spleen. That would have to come out.

The intestines were also damaged. He'd have to remove a small section. The trauma to the intestines would be a post-op concern as injuries of this sort often were, especially when the intestines have been outside the body cavity and subjected to the battlefield environment. In fact, wounds like the one in Jake's abdomen often resulted in life-threatening infections.

Captain Barnes saw no other complications. He mentally calculated the operation would take about two hours. Barring any unforeseen difficulties this man was going to live to fight again.

4

SARAH CRAWFORD WAS working the 3-11 shift at Balboa Naval Hospital in San Diego. A Navy nurse with eight years experience, she was reveling in the attention she'd been getting for the past two days. She remembered clearly the phone call that had placed her in the spotlight. She was sleeping late after working overtime the night before when the telephone rang. "Oh no, please don't let it be the hospital. I can't come in early today," she thought. Her alarm clock read 11:23 a.m. She was already trying to think of a way to tell the head nurse she couldn't report early when she picked up the phone.

"Lieutenant Crawford, this is Georgia in Captain Walter's office. The captain would like to see you at 1500. Please wear your Summer Whites," said a somewhat bored sounding secretary.

"Georgia, what's this all about?" asked a nervous Sarah. She was nervous because Captain Walters was the Commanding Officer of the naval hospital.

"I am not permitted to say, Lieutenant. May I relay to the captain that you will be present?"

"Of course, Georgia. I'll be there," replied Sarah. How could she say no? The United States Navy frowned upon lieutenants telling captains no.

Sarah's mind was racing. What had she done? She'd been stationed at Balboa for fifteen months and the only time she'd met the commanding officer was the day she checked-in. Perhaps she'd made a mistake on her charts. No, the CO wouldn't call her in for that. Maybe she'd been named in a Naval Investigative Service investigation, or Naval Criminal Investigative Service, as they were calling themselves now. Oh well, whatever the cause of the summons she knew she wasn't going to get anymore sleep.

After showering she picked out a fresh set of summer whites that were still in the dry cleaner's bag. It was always wise to have an "inspection ready" uniform in the closet. She was happy she'd adopted the practice. Too many of her friends had been embarrassed by short notice inspections when all of their uniforms were in the cleaners. The clock showed 1455 as Sarah entered Georgia's office. "I'm Lieutenant Crawford," said Sarah.

"Good afternoon, Lieutenant. Please have a seat. I'll let the captain know you're here."

Sarah took a seat next to the door and waited for her appointment. Two minutes later the door to Captain Walter's office opened and an exuberant Jan Swanson strode out. Jan was a good friend who'd joined the Navy two years before Sarah.

"Hi, Sarah." Jan beamed as she happily rushed past her and quickly exited the outer office. Something was out of place as Jan breezed past, but right now Sarah was too nervous to try to figure it out.

"Lieutenant Crawford, Captain Walters will see you now," Georgia intoned pleasantly.

Nervously, Sarah stood up and smartly entered the CO's office.

"Lieutenant Crawford, reporting as ordered, Sir," Sarah reported in her most military voice. She noticed that her department head was also in the office as well as an enlisted woman with a camera.

Captain Walters smiled broadly and said, "Relax, Lieutenant. Sorry to bring you over here on such short notice. I was reading my message traffic this morning and I ran across your name. I thought it would be appropriate to call you in and personally let you know why your name was in my message traffic." The captain was obviously enjoying himself.

"Lieutenant Crawford, come to attention," ordered her department head. Sarah popped tall; still not knowing what this was all about. "Sarah, it is my distinct pleasure to inform you that the Department of the Navy has promoted you to the rank of lieutenant commander. I am authorized to frock you to that rank. That means you are entitled to wear the rank and enjoy all privileges of rank, with the exception of those relating to administering punishment under the Uniform Code of Military Justice," said the captain.

Sarah was dumfounded. "Sir...there...uh...there must be some mistake," Sarah stammered. "I have to wait another two years to be in zone for lieutenant commander."

Captain Walters, still wearing his well practiced smile, said, "Sarah, you don't understand. You've been 'deep-selected' for O4. That means the Department of the Navy is so impressed by your record that they selected you for promotion two years ahead of your peers."

"Sir, I don't know what to say." Sarah was blushing. How mortifying. She hated it when she turned red.

"Then don't say anything. Just smile for the camera as Commander Van Kirk and I snap on your new shoulder boards," Captain Walters said, vainly trying to put Sarah at ease.

Standing to either side of the Navy's newest lieutenant commander,

Walters and Van Kirk removed her old shoulder boards and ceremoniously replaced them with the new ones. The photographer was taking pictures non-stop.

"Congratulations, Sarah," said Captain Walters as he posed for yet another "grin and grip" picture.

"Congratulations, Sarah," parroted Commander Van Kirk, shaking her hand firmly.

"Thank you sir, ma'am."

"Lieutenant Commander Gibson, thank you for your time. Please tell Georgia to send in my next appointment," Captain Walters ordered. Obviously, the ceremony was over. The CO escorted Sarah and Commander Van Kirk to the door still wearing his big, friendly smile. "Boy, it must really hurt to have your face frozen like that" Sarah thought as she hurried out of his office.

* * *

TWO DAYS HAD passed since she'd seen the CO and she was still enamored with the new rank. She was beginning to develop a stiff neck from looking at her new shoulder boards. She'd never realized how badly she'd desired to wear the two half inch and one quarter inch gold stripes.

Sarah wasn't power hungry. She cared little for the way people were now going out of their way to salute her. What she did appreciate though was that now people listened to her opinion. It was as if she'd suddenly become much wiser. One day she was just a wet-nosed lieutenant and the next day she was an all-knowing expert.

However, the real reason Sarah was excited about her promotion was that finally people were looking at her and seeing a professional naval officer. It was a great honor to be promoted two years ahead of your peers. Less than one percent of all naval officers ever receive such special recognition. The entire hospital staff now treated her with a new respect.

Sarah had always been smart. As her early promotion testified, her professional abilities were widely recognized as superior to others. Her fitness reports consistently singled her out as the number one performer.

In spite of all this the first thing people thought when they met Sarah Crawford wasn't what a great nurse she was. It was hard to think about anything when you met Sarah. Men normally stopped what they were doing and stared. Women gave her the once over and immediately label her as a threat. Simply stated, Sarah Crawford was a "looker". She was five feet seven inches tall and weighed one hundred twenty pounds with light brown hair and amazing green eyes. Her bubbly personality and sharp intellect were wrapped in a package that overshadowed all of her other strong points.

She'd spent most of her adult life trying to convince people that she had a brain. Now that the whole hospital was talking about her early promotion perhaps she'd finally be viewed as just another good nurse. She wanted that more than anything.

Commissioned as an ensign in the Navy Nurse Corps eight years earlier, she'd dedicated her life to becoming the best nurse she could possibly be. She was driven by a craving to be recognized as something other than a "babe." She heard men call her that so often she was beginning to wonder if it was on her nametag.

Sarah was consumed by her work and medical studies. She made time for nothing else. In fact, she hadn't been on a date in over a year. It wasn't that she disliked men, she just didn't have time for them. Besides, all the men she knew were so shallow she couldn't imagine trying to have a meaningful conversation about anything other than work. She certainly wasn't interested in the playboy jock kind that was always hitting on her.

Sarah was making rounds with the day shift nurse and getting briefed on each patient prior to shift change. The orthopedic ward normally didn't have any patients with life threatening conditions. Most of her patients were recovering from surgery or undergoing physical therapy of some sort.

"Have you heard about our new patient in room 618?" asked Lieutenant Commander Brenda Howard, the day shift Charge Nurse.

"No, what's the problem?" asked Sarah.

"Oh, nothing's wrong. It's what's right."

"Whatever are you talking about?"

"Sarah, I can't believe you haven't heard about our newest rehab patient."

"OK, I give. Are you going to give me a brief, or what?" Sarah asked, exasperation evident in her voice.

"Sure, here's his chart'" Brenda said between giggles.

"Brenda is acting very strange," thought Sarah as she read the chart. Hmm, nothing life threatening — six feet, four inches, 234 pounds — wow, he's a big one! "Apparently this patient had reconstructive surgery to correct some kind of damage to his shoulder," Sarah said.

"Yeah, bullet hole kind of damage," replied an excited Nurse Howard.

"Bullet holes? We don't get many of those. What happened?" Sarah asked, her interest now piqued.

"Sarah, don't you know anything! This is him! The guy who rescued that ambassador in Africa!" Brenda whispered as they approached the patient's door.

Yes, now she remembered. Sarah was almost religious about watching CNN. With her busy schedule she didn't have time to read the newspaper, so like the advertisement said, CNN was her "window to the world." She'd been following the developments in Ethiopia. When the reporters described the rescue that had taken place three months earlier she'd cried. Sarah was always emotionally affected when she heard reports about people risking their lives to help others. Maybe she was just old fashioned, but she admired people like that.

Sarah's heart nearly jumped out of her chest when she entered the patient's room. Lieutenant Commander Jacob Arlon Gregory was standing with his back to the door gingerly exercising his wounded shoulder as he stared out the window.

Turning around slowly Jake saw the two nurses standing in the doorway with their mouths open. "Evenin', ladies," he said, pouring on his best southern charm.

SARAH FELT HERSELF turning red. "What do you think you're doing?" asked Sarah, trying to take the offensive and keep him from noticing her embarrassing red face. "Put your shirt on and get back in bed," she ordered. Boy, did she hope he would put his shirt on. She was embarrassed to find herself staring. This guy had shoulders wider than the door. His stomach muscles looked like a washboard and his arms and chest were huge. She was so flushed she didn't even notice the scars.

"Sorry, Ma'am," Jake said apologetically. "I didn't mean to make you mad."

"I'm not mad," Sarah insisted.

"If you aren't mad then why is your face so red?" Jake asked innocently.

"My face isn't red!" Sarah said bitterly. "Now then, I'm Lieutenant Commander Crawford," Sarah said as she subconsciously adjusted her uniform. "I'll be the Charge Nurse for the next shift. If you need anything just push the call button," Sarah said as she spun around and quickly exited his room.

"What'd I do?" a puzzled Jake asked Nurse Howard.

"Oh, nothing, nothing. Lieutenant Commander Crawford was just a little surprised you were out of bed. Well, gotta go. I'll check in on you tomorrow, bye," Brenda said as she backed out of the room.

"Real smooth, Sarah. I must say you handled yourself very well," Nurse Howard chided.

"What're you talking about? I was just establishing the proper patient-nurse relationship. You've got to let those hero types know who's in charge," Sarah asserted.

"Don't try that lame excuse with me. I saw you turn beet red. You're just embarrassed you're attracted to him," Brenda said.

"Brenda, you think I'm attracted to *him?*" she said, emphasizing the "*him*" as if he were some type of insect. "How could I be attracted to someone like him? Did you hear that thick southern accent? He sounds dumb as a tree. I'll bet he didn't even graduate from high school."

"Sweetie, don't give me the wounded pride routine!" Brenda stated defiantly. "I've known you for a year and a half and you've never so much as looked at a man. Today, you walked into Jake Gregory's room and acted like a thirteen year old girl who'd just been kissed for the first time."

"Brenda Howard, how dare you speak to me like that! My demeanor was nothing less than the picture of professionalism," Sarah huffed.

"Sure, honey, that's why you were blushing like a new bride and stuttering like a fool. Oh, and don't think he's some kind of dummy just because he got a country twang. His commanding officer visited this morning and provided a wealth of information. It seems our cute mountain man graduated from the Naval Academy, earned a Masters Degree in Foreign Affairs from the Naval Postgraduate School and another Masters in European Affairs from George Washington University. He also speaks fluent Arabic and Russian. If you ask me, that makes him sort of an Appalachian Renaissance Man," Brenda said coyly.

"I don't care if he has a Ph.D. in Nuclear Physics. I'm not interested!" With that, she stormed off and busied herself with her charts.

JAKE SAT IN his bed thinking about Lieutenant Commander Sarah Lynn Crawford, United States Navy Nurse Corps. She had a strange affect on him; one he hadn't experienced since he was a teenager and madly in love with Samantha Tracey, a freckled-faced cheerleader at Hayes Junior High School. Jake wasn't sure if he knew what to make of his feelings. Logically speaking his present train of thought bordered on insanity. He'd seen a nurse for three or four minutes, been lectured like a school child, and now was unable to think of anything else.

Was this love at first sight? Perhaps he'd just been away from the real world for too long and was infatuated with the first pretty woman he met. Whatever the root cause, one thing was certain, he was going to find a way to get to know her better.

THE FOLLOWING MONTHS were painful for Jake in many ways. The orthopedic surgeon determined that his shoulder blade hadn't healed properly and performed another operation in which he broke the partially healed bone and reset the pins. Jake was beginning to think he'd never again enjoy full use of his left shoulder and arm. After suffering through three separate surgeries he still had two metal pins in his shoulder. The pins would have to be removed at a later date in yet another surgery.

That was just his orthopedic problem. Plastic surgeons were repairing the unsightly jagged scar on his back. The other wounds had healed very nicely but the exit wound in his back looked more like a badly healed burn than a bullet hole. Deep pits had developed in whitish scar tissue that stretched unevenly across his lower back. The ghastly looking skin was the diameter of a softball and set slightly to the right of the small of his back. His plastic surgeons planned to take skin from his buttocks and graft it over the site once his other injuries were completely healed.

Jake could deal with the physical pain. This wasn't his first combat injury. He'd earned a *Purple Heart* during Operation Iraqi Freedom as well. This pain was much deeper — internal —something no doctor could fix with a scalpel or a pill. It was like an emotional cancer eating away his desire to live and robbing him of the sense of purpose he'd possessed since his early teens.

Try as he might he couldn't figure out what was eating at him. He felt a growing cynicism toward life in general. Since being carried off of the rooftop in Ethiopia he'd begun to question where his life was heading and if what he did made any difference. His neatly arranged concept of good and evil was badly shaken. And then there was the dream that kept haunting him several nights a week. He couldn't remember all of it, only the overwhelming fear that came over him and that death was very near, reaching out its ugly hand to snatch away his life.

And then there was Sarah. No matter how hard he tried to reach out to her he was rebuffed. She was the only bright spot in his otherwise miserable day. He could think of little else.

When Sarah came into his room to check on him she wasn't rude but it was obvious she didn't like him. "What have I done to offend her?" Jake thought. "I've done everything I can to let her know how special I think she is, but it just seems to drive her further away."

As the weeks rolled by Jake's arm and shoulder gradually began to regain their strength. The surgeon said he was satisfied his patient was well enough to be released from the hospital and placed on limited duty. Physical therapy would be required for another three months but that could be accomplished on an outpatient basis. The plastic surgeons wanted to do some more work on his back but Jake would have no part of it. He wanted to go back to work. Maybe that would make him feel better.

Jake was informed of his impending release from the hospital and was surprised to find that he was filled with mixed emotions. Now he could return to Coronado and rejoin his SEAL team. He could start working out again and taking his daily six-mile run. The doctor had even encouraged him to start swimming again.

Normally, Jake didn't require much more than this to be happy. But Jake Gregory was not happy. The thought of never seeing Sarah again was more than he could bear. He decided to bring things to a head. Sarah would probably tell him to get lost but he was going to ask her for a date. He'd probably go down in flames but it was worth a shot.

"Hi, Sarah," Jake said as she entered his room. "Doc says I can go home today."

"Yes, I know. I have your paperwork all ready. You may leave any time you like."

"OK, but before I go I'd like to have a few words with you if I may," Jake said nervously.

"Sure Jake, what can I do for you?" asked Sarah.

"Jake! She called me Jake. She's never done that before. Maybe there is a chance!" Jake thought.

"Sarah, I appreciate how well you've cared for me the last couple of months."

"That's my job. I'm a nurse, remember?" Sarah said.

"Yeah, I know. Look, I'm a little nervous so I'll just speak my mind."

"Yes, why don't you. I do have a few other patients on the ward," Sarah said coolly.

"OK, here goes. I've wanted to ask you out for months but I've been too chicken. I'm checking out today so I figure it's now or never. So, how about it?" Jake said.

"How about what?" she asked.

"Gonna make it hard for me are you? OK, Sarah, will you go out with me?" Jake begged.

"I make it a policy never to date patients. However, since you're checking out I guess you are no longer a patient," Sarah said, smiling at Jake for the first time.

"Does that mean yes?" Jake asked hopefully.

"Yes, Jake; that means yes," Sarah answered tenderly.

Jake, for once, didn't know what to say. He'd been trying to find the courage to ask her out for months. He'd thought about a hundred different things he wanted to say to her but now he was speechless. She'd agreed to go out with him and all he could do was stare into her deep green eyes and grin stupidly like a gargoyle.

Sarah laughed. The laugh was not unkind but rather the type that escapes a heart that's finally free to express emotions that have been long repressed. Sarah had been fighting the way she felt about Jake since the first day that she met him. When Jake asked her out it took her by surprise. She'd done all that she could to discourage him but her resistance melted when she saw the sincerity in his eyes.

Sarah decided to break the awkward silence. "Let me give you my telephone number," she said as she scribbled it down on a scrap of paper she pulled from her pocket. "I'm off this weekend. Maybe we can do something."

"Yeah, sure; thanks," Jake said sheepishly.

"Well, I have to get back to my patients. I'll see you this weekend. Bye, Jake," she said, reluctantly moving toward the door.

Jake couldn't remember a time he'd felt more foolish. "I'm thirty-four years old, been shot twice, faced death a dozen times, and I'm so nervous I can't even carry on a coherent conversation with a pretty lady," Jake thought. Whenever Sarah Crawford was near him his mind seemed to disengage. "Man, I've got it bad!" Jake said to the wall as he packed his belongings.

* * *

SARAH CLEANED HER apartment for the second time in three hours. It was Friday afternoon and Jake was going to pick her up in an hour. She was a nervous wreck. Jake had been on her mind all week and she couldn't wait to see him. He'd called around noon and said he had a special evening planned. No matter how hard she pressed him he wouldn't tell her where they were going. All he said was to dress casually and bring a jacket.

Jake obviously didn't understand what he was putting her through. How was she supposed to know how to dress? Casual in California can mean anything from shorts and flip- flops to a business suit. After tearing through her closet and trying on one third of her wardrobe she settled on a knee length khaki skirt and a royal blue silk blouse. Shoes were another problem. Since she wasn't sure what the evening held she settled on a pair of brown dress leather sandals. "Jacket — hmm — this will do," thought Sarah as she selected a dark blue *Tommy Hilfiger* windbreaker.

After what seemed like days the doorbell rang. Sarah opened the door and was relieved to see Jake dressed in khaki slacks, white shirt, blue blazer, and Dockers, (no socks of course).

"Please come in."

Jake paused to drink deeply of her beauty when he saw her standing in the doorway smiling up at him. She had the most beautiful smile he'd ever seen. Her big green eyes sparkled like emeralds, radiating a warmth that melted his heart. His pulse was racing. "OK Jake, get a grip on yourself. Don't blow this chance," he thought.

"Sorry, we don't have time for me to come in. If you're ready we really need to get going. I have reservations for an hour from now and we can't be late."

"I'm ready if you are," Sarah said as she naturally slipped her arm through his as Jake escorted her to their waiting coach, in this case a 1964 *Corvette* convertible.

Sarah was pleasantly surprised Jake owned such a car. She was ashamed to admit it but for some reason she was expecting Jake to show up in a rustedout four-wheel drive truck. The more she found out about Jake the more he confused her. Most people fit into neat little molds - standard packages that fit a personality type. Jake didn't fit into a mold.

"So, where are we going?" Sarah asked.

"Sorry, I want it to be a surprise."

"Whatever you say. You're driving."

Sarah's apartment was in La Jolla, an upscale neighborhood north of San Diego. Jake headed toward Interstate 5 and accelerated down the southbound on ramp. Fifteen minutes later he parked the car on Harbor Drive across from the *Star of India*, a nineteenth century sailing ship that was the centerpiece of San Diego's Maritime Museum. The commercial pier was to the left of the *Star*. Jake led her down the pier to another more modern sailing ship, *The Hornblower*. *The Hornblower* sailed daily on whale watching tours and nightly on dinner cruises around scenic San Diego Harbor.

"I hope you don't get sea sick," Jake said. "I reserved two tickets for tonight's dinner cruise. I hope you don't mind."

"Jake, it's a wonderful idea. I've always wanted to go out on the *Hornblower*."

"Great, I was a little scared you might not like going out on a ship."

"Are you kidding," she replied. "Why do you think I joined the Navy? I only wish you'd warned me we were going on a dinner cruise so I would've known what to wear."

"Sorry. I guess guys don't think about things like that."

Hand in hand they strolled onto the old twin-mast sailing ship. The dining room was already full as they made their way to their table. Jake made a show of helping his date into her seat. Bowing in a greatly exaggerated motion, he said, "Your seat, my Lady."

"Kind of corny Jake, but still, I think its charming."

"I aim to please, my dear."

The waiter approached carrying a long box. "Miss Crawford, these are for you," he said as he handed her a box containing a dozen long stem roses.

"Oh Jake, they're beautiful. You're so thoughtful. Thank you."

Jake stared hard into her smiling eyes and said, "I don't know why but for some reason I seem to have trouble expressing my feelings with words. I hope the flowers tell you how special you are to me."

"Jake, I have something to confess. I haven't been completely honest with you."

"What do you mean? You aren't sorry you came are you?" Jake asked with a wounded look in his eyes.

"Oh no. Quite the contrary. I've been walking on cloud nine ever since you asked me out."

"Yeah, me too. So what do you want to confess?" Jake asked, once again smiling his best smile.

"Well... it's a long story, but I think you need to know. I haven't dated a lot of guys recently. Men are always hitting on me and I've become pretty callous. I hear them talking about me when they think I can't hear and I guess that maybe I've stopped trusting them. I'm not interested in the kind of relationship most men want.

Sarah's eyes were rimmed with tears as she continued, "I know I should be flattered that men find me attractive but it makes me feel cheap when I'm constantly bombarded with their dirty little innuendo's.

"I'm sorry for laying all of this on you but I don't want to start something that will end up hurting us both. I had a long string of boyfriends when I first came in the Navy and maybe I was a little disillusioned by the experience. They were either looking for a good time or a trophy wife. I'm not looking to be either."

Jake silently listened as Sarah poured out her heart. The smile was now gone. He could feel her pain. How many times had he ignorantly inflicted the same thing on women? Jake reached across the table and clutched her hand. "Sarah, I don't think you're cheap and I'd never knowingly hurt you. You're one of the most wonderful people I've ever met."

"Thank you. I knew the first day I met you that you were different. I've spent the last eight years trying to prove to people that I'm not some kind of dumb bimbo. I hate that word, but I know what most men are thinking when they see me." Tears were now streaming gently down her face.

"Jake, when I walked into your room I felt more alive than I have in years. I know I acted like I was a cold-hearted witch, but the truth is, I was trying to hide my true feelings for you. Can you forgive me?" Sarah asked with pleading eyes.

An impish smile quickly spread across Jake's face. "That depends," he said.

"Depends? On what?" Sarah asked.

"It depends on what the true feelings are that you were trying to deny."

Sarah laughed. It was good to see her laugh. "Jake," Sarah said with a hint of exasperation in her voice, "I think someone wasted a lot of money sending you to college. I guess I have to spell it out for you." Now it was Sarah's turn to be serious. "What I'm trying to say is that I really want to get to know you better. I know I'm out of my mind to tell you all of this on our first date, but I think you're special, and I just wanted to let you know where I'm coming from. If we're going to have any chance to build a relationship I thought you had to know. I hope I haven't scared you away."

Things were going better than Jake had dreamed possible. Earlier in the morning he'd worried he was moving too fast. He knew he loved her and was afraid that if he didn't move fast he'd lose her to someone more deserving. One thing was for sure; Jake Gregory wasn't one to beat around the bush. He firmly believed that once you made your mind up the best course of action was to act swiftly and decisively. Second thoughts were for losers and Jake didn't intend to lose this battle.

"Sarah, when I asked you out I didn't know how you felt about me. I tried to get through to you the whole time I was in the hospital. I thought you weren't interested but I couldn't get you off my mind. When you agreed to go out with me I was shocked. I thought that perhaps this was a sympathy date. All week long you've been all that I could think about. I know this may sound presumptuous, but I came to realize that I don't want to live the rest of my life in a world that doesn't revolve around you. You're the only ray of light I have in my life right now."

Jake was surprised to hear himself speaking his heart to Sarah. They were only thirty minutes into their first date and already he felt like he'd known her for years. He felt like she belonged beside him - as if God had made her especially for him. Indeed, the evening couldn't be going better if God had planned it himself.

Jake had developed two possible scenarios for tonight's date. Plan A was a long shot but it was what he really hoped to accomplish. Plan B was a scaled down version of Plan A in which he would try to get Sarah to go out with him again. His plan was to play it by ear and see which way the wind was blowing before he decided which plan to implement. The wind was definitely blowing in the direction of Plan A.

"Sarah, I have a confession to make too. I wasn't sure how you felt about me, but I was hoping for the best," he said as he took her hand in his. "Honey, I'm head-over-heels in love with you. You were worried about my commitment and intentions but I'm way ahead of you," Jake said as he reached in his pocket and retrieved a small velvet covered box. He opened it and pushed it across the table to Sarah. "Sarah, I love you.

Will you marry me." Sarah's surprise was total. Jake was holding his breath waiting for an answer.

"Oh! Jake, it's beautiful!" She leaned over the table and kissed him. "This is so overwhelming. I mean, this isn't what I expected on our first date. I don't know what to say. ` "

"Just say yes, and I'll spend the rest of my life trying to make you happy," beamed Jake.

"I need some time to sort all of this out. Please, don't be mad. I think I might be in love with you. No...I mean...I probably am. I just need some time," pleaded Sarah.

"Sure. A 'maybe' is better than a 'no'. Spend a little more time exposed to my irresistible charm and you'll come around," said Jake teasingly.

The rest of the dinner cruise was spent laughing and talking as they finished their meal, followed by a romantic stroll around deck. The night was perfect. The calm Pacific was illuminated by a full moon; a gentle salt breeze caressed them playfully as they stood silently by the rail. Sarah held tightly to Jake's arm feeling complete for the first time in her life. There was no need to ask him if he really loved her as much as she loved him for their hearts now spoke to one another with voices louder than words.

The Hornblower moored at Pier One as scheduled at eleven p.m. Jake and Sarah happily scampered across Harbor Drive heading for the public parking lot. Sarah carried her roses in one arm and held Jake around the waist with the other. A perfect ending to a memorable evening.

HECTOR RAMIREZ WAS from a good Catholic family in Southeast San Diego. His father was a hard working man who prided himself in never missing a day's work. He earned a meager living as a welder for a local shipyard with an hourly wage slightly higher than the average welder's because he worked the evening shift.

Although he earned a decent wage, supporting eleven children cost a lot of money. The family didn't lack the basic necessities of life but there wasn't much money left over after the bills were paid to purchase many conveniences. Hector's dad did the best he could and everyone was grateful they had food, clothes, and a solid roof over their heads. Everyone except Hector.

Hector was a strong-willed, rebellious teenager. His dad managed to keep him in line when he was younger but now that he was working evening shift Hector was pretty much doing whatever he wanted and hanging out with the wrong crowd. His dad suspected he may have joined a gang but Hector denied it vehemently.

Lately, his mother complained that Hector was acting strangely. Hector had even overheard her complaining to his father that she thought he was on drugs. Hector's mother's worst fears were well founded. He had a one hundred-dollar a day heroin habit.

Hector crouched between a Dodge van and a hot looking classic *Corvette*. He hadn't had a fix in five hours and was getting the shakes. All he needed was a quick score and he could once again put all his troubles behind him. He could almost feel the hot drug coursing through his veins, but that would have to wait. First, he had to liberate some money from some fat, rich *Gringo*.

Hector saw them walking toward him as he crouched in the darkness. This was going to be easy. The love bugs wouldn't know what hit them. Hector had the gun in his hand and was already anticipating pulling the trigger and blowing away the big guy. No use taking any chances. Just shoot them, grab the money, and drive their car downtown and buy more smack. No big deal. He'd already done the same thing once before.

Jake and Sarah were holding hands and smiling as they walked to the car. He released her hand as he approached the passenger side. Jake was forever the gentleman. Ten paces from the rear bumper Hector sprang from the darkness. He pointed the gun at Jake's head and yelled, "Give me your money man, or I'll blow you away." A scream froze in Sarah's throat.

Hector's eyes were playing tricks on him. People couldn't move as fast as the big man was moving. For some reason he hesitated in killing his prey. As his clouded mind started to work he realized his mistake. "OK, if this guy wants to play tough guy, I'll just ice him," Hector thought as he pulled the trigger.

Jake was angry. How dare this "smack freak" threaten the woman he loved? He clicked into automatic. His left hand grabbed the barrel of Hector's .44 Magnum and pushed it away while his right hand grabbed the gun slightly in front of the trigger guard. BOOM! The big gun went off opening a large hole in the Dodge van next to him! Jake back-peddled with his right foot and yanked his right hand backward with all of his might. Hector screamed as the trigger guard severed his index finger at the first knuckle. Jake slammed the gun handle down on Hector's head causing a loud CRACK! He picked up Hector's limp body and threw it aside.

"Sarah, get in the car!" Jake ordered.

Sarah jumped in as Jake ran around the car and angrily climbed into the driver's seat. He put Hector's gun under his seat and started the engine. As they drove away Jake saw Sarah looking at him. He recognized what was in her eyes – fear!

They drove in silence each deep in their own thoughts. Jake was concerned that Sarah would never go out with him again. If that dope addict caused any problems between them he'd track him down and kill him! He was sure Sarah would never marry someone who could hurt another human being the way he'd hurt Hector. She was such a delicate woman and he knew women were repulsed by violence. It didn't occur to him that he'd not spent one second thinking about how close he'd come to killing the attacker. Jake viewed the attacker simply as something that threatened to come between him and Sarah.

Sarah wasn't repulsed. She was awestruck. Emotionally she was all mixed up. Terror. That was one emotion she was experiencing. She was well aware that she'd had a close brush with death. If she'd been out with anyone else both of them would probably be lying dead in the parking lot. Instead, she was alive, sitting in a car next to the man she loved.

Sarah felt a little silly as she realized how safe she felt with Jake. She felt like saying, "You Tarzan, me Jane." Of course she'd really never say something like that but Jake did make her feel protected. What bothered her the most was that she enjoyed the feeling. Jake was a dangerous man, capable of killing another human. She was scared of him but attracted to him at the same time. She'd always thought she was above that sort of thing. Maybe she wasn't as liberated as she had once thought.

Jake pulled up in front of Sarah's apartment and stopped the car. When he looked at Sarah his expression was that of a man who'd lost something that could never be replaced.

"Sarah, I'm sorry you had to see that. If you don't want me to call you anymore, I'll understand," said Jake.

Sarah began to cry. Jake mistook the reason for the tears and started to apologize again. Sarah reached across the center console and took his hand. "Jake, that man was going to kill us. You saved my life!" she said. She leaned over and kissed him on the cheek.

Jake felt a warm tide sweeping through his body. He was embarrassed. He was shocked. He was happy. He was giddy. He didn't know what he was but he was glad she'd kissed him. Sarah made him feel as no other women ever had before. He couldn't think straight around her.

His thoughts were interrupted when Sarah said, "Well, aren't we going in?"

"Oh, yeah," Jake said, realizing that he'd been sitting with his mouth open like an idiot for about ten seconds. "Man, I've got to get a grip on myself or she's going to think I'm nuts," Jake thought.

Once inside, Jake called the San Diego Police Department and reported the attempted mugging. The police were full of questions. Yes, he'd press charges. No, he wasn't hurt. The mugger? Well, he might need an ambulance. Yes, he still had the gun. Yes, he could come down and fill out a report. Yes, he'd be sure to bring the gun with him.

Jake hung up the telephone and turned to Sarah, "Well, I guess I'd better go downtown and see the police."

"Do you want me to go with you?" asked Sarah.

"No, I don't think that will be necessary. I sorta forgot to tell them there was anybody with me when I got jumped," Jake said with an impish grin.

"OK, call me tomorrow," Sarah said as Jake backed toward the door.

He felt so awkward. What should he do? Should he kiss her good night or just leave? Man, this love stuff was complicated. He decided to compromise. He walked over and kissed her on the cheek and said, "See ya tomorrow."

6

JAKE FELT HIMSELF growing stronger as the days and weeks melted into one continuous flurry of activity. Although busy with their naval careers, they managed to find time for each other almost every day. Sarah's schedule was more of a problem than Jake's. She worked the 3-11 shift at Balboa Naval Hospital and had to work most weekends but she was happy to spend what little time she had with Jake.

Jake's time with Sarah was the highlight of his week, and for some reason, that bothered him. His growing love for her made it all that much harder for him to untangle the warring feelings that were tearing at his mind. He'd been through a lot the last few weeks and hadn't had time to sort it all out. Sitting in the familiar surroundings of his office in Coronado he tried to make sense out of it all but wasn't making much progress.

The whole time he was in the hospital he was anxious to get back to his command and resume the life that had always made him happy and provided him with a sense of purpose and belonging. Jake shivered when he recalled that his career had nearly come to an end a few weeks earlier when a team of doctors walked into his hospital room and asked him to accept a medical retirement. Jake couldn't imagine life outside of the SEALs. He'd been a SEAL his entire adult life — it was who he was.

Jake threw a fit, somehow convincing the doctors that he would in fact overcome his injuries and make a full recovery. Jake pled for them to hold the paperwork long enough to see if physical therapy would make a difference.

The evenings that he wasn't with Sarah were devoted to getting back into shape. He pushed himself relentlessly.

Swimming, running, and weight lifting became an obsession. Soon he was in better physical shape than before he was wounded.

His recovery was remarkable. He regained full range of motion and strength in his left arm and right leg. The only indications that he'd nearly lost his life were the massive scars; one covering most of his shoulder and extending down the left arm almost to the elbow, and the other a softball sized maceration of flesh in the small of his back. He was examined by the orthopedic surgeon and released from limited duty.

Now that he was back at work it just wasn't the same. He felt something was missing. Normally, he felt a sense of excitement about getting up in the morning and going to work to face the day's challenges.

He wasn't looking forward to doing his job any longer. Instead, he felt a strange mixture of disappointment and boredom. Doing what he did just didn't seem as important as it once had. What was the use? People got killed and nothing changed. And that stupid dream was getting worse. He didn't dare say anything to the shrinks at Balboa about it or they'd certainly reconsider his fitness for duty. If it hadn't been for Sarah his life would've been complete drudgery.

Sarah threw a surprise party a few days later to celebrate his return to full duty. In an unusual show of support almost everyone who'd provided medical care for Jake at Balboa attended the party. Captain Barnes couldn't attend but sent a message wishing him well. Jake's command turned out in force as well. Everybody that considered Jake to be a friend was there. Although he tried to hide it he was deeply moved by all the people who showed up to help him celebrate.

The party was in full swing when Sarah took a spoon and tapped her glass to get everyone's attention. The crowd of well-wishers fell silent. Clearing her throat, she said, "Jake, these friends that have assembled here tonight didn't come just to have a party at your expense. They wanted to let you know that you've touched their lives and made them better people."

The SEALs began shouting words of endearment at Jake. Only those familiar with the club understood that the comments were intended to be an encouragement. Sarah laughed and said, "OK fella's, enough snide remarks from the snake-eaters." Sarah continued. "Jake, everybody here has been pulling for you and wants you to know how much you mean to them."

Sarah fell silent as Jake took his cue, "Thank you all for coming tonight. You're all very good friends and I consider myself fortunate to have had the opportunity to get to know each and every one of you. I don't know if the experience was worth getting shot for but you're all OK in my book."

When Jake finished speaking, Sarah said, "And now I have one more surprise for you. Someone very special would like to speak to you on the telephone." Being forewarned, the crowd parted as Sarah led Jake to the phone.

"It's on speakerphone," Sarah warned.

Jake sheepishly looked around the room and said to whomever was on the other end of the telephone, "Hey! This is Jake!"

"Hello, Jake. This is Theo McClintock. When Sarah called and told me she was throwing a party for you I didn't want to be left out. Things have been moving fast for me since I returned from Ethiopia and I haven't had a chance to properly thank you for saving my life."

"Thank you, Ambassador, but it was no big deal, sir. I figured that since I was in the neighborhood I might as well make myself useful," Jake joked.

"Jake, I've got some good news that even Sarah doesn't know anything about. I wanted it to be a surprise. I was on a conference call with the Secretary of State and the Secretary of Defense yesterday and your name came up," the ambassador taunted.

"My name came up when you were talking to them?" Jake asked incredulously. "Why?"

"Jake, it's my distinct honor to invite you to Washington, D.C. as my guest. I am to escort you to a ceremony," the ambassador said, still toying with him.

"OK, I give. What kind of ceremony?" Jake asked innocently.

"Commander Gregory you are to be awarded the Navy Cross. Following the awards ceremony it will be my pleasure to introduce you to the President of the United States. He's been dying to meet you. I've made arrangements for you to bring Sarah, too."

A momentary hush fell over the room but it was quickly replaced by dozens of excited voices shouting congratulations. Jake and the ambassador exchanged a few more personal pleasantries and said good-bye. It was three in the morning before he managed to say good-bye to his guests.

* * *

A FEW WEEKS LATER after they returned from Washington, Sarah walked in the door of her apartment after work and heard the telephone ringing. "Who'd be calling me at this time of night? "

"Hello."

"Sarah, this is Jake. Do you mind if I come over? Something has come up."

It was obvious from his tone of voice that whatever had come up wasn't good.

"What is it Jake?"

"I don't want to tell you over the phone. I'll be there in thirty minutes," Jake said. The line went dead on Sarah's end.

Jake arrived in twenty-five minutes. Obviously, he hadn't obeyed the speed limit. "Sarah, I've got bad news," he said as she opened the door.

"Come in and sit down," Sarah said in a voice much calmer than she was feeling. "What is it?"

"Tom Barnes broke his leg on a training jump yesterday," Jake blurted. Tom was a mutual friend who was the Officer in Charge (OIC) of a detachment of SEALs in Riyadh, Saudi Arabia. He was responsible for training the Special Forces from the various Gulf Coalition Countries (GCC).

"Jake, Tom is a friend of ours and I'm sorry he's been hurt, but why did you think you had to come over here at midnight to tell me."

"I've been ordered to replace him. I leave in two days!" Jake's words took Sarah's breath away. She couldn't imagine being without him.

"How...uh, ...how long will you be gone?"

"I imagine the orders will be for at least six months. It'll be difficult to find a permanent replacement. That part of the world isn't very hospitable so I wouldn't expect a lot of people to volunteer."

Sarah's only reply was to hug him around the neck and softly cry.

Dhahran, Saudi Arabia

T HE HEAT WAS unbelievable when Jake stepped off the C-5 *Galaxy* in Dhahran. Arriving at 2330 he'd expected it to be much cooler. It had to be at least ninety degrees and the humidity was suffocating. He'd never experienced a summer night quite like this one.

During Operation Iraqui Freedom he'd spent his nights much further north in Iraq. The temperatures at that time of year were much different. In fact, a couple of Army Rangers who'd made the same high altitude, low opening (HALO) parachute jump on the night he was inserted into Iraq died of exposure. It was hard to believe a couple hundred miles could make so much difference in the weather.

Lieutenant Sammy Black met Jake at the bottom of the ladder. Sammy was the next senior SEAL in Jake's new unit. Sammy didn't look like an elite commando. He was six feet tall and looked to be thin at first glance. He had hair so blond it was almost white with steel gray eyes. Jake thought he looked much more like the California surfer type than a naval officer. The five other SEALs assigned to the training detachment were all enlisted men.

On the way to the barracks Sammy briefed Jake on what to expect. He filled him in on what the Saudi Special Forces were interested in learning and what their strong points and weak points were. Sammy spent most of his time on the latter explaining the situation in a uniquely pungent and witty manner. Jake could tell he was going to like this brash young lieutenant.

The workday started for Jake and his crew at 0600 Sunday morning. The Arabic world operates Saturday through Wednesday, with their weekend being Thursday and Friday, much like the Jewish Sabbath. Historically, the custom originated in 620 AD when Muhammad, who'd been spurned by the Arabic people in Taif, attempted to gain the support of the Jewish merchants living in the area. He even adopted the Jewish holiday.

Later, when he'd gained the support of the Arabic population and the Jews fell out of favor with him he changed the days of rest to Thursday and Friday. This caused the Jewish merchants to lose business as they now had no Arabic customers on Thursday and Friday and they were closed to observe the Sabbath on Saturday. The SEAL detachment's routine was to get in two hours of physical training before their Arab students arrived. This schedule accommodated the Islamic student's morning prayers and allowed the SEALs to exercise before the sun pushed the temperature over 100° Fahrenheit.

Jake was pleased with what he saw when the Saudi troops arrived for training. They appeared to be in excellent physical condition. His initial impression proved to be accurate. More surprising still was their expertise with small arms. Each soldier proved to be proficient with several weapons.

One small wiry looking Saudi asked Jake to demonstrate some American hand-to-hand combat techniques. Jake noticed all the Saudi's were snickering as he produced a rubber training knife. So, they had a resident martial arts expert! Well, he had a few surprises of his own.

The little Arab feinted and slashed at Jake's chest with the knife. Jake ducked under the arc of the knife and brought a knee up into the attacker's midsection nearly knocking the air out of him. As the man bent over momentarily to catch his breath Jake hammered the back of his head with both fists. He went down like a rock, but to everyone's surprise jumped up and jabbed at Jake with the knife. The snickering stopped abruptly as Jake grabbed his arm and their "expert" screamed out in pain as Jake applied pressure in an elbow joint lock. The rubber knife fell to the ground and Jake kicked it across the room. He looked the Saudi in the eye and saw that he'd had enough.

Jake was an instant hit with the Saudi troops. They quickly forgot that he was a foreigner and trained hard trying to please him. Jake genuinely respected their abilities and concluded that their shortcomings weren't due to a lack of desire. In fact, they'd make formidable adversaries if they received the proper training. Their most glaring deficiency was their inability to fight as a unit. They lacked the *esprit de corps* and cohesion required to be successful in their chosen line of work. But that was something he could fix.

AFTER LUNCH JAKE was introduced to the Saudi Commander of Special Forces, a tough looking man of about forty. Jake was good at judging people and could tell that this man had mettle. Colonel Muhammad bin Abu Talib and Jake soon became fast friends. The colonel saw in Jake what he wanted his men to become.

Colonel Talib spent the next three hours telling Jake what he wanted him to teach his men. The colonel's understanding of his men's weaknesses impressed Jake. There was no attempt to hide their problems. The colonel was concerned with only one thing: he wanted his men to be the finest Special Forces Corp in the Arab world. Jake could work with this man.

Jake threw himself into the task that was before him and the Saudi forces were eager to learn the skills Jake taught them. They studied the art of concealment, how to conduct an ambush, how to direct their fire at night, and how to take down a fortified enemy defensive position. Jake demonstrated how to plant explosive charges on tanks and armored vehicles without getting yourself killed in the process. Most importantly, he taught them how fight with their minds. The key to survival and success in combat was to fight smarter than the enemy, not necessarily harder.

ADMIRAL JEFFREY TAYLOR stood before the assembled troops in the hot midday sun as he prepared to read his official orders giving him command of all naval forces in the Middle East. Admiral Taylor still couldn't believe it. He was chosen for the job ahead of nearly two dozen of the Navy's more senior officers. The events that led to his selection were bizarre to say the least.

Several months earlier when his Amphibious Task Group returned from a deployment to the Arabian Gulf and Northern Africa, Admiral Taylor and his wife were invited to lunch by the Chief of Naval Personnel, Admiral Edward Stevens. Admiral Stevens and Admiral Taylor had been friends since the days when they were both lieutenants serving in Vietnam. The Taylor's simply thought they were having lunch with an old friend. During the course of the afternoon Admiral Stevens asked Mrs. Taylor as many questions as he did Admiral Taylor. Admiral and Mrs. Taylor thought he was just being polite and trying to include her in the conversation. Actually, he was interviewing them as a husband and wife team to see if they were suitable to represent the United States as the next Commander, United States Naval Forces Central Command.

Legally, promotions must be based solely upon the performance of the person on active duty. However, everyone knew that was not the case, especially among flag officers. Admirals spend most of their time entertaining dignitaries and an admiral's wife is subjected to pressures that would drive the average housewife insane. The United States Navy wasn't going to impose such rigorous demands upon an unwilling participant.

Two weeks later Admiral Taylor received a call from Admiral Stevens. "Hello, Jeff; this is Ed Stevens."

"Admiral Stevens, good to hear from you. To what do I owe the pleasure of this call?" asked Admiral Taylor.

"Well, unofficially of course, I wanted to be the first person to let you know you passed."

"Passed what?"

"I've got a confession to make. A couple weeks ago when I asked you and Tina to lunch it was more than a social call," said Stevens.

"Sir, what're you trying to tell me?" Taylor didn't like it when people beat around the bush. A more junior person would've been told this in a more direct manner.

"Jeff, I've just come from a meeting with the Secretary of the Navy and the Chief of Naval Operations. If you're agreeable, you're going to replace Admiral Pierce as Commander of U.S. Naval Forces, Central Command (COMUSNAVCENT)."

The light came on in Admiral Taylor's mind. "Excuse me, sir, but that's a three star's job," Taylor said hopefully.

"I know, Jeff. We're already working on taking care of that little detail. You've been nominated for Vice Admiral."

Admiral Taylor felt like jumping out of his seat and dancing around the room, but three star admirals didn't do things like that. He couldn't wait to get off the telephone with the Chief of NAVPERS so he could call Tina and give her the good news. Well, at least she'd like the part about the promotion. He wasn't so sure about what she'd think when he told her they'd be moving to Bahrain. Tina was an attorney with a thriving law practice in Rancho Santa Fe, California.

Admiral Taylor may have had reservations about accepting his promotion to Vice Admiral had he known what the future held. His naval career had been one adventure after another and he wouldn't have had it any other way. Yet, he most likely would've opted to sit the next adventure out had he known the dangers that lay ahead.

7

THE WIND HOWLED fiercely through the leafless trees surrounding the secluded dacha. Nestled deep within the Ural Mountains the small house was lavishly outfitted with the latest western conveniences. The naive would've thought it was simply a retreat where some wealthy members of parliament tried to escape the stress of Moscow. Perhaps it was the secret hide-away of a high-ranking member of Chelstenov's cabinet, but it wasn't safe to speculate out loud. Yes, some things had changed in the years since *Perostroika*, but people still disappeared if they asked too many questions.

Gathered in front of a roaring fire were three of Russia's ruling party's elite, purportedly on a hunting trip to the mountains. The fact that these three men had never hunted before in their lives was not important. Nobody was going to ask any questions. The mere mention of their names would strike fear into the heart of anyone who might question why they were on a hunting trip in this kind of weather.

A closer look around the dacha would also reveal that the men around the fire had more than hunting in mind. Concealed in a poorly built barn-like building behind the main house was an armored personnel carrier with its engine running to keep ten heavily armed *Spetsnaz* soldiers from freezing to death. The officer in charge of the unit wasn't worried about CO_2 poisoning, not with the way the wind whipped through the walls.

Motion detectors were installed in the surrounding forest and the only road leading to the dacha was monitored by a dozen video cameras. The men inside didn't want to be disturbed.

At a quick glance, two of the men in the room could've been confused for brothers. Sergi Valshenko and Vladimir Masavich were both of medium height, barrel-chested and slightly pudgy. Their dark brown eyes were almost obscured by thick, bushy eyebrows, peering out from faces that seemed much older than appropriate for men who were barely sixty.

Alexi Yanochev hadn't changed much over the years. He still looked like an American movie star. He'd managed to keep his body in exquisite shape and, if anything, his boyish good looks had given way to a more mature and ruggedly handsome appearance.

"Comrade General," said Deputy Defense Minister Sergi Valshenko, "the *Rodina* is laid waste by the incompetence of our own countrymen. Our economy has collapsed. The Red Army is a hollow shell, raped of its power by gutless politicians who did not understand the consequences of removing the means for order in our society. What no foreign army in history could accomplish we have done to ourselves. I say it is time to act."

"My dear friend, Sergi; on the grand scale, your strategy is indeed attractive, but do you realize the full ramifications of your recommendation? Nothing in history has been so ambitious," cautioned

General Vladimir Masavich. Valshenko esteemed Masavich's opinion. After all, he was the commanding general of the motherland's armed forces.

Alexi Yanochev sat in front of the fire and quietly listened while Sergi Valshenko ranted about his master plan to restore Russia to political prominence. It did have its merits. Sergi's idea was good, yet fraught with risk. However, Alexi Yanochev had been known to throw caution to the wind and play the odds on occasions. It had been just such a gamble that had placed him at the helm of the KGB. (Although the Foreign Intelligence Service had replaced the KGB everyone still called the intelligence organization "the KGB.")

A series of accidents had claimed the lives of two political rivals vying for the post he now held, considered by many to be the nation's most powerful cabinet position. One man supposedly slipped in the shower and broke his neck. Another candidate's body had been discovered in a forest with his hands tied with a 9x21mm SP-10 armor piercing bullet from a Gyurza pistol lodged in his head. The planning and execution of the assassinations had been so skillful that Alexi wasn't even questioned when authorities investigated the deaths. Yes, Alexi Yanochev was willing to gamble if the stakes were high enough.

"Comrade General, Deputy Valshenko," Alexi began, "I must agree with Sergi's assessment that immediate action is required. We were idle while the great Soviet Empire was dismantled before our eyes, replaced by the anemic Confederation of Independent States. We were idle while our leaders vainly attempted to impose democracy upon our people. The revisionist dreams of Gorbachev and his followers have failed!" Alexi's voice reached a crescendo.

Everyone in the room knew Alexi was right. The Soviet Union had come apart at the seams. The Baltic Republics had proclaimed their independence years earlier and Russia was on the verge of a civil war in Georgia. Chelstenov attempted to establish a *sodruzhestvo*, or loose relationship, of independent states. He'd hoped to forge some type of economic and military agreement between the members of the former Soviet State, but it was not to be.

Chelstenov couldn't even convince the now independent states to agree to a weak unified command of troops similar to the United Nations which would provide a common defense from outside aggression. It wasn't entirely Chelstenov's fault. His predecessor had signed legislation on May 7, 1992 forming a Russian Ministry of Defense with the breakaway republics and had installed himself as Commander in Chief. His lack of respect for his new partners had offended all of them and sounded the death knell for any hopes of a joint defense pact. When Russia tried to convene a meeting of the new alliance on May 15, 1992, only four states attended and signed the joint pact.

The remnants of the former Soviet armed forces were totally confused as to who was in charge. Russia claimed all the armed forces as their own. Ukraine contended that all forces within their borders were now Ukrainian and nationalized the 350 navy ships homeported in Kiev. Soldiers and sailors were receiving orders from two different countries. Pandemonium ensued.

Things were so bad that Russian military commanders stationed in the now hostile states began selling their equipment to the highest bidder. Regimental commanders sold tanks, armored personnel carriers, and rocket launchers to anyone who wanted them. Business was so good that they went so far as to form a military hardware stock exchange.

"Our country is on the verge of anarchy," Yanochev continued quietly. "Those of us who love our nation must act quickly if there is to be anything left to save. Communism and Democracy must both be laid to rest in the same grave. We must glean the things from each system that made them strong and move forward to forge a 'New Russia.'"

Alexi was a powerful speaker but he possessed much more than simple charisma. His intellect was frightening. He had the ability to listen to the ill-conceived ideas of lesser men and transform them into inspirational strategies that were virtually foolproof. Scarier still, he had a knack for planting his ideas in the minds of those around him. Sergi's brilliant plan was a perfect example. Alexi had been steering Valshenko for months, kindling a patriotic fervor and fanning the flames in the direction that led to tonight's meeting.

Alexi already knew the basics of what he wanted to accomplish. The final plan came to him as Vladimir was complaining about the risk involved in Sergi's plan. Yes, Sergi's plan was basically flawed, but all Alexi wanted was for him to broach the subject so that he could solve the problem. The other two men sat spellbound as Alexi unfolded his master plan for the "New Russia" that would forever change the course of history. The plan's genius lay in its simplicity. The groundwork had already been laid unwittingly by those who would soon be deposed from power. Their incompetence had created the exact conditions required to ensure the plan's success. Now, all Alexi had to do was exploit what others had done.

Returning to Moscow that same night the conspirators began the task of organizing the coup. Seizing power wouldn't be a problem. The army was already under their control as were the KGB and several other key cabinet positions. The President's popularity had declined to the point that very few members of parliament remained loyal. The only question that remained was the timing. Alexi knew that timing was everything.

Washington D.C.

AMBASSADOR MCCLINTOCK SAT in his plush new State Department office in Washington, D.C. The recent episode in Ethiopia had caught the attention of the President of the United States, and therefore, the Secretary of State. The President fancied himself as a fighter and when he read the after action reports from the attack on the American Consulate he decided that he had to meet the gutsy old ambassador in person.

Invited to dinner at the White House, McClintock quickly proved to be much more than just another aging diplomat on a twilight posting. The man was intelligent, aggressive, courageous, and well versed on foreign policy. His views on the Middle East were insightful. In fact, the President expressed the opinion that McClintock probably knew more about that particular region of the world than all of his "expert" advisors combined.

Shortly after his dinner at the White House, Ambassador McClintock received an invitation to have lunch with Secretary of State Margaret Clark and Congressman Hank Massey, the Speaker of the House. After the usual pleasantries he was informed that the President was considering nominating him to replace the current Under Secretary of State for Middle Eastern Affairs.

Carson Jefferson had fallen out of favor with the President after a string of embarrassing foreign policy failures. Jefferson couldn't escape responsibility for the failed initiatives because all of them were his brainchildren. He'd used his office to ride roughshod over those who cautioned the Secretary of State to reconsider his "informed recommendations."

The Secretary had allowed himself to be swayed by his deputy and forwarded the ill-fated proposals to the President. They were an immediate disaster. The Arabs were outraged by the insensitivity of the American proposals and were now discussing expelling all American troops from their soil. Years of hard work were quickly unraveling. Something had to be done, and in Washington, that meant someone had to take the blame.

The Secretary of State pulled Jefferson's standing letter of resignation from his files and called him in for a chat. After a long conversation Jefferson signed his letter of resignation and slid it across the desk to his boss. The resignation would take effect as soon as a suitable replacement could be found.

The President announced the resignation at his weekly press conference. He looked especially sober as he said, "It is with deep regret that I have accepted a letter of resignation from Carson Jefferson, the Under Secretary of State for Middle Eastern Affairs. Carson has been a good friend and it causes me great sorrow to accept his resignation. When I telephoned Carson to find out what this was all about, he told me the demands of the job were causing him to be away from his family more than he thought prudent. After talking with Carson and his wife Joan I believe it is in the best interest of his family that I accept his resignation. We will miss him sorely, but we certainly understand his concerns."

McClintock was unquestionably overqualified for the position. He'd spent over twenty-five years as a diplomat in the region and had published numerous highly respected articles on Arab-American relations. Fluent in Arabic and Farsi, he was highly esteemed by the friendly Arabic gulf countries and was a frequent dinner guest of King Abdullah bin Abdul Aziz al Saud of Saudi Arabia.

Still, McClintock was mildly shocked when his nomination was unanimously approved. He still felt awkward when he read the gold letters on the door to his office, *The Honorable Theodore McClintock, Undersecretary of State for Middle Eastern Affairs.*

However, feeling awkward didn't stop McClintock from diving headfirst into his duties. Whereas Jefferson had been primarily a political opportunist McClintock was a nuts-and-bolts leader committed to serving the best interests of his country. Changes in his office were rapid and far-reaching. People who shared the new undersecretary's vision and work ethic replaced those who didn't shift gears to his way of doing business fast enough. In a matter of weeks, McClintock had the most productive, hard working staff at the State Department.

"Ambassador" was a title that seemed to fit the dignified looking undersecretary. Although everyone observed the appropriate protocol on official occasions, privately, people still referred to him as "Ambassador". McClintock didn't mind. After twenty-five years he was comfortable with the label.

One of the first things McClintock did after assuming office was to schedule a junket to the Middle East to try and reestablish the mutual goodwill that had once prevailed. His first meeting was with the rulers of Saudi Arabia, Bahrain, Qatar, the United Arab Emirates (U.A.E) and Oman. These Gulf Coast States were of vital interest to the United States.

Since the end of Operation Desert Storm, America had slowly built an aggressive schedule of multi-national military training exercises. These exercises achieved a number of political as well as military goals. Primarily, they fostered mutual respect among the Arab-American participants. America provided military training in exchange for utilization of Arab military bases in emergency situations. Some countries, such as Bahrain, even permitted the United States to forward deploy U.S. forces on their soil.

This was no small achievement when dealing with an Islamic country. Islamic laws, and therefore Muslims in general, view Americans as infidels. According to various Hadith and Sharia infidels are thought to defile the sacred ground of Islam. Muslims hold the Quran to be Allah's divine instructions to mankind for the conduct of all aspects of life. Hadith are things that Allah's prophet Muhammad said or did as recorded by a companion prophet. The Quran and the Hadith taken together are called "Sharia", or Islamic law. A leader risks starting an insurrection by the devoutly Islamic population if he violates the Sharia.

Americans were allowed on Islamic soil during the Gulf War as a necessary evil. King Fhad of Saudi Arabia showed great courage when he invited the multi-national coalition to stage the liberation of Kuwait from his country. Although the reason King Fhad allowed foreign troops to be based in his country was because the United States convinced him that Saddam Hussein's true goal was to seize all of the oil fields in Kuwait and Saudi Arabia, he still put his life at risk when he did so.

He not only violated religious custom but also dared to put the welfare of his country before the holy commands of the Quran. "*O ye who believe! Take not the Jew and Christian for friends. They are friends one to another. He among you who taketh them for friends is (one) of them. Lo! Allah guideth not wrongdoing folk.*" Surah al Ma-idah 5:51.

America built upon this new relationship after the war. In fact, the U.S. still had several Air Force fighter squadrons based in Dhahran, Saudi Arabia, and a squadron of AWACS in Riyadh. Now, thanks to Carson Jefferson's miscalculation of Arab sentiment the arrangement was in jeopardy.

McClintock and the Arab leaders met at Sheik Isa bin Al Khalifa's summer palace in Manama, Bahrain. The palace was situated on a picturesque expanse of land overlooking the Arabian Gulf. The Grand Mosque was across the street and provided a befitting backdrop for the conference.

Bahrain is a beautiful island in the Arabian Gulf just off the coast of Saudi Arabia. Ambassador McClintock was elated that the Gulf Coast Countries leaders had selected this particular Arab country to host the conference because it's the most pro-western in the region. It's an Islamic country but it is not repressive in the least. They have a thriving expatriate community who are free to live as they please so long as they don't interfere with the Islamic population.

McClintock was upbeat as he registered at the *Gulf Hotel* which is within easy walking distance of the palace. His position prohibited him from walking but he liked the thought of lodging near the site of the conference. Although he was filled with confidence, there was a small voice in the back of his subconscious mind telling him something was amiss.

Something was wrong with the picture, but he couldn't put his finger on it. He'd thought it strange when the meeting was scheduled for Bahrain. He'd presumed the conference would be held in Riyadh. Saudi Arabia had long ago established themselves as the spokesman in issues dealing with the Arabian Peninsula. Was that what was bothering him?

McClintock arrived at the palace in the usual Arab manner. His motorcade was complete with twelve motorcycle security guards dressed in dress white uniforms and red aigrette. His limousine was so lavish it was obscene — even by Washington standards. A less experienced diplomat would've objected to all of the expense and inconvenience the procession imposed upon his host. McClintock didn't object. He knew the extravagant show wasn't solely for his benefit. It would be an insult for a diplomat to refuse such an honor. The motorcade was an opportunity for the host government to show its people that they were meeting with someone important. Arabs derive their importance not from what they accomplish but from whom they meet. Important leaders meet with important people. That's why their newspapers are filled with endless pictures of the royal family receiving foreign dignitaries.

McClintock entered the lavish reception room and shook hands with the official party. Arab culture dictates that any business must be preceded by hours of socializing. McClintock smiled pleasantly as elaborately dressed servants served tea and finger foods. He smiled and nodded at the appropriate times during the introductions and endless questions about his health and well being. He was a most gracious guest during the obligatory exchanging of gifts. Finally, they were all seated around the oversized oval conference table and ready to start discussions.

Sheik Muhammad Isa bin Al- Khalifa of Bahrain, son of the former Emir, now the small country's new King, opened the conference. After thanking the participants for being so gracious as to accept his invitation on such short notice, he introduced the Honorable Theodore McClintock of the United States of America.

McClintock acknowledged each leader by name as he made his opening remarks. He spent a full twenty minutes reviewing the great strides the Gulf Coast Coalition had made through their participation in the joint U.S. - Arab military exercise program. Transitioning smoothly into the significant contribution the forward deployment of American forces had made to the defensive posture of each nation he presented a masterful argument for their continued presence in each country.

The assembled dignitaries sat stone-faced as McClintock presented his offer of increased American assistance in defending their countries against further aggression by their mutual enemy to the east as well as significant discounts on American military hardware.

Sheik Al-Khalifa stood and thanked Secretary McClintock for his kind words and offer of assistance. McClintock was beginning to think there was a glimmer of hope for his initiative when Al-Khalifa said, "However, we are but the servants of our people. We have had thousands of loyal subjects marching in our streets demanding the expulsion of all foreigners. Secretary Jefferson's proposal to form an Arab-American League of Nations under Saudi leadership threatened our national sovereignty. I fear it will be years before the breach of trust can be repaired."McClintock was both shocked and honored by Al-Khalifa's openness.

Al-Khalifa paused for affect. The room was charged as if lightening had struck. The sheik continued, "Those of us in this room fully appreciate the past contributions of America in the defense of the Arabian Peninsula, but we must appease the will of the people. Therefore, I am afraid we will be forced to order the immediate withdrawal of American forces from our soil and cancel all further military exercises until the sentiment of the people is assuaged."

So, that was that. McClintock didn't have to wonder why there'd been no discussion among the Arab leaders. Obviously, they'd met privately before he arrived. This meeting was just a formality at which they intended to inform the United States of their decision.

McClintock decided to make one last ditch effort to get some type of small concession. "America will continue to cherish your governments as our loyal friends regardless of the outcome of this meeting. We fully appreciate the precarious position my predecessor placed you in, but there may be a way to appease the anger of your people and still maintain a strong defensive posture."

McClintock was playing this by ear. "Perhaps we could highly publicize the cancellation of all joint exercises and announce a phased withdrawal of American forces. However, the phased withdrawal could prove to be a lengthy process - possibly as long as a year or two. If we pursue this course of action there is a possibility your people will be satisfied that you have adequately dealt with the problem. Our forces will remain on alert within the perimeter of your military bases and be available if you need them to defend against outside aggression," McClintock said.

"We will continue to provide technical advisors, intelligence support, and other low profile help that will not incite your people. We will be careful to remain out of sight and not draw attention to our presence."

Ambassador McClintock could tell by the way that the leaders were exchanging nods that he'd hit upon something. "My friend," said Al-Khalifa, "your proposal is most interesting. Allow us an opportunity to discuss this matter privately."

McClintock excused himself and was escorted by a servant to the anteroom. Two hours later he was invited to rejoin the assembled leaders. They'd agreed to his plan with a few modifications. The American Secretary of State was to submit a letter of apology to each country involved which would be published in their newspapers. Each country was to be forgiven the unpaid balance of American military sales as well. McClintock could live with the agreement. He was on an aircraft bound for Washington two hours later to present the proposal to the Secretary of State.

GREGOR STANISLOV SAT silently in the back seat of the aging Peugeot sedan. His young Iranian driver did his best to miss most of the potholes filling the long neglected highway leading to Tehran. He was sweltering under the summer sun, and of course, the car had no air-conditioning. Gregor could stand the heat, but the smell was something else entirely. He didn't know which was worse, the body odor of the driver or the smell of raw sewage assaulting him through the open windows.

Gregor had readily accepted the mission that had brought him here. How could anyone refuse a personal plea from the head of the Russian Intelligence Service? While most young agents could only reflect upon the accomplishments of their predecessors he was making history. He understood the importance of his task. Although he hadn't received any specific promises, Gregor knew that if he were successful Alexi Yanochev would reward him with a position of prominence in the new Russian government.

Gregor was a little disappointed when the young driver met him at Mehrabed International Airport. He'd expected to be received by some government official. No matter, he wasn't here to be entertained by the Iranians. He only wanted to deliver the message and go home.

They drove for over an hour through deteriorating neighborhoods and run down city streets. Gregor knew the driver was going in circles, but he figured it was all part of the game. The young man probably had instructions to make sure Gregor couldn't retrace their route when he was debriefed. That was no problem at all. He was totally lost the moment he got off the plane.

Finally, the car stopped in front of a dilapidated mosque. Gregor got out and was escorted inside by his driver. Inside the mosque Gregor got the impression that the game was over. A large bearded soldier shoved him roughly against a wall and searched him paying little homage to his privacy. Gregor was big at six foot tall and one hundred eighty pounds but this guy dwarfed him. Search complete, he was placed in an empty chair next to an overstuffed sofa.

A curtain parted and an elderly mullah stepped through it and took a seat next to him. Speaking French, the old man said, "I hope you bring good news from my old friend Alexi Yanochev."

Gregor was momentarily confused by the French speaking mullah. He thought he'd been given this assignment because he was fluent in Farsi. Perhaps the mullah was speaking French because he didn't want his security guards eavesdropping on their conversation. Oh well, Gregor was just as comfortable with the French language, courtesy of three years duty at the Russian Embassy in Paris.

"I do indeed," replied Gregor. "Comrade Yanochev wishes to discuss a mutually beneficial arrangement. He has a small problem that you may be able to help him solve. He in turn will help you achieve a goal you have discussed with him in the past."

"And what is it that I can do for my old friend Alexi Yanochev?"

Gregor quickly outlined Yanochev's proposal. The mullah sat back in his chair and stroked his beard. Stanislov knew that the mullah already knew parts of what Alexi Yanochev was planning. Alexi had sent a diplomatic communiqué via the embassy earlier in the week with a rough skeleton of the plan.

Gregor tried to read the clerics face to no avail. The wizened old man was apparently a master at this sort of thing and wasn't giving anything away. Perhaps the beard stroking implied the Ayatollah was impressed by the way Yanochev had worked out all of the details. And why wouldn't he be? The Revolutionary Council would undoubtedly agree to such a plan without hesitation. Hadn't they prayed that Allah would help them accomplish exactly what Yanochev was promising?

Yes, the Iranians were going to agree to the plan! These backward, self-righteous, zealots couldn't see past their hatred for the Jews and the Americans. Yanochev was playing them like a fine instrument. They would perform exactly as planned.

The mullah hurriedly dismissed Gregor and picked up the telephone. "Inform the ruling Mujtahid I must see them at once. My meeting with the Russian was more profitable than we had hoped."

The Kremlin

ALEXI YANOCHEV SAT across from President Chelstenov. Opening a folder marked "Top Secret" he said, "I have disturbing news. Our signal intelligence section in Azerbaijan has intercepted a communiqué from Tehran," reported Yanochev. "Apparently, the Azerbaijani rebel leader has struck some type of deal with the Iranians," he said as he slid a sheet of paper across the desk. "The message you hold in your hand is a copy of the interception."

"What do you make of this, Alexi?" asked Chelstenov. "I'm not an intelligence man."

"Since we only intercepted the reply from Tehran a few hours ago we can't be sure of the exact nature of the agreement, but it appears that Iran is promising to send troops and weapons to assist their Islamic brothers in Azerbaijan."

"Do you consider this a serious threat?" a concerned Chelstenov asked.

"Yes, sir; we have corroborating intelligence that indicates Iran is staging armor and equipment near their northern border at this very moment," Alexi said. "Additionally, the official IRNA news agency carried an article reporting a rally at Tehran's *Azadi* (Freedom) *Square*, with large crowds chanting 'Death to Russian Invaders.' Our agents in Tehran report there were over two hundred thousand people in attendance."

"Have you reported this information to the Army Chief of Staff, Vladimir Masavich?" Chelstenov asked.

"Yes, sir; he is preparing a request for reinforcements."

"Reinforcements? We are just now beginning to get the situation in Azerbaijan under control. Now that the Azerbaijani leadership is talking peace I don't intend to escalate hostilities by sending in more combat troops!" a defiant Chelstenov stated.

"Sir, we must take this new threat seriously. I only collect intelligence, but I recommend that you consider discussing the matter with General Masavich."

Chelstenov frowned as he considered what the West would do when they heard he was sending more troops to Azerbaijan. He was just starting to normalize relations with the Americans after years of antagonizing them at every opportunity.

His position as President had been severely undermined when he failed to crush the rebels in Baku. Yes, he'd sent troops to deal with the problem, just as his predecessor had sent the army to deal with Chechnya. People at home and abroad had criticized him for his brutality and seeming lack of control over his armed forces. He couldn't allow that to happen again. Neither could he allow the Iranians to assist the Azerbaijani rebels. If that happened he'd be forced to withdraw Russian troops and concede defeat or fight a prolonged, bloody war.

As Chelstenov considered his options he realized that if Iran came to the aide of Azerbaijan he'd have little choice but to commit more troops. Perhaps if he placed an overwhelming superior force on the Azerbaijani border the Iranians wouldn't be so anxious to help their Muslim cousins. He knew that Georgia, the former Soviet republic to the west of Azerbaijan, wouldn't offer any meaningful resistance to an Iranian invasion of their tiny neighbor. Only Russian troops could provide a credible deterrent.

Whatever course of action he chose he knew he must take the high moral ground in the Western press. That would require a trip to Washington to meet with the President of the United States. An emergency session of the United Nations Security Council would also be in order. Yes, this time he would appear to be the injured party. Surely, no one would blame him for committing troops in order to prevent further bloodshed.

MIKHAIL KOLSTOY HAD only been Foreign Minister for eight months. His aging predecessor had suffered a stroke and was now enjoying retirement in a two-bedroom Moscow apartment. Chelstenov had elevated Kolstoy to his present position for one reason - loyalty. The President was running out of men he could trust.

Kolstoy had labored faithfully at Chelstenov's side as the President rose through the ranks, ultimately gaining Russia's highest office after Gorbachev, Yeltsin and Putin's political demise. There were a number of men who were more qualified but their allegiance to Chelstenov was questionable. Chelstenov was confident Kolstoy would carry out his foreign policy directives. More importantly, he felt that he'd do so without trying to use his position to seize the Presidency. Others he was not so sure about!

Foreign Minister Kolstoy arrived at Chelstenov's office within thirty minutes of being summoned. He found the President slumped in his chair halfway through a bottle of vodka. He wasn't alarmed in the least. He'd been a personal friend of the aging politician for over thirty years and they'd spent the day drinking themselves into oblivion on more than one occasion.

"Mikhail, it is good to see you, my old friend," Chelstenov said without the slightest trace of a drunken slur. "Please, join me in my miseries," he said, sliding the bottle and an empty glass across the desk.

"Thank you for your kindness. How may I be of service?" asked Kolstoy as he poured himself a drink.

"Mikhail, I have much upon my mind. These are dark days for Mother Russia. As you well know, I don't have many friends left so I must rely on those that I have."

"Don't be so hard on yourself, sir. You have more friends than you think. Many in this great nation are still grateful for all you have done."

"Thank you, Mikhail. You're a good friend." Chelstenov paused before continuing. "I have just received some disturbing news from Alexi Yanochev." Kolstoy waited patiently for almost a full minute as Chelstenov stared blankly at his drink. "We have reason to believe that Iran is preparing to enter the Azerbaijani War."

"Are you sure?" gasped a visibly shaken Kolstoy.

"Fairly so. Alexi has received intelligence from a number of sources that indicates they're planning an invasion in the near future. Our options are very limited. I believe we must commit troops along the Azerbaijani border. "

"I concur," Kolstoy said. "We cannot permit the rebels to be reinforced. Iranian intervention would put victory out of reach. We'd be forced to wage a long term, bloody war to win. That's something we have neither the money nor the national will to accomplish."

Although he'd been in office only a short time, Mikhail Kolstoy had quickly demonstrated an appreciation for the dynamics of national policy. He'd lectured the Parliament on several occasions how that military intervention cost money and it cost lives. Soldiers had families. If a protracted war was to be won the citizens of the warring nation must understand the necessity for bloodshed and be willing to sacrifice their loved ones to achieve victory.

"Those are my thoughts exactly," replied Chelstenov. "We are barely able to feed our army much less fight a large scale war. We must move quickly if we are to avert further bloodshed. I want you to schedule a trip to Washington at once. I'll arrange to speak to the President of the United States. I want you to call an emergency session of the United Nations Security Council. Contact Alexi and have him provide you with the intelligence reports and satellite photographs. I intend to show the Americans everything we have. We must have their support."

Vladivostock Naval Base,
Vladivostock, Russia

DEPUTY DEFENSE MINISTER Sergi Valshenko and General Vladimir Masavich arrived at the Vladivostok Naval Base shortly after sunrise. Their meeting with Admiral of the Fleet Anatoly Rybakov had been arranged two months earlier only hours after they'd returned from their secret meeting in the Urals.

Admiral Rybakov and General Masavich were boyhood friends who'd maintained their friendship as they rose through the ranks. They corresponded often and made it a point to spend time together whenever their busy schedules allowed.

Recently, their conversations revolved around the terrible state of their beloved country. They'd watched in horror helplessly as the awesome military might of the Soviet Union became a casualty of democratic reforms. The great military machine that lifted Russia to super-power status had fallen victim to the economic failure of Chelstenov's government. The army could no longer feed itself. Vladivostok Naval Base frequently suffered through weeks without electrical power because his government couldn't pay the utility bill. The increasing number of senior officers being dismissed from service by Chelstenov also alarmed them. The Chief of Staff of the Russian Army and the Commanding General of the Azerbaijani campaign had been relieved for cause within the last year.

The fact that General Masavich had been promoted to his new position as a result was no comfort. They both knew he could easily be the next victim of Chelstenov's axe. Senior officers in all services felt threatened. No one felt safe any longer. Men with thirty and forty years of faithful service to their country were being dismissed in dishonor. This fact more than any other accounted for the widespread sentiment among all branches of the military that something had to be done about Chelstenov. The purpose of General Masavich's and Deputy Defense Minister Valshenko's visit was to discuss with Admiral Rybakov the specifics of what his part of that "something" was going to be.

The Pentagon

ROGER HARTLEY WAS on his third pot of coffee and it was only 6:00 am. The fifty-eight year old Secretary of Defense had been up all night. In fact, he'd not been to bed in seventy-two hours. He'd been looking forward to spending some time with his wife and family this weekend. He'd made reservations at the *Greenbrier* in neighboring White Sulfur Springs, West Virginia - a posh hotel that catered to Washington's elite. Just as he was beginning to wind things up on Friday afternoon the phone started ringing.

Things didn't look so bad at first, just some unannounced Iranian troop movements. Then the intelligence reports started pouring in. Something big was happening and he had no idea what it was. Satellite photographs, communication interceptions, human intelligence, and his pounding headache, all told him that the world was about to enter its next crisis.

Less than twenty-four hours after the Iranians started moving troops north the Russians began mobilizing their reserves. Russian military bases were on full alert and the Russian Air Force was heading south. Three Russian bomber regiments were already in varying stages of redeployment to an airfield in Azerbaijan. Iranian armored convoys were heading north to Tabriz, a city close to the northern border. All this, and not a word from Iran or Russia that anything was out of the ordinary.

Two days after it all started the President was acting like a man with his hair on fire, screaming for answers. Roger Hartley had none and neither did the CIA or NSA. Everyone could tell the President how many troops were going where but nobody knew why.

That was when the President got the call from Boris Chelstenov requesting a personal meeting and an emergency session of the UN. He briefly explained to the President why Russia was sending so many troops to Azerbaijan and promised more information when he arrived on Tuesday. There was no attempt to determine if the President was free on Tuesday, just a flat statement that he'd see him then. Hartley remembered thinking, "OK, good, this is something between Russia and Iran. Doesn't involve America. All I've got to do is keep an eye on things and we'll be fine."

He redirected America's national sensors to cover the converging armies. America's entire intelligence community was boresighted on Azerbaijan when a new wrinkle developed. Monday afternoon's satellite surveillance revealed that most of Russia's Pacific Fleet submarine pens were empty. Almost every submarine that was seaworthy had simply disappeared. Initial estimates were that over eighty subs were now at sea. Russia didn't need submarines to fight a land war with Iran.

Something was very wrong!

THE PRESIDENT WAS notified at 3:00 am Tuesday that the situation had changed. He assembled his key national security advisors at the White House at 7:00 am. Roger Hartley went down the list of what subs were underway and the weapons carried by each. He was visibly embarrassed when the President asked for locating data on the Russian submarine fleet. He was able to provide locating data on fewer than thirty submarines, and they were heading southeast, directly toward the American coastline. The CIA was adamant that the missing submarines posed no threat to the United States, but they were at a loss when asked to provide another plausible explanation.

Roger Hartley was impressed by the President's composure as he slowly twisted in his chair in the Situation Room. This was the first time he'd faced a direct threat to the United States. When he was informed that several of the missing submarines were *Typhoon* Class ballistic missile submarines, he was cool as ice. "Gentlemen," the President announced, "we are now at DEFCON II. Until I hear from the Russians we're going to assume the worst. Mr. Hartley, your only job in life is to locate those submarines. I want reports every four hours. If you don't feel you can provide me with satisfactory answers I'll find someone who can. Do I make myself clear?"

"Yes, sir!" Hartley managed to say.

"General Freeman," the President said as his eyes bored holes in the

Director of the CIA (DCI), "I expect every national sensor at our disposal to be assigned to this endeavor. You are to coordinate efforts with the National Security Agency (NSA) and the Defense Intelligence Agency (DIA). If they have any problems with that arrangement, let me know."

General Marshall Freeman nodded his head indicating he understood.

"Margaret," the President said addressing the Secretary of State, "use every means at your disposal to make contact with Chelstenov's government and try to find out what they are doing. There doesn't seem to be anyone on the other end of my red phone."

"We'll meet again in four hours. Plan to have lunch in the Situation Room." The President stood and strode out of the room.

No one spoke for a full minute. The Vice-President broke the silence and said sheepishly, "Well fella's, I guess we'd better get to work. General Freeman, please join me as I walk back to my office."

Outside the Situation Room when Vice-President Braxton was sure they were alone, he asked the DCI, "How are we progressing on our project?"

"Everything is proceeding on schedule. The patsy has been selected and the groundwork is laid for the cover story. It should go like clockwork. We're just waiting for word from you to execute the plan."

"OK. It's almost time. Get things started on your end. Expect to hear from me in the next few days."

Moscow

SEVERAL THOUSAND MILES away in Moscow, Defense Minister Andrei Nicklochev spent the evening going over the most recent intelligence reports. There was something that didn't make sense about the Iranian troop movements. Critical pieces of information that would normally be available were missing from the reports. It was almost as though someone was keeping something from him, but that couldn't happen. There were too many agencies involved in reporting intelligence. If someone in Army Intelligence were trying to keep him from seeing certain information the KGB would surely get the information to him. That was the reason for dual reporting.

Nicklochev picked up his secure telephone and dialed Alexi Yanochev's direct number. "Alexi, my good friend. This is Andrei Nicklochev," said the Defense Minister. "I've been studying the intelligence reports on the Iranian troop movements. The reports I'm getting appear to be missing information. I was wondering if you could answer some questions for me."

"Certainly, Comrade Nicklochev. What are friends for if not to help each other in time of need?" replied Alexi. "What questions do you have?"

"Well, I haven't seen any reports of the Iranian Air Force pre-positioning their aircraft near the front. If they plan to invade, wouldn't they utilize their air power? Considering the number of aircraft we've moved to the area I would think they'd attempt some type of response," said Andrei.

"Yes, you're right. The KGB does indeed have imagery of the Iranian Air Force pre-positioning to the front. I'll have copies delivered to your office in the morning," Alexi said. It was a lie. The Defense Minister was a little bit too smart for his own good.

"Another thing that bothers me," Nicklochev continued, "is that the Iranians haven't massed their armor on the Azerbaijan border. Instead, they have their tanks staged in Tabriz. It would make more sense to have them in front of their troops."

"Comrade Nicklochev, that is a brilliant deduction. I hadn't noticed. We must discuss the ramifications of your observation. I think we need to meet first thing tomorrow morning. Would that be convenient for you?" asked Alexi.

"Certainly, comrade Yanochev. Shall we say eight thirty?"

"Eight thirty will be fine," replied Alexi. It was an appointment Alexi didn't intend to keep.

"How could I have been so stupid?", thought Alexi. He'd carefully scripted the intelligence reports that were sent to the Russian leadership who weren't part of his secret group of consirators. The Director of Army Intelligence was one of his most loyal supporters. Alexi had complete control over all aspects of intelligence reporting.

People only saw what he wanted them to see. He could make people believe things were happening when they weren't. Such was the case with the phony intercepted message from Iran to the Azerbaijani rebels. Yet, he'd failed to anticipate the questions that Defense Minister Nicklochev had just asked. The Defense Minister's questions threatened Alexi's entire game plan.

IT WAS ALMOST midnight and Andrei Nicklochev was beginning to succumb to the late hour and his advancing age. He called for his driver and twenty minutes later was dropped off at his doorstep. He was deeply troubled by the problem with the intelligence reports. Never before had such important information been overlooked. The Russian intelligence apparatus was one of the best in the world. What could've gone wrong? Why was he denied critical reports? Oh well, he would think on this again in the morning.

As he was preparing for bed he felt a draft and saw that his bedroom window was open. "Stupid Ukrainian servant," he hissed as he walked to the window. The vinyl shade was flapping in the breeze. Lifting the shade he put both hands on the window and slammed it shut. "Strange, I've never before seen this hole in the glass," he thought. Andrei

Nicklochev felt no pain as he fell dead in front of the now closed window, a small hole in his forehead leaking blood.

Across Cherkassky Street from the late Defense Minister's house a lone figure rose from his hiding place and walked to a waiting car parked on Lubyansky Street two blocks away. As the car sped away, the army sergeant disassembled his sniper rifle and placed it in a canvass bag. Soon the rifle would be part of the foundation of one of Moscow's newest buildings. For that matter, so would the sniper.

9

THE SECRETARY OF Defense was taking the President's orders seriously. He'd tasked two Cruiser Destroyer Groups and three P-3C Patrol Squadrons to locate the Russians. That accounted for over twenty capital ships, fifteen Anti-Submarine Warfare (ASW) helicopters, two aircraft carriers with forty-eight S-3B ASW jet aircraft, and twenty-seven long-range shore based Lockheed P-3 *Orion* aircraft.

Two specially equipped civilian SURTASS "oceanographic research" ships were committed to the search as well. These were slow moving vessels that towed a long linear hydrophone array. They were strategic assets designed to track enemy nuclear ballistic missile submarines at extreme ranges and weren't normally assigned to a battle group. An exception was made in this case because an admiral by the name of Skip Warren had found a way to utilize them in conjunction with his aircraft and tactical towed arrays to reliably track anything that put noise in the water.

Additionally, the Secretary of Defense directed the entire Integrated Underwater Surveillance System (IUSS) to be dedicated to the effort. This system relied upon a number of national sensors, but primarily, it consisted of a vast network of underwater cables connected to huge hydrophone arrays called SOSUS.

These systems had been used primarily for oceanographic research since the end of the Cold War but they could still track submarines. The long hydrophone array cables were connected to equipment that converted noise in the water into frequency specific lines on thermographic paper. Technicians then expanded the frequency spectrum they were analyzing and determined the direction and exactly what type of submarine they were "hearing." By tracking the sub on different arrays and recording where the lines of bearing crossed they could get a fix on the target's location.

The Secretary of Defense meant to find the Russian submarines. He committed every resource at his disposal to detecting, localizing, and tracking each and every one of them. He wasn't concerned simply because the President had made finding them a condition of continued employment, but because he understood the threat posed by the unlocated submarines.

Among the missing Russian submarines were several ballistic missile platforms which carried nuclear missiles capable of reaching any city in America. What made the subs particularly dangerous was that they could launch all of their missiles without coming to the surface, making it impossible to detect a missile launch until it was too late. No one knew why Russia had sortied all of their submarines, but until they were found they were a matter of grave concern.

Aboard the USS Abraham Lincoln CVN-72

REAR ADMIRAL DOUGLAS "Skip" Warren was a living legend in the U.S. Navy. The common sailor revered him for his straight talk, well-deserved reputation as a warrior, and his tenacity in fighting to improve the life of the average enlisted sailor. Lean and muscular, the blond six foot surface warrior was a man that inspired confidence.

His widespread reputation as the navy's foremost expert in ASW was no exaggeration. Years earlier he'd developed most of the current tactics for finding submarines. An expert in oceanography, he had a natural talent for knowing what a submarine commander would do in virtually any given situation.

Eight years earlier he was the commanding officer of a *Spruance* Class Destroyer outfitted with the *SQR-19* towed array sonar system. At that time, most people in the navy didn't fully understand the potential of the new system. That was something Skip Douglas quickly rectified. He surprised everyone by developing tactics that dramatically increased his Destroyer Squadron's effectiveness in locating enemy submarines. Under his command, his crew set a record for the number of hours logged tracking enemy nuclear submarines, which no other ship had surpassed in the eight years that had elapsed since his destroyer command.

The fifty-one year old Admiral Warren didn't rest on his laurels after he was relieved as commanding officer. He served two tours in Washington DC and completed a command tour aboard an *Aegis* Cruiser. Now he was serving as Commander, Cruiser Destroyer Group One, a position that gave him command of an entire battle group. Warren called his CO's together two hours after receiving the top-secret orders calling for an immediate sortie of his battle group. Directed to proceed at top speed to the Northern Pacific Ocean (NORPAC) to locate and track the Russian submarine fleet, he made sure all of his commanders understood their orders.

Admiral Warren was an ardent student of naval history and loved to read biographies of great naval leaders. Much of his leadership style was developed through studying those who'd fought great sea battles successfully in the past. One of his favorite heroes was Admiral Lord Nelson of Great Britain. Admiral Warren adopted Lord Nelson's philosophy of training his captains to think as he would think and fight as he would fight. That way, when the original battle plan fell apart in "the fog of war", his CO's would know instinctively what he'd do if he were in their place. With that thought in mind, he told his assembled captains everything he knew about the looming Russian- Iranian war, the Russian submarine fleet, and his version of what was going on in Washington.

Had the situation not been so serious Admiral Warren would've laughed. For years he'd been telling people the Russian submarine fleet was still a threat but no one would listen. They labeled him as another career military man trying to justify his existence. When communism fell America was anxious to realize the so-called "Peace Dividend." Politicians told the American people that Russia was no longer a threat. They were now proclaimed to be freedom loving people. Years ago, the Russian reformer Gorbachev was named "Man of the Year." The press used that to lambaste anyone who dared contradict the party line and say Russia might not be all they appeared to be.

The big secret that everyone in the military knew was that Russia continued to build nuclear submarines at the same pace they did before the so-called "demise of the Russian Bear." Naval leaders tried to warn Congress and the American people that America was dismantling its Anti-Submarine Warfare forces too quickly, but no one would listen. Politicians were eager to divert money from the defense budget to their favorite social programs and the press was busy writing articles about the

"New World Order". The truth didn't fit their agenda so it was ignored.

When communism fell America let out a great sigh of relief. The cold war was over. Now that the Soviet Union was no longer a threat there was no need for a large standing army or such a large navy. President Reagan's dream of a six hundred ship navy was scaled back to a two hundred and seventy ship navy. America's navy no longer had the ability to meet simultaneous commitments simply because there weren't enough ships or sailors.

Entire classes of ships were deactivated in the rush to save money. The *Knox* and *Garcia* class frigates were scrapped. The *Belknap*, *Virginia*, and *Long Beach* class cruisers were retired. Numerous attack and ballistic missile submarines were decommissioned as well. These vessels weren't taken out of the inventory because they'd reached the end of their service life. They were mothballed for one reason- to save money. The defense budget was slashed so deeply the navy had no choice but to eliminate ships.

Admiral Warren allowed himself a few sarcastic thoughts. Where were all of the "defense experts" that assured America that Russia was not a threat? Why weren't there any stories in the news about liberal congressmen apologizing to the American people for misleading them?

Somewhere over the Atlantic Ocean

B ORIS CHELSTENOV AND Foreign Minister Kolstoy sat in the plush cabin of their official aircraft as it approached the American coastline. The flight was long and arduous but no one had fallen asleep. Everyone aboard understood the importance of their mission. The democratic revolution hadn't lived up to the expectations of the Russian people. They'd heard exaggerated stories about democracy and thought they'd automatically have enough money to buy whatever they needed once communism was abolished, equating freedom with all the material things they saw in the West.

While democracy didn't deliver all of the things they'd expected it did make some important changes. One change that President Chelstenov was slowly learning to deal with was "freedom of the press". The Russian people were getting the whole story for the first time in recent history. No other Russian leader had been forced to deal with the press, especially the foreign press. Chelstenov was a slow learner in this department but the light was beginning to come on. He was beginning to see the connection between public opinion, which is created in the press, and the success and longevity of governments.

He'd experienced the wrath of the western press on numerous occasions. This time he was determined to put the proper spin on what he was doing. Chelstenov was beginning to learn how to use the press to his advantage. Who could tell, perhaps he could even convince the United Nations to send peacekeeping troops to the Azerbaijani border.

"Mikhail," said President Chelstenov, "you're not looking well. You're white as a sheet."

"I'm not feeling very well," confessed Kolstoy. "I started getting weak about thirty minutes ago. Perhaps it was something I ate."

"We have another three hours before we land at Andrews Air Force Base. Why don't you go lie down? I'll have someone wake you before we land," a genuinely concerned Chelstenov said.

"Thank you. That's very kind. I believe I'll take your advice." Mikhail Kolstoy was indeed seriously ill. He was sweating profusely and extremely nauseous.

Chelstenov's aircraft was one hour out of Andrews Air Force Base when an orderly knocked on the door to Mikhail Kolstoy's sleeping quarters. Receiving no answer he knocked again and opened the door.

"Comrade Kolstoy, time to wake up. It's almost time to land." Mikhail was lying on his bunk in the fetal position still fully clothed. The orderly reached down and shook him gently by the shoulder.

"Sir, time to get up." The orderly was getting ready to shake him harder when a chill ran down his spine. Kolstoy's eyes were wide open. The orderly bolted out of the room yelling, "He's dead! He's dead!"

Security agents responded instantaneously. The tiny compartment was barely large enough to accommodate a bed and a washbasin but two KGB security officers drew their pistols and managed to crowd themselves into the room. People stood ten deep in the narrow aisle leading to the Foreign Minister's compartment trying to see inside. One of the KGB men came out of the room and motioned for Chelstenov's private physician.

The doctor carefully examined the Foreign Minister, narrating his findings as he worked as if he were conducting an autopsy and recording his findings. "Pupils fixed and dilated, finger nails and lips blue. No pulse or respiration. Judging from the lividity of the body Foreign Minister Kolstoy has been dead for at least an hour."

The pilot notified Andrews that there had been a death onboard their aircraft. The diplomatic communications section onboard tried in vain to reach their counterparts in the Kremlin but the radios yielded nothing but static. Something very strange was happening.

Chelstenov's aircraft was equipped with the latest satellite communications suites. Technically, they should've been able to establish secure radio communications instantaneously. They had back-up radios and back-up circuits. The technicians conducted self-diagnostic equipment checks and found their radios to be in perfect operating order.

The senior KGB officer reported the communications problem to Chelstenov's Chief of Staff. Boris Ilyshin's face lost all expression. A forty year Kremlin veteran, he knew immediately what was happening.

President Chelstenov was sitting across from his physician as the doctor hypothesized about possible causes of Kolstoy's death. Boris

Ilyshin interrupted the doctor in mid sentence.

"Comrade President, we need to speak privately. It can't wait," Ilyshin said.

"What is it Boris?" Chelstenov slurred. He was beginning to show the effects of his vodka.

"Doctor, if you will excuse us," Boris said as he glared at the doctor. The doctor took the hint and left the President's private compartment.

"Comrade, if you want to live, sober up!" Boris Ilyshin shouted as he grabbed the President's arm. A security guard opened the door and looked at the President. Chelstenov cautiously waved him away. He was quite sober now.

"What is so urgent that you speak to me in this manner?" an agitated Chelstenov asked.

"Comrade, your life is in danger. I believe a coup is underway. Foreign Minister Kolstoy has just been found dead and now we can't raise anyone at the Kremlin on our radios." The Chief of Staff was frantic.

"Are you sure our radios aren't malfunctioning?"

"Sir, that's impossible. We've checked them. Someone's turned off the radios in the Kremlin. We've tried to reach the National Command Center on the Emergency High Frequency circuit. They don't answer either. That can mean only one thing- we are no longer who they are taking orders from," Ilyshin stated flatly.

Chelstenov sat motionlessly for almost a full minute staring at the far wall. "There's one way I can tell if we're in the trouble you say. Have your men connect me with the President of the United States."

The White House Situation Room

PRESIDENT CHRISTOPHER BAINES Carpenter was entering his third day without sleep. He was drinking coffee in the Situation

Room with Secretary of State Margaret Clark, Secretary of Defense Roger Hartley, National Security Advisor Franklin Samuelson, and Director of the CIA General Marshall Freeman. They were seated in comfortable high-backed chairs on an elevated platform intently staring at a large screen display. A United States Navy captain was briefing them on the progress of the search for the submarines when the President's military attaché interrupted and approached the President. Lieutenant Colonel Tom Morris leaned over and said, "Sir, President Chelstenov is requesting to speak with you. He's thirty minutes out of Andrews Air Force Base at this time. We've patched him through to your handset." The President looked at the Secretary of Defense and arched his eyebrows and said, "Well, gentlemen, I guess now we'll find out what this is all about."

USS Abraham Lincoln CVN-72
The Central Pacific Ocean

ADMIRAL WARREN, SEATED in his chair in the Flag Command Center aboard the carrier *Abraham Lincoln,* was carefully studying the Joint Over the Horizon Targeting System large screen display. This system, called JOTS III, provided Admiral Warren with a composite overlay of all tactically significant information at the admiral's disposal and was gathered from a host of different sensors and sources. He could see the exact location of every ship and aircraft held on radar by any naval ship or aircraft. Intelligence information from multiple sources could also be displayed.

The watch team continually updated the positions of all known Russian submarines along with their course, speed, and predicted track. So far, they'd located all but about two dozen subs. They were prosecuting submarines from the Kamchatka Peninsula to the Central

Pacific Ocean.

Initially, the American response had been limited to utilizing SOSUS to establish a large area of probability, called an LOP, and then sending a P-3 *Orion* out to find the sub. Now, less than twenty-four hours after the Russian subs left port, Admiral Warren's battle group was sprinting toward the largest concentration of enemy submarine contacts. Another battle group from Pearl Harbor was steaming toward a cluster of Russian boats further north.

It's not very difficult to launch an aircraft to look for a submarine but it's an entirely different story when you have to send a ship. Fortunately, it was late Monday afternoon when the fleet was ordered to get underway within eight hours and the ships were fully manned. All that was required to get underway was to cast off the mooring lines. They could top off with fuel and take on all the other required supplies via replenishment at sea.

People unfamiliar with anti-submarine warfare would've thought it was quiet an accomplishment to locate so many submarines in such a short amount of time, but the admiral knew the accomplishment wasn't as astonishing as the statistics indicated. Nearly half of the submarines had simply come to the surface and radiated their radars, thus telling the world where they were located.

Admiral Warren was receiving "Well Done" messages from higher command, "Bravo Zulu's" in Navy jargon, but he didn't feel like celebrating. Studying the composite display, he got the feeling someone was playing him for a fool. He didn't like being a fool.

Try as he might he couldn't figure out the Russian strategy. They had to have one. You didn't sortie your entire submarine fleet unless you had a strategy. He'd studied Admiral of the Fleet Rybakov and knew he was a brilliant strategist. "OK, Admiral", Warren thought, "if I were you, why would I send my submarines out of port at full speed. You know that makes a lot of noise. You've undoubtedly studied my capabilities, just as I have studied you and yours. Why would you do something so stupid? We found two thirds of your subs without effort. Then you had them surface and turn on their radars. We had aircraft overhead immediately."

As Admiral Warren studied his JOTS display he noticed that all the Russian ballistic submarines had fanned out and headed toward the American coast. This was alarming, especially since many of the boats were front-line SSBNs. Surely, the Russian admiral knew America couldn't allow submarines capable of launching nuclear missiles to approach the American coastline unchallenged.

Many in Washington were wringing their hands- sure that Russia was preparing to unleash a nuclear attack upon the United States. Admiral Warren knew better. If that'd been the case the submarines would've done what submarines do best - approach their target unobserved. Far in the back of his mind a plausible explanation started to form. It wasn't based so much upon what he saw on the display as what he didn't see. He mentally kicked himself when it dawned upon him. He'd been suckered. Admiral Rybakov was indeed a worthy adversary.

Part of being a leader is knowing what questions to ask. He'd overlooked one very important question. How long could the Russian Fleet stay deployed? This question was usually answered by overhead imagery depicting trucks and crates on the piers. You could determine what type of weapons they were carrying by what types of crates were left on the pier. You knew how long they could stay out by how much food they onloaded.

"Watch Officer, get me the Intel Officer," snapped Admiral Warren.

"Aye aye, sir."

Four minutes later Captain Andy White, the Group Intelligence Officer, stepped through the hatch. "Yes sir. You wanted to see me?"

"Andy, how many pictures do you have of Vladivostok the day

before the Russians sortied their submarine fleet?"

"Quite a few, sir; why do you ask?"

"How many of those pictures show submarines onloading supplies or weapons?"

"Well, none of them do," replied the captain.

"Didn't that fact strike you as rather strange? Don't sailors have to eat?" asked the admiral.

"Yes, sir; now that you mention it, it's very strange. Normally, we get numerous reports of pier-side activity before a major deployment." Captain White was embarrassed and the admiral knew it.

"What does that tell you?"

"Admiral, it means either they don't intend to stay out very long or they plan to resupply somewhere else." The captain figured his best defense was to give the admiral straight answers.

"I'm sorry, Andy. I'm not upset with you. I'm just mad this didn't occur to me earlier," the admiral said apologetically. "I concur with your assessment for the most part. I'm beginning to wonder if both of your answers are not the case."

"I'm not following you, Admiral," confessed the Intel Officer.

"Andy, I hunted deer as a kid. I remember one cold November day I was sitting with my back against a tree hoping to bag my first buck. I'd been there about two hours when a couple of doe walked out of the woods and strolled right up to where I was sitting. I couldn't believe it. I sat real still and watched the female deer for about five minutes. Suddenly, I heard shots behind me. I got up and ran toward the noise. My dad was standing over a ten point buck he'd just shot. He smiled and thanked me for letting him have the shot. Later, he explained to me that a buck will often send the doe out into the open to attract a hunter's attention while he slips away in another direction. I don't know if that's really true, but I've got a sneaking suspicion that's what the Russians have done to us."

The Intelligence Officer's face broke into a wide grin. "Admiral, I've got to hand it to you. The entire national intelligence community has been concentrating on what we've been finding but no one has been looking into the significance of what we're missing."

Admiral Warren pressed his fingers together in front of his face. He was deep in thought and Captain White knew better than to interrupt him. The admiral leapt to his feet and began pacing back and forth. His predisposition toward pacing was a characteristic that got a lot of mileage at parties when his staff wanted to have some fun at the admiral's expense.

"Andy, let's pretend we are Admiral Rybakov for a moment," the admiral said. "If I wanted to send 'x' number of submarines someplace surreptitiously and I knew it was unlikely I could get them out of port undetected, what would I do?"

The admiral continued without waiting for an answer. "One way I could sneak my best subs out would be to overwhelm my opponent with targets. Give him what he is looking for and lead him away from the subs I'm trying to hide. I think Admiral Rybakov played upon our fears by sending large numbers of his "Boomers" (ballistic missile submarines) toward our coastline knowing we'd have to follow them."

"But wouldn't that run the risk of starting a nuclear war?" Captain White interrupted.

"Not the way he did it," Admiral Warren continued. "He had them leave port at full speed. You and I both know that a submarine can't fire its missiles going that fast. Furthermore, they know as well as we do that the faster you go the more noise you make. They put so much noise in the water that a deaf man could've followed them. Now, after leading us two days out of the way they have all their subs surface and radiate their radars. We congregate around them like flies on a watermelon while the other subs sneak off to wherever it is they are going!"

"I don't know, Admiral; your logic makes a lot of sense, but we don't have one shred of evidence to support your hypothesis," commented a skeptical Captain White.

"Andy, get the OPS Officer up here. I want to run this by him and see what he thinks," Admiral Warren ordered.

Captain Cliff Nelson was reviewing the admiral's operational brief prior to the afternoon presentation. Nelson was a hard man who didn't tolerate mistakes. Woe to the unfortunate junior officer who had a slide out of order or a spelling mistake. The captain believed an admiral deserved a flawless, professional brief. Any mistakes eroded his credibility. When dealing with admirals, credibility was your most valuable commodity.

Captain White called the Operations Officer from the telephone on the Battle Watch Officers console in the Flag Command Center. "Cliff, this is Andy. The admiral wants to see you in FCC right away."

"Roger, tell him I'm on my way," said the fifty-four year old OPS officer. Captain Nelson's cabin was one deck below FCC and it only took him a few moments to cover the distance.

"Good afternoon, Admiral. What's up?"

Admiral Warren quickly rehearsed his theory to the OPS Officer and said, "Cliff, I'd like you to get on the horn to SUBPAC (Submarine Forces Pacific) and run through what we've discussed. See what Admiral Fuller thinks. I'd like him to monitor the normal choke points and let me know if there's any Russian activity. Ask them if they can cover the Malacan Straits and the Strait of Hormuz. I've got an idea the missing subs are heading west."

The White House

THE PRESIDENT WAS pacing the Oval Office, something he never did. He needed a shave, his shirttail was partly out in the back, and his trousers looked as if they'd been slept in. His advisors watched quietly as he ran his fingers through his thick gray hair for the tenth time in five minutes. Clearly, he didn't like the news he'd just heard.

"So what you're telling me is that the Speaker of the House is going on the talk-show circuit and telling people we don't have a handle on the Russian problem?"

"That is correct, Mr. President," answered his newly appointed Press Secretary, Erline Frazier. "He just finished taping *Meet the Press* and will be on the *Larry King Show* tomorrow evening."

"That's all we need. People are already petrified. I can't believe Hank Massey is going to inflame the American people simply to try and take my job," lamented the President. "No wonder nobody trusts politicians!"

Erline Frazier held up her hand like a school girl and said, "Sir, I think we need to go on the offensive on this issue. I think we can steal Congressman Massey's thunder."

"Yeah, and what are we going to say. Maybe something like, "Yes, a crazy man has taken over Russia and he has every nuclear missile submarine he owns off our coast. But don't worry, I have everything under control". I don't think that would help very much Erline," exploded the President. The National Security Advisor arched his eyebrows and folded his hands together as the Secretary of Defense nervously cleared his throat. The President was operating on the edge of his ability and everyone in the room sensed it, with the possible exception of Erline Frazier. She was too new. Normally, a decisive and unemotional problem solver, he was losing his ability to sort things out. What a mess!

As everyone was filing out at the conclusion of the meeting, Vice President Braxton pulled Erline Frazier aside. "Erline, I think you're on to something that can really help. A press conference might be just the thing. I'm not thinking about the normal press room routine, though.

Let's do it right and make the boss look good in front of the public."

"What did you have in mind?"

"I think we ought to use this crisis to launch the President's re-election campaign," replied the Vice President. "Let Massey blow steam for the next week or so without the usual denials from our side. Then, we'll upstage him with something big of our own."

"I don't get it. How could we do something like that? If we let the public know the President is even remotely thinking about politics during a time like this it'll ruin any chance he has for re-election," retorted Frazier.

"Not if it's done right. We'll make it a big flag-waving affair. Show the President taking a tough stand against aggression, all that stuff. I know just the place to use as a backdrop too, the *Greenbrier*."

"That's a beautiful country setting. Maybe we could surround him with school children, union workers, and have a bunch of Marines in dress uniform standing around," offered the Press Secretary.

"That's the ticket, Erline. Why don't you come by my place this evening around 9:00 p.m. We can brainstorm the idea. I'm having General Freeman and a few other friends over. They might be able to help."

"Sure thing. I'd be honored," replied the Press Secretary. Honored was not the word. She was flattered and exhilarated all at the same time. She'd come a long way since her days at NBC anchoring a small market news program in Clearwater, Florida. She was finally moving in the right circles. If she played her cards right, she might be able to land a cabinet position during President Carpenter's next term.

10

USS Houston SSN-713
Malacan Straits

COMMANDER JASON BRUSTER was standing over the Senior Chief Sonar Technician's shoulder staring in disbelief at the sonar's waterfall display. He'd been patrolling four miles off the coast of Kuala Lumpur, the narrowest part of the Malacan Straits, for over a week and hadn't detected one submarine. Then, out of nowhere, he'd detected four Russian submarines in the last thirty minutes. Under normal circumstances he would've been elated to get some time tracking a potential enemy sub, but not after the message he'd just received from Admiral Fuller.

He had the message in his shirt pocket but the words were still fresh in his mind, "Detect and track all Russian submarine contacts. Hostile intent likely. Peacetime Rules of Engagement in effect modified as follows: Authorized to attack with MK-48 torpedoes if you are detected and enemy contact floods torpedo tubes or goes active on sonar. President of the United States ordered DEFCON II."

COMMANDER BRUSTER KNEW he was good at what he did. Judging from the message he'd just received from SUBPAC he was about to be given the opportunity to prove how good he really was. He'd been commanding officer of the USS *Houston* for fifteen months and knew his boat like the back of his hand. His crew was well trained and had always performed well in the attack trainers, but this was different. This time the enemy could shoot back. If they made any mistakes today it wouldn't cost them points - it would cost their lives.

The executive officer was leading the Fire Control Plotting Team a few feet away. He looked up and said, "Captain, contacts Alpha One and Alpha Two have reversed course and slowed to four knots. Alpha One and Alpha Two are both *Akula* Class attack submarines. Bearing and range to Alpha One is 035 degrees at 18,500 yards. Bearing and range to Alpha Two is 060 degrees at 17,000 yards."

"Very well. Update Alpha Three and Alpha Four," ordered the CO.

"Alpha Three is *Oscar* Class, bearing 038 degrees at 16,000 yards. Alpha Four is *Oscar* Class bearing 065 degrees at 16,500 yards," the XO reported.

Commander Bruster's submarine was creeping toward the enemy submarines at two knots. His mind quickly evaluated the tactical situation. They were in seven hundred feet of water. The thermal layer was at two hundred thirty-five feet and he'd set his depth at three hundred feet. Acoustically, he was in the best position to prevent detection by a surface ship. However, all four of the enemy submarines were on the same side of the thermal layer which made him somewhat vulnerable.

It was too late to change depth so he'd have to depend upon stealth to remain undetected. *Los Angeles* class submarines were the quietest in the world, with the exception of the new *Seawolf* class that the United States had recently put to sea, and he was confident he could avoid detection. Following Russian submarines at close range was standard fare for American submarine commanders and he didn't expect this time to be any different. All he had to do was wait for them to pass,and then maneuver his boat into their baffles. Once he was in their sonar's blind zone he could track them for days and they'd never know he was there.

Bruster was starting to breathe easier. This wasn't going to be all that taxing after all. He walked over to his chair in the control room and belted himself into the seat. He was reaching for his coffee when the Senior Chief yelled, "Torpedo bearing 035 degrees."

"All ahead flank, hard right rudder, fire decoys, dive," ordered the Officer of the Deck.

"Belay those orders," shouted the captain. "They don't know we're here. Sonar, what's the track on the torpedo?"

"Torpedo bears....Second torpedo launch, bearing 060 degrees," reported an excited sonar tech. "Sir, first and second torpedo are tracking away from our position. First torpedo was from contact Alpha One. Second torpedo was from Alpha Two. Designate first shot as Tango One. Second shot as Tango Two. Run time on Tango One is one minute thirty seconds. Run time on Tango Two is...forty-five seconds," reported the sonar watch.

"Sonar, have torpedoes switched to acquisition mode?" asked Bruster.

"Negative, sir."

"XO, are you tracking anything that could be a potential target?"

"No, sir; no surface tracks within range," replied the XO.

Forty seconds later sonar reported, "Sir, Alpha One firing second torpedo." The Fire Control Team designated the third shot as Tango Three. The Russian submarines continued firing torpedoes every thirty to forty seconds. After twelve torpedoes the firing stopped. Sonar reported that the torpedoes were running in a straight line which meant they weren't in a search mode. After three minutes run time the torpedo motors shut down. The two *Akula* submarines fired six torpedoes apiece. The fire control team plotted the firing platform's position, torpedo tracks, and torpedo run times. Once this information was plotted they marked the approximate position of where the torpedoes shut down. These positions were then double-checked and marked in red. When this task was complete the XO looked up and said, "Captain, you need to take a look at this."

"What is it, Bill?" asked Bruster.

"Sir, the two *Akula's* fired twelve shots total. At first I thought it sorta strange that there were no obvious targets. It just occurred to me that we also did not detect any torpedo sonar," the XO said.

"You're right. I was so busy making sure nothing was headed for us I didn't notice none of the torpedoes lit off a sonar," exclaimed Commander Bruster. "Then that can mean only one thing."

"Yes, sir; the Russians have mined the Malacan Straits," the XO replied.

"OK, have Lieutenant Rogers prepare a message informing SUBPAC about what's going on. As soon as the *Akula's* are P&O (passed and opening), we'll drop back and transmit using the trail wire antenna. Meanwhile, keep a good track on the *Oscars*. Folks, I think this means we are at war!" commented the CO dryly. "XO, trail the Comm wire and fire off a FLASH message to SUBPAC as soon as it's deployed. Let them know what's going on. This can't wait until our next communication cycle."

Thirty minutes later, Top Secret message boards were being

delivered to top ranking military officers throughout the Pentagon as well as the CIA, NSA, DIA, and various military intelligence commands. That was routine. What was unusual was that the message was sitting on the desk of Alexi Yanochev as well, courtesy of a highly placed friend in the United States.

The White House Situation Room

THE PRESIDENT LIFTED the handset mounted on the arm of his chair, "President Carpenter here. I've been trying to reach you for the past twenty-four hours." He was in no mood to be polite. The world was teetering on the brink of nuclear war and Chelstenov had been "unavailable."

"President Carpenter, I apologize for not calling you earlier, but I have experienced a few difficulties. My staff just found Foreign Minister Kolstoy dead in his cabin and my communications relay with Moscow has been, shall we say, interrupted," said Chelstenov.

"We'll discuss apologies later. I want to know why you've sortied your submarine fleet out of Vladivostok!" demanded the President.

There was silence on the other end of the line. After approximately forty seconds had elapsed, President Carpenter became impatient. "President Chelstenov, are you there?"

"Uh... yes. Forgive me. Mr. President, It seems we have a problem. I did not order any submarines to sea. It would appear that my country's military is taking orders from someone other than me," confessed Chelstenov.

"What are you talking about?" the President asked suspiciously.

"President Carpenter, I believe there is a coup in progress. Someone waited until I got on this airplane to order Russian submarines to sea. Then they killed my foreign minister and sabotaged my communications. I fear this is not the worst that will happen. Whoever is attempting to seize power has other things in mind as well," Chelstenov said.

"When will you be on the ground?"the President demanded.

"We will be landing at Andrews Air Force Base in about twenty minutes."

"Good," replied the President, "I'll make arrangements for a limo from your embassy to be allowed on base to pick you up. Secretary Clark will meet your plane upon arrival and brief you on what's happened while you've been in the air."

"Mr. President, I am embarrassed to ask, but I don't know who I can trust at the moment. I would prefer to forgo meeting anyone from my embassy until I can ascertain their loyalty. Would it be possible for you to provide my official party with a temporary safe haven?" asked Chelstenov.

The Russian President knew U.S. law required American officials to provide safe haven to foreign citizens when there was an immediate threat to their personal safety. President Carpenter had to admit that Chelstenov was probably in danger from his own countrymen.

"Your request for safe haven is granted. I'll have the State Department make the arrangements," Carpenter said with a small grin tugging at the corners of his mouth. How ironic that the President of Russia was safer in a foreign capital than in his own.

"Is there anything else I can do for you?"asked the President.

"Yes, I would like for your pathologists to examine Foreign Minister Kolstoy's body. I suspect he was poisoned," said Chelstenov.

"We'll be happy to be of assistance. I'll need to see you as soon as possible after you land. Secretary Clark will escort you to the White House. I'll meet you there in two hours. Carpenter out."

"What do we do now?" asked the President to no one in particular. "We've got Russian ballistic missile submarines all over the ocean doing who knows what, a full blown land war ready to start in Russia, and we don't even know who's in charge over there."

Somewhere over the Malacan Straits

COMMANDER KEVIN LEWIS and his SEAL Team were strapped into their seats aboard a Navy C-130 as it cruised at 9,000 feet over the Malacan Straits. The *Houston* was on the surface radiating a homing beacon guiding the aircraft to their position. Lieutenant Morris switched the intercom to the "All Stations" position, keyed his mike, and checked his communication panel lights to make sure he wasn't transmitting outside the aircraft, and said, "Commander Lewis, we have a lock on the *Houston*. I have her 35 nautical miles out. I'm turning to heading now. Recommend you prepare for your jump. Dropping to 5000 feet AGL. I'll open the aft door on your command."

"Roger, copy all," Lewis replied as he stood to his feet. "Any hits on the ESM gear?"

"No air search radars detected. I've got numerous surface navigation hits from the tankers you see out the window, but nothing in the threat category. Looks like we've arrived undetected."

"Good job. I'll buy you a beer when we get back," said Lewis as he motioned for his team to stand up and head for the back door.

They formed a line at the ramp and each man checked his jump partner. This was not going to be a static jump and it was under cover of darkness. Night jumps were always dangerous, but a night jump over water was especially hazardous. There were so many things that could go wrong. They were loaded with close to seventy pounds of combat gear and their own personal diving equipment. In addition to their personal gear, they were dropping a large supply of shaped charges and extra dive tanks. If they weren't careful they could easily become entangled in their gear, or more likely, their parachutes. Normally, the team would've released their Koch fittings on their shoulder harnesses to free themselves of their chutes about five feet before impacting the water. At night, it was too easy to misjudge the distance. They'd have to take their chances.

"Open cargo door," Lewis ordered over the intercom.

When the door was completely open Lewis gave the signal and six men stepped out of the aircraft into the waiting darkness. Once the last man was out the Jump Master closed the door and notified the Pilot-In-Command that the jumpers were clear.

Lieutenant Morris keyed his mike and listened for the beep to confirm he was on a secure circuit. After checking to ensure the green light was illuminated on his communications panel, a secondary indication that he had a secure circuit, he said, "*Houston*, this is C6T...Over."

"Roger. C6T, this is *Houston*, ...Over."

"Roger, *Houston*. The SEALs have jumped and are inbound your position...Over."

"Thanks for the info, C6. I'm ordering the flare as we speak." A green flare appeared on the water five miles behind the aircraft. Commander Lewis and his SEAL team spotted it immediately and used their risers to steer toward the pick-up point. The flare was timed to burn for three minutes, plenty of time to ensure the SEALs hit the water in close proximity to the circling zodiac waiting to pick them out of the water.

Commander Lewis watched as each man switched on his battery powered flashing light upon entering the water. It was a clandestine jump but there was very little chance a passing tanker would see their lights bobbing in the water. Besides, there were so many lights in the Malacan Straits one more wouldn't draw much attention. If anyone did see them they'd probably think they were looking at a fishing buoy marker. Now all his men had to do was float in their inflatable life vests until the *Houston's* zodiac crew picked them out of the water.

The *Houston's* CO was waiting on the open bridge when Lewis climbed out of the raft. "Welcome aboard, Commander. I'm glad to see your team made it in one piece."

"No problem, Skipper; just another day at the office," replied Lewis.

"Better you than me. After you stow your gear and get cleaned up join me in the wardroom. I'll have a hot meal and some coffee ready. After you eat we can discuss your mission."

"Roger that, sir; I'll be right with you." With that said, Commander Lewis and most of his TEAM followed a Petty Officer to their quarters. One of Lewis' men stayed with the gear and prepared it for the upcoming dive. Thirty minutes later after a quick shower and a change into dry uniforms they were seated in the wardroom drinking hot coffee and debriefing their jump.

"Attention on Deck!" barked the Chief of the Boat as he and Commander Brewster burst through the door to the wardroom.

"Seats. I understand you gentlemen were briefed stateside concerning the number of mines the Russians planted and believe they are CAPTOR mines. My crew and I concur with the assessment."

Lewis stood up and moved to the bottom topography chart mounted on the bulkhead. "Captain, Gentlemen," Lewis said as he looked around the crowded room at the assembled officers and key crewmembers. "If you'll notice the plotted positions of the mines you will see that they're intended to block the deep water passages through the Straits. The Malacan Straits are a vital choke point that can effectively deny our navy the ability to project power in the Pacific Ocean. If we are denied passage through the Straits we are effectively limited in our ability to respond to a crisis by whatever assets we have in place in the Western Pacific Theater of Operations."

"Furthermore, we're not only denied access to our vital strategic concerns in the Pacific Basin, but we're also limited in our ability to respond to a crisis in the Indian Ocean and Persian Gulf Region. We can transfer assets to the Indian Ocean via the Suez Canal, but we must assume that if Russia has taken the trouble to mine the Malacan Straits the Suez Canal may also be in jeopardy. You may be interested to know that SEAL and EOD teams have been dispatched to covertly search those waterways as well."

"But if these waterways are mined, why aren't ships that pass through them blowing now?" asked a Quartermaster Second Class.

"Good question, sailor," responded Lewis. "The Russians have spent a great deal of time and money developing smart mines. Most people are familiar with the old fashioned contact mines that the Iranians and Iraqis used in the Persian Gulf in the eighties and nineties, but most modern navies use influence mines. Normally, these mines are triggered by the magnetic influence of a ship as it passes in close proximity and would explode anytime a vessel's magnetic field came in contact with the mine's firing circuit.

"However, there are a number of deadly variations to these mines. Depending upon how much money the mine's builders are willing to spend, they can be built to explode only under a combination of conditions that very few ships can produce, such as an aircraft carrier or super tanker. They can also be set to explode after a certain number of ships pass over them or be set to activate and deactivate after a set number of days.

"The mines that we are expecting to find tonight are a combination mine and torpedo, called *CAPTOR*, which stands for Encapsulated Torpedo. When the mine's firing circuits are triggered a torpedo is launched at the target. If our *CAPTOR* mines are also built with a time delay the delivery vessel could seed the minefield and retreat to safe haven before the mines activate. These type of weapons are often used when a nation expects to start offensive military operations on a specific day."

"Sir, why use *CAPTOR* mines instead of the more traditional fixed mine?" asked Ensign Mallory, the *Houston's* Communications Officer.

"There are primarily two advantages to *CAPTOR* mines. The first is that the torpedo in the CAPTOR mine will attack a ship and follow it through evasive maneuvers making a kill more likely. The second is that warships in the area will detect the torpedo's active homing sonar and believe there are enemy submarines in the area. That dramatically changes the tactical picture. Ships will spend hours or even days searching for submarines that aren't there. Thus, the ships being attacked will be neutralized from conducting free offensive actions," Lewis explained.

"Now, I'd like to introduce Lieutenant Commander John Parsons, our resident Explosive Ordnance Officer. John is on loan from Subic Bay where he is helping the Philippine Navy remove unexploded ordnance from the area around Grande Island. John, the podium is yours."

"Thank you, Commander. Captain, Gentlemen, if I may direct your attention to the chart on the bulkhead I will proceed with the mine clearance brief. I expect this operation to take approximately twelve hours if all goes well," said Lieutenant Commander Parsons.

The brief lasted two hours and twenty-five minutes and covered every minute detail of the operation. Which divers were assigned to each mine, disarming and safety procedures, depth of water, depressurization guidelines, communication plans, placement of explosive charges, and procedures should disarming prove unsafe or overly time consuming, were covered in detail. Nothing was left to chance or assumption. An hour later divers were in the water and the clearance operation had begun.

Ten thousand yards astern of the USS *Houston* a rusting tramp steamer built in the early fifties was slowly steaming north. No external lights were visible with the exception of a green starboard running light, a masthead light, and a dim bow light. The *Houston's* Executive Officer had seen the ship in the periscope as he cleared the surface of contacts prior to surfacing to discharge the divers but quickly dismissed it as one of the hundreds of commercial vessels plying the Straits this night.

A quick check with the sonar watch confirmed the ship was an aging Russian merchant with a single screw and a steam propulsion plant. ESM reported no radar transmission coming from her so it was unlikely she would detect the *Houston* when discharging the SEALs. Little did he know that the steamer was putting divers into the water at precisely that moment, a fact that no one aboard the *Houston* would discover until it was much too late.

11

KATHLEEN HAYES, CNN's Moscow corespondent, knew
something important was about to happen. She'd been notified a
couple of hours ago that there was going to be a press conference at the
Kremlin at 3:00 p.m. She dropped what she was doing and rushed a
camera team to the designated room. The Russian government seldom
held press conferences and when they did it paid to be there.

Every foreign correspondent in Moscow was in attendance, the room
quickly filling to capacity. Television camera tripods and lights were
everywhere and reporters were standing around self-consciously primping
themselves knowing that soon their faces would be nationally televised.

Excitement filled the air. Rumors had been flying for days that there
was some type of trouble in the Chelstenov Cabinet. Some of the rumors
seemed to be quite plausible. Most of them were nothing more than
vague comments about a vote of no confidence resulting from

Chelstenov's handling of the Iranian crisis. However, all official inquiries were vehemently denied. Perhaps now the world would get some straight answers.

A few moments later a door opened and a dozen of Russia's top leaders entered the room and walked up the stairs of the small platform and formed a line against the back wall. They were all facing the camera standing shoulder to shoulder with somber faces in a contrived show of unity. "This is going to make a great camera shot", thought Hayes.

The Russian Army Chief of Staff, the Deputy Foreign Minister, the Deputy Defense Minister, leading Members of Parliament, and most of Chelstenov's cabinet were standing quietly before the assembled news media. Camera flashes erupted like machine gun fire. Television programming was interrupted all over the world with an important news flash. Judging from the people standing on the platform the world was about to write another page in its tumultuous history.

Alexi Yanochev had painstakingly choreographed the press conference. He'd assembled all of the players and rehearsed every aspect. He told them where to stand and how to stand. He told them what to wear and how to look at the cameras. He'd watched hours of American news conferences and took copious notes. He wanted to make sure he left nothing to chance. This little show was going to propel him to center stage in world events.

Alexi stood behind the door listening to the excited voices of the reporters. He waited until the crowd of international journalists had time to soak in the significance of what was about to happen, wanting to let the excitement and anticipation climax before he entered the room. When he felt the moment was right he opened the door and walked briskly to the podium.

Alexi Yanochev was an impressive figure as he stood silently before the expectant audience. Standing well over six foot three inches tall his remarkable athletic appearance helped conceal the fact that he was fifty-seven years old. He always made a good first impression. When people looked at him they saw an intelligent, dedicated, and competent leader. His charisma was infectious and people trusted him on sight. Tonight, he'd make good use of these inherent characteristics.

Alexi stood quietly for several moments. Television cameras were rolling and everyone was waiting for him to speak - but he just stood there. Finally, when he knew he had the audience where he wanted them he spoke.

"Ladies and Gentlemen, I have called you here to document the most significant event in Russia's recent history. Today, I am announcing to the world what they already know. The truth can no longer be swept under the rug. It is with much sadness that I announce that Russia has been destroyed.

"Destruction did not come from without but from within. Our leaders hid their eyes while our economy collapsed. We can no longer feed our people. Our national infrastructure has collapsed. We have inadequate hospitals, schools, transportation systems, and housing. Our system of government no longer works.

"There are many who love Mother Russia and are willing to make the sacrifices that are required to rescue our nation from complete anarchy. We cannot sit by idly while our people starve to death.

"Therefore, for the good of the people, a coalition of concerned national leaders has formed a new government. The men standing behind me are but a small representation of the widespread support for this bold move among all true Russian patriots.

"As of this moment Boris Chelstenov is no longer the President of Russia. I have been appointed as the new head of state. The rest of the new government will be announced shortly. Additionally, after careful consideration, we have decided that it is in the best interest of our country to suspend the existing constitution. We will be taking drastic and necessary moves in the very near future to rescue our country from the brink of total collapse. We can no longer afford to waste time talking and arguing about what is the best remedy for our ills. If Russia is to continue to exist immediate action is required.

"We are prepared to take that action. Let me be very clear about one thing: I am taking this course of action because Russia is dying. She is already in her final death throes and I intend to save her. Any move by a foreign power to interfere with my initiatives will be considered a direct attack upon Russia. I will use every weapon at my disposal to resist such an attack."

Alexi dramatically turned and walked off stage. The room emptied in seconds as reporters raced for telephones to call in their stories. Television reporters quickly set up outside the Kremlin pushing and shoving like school children as they fought for the best back-drop. The attention of the entire world was now focused on Russia.

Alexi hadn't told the complete truth at the press conference. There was not the widespread consensus among Russia's leaders that he'd indicated. Yes, people were fed up with the stagnant bureaucracy and incompetence of the Chelstenov government. People were indeed desperate to try anything that promised to feed their families and heat their homes in the winter.

Alexi had only explained bits and pieces of what he had in mind to a small group of Russia's most powerful leaders. They were the people who controlled the military, the intelligence services, the national police, and select members of Parliament. They had in turn enlisted the help of key people within their organizations without divulging the details of the plot. The only people who knew the entire plan were the three men who'd met in the Ural Mountains months earlier and Admiral of the Fleet Rybakov.

It had been necessary to limit the number of people involved at first. However, now that the coup had been successful and he was firmly in charge of the country, it was time to enlist as many supporters as possible.

The members of Parliament were not stupid. They understood the essential elements of survival. Seventy years of communism had taught them to keep their mouths shut and go with the flow. Alexi Yanochev had the support of the military and the KGB, and therefore, he had the support of Parliament.

Alexi wasn't one to waste time. Less than one hour after the press conference he was sitting before a crowded room of recently unemployed members of parliament. He carefully explained to them their options. They could continue to represent their people as a loyal member of his government or they could retire to a work camp in Siberia. The choice was theirs.

The decision to join Alexi's government was unanimous and everyone present was more than happy to sign an affidavit pledging their undying support. Alexi smiled and thanked them for their loyalty. The document would be faxed to leaders around the world before the night was over.

After dismissing the assembly Alexi asked three dozen representatives and a few military officers to stay behind for private discussions. These were men that he knew he could count upon. They'd all indicated their support for the coup before it had taken place. In order to ensure their loyalty Alexi had spread their names around for the sole purpose of incriminating them if the coup was a failure. They all knew that if Alexi went down they would go with him.

The small group of officials were directed to seats in one section of the cavernous room that had earlier held the entire Parliament. Standing in front of the first row of seats Alexi said, "Friends, please take your seats." Alexi had to shout to be heard above the din of the small crowd. He spoke without the aide of the sound system. He didn't want anyone outside of the room to overhear what he was about to say.

"I know all of you have many questions but first, allow me the opportunity to give you an overview of how I intend to save our country,"

Alexi said. He had their undivided attention. "I don't need to waste time telling you how desperate the situation is in the *Rodina*. Let me begin by outlining the initiatives that are already underway. I will tell you everything, so please, save your questions until I am through." Alexi explained how he and the other two "patriots" had met in the dacha in the Urals months earlier and determined that Russia was doomed unless someone took action.

Everyone in the room felt the same way but had felt powerless to do anything about it. They were eager to hear Alexi Yanochev's plan. They hoped and prayed it was a good one, after all, their lives were on the line as well as Alexi's. He didn't disappoint them.

"Fortunately," Alexi continued, "the incompetence of Chelstenov created just the opportunity I needed to set in motion the events that will salvage our great country. The desperation felt by mothers trying to feed their starving children will work to our advantage. Men who have not been able to provide the basic necessities for their families will rally behind us. When the people learn of our vision they'll be willing to die in our behalf.

"Now, enough philosophy. Let me give you the details. As you all know, what Russia needs more than anything else is hard currency. We need a massive infusion of capital. The bad news is that we are bankrupt and have no capacity to produce goods that can compete on the open market. However, I believe I have found a way to get the capital required to rebuild our country and feed our people.

"Recently, we've been sending troops to Azerbaijan to prevent an invasion by the Iranians. I am pleased to inform you that Iran has no intention of invading Azerbaijan. I've been in constant communication with Iran for the past two months. They are not our enemies. They are our allies." Alexi paused to let his last statement sink in.

"Iran has agreed to commit their military to a joint invasion of the Arabian Peninsula. We've been massing our troops in preparation for just such a campaign. We'll attack as soon as all our troops are in place.

"The entire story about an imminent invasion of Azerbaijan by Iran was a ploy to divert the world's attention as we prepared for the real invasion. Foreign intelligence services have been led to believe we are staging troops and weapons to defend Azerbaijan when in fact we are preparing to stage the invasion of the Arabian Peninsula out of Azerbaijan."

"OUR OBJECTIVE IS to seize the oil wells for our own. We will begin with a massive bombing campaign of Saudi Arabia, Iraq, Kuwait, and the other Gulf countries. While the bombers are still in the air we will airlift troops and armor into Kuwait. From there we will deploy our invasion force and strike deep into Saudi Arabia and annihilate all opposition. Iran will be allowed to govern the people of Arabia and subject them to their own particular brand of Islam and later, we'll help them avenge themselves on their ancient enemy Israel. All we want is the oil.

"General Masavich has developed a brilliant battle plan which anticipates the Arab's every move. I don't foresee any problems with the Arabs. They have only a token military and are poorly trained."

A general on the front row pensively held up his hand.

"Yes, General," said Yanochev.

"Sir, what about the American Navy? They have two powerful carrier battle groups underway as we speak, not to mention their potent Amphibious Warfare ability. What is to stop them from landing Marines and attacking with their carrier bombers?"

"Good question, General," replied Alexi. "We've already taken steps to keep the Americans out of the picture for a while. We're taking control of all of the choke points leading to the Arabian Peninsula and will keep the American carriers out of striking range. We've already mined the Malacan Straits, the Straits of Hormuz, and the Suez Canal.

The mines will activate in seven days. Admiral of the Fleet Rybakov has assured me that the mines will be sufficient to keep the Americans at bay until it is too late for them to be a serious threat to our invading forces.

"Additionally, we have attack submarines patrolling the lines of communication leading to the area and missile submarines lying in wait for any warships that might try to enter the fray. If our submarines off their coast don't fool the American Navy and they turn and head for the Malacan Straits we'll destroy them with our long range bombers and submarines long before they arrive. If that fails the mines will stop them."

"OUR ATTACK PLANS call for the immediate seizure of all Arabic air fields. The initial attack will consist of saturation bombing followed by a paratrooper assault. When the troops have control of the airstrips we will bring in our transports with heavy armor. Once the military airfields and installations are in our control we will have air and ground superiority. Our bombers can then begin to dismantle the Arab population centers and our fighters can resist any long-range attacks by Western bombers. The combined ground forces of Iran and Russia will occupy the major oil fields within the first week of the conflict.

"We have carefully studied the American strategy from Operation Iraqui Freedom. They won the war because Iraq made three fatal mistakes. First and foremost, the Iraqi's did not anticipate the American resolve to protect the Arab oil supply. Secondly, they conceded control of the skies to the Americans. Thirdly, they did not prevent American access to major seaports in the region. That allowed the Americans to deliver an endless stream of supplies to support their war effort.

"Our strategy will not make things so easy for the Americans. I admit, we do expect America to make a concerted effort to forcibly expel us from Arabia. However, they will soon find that they have been out maneuvered and have little recourse. They will be forced to capitulate and buy their oil from us just like every other industrialized nation in the world.

"When we control the Arabian oil fields we will use the revenues to resurrect our economy. We will be the richest country on the face of the earth. Like the mythological phoenix of old we will rise from the ashes of destruction to become the greatest nation on earth."

Alexi was pleased with himself. The select group before him was obviously impressed. They were momentarily speechless as they considered what he'd said but it was apparent they considered it to be a good plan. Bold yes, but try as they might, they couldn't find anything Alexi had overlooked. It was exactly the kind of plan that was needed. Anything less wouldn't be able to save the country from self-destruction.

Russia was living on borrowed time and this seemed like just the thing to give her a new start. Besides, what did Russia have to lose? If they did nothing, the country would soon cease to exist. If they tried Alexi's plan and failed, the country would also be destroyed. But if the plan worked they would be heroes. There was everything to gain and nothing to lose. Yes, if necessary, they would give their lives to help Alexi Yanochev.

As Alexi had hoped no one challenged his assertion that the Iranians had agreed to help Russia for expansionist and religious reasons. They swallowed the story without thinking. If they'd pressed him hard enough he would have revealed the real reason Iran was willing to let their brave young soldiers die for Russia. They were getting something they wanted much worse than territory. But since he didn't have to tell them he would keep the information a secret. No one except the major players needed to know the whole truth.

Washington, DC

THE PRESIDENT SAT spellbound as he watched the CNN video of the Russian press conference for the third time. His ulcer was beginning to bleed. What else could go wrong? He was beginning to wish he'd lost the election. That way he could sit in his easy chair fat, dumb, and happy and not have to worry about enemy nuclear submarines running around all over the ocean and some lunatic KGB officer with his finger on the nuclear button.

He'd already tried to reach Yanochev on the so-called "Hot Line" to no avail. The only word he'd received out of Russia was from the Russian ambassador. The ambassador had delivered a message about twenty minutes ago from the new Foreign Minister. The message read as follows:

THE RUSSIAN PEOPLE HAVE DENOUNCED THE FAILED POLICIES OF FMR PRES BORIS CHELSTENOV XX THE RUSSIAN PARLIAMENT VOTED THIS MORNING TO REMOVE HIM FROM OFFICE AND FORM A NEW GOV XX ALEXI YANOCHEV IS NOW THE ACTING HEAD OF STATE XX AS SUCH HE HAS LAUNCHED A SERIES OF INITIATIVES AIMED AT IMPROVING THE QUALITY OF LIFE OF THE RUSSIAN PEOPLE XX ANY ATTEMPT TO INTERFERE W/ THESE INITIATIVES WILL BE MET W/ FORCE XX RUSSIA WILL RESPOND IN KIND TO ANY MILITARY REPRISAL XX FOR THE PRESIDENT NICKOLEI ANDROSTOV FOREIGN MINISTER
END MESSAGE

BREAK***

President Carpenter had met briefly with Boris Chelstenov when his plane landed. He tried to gain some understanding about what was going on in Russia but Chelstenov was no help. The coup had caught him totally by surprise. Yanochev and General Masavich had duped him into coming to America.

While the coup had caught Chelstenov by surprise he was able to provide the President with some valuable information. He told the President all about Alexi Yanochev bringing him the intercepted message from the Iranians. He explained in great detail the discussions he'd had with his military leaders about how to best handle the situation, which explained why Chelstenov had agreed to mass his troops and bombers in Azerbaijan.

Everything Chelstenov said made sense to the President. All the pieces fit nicely together. All except one. Why were the Russian submarines at sea? Chelstenov didn't know but what he said next sent chills down the President's spine. He asked a number of hypothetical questions, "Let us suppose that Yanochev fed me false intelligence to get me to leave the country so that he could seize power. If that is the case, why are the Iranians massing troops on their northern border? Secondly, what is Yanochev's real reason for sending troops to Azerbaijan? Thirdly, how does the Russian submarine fleet tie into all of this?"

These were difficult question. "Better call in General Freeman from the CIA and get his read of the situation", thought the President. "Maybe he can make some sense of all of this!"

12

SERGEANT ELI WASHINGTON joined the Army the day after he graduated from St. Albans High School. Coming from a working class family, he didn't have very many other options. Jobs were scarce and he didn't have any money for college so the Army looked attractive.

That was nearly six years ago. He had three months to go on his enlistment and then planned to get out of the Army and enroll at West Virginia Technical College and study Chemical Engineering. There were plenty of jobs in the Kanawha Valley at the area's chemical plants and he planned on getting a good one.

After boot camp Eli was sent to the Army's Chemical Warfare School at Ft. McClellan, Alabama. Although he was an enlisted man, he'd learned a great deal about chemical engineering by attending every school the Army had to offer in anything related to chemical warfare. He'd even taken a few chemistry classes at night school.

THE ARMY HAD been good to him. His superiors did everything possible to accommodate his desire to improve himself, especially in the areas relating to his Army duties.

The best thing they'd done for him, at least in his opinion, was assigning him to the Army Reserve Center in South Charleston, West Virginia. The sign in front of the armory described the facility as a mortar battalion, but that was only partially true. The facility was in actuality one of twelve secret Chemical Warfare Depots scattered throughout the United States.

South Charleston, West Virginia is known as the "Chemical Capitol of the World." Situated on the Kanawha River it is home to a number of the largest chemical plants in the world. Monsanto, Dupont, FMC, and Union Carbide all maintain large manufacturing and processing plants there.

Union Carbide was the Army's largest suppliers of chemicals. The relationship was cemented in the early sixties when Carbide took the lead in manufacturing binary chemical weapons. These weapons utilize chemicals that are perfectly harmless by themselves, but when mixed together, they become a potent weapon of mass destruction.

The chemicals are stored separately and are most often mixed after the weapon has been deployed. They are commonly placed in artillery or mortar shells and mixed when the projectile is fired, or they can be stored in two separate tanks aboard an aircraft and mixed when sprayed.

The Army Reserve Center in South Charleston was the first stop for the binary chemicals on their way to the eleven other storage sites. Shipped in fifty-gallon plastic drums, they were transported from South Charleston to the other East Coast storage facilities by truck, and by rail to the Denver Army Reserve Center for distribution to the other West Coast sites.

The twelve Army Reserve Centers designated as binary chemical storage facilities were not equipped with the usual ammunition bunkers but rather large rooms with secure storage areas designed to warehouse chemical filled drums. No actual weapons were kept in the depots; only the chemicals were present. People driving by a storage site could see nothing to indicate the presence of deadly chemicals. The Army's reasoning was that the best place to hide them was in plain view. Since there were no high explosives involved and the chemicals were perfectly safe as long as they were separated the powers that be approved the storage plan.

Security at each of the twelve sites was identical. A twenty-four hour a day armed security team provided continuous protection for the binary chemicals. Each team consisted of four active duty personnel from the Chemical Warfare Battalion stationed at the Reserve Centers. These soldiers, three non-coms and one senior enlisted, were given additional training in security and anti-terrorism to equip them to handle a wide variety of threat situations.

The Watch Officer's desk was situated in a small cubicle in front of the heavy steel door that served as the only entrance to the secured storage site. There was a large sliding cargo door in the rear of the facility which was constructed of three inch steel. It was alarmed and operated by a motor controller to which only the watch officer had a key. It would take a tank to gain entry through that entrance. So effectively, there was only one way in and the Watch Officer sat in front of that door.

Two men patrolled inside the enclosure; more concerned with leaking storage drums than intruders. The area they patrolled was really nothing more than a large vault with one large cage for each kind of chemical. The fourth man patrolled the perimeter of the building.

Their job was to safeguard five hundred barrels of chemicals. Two hundred and fifty barrels of the binary chemicals were stored in each of the two separate secure enclosures. To the untrained observer the supply of binary chemical weapons would seem rather meager, but when combined and vaporized, there was more than enough to meet any conceivable contingency the country might encounter.

SERGEANT ELI WASHINGTON sat behind the Watch Officer's desk looking at his security camera monitors. His two secure radios and STU-III secure telephone were silent. His cubicle resembled what one might expect at a bank drive-up teller. There was a small window with a metal drawer that he extended for visitors to place their ID badges in. He would then close the drawer, extract and examine the badge, compare it to the authorized entry list, and then return the badge to the owner, all the while protected behind the bulletproof glass of his cubicle.

Security cameras monitored every square inch of the complex so Sergeant Washington had no real need to leave the desk during his watch. Tonight he had the midnight to 0600. It was tough staying alert all night but he had a routine to keep that helped keep his eyes opened. He was fortunate in that Sergeant's were only assigned the midnight watch once every two weeks. The lower enlistees drew the mid-watch every five days.

Tonight's watch team was all regular Army like himself. Private Jimmy Engle was the roving sentry on the perimeter. At six foot six inches tall and one hundred and forty-five pounds he presented a rather gangly appearance, but was nonetheless a dedicated young soldier with a lot of potential. Corporal Steve Pearson was twenty-two years old and a three-year veteran. Private Armando Ruiz was eighteen years old and fresh out of Chemical Warfare School at Fort McClellan, Alabama. He and Corporal Pearson were providing security in the vault complex.

At 0200 Sergeant Washington picked up his walkie-talkie to conduct his half-hourly check of the sentries.

"Post One...report."

"Post One...Conditions Normal," Private Ruiz reported.

"Post Two...report,"

"Post Two...Conditions Normal," Private Engle responded.

Washington made the proper entries in his logbook, conducted a circuit check on his secure radios, and poured himself a cup of coffee. It would be his last.

Six black clad men lay in the darkness outside the perimeter of the building with their eyes glued on the lone sentry. Another was on the depot's roof wiring a VCR into the external security camera circuit. A tape showing a deserted parking lot replaced the live feed. Sergeant Washington noticed a momentary static on the monitor but it cleared up immediately, so he thought nothing of it.

Private Engle's radio crackled to life. He seemed bored as he pulled it from its belt-mounted holder and pressed it against his ear. One of the men in black rose from his position and crept silently into position behind the sentry.

"Post Two... Conditions Normal," Private Engle reported.

He placed the radio back in its holder and reached for a stick of gum from the pack he kept in his breast pocket. As he lifted the gum to his mouth, a hand pulled his head back and a garish looking knife cut a deep gash in his throat severing his windpipe and carotid artery. Engle's killer quickly drug his body behind the shrubbery lining the building and joined the other five men as they ran to the back of the building.

Two of the intruders carried a large canvass bag between them and were visibly straining under its weight. The other three men carried smaller bags in each hand. When they reached the back of the building they sat down their loads and with deadly speed began completing a much practiced checklist.

All were equipped with hands-free radios with earpieces- the man who'd killed the sentry was whispering orders to his elite team. The man to the killer's left spun and used his silenced 9 mm pistol to shoot out the two spot lights illuminating the back of the building. As one man they all donned night vision goggles over their gas masks and began unloading their bags.

Another found and cut the building's telephone line as two others inserted a long bit into a high powered, silent running masonry drill and began drilling a hole in the back of the chemical storage vault. The drill motor was so quiet it couldn't be heard beyond a few yards.

While two men drilled the hole two others assembled a strange looking rig with two tanks and a long, thin nozzle. The remaining two men took up defensive positions with AR-15's, a civilian version of the M-16 with collapsible stocks, long curved banana clips holding 30 rounds each, and wicked looking silencers.

Inside the storage vault Private Ruiz stopped and cocked his head to one side. Corporal Pearson was less than thirty feet away.

"Hey, Steve; you hear anything?" Ruiz asked.

"No. What's up?"

"I don't know. I just thought I heard something."

"Then let's go check it out," Pearson said.

They walked quickly toward the end of the vault from where the sound had come. Fifty feet from the back wall they heard a faint noise. Before they could identify the sound, it abruptly stopped.

"Did you hear that?" whispered Ruiz.

"Yeah. Whatever it was it stopped. It was probably a rat scratching on a wooden pallet but I still want to check it out. It might not be anything, but we don't get paid to assume," Pearson said.

They continued walking toward the back wall and turned left down the walkway between the back wall and a line of barrels. Something looked out of place to Corporal Pearson, but he couldn't place it. Just as he was about to walk away he saw something out of the corner of his eye. "Hey, Ruiz. What's that by your feet?"

"Where? I don't see anything."

Pearson knelt down beside Ruiz and ran his hand along the floor and raised it to where Ruiz could see. "Looks like grit, or sand or something," he said.

"Hey, look!" Ruiz shouted.

Pearson looked where Ruiz was pointing and saw a thin tube of some type come through a hole in the back wall. "What the heck! Ruiz, call the Sarge!"

Ruiz didn't have time to act. A mist came out of the end of the tube and both men instantly fell to the floor and began convulsing. Ruiz's radio clattered to the concrete floor and landed on the key button. The radio was keyed for only a split second.

Sergeant Washington realized he was dozing off the third time his head bobbed toward his desk. He shook himself awake and silently cursed his lack of discipline. "Maybe I ought to go to the head and wash my face," he thought.

He pushed his chair backand stood up and stretched. After a yawn he walked in the direction of the men's restroom. He pushed the door opened and started to go in when his radio emitted one short beep. Something caught his ear. He waited to see if he was being called by one of the sentries, but.... nothing. Was somebody keying the radio? Probably nothing to it, but something in the back of his mind was making him feel uneasy. "Better check on my men, just to make sure everything's OK," he thought. He walked back to his desk and picked up his walkie-talkie.

"Post One, Radio Check...Over." No response.

"Post One, Radio Check...Over." Still no answer.

Sergeant Washington's voice raised noticeably as he keyed his radio again. "Post Two, Radio Check...Over." No response again.

"OK, before I panic, I'll go check on Ruiz and Pearson. Maybe my radio's on the blink," he thought.

Drawing his pistol, he slowly opened the door to the vault and stepped inside.

"Pearson, you guys OK?" he shouted. "Better get out and call this in," he thought. He tried to turn around and open the door, but his body wouldn't listen. Suddenly, his legs gave way and he crashed to the polished concrete floor. Blackness closed around him as he vaguely felt his body thrashing about wildly. Somewhere off in the distance he thought he heard an explosion — then nothing.

Four men in black rushed through a large gaping hole they had just blown in the back wall of the vault. Guns extended, they quickly made sure the room was clear. One man put a bullet in the forehead of each downed guard just for good measure. Two other men cut the locks on the cages holding the binary chemicals while two others cut the lock on the main gate outside before driving a paneled two ton truck around to the back of the building.

"OK team, find out which of the stiffs has the key to the cargo door. Johnson, take out the alarm," barked the leader.

The door was opened in less than five minutes. While the team loaded chemicals onto the waiting truck the leader extracted a small plastic bag from his utility vest and placed two human hairs near the body of Sergeant Washington. He then dipped a finger of a glove in Washington's blood and placed the glove in the plastic bag from which he'd taken the human hair samples. Seven minutes later the two-ton truck was on I-64 heading east.

13

AMBASSADOR MCCLINTOCK SAT in the Gulf Region Joint Task Force (JTF) conference room. Located in an underground bunker in Riyadh the room was comfortably furnished with high-backed leather swivel chairs situated around a large oval table. Built in the late eighties to facilitate American commanders in defending *the Kingdom*, the conference room was constructed so that its occupants could sit and talk while looking out over the Air Tactical Operations Center (ATOC). This was accomplished by building the room slightly above and to the rear of the ATOC. The wall facing the ATOC was made out of glass, thus providing an unobstructed view of the command center.

In its heyday, the ATOC was the nerve center for the air war against Iraq during *Operation Desert Storm*. There were two large screen displays standing twenty feet tall that displayed the air picture from southern Saudi

Arabia to Turkey. A number of smaller screens displayed flight schedules, communication plans, and various other important information. A bank of television monitors was perpetually tuned to CNN and the BBC. The watch team controlled aircraft, monitored different sections of airspace, and communicated with the airborne AWACs from three rows of consoles set in the middle of the dimly lit room.

A small corner of the room was occupied by the Saudi Arabian Air Force. They had a scaled down version of the American equipment and under normal circumstances flew only one or two AWAC missions a week. The rest of the time they provided *oversight* for the American operations.

The United States Air Force, with the help of U. S. Navy airwing assets, had been providing Saudi Arabia their only meaningful air defense for a number of years. The Saudi Air Force's main contribution was to stay out of the way. They had neither the desire nor the sophistication to do a credible job. In the past that had never been a problem because the USAF took up the slack. However, things were quite different now.

The ATOC should've been crowded with USAF Air Controllers, Engagement Coordinators, Weapons Coordinators, and Watch Supervisors. Instead, the room was virtually empty. The strained relations that had canceled all joint training were having a devastating effect on America's ability to monitor the air picture in the Gulf region. With the USAF AWACS sitting idly on the flight line there wasn't much to do in the ATOC except monitor the air picture provided by the U. S. Navy's E-2C flying over the Northern Gulf.

The carrier *George Washington* was conducting flight operations from the Northern Arabian Gulf - called the NAG in navy-speak. The ship carried eighty-five aircraft but only thirty-six were fighters. Five E-2C *Hawkeye* aircraft provided the carrier with airborne radar surveillance.

The only problem with the Navy E-2 was that its radar didn't have the range of the *E-3 Sentry* AWACS. While the Navy assets could provide limited coverage of the skies over Northern Iran they couldn't plug all the holes left by the idle Air Force AWACS.

Ambassador McClintock was receiving a briefing on these very problems from Lieutenant General Bull Phillips, the JTF Commanding General. Also present was Vice Admiral Jeffrey Taylor, Commander, U.S. Naval Forces, Central Command or Fifth Fleet as his command was now being called. These two officers were the men in charge of all American military operations in the Arabian Gulf region.

"My biggest concern is that we have inadequate assets to protect our own forces should the Russian problem with Iran get out of hand," commented General Phillips.

"I concur with Bull," said Admiral Taylor. "Intelligence reports confirm that Russia presently has over six hundred aircraft in Azerbaijan. That scares the living daylights out of me. The *George Washington* has a cruiser escort, but there's no way we could protect American interests against a concerted Russian attack."

"Gentlemen, I understand your concerns. However, we have had no indications that Russia intends to do anything with their forces other than what they have stated. They have repeated numerous times their assertion that they're simply massing an overwhelming defensive force in Azerbaijan to discourage the Iranians from getting involved," replied McClintock.

"Sir, I think the people in Washington are sticking their heads in the sand," Bull Phillips blurted. "I learned a long time ago that if something feels wrong, something *is* wrong! Right now, I have a real bad feeling about this whole mess!"

"General, what do you expect me to do? Our hands are tied. The Arab nations are united in their refusal to allow us the use of their military facilities. We can't fly the aircraft we have in country much less bring in reinforcements. What else can we do?"

"You can get us out of Dodge!" exploded Phillips. "If we aren't going to be allowed to defend ourselves when things go south then we need to load up our toys and go home!"

"General, I think you're over reacting. Until the State Department gets some indication that the Russians have hostile intent we will direct the Department of Defense to maintain the status quo in the Gulf. Any move to withdraw American forces from this part of the world now would serve only to exacerbate the problem. If Russia has hostile intent as you say, any reduction in American presence would give them a clear signal that we are willing to capitulate."

Admiral Taylor almost came out of his chair when McClintock downplayed Russia's hostile intent. "Mister Secretary, how much hostile intent do you need to admit we have a problem here? Just between you and me, I've had a belly full of hostile intent! I call mining the Malacan Straits hostile intent. I think surging their entire submarine fleet is hostile intent. You combine those moves with the recent overthrow of the Chelstenov government and I think they've displayed enough hostile intent to warrant your concern. I'm not willing to sacrifice the lives of my people waiting for the State Department to figure out what's going on!"

Admiral Jeffrey Taylor was walking a thin line and he knew it. Even though he was an admiral he knew better than to speak to the Undersecretary of State for Middle Eastern Affairs in such a belligerent and disrespectful tone of voice. He was banking on his credibility and friendship with McClintock to spare him a formal reprimand.

However, at this point, Taylor didn't care. If he was called on the carpet for his words, so be it. Somebody had to let the President know things were about to get nasty and McClintock was the logical choice. That was why General Phillips and he had requested McClintock make a personal visit in the first place.

"Jeff," McClintock said calmly, "let me assure you that the President is watching the situation very closely. There is more to this thing than meets the eye. I know that you already know much of this, but let me lay out the whole scenario for you. As you were so quick to point out, the Malacan Straits have indeed been mined. According to International Law that's an act of war.

"Under normal circumstances the United States would hold the government of the offending country responsible. We would impose economic sanctions, and if necessary, take the appropriate military action. A number of factors prevent us from implementing those actions at this time.

"The primary reason we are reticent to take any overtly provocative steps is that the government of Russia is unstable. Yanochev can't be counted upon to act in a responsible manner. He's struggling to consolidate power and any military move against him would strengthen his hand. His opposition would unite behind him to repel any perceived threat to the "Motherland."

"The Russians are fanatical about protecting their country from outside aggression. If they think our actions are a serious threat to their national security we'll very likely elicit a nuclear response. Please remember that they have about three dozen ballistic missile submarines at sea in the Pacific as we speak. This is an unprecedented move on their part. Even at the height of the cold war they never did anything like this.

"Yanochev has nothing to lose. You heard his speech on CNN. He envisions himself as the savior of Russia. The President doesn't want to do anything to provoke him," said McClintock.

"Yes, sir; I understand his concerns," Taylor said. "I just don't want our people to be the sacrificial lamb if the President's conciliatory gestures don't do the trick."

McClintock shared the admiral's concern for the safety of his troops but there wasn't much he could do to help. "Admiral, I've explained the President's concerns. What do you expect me to do?"

Admiral Taylor didn't hesitate. "Sir, Central Command has been begging SECDEF for more assets since this thing got started. Perhaps you could put a bug in the President's ear and see if he would be willing to bring the *Truman* Battle Group around from the Mediterranean. The Pacific Fleet is out of the picture until the mines are cleared from the Malacan Straits and Straits of Hormuz. The Atlantic Fleet is locked out until the Suez is cleared. Our only option is to clear the Suez ASAP and get help from the Med. The *Truman* Battle Group has two *Aegis* Cruiser escorts and two Tomahawk equipped *Spruance* Destroyers. That would more than double our defensive capability and give us enough attack aircraft to keep an enemy offensive at bay until help arrives."

"General Phillips, what's your input?" asked McClintock.

"Sir, I've got two squadrons of fighters that have been grounded since your last trip over here. I doubt very much that we'd even get them off the ground if the Russians launched an air attack. Without our AWACS we wouldn't detect the incoming raid until they were almost upon us. The Navy E-2 radars can see a couple hundred miles and that's a big help. The problem with the E-2 coverage is that they can't stay on station twenty-four hours a day. If we're attacked while the *Hawkeyes* are on deck we'll never know what hit us. We desperately need the additional air assets and radar coverage the *Truman* can provide."

"What about the Saudi AWACS?" asked McClintock.

"Sir, they aren't reliable. Most of the time they can't even get their radars turned on. Even if they manage to bring up an operational radar they don't have the experience to control an air battle. They're only about fifty percent effective when U.S. crewmen fly on their aircraft and work most of the stations for them. Now that we aren't allowed to help them they're pretty useless, " said the general.

"Sir, both Admiral Taylor and I know how to follow orders. If we don't get any help, we'll sit tight and do the best we can. But I want to go on the record as saying that we don't have sufficient resources to carry out our assigned mission. If we get into a shooting war a lot of our people are going to die!"

McClintock agreed. He was becoming more skeptical of the Russians with each passing day. He'd bought the Russian story hook, line, and sinker when he first heard it. Now he was having serious second thoughts. Things just didn't add up.

The more he thought about it the more he was convinced Russia was up to something bigger than simply reinforcing their troops in Azerbaijan. Another thing bothering him was the Iranians. They were acting out of character. They'd never demonstrated any previous aspirations to help other Muslim nations. In fact, they'd always been outright antagonistic. Ayatollah Khomeini and his clerical associates had proclaimed in 1979 that all Muslim countries in the region were corrupt, unworthy, and un-Islamic, and therefore deserved to be overthrown.

McClintock remembered an excerpt from one of Khomeini's speeches. The Grand Ayatollah was quoted as saying, "We have in reality then no choice but to destroy those systems and governments that are corrupt in themselves and also entail the corruption of others, and to overthrow all treacherous, corrupt, oppressive, and criminal regimes. This is a duty that all Muslims must fulfill in every one of the Muslim countries, in order to achieve the triumphant political revolution of Islam. We see too, that together the imperialist and tyrannical self-seeking rulers have divided the Islamic homeland. They have separated the Islamic umma from each other and artificially created separate nations."

Khomeini was dead but his Islamic Revolutionary Council still ruled the country. The West rejoiced when Khomeini passed from the scene, thinking that his death would end the world's problems with Iran. McClintock knew better. He'd been closely following Iran as they quietly rearmed. The world had been focused on Iraq for decades and nobody seemed to care about Iran. Iran was using the media's apathy to their full advantage.

McClintock felt a shiver run down his spine as a fleeting thought danced across his mind. What if the crisis between Iran and Russia were only a feint? How would that possibility line up with recent developments? Admittedly, the idea was ludicrous, but just suppose there was some type of collusion. What common goal could they have?

Suddenly, a flood of previously unrelated events began to replay in his mind. Iran had purchased three *Kilo* submarines from Russia a couple of years ago for "defensive purposes." They still had Russian advisors training Iranian submarine crews. Why hadn't the Russians been expelled when tensions between the two countries threatened to erupt into an armed conflict?

Another disturbing fact was that Iran had fortified three islands in the mouth of the Straits of Hormuz. The Tumb Islands and Abu Musa are strategically located so that they can easily control all shipping entering or leaving the Gulf. Iran brought in *Hawk* anti-aircraft missiles, SA-6 surface to air missiles, 155mm artillery, and over 4,000 troops. This recent development, coupled with Iran's *Seersucker* anti-ship missiles on the mainland gave them complete control of the waterway.

Perhaps Iran had conspired with Russia to bring about a new Islamic dynasty. What if they considered an alliance with Russia as the only way to reunite all the Arab Islamic countries under a truly Islamic government? If so, what was in it for Russia? McClintock would have to give his fledgling theory more thought. Whatever was going on he was convinced he had to do all in his power to convince the President to increase American military presence in the region.

"OK, I tell you what I'm going to do. I'll call and get permission to withdraw the *Washington* and her escorts from the Gulf. We'll keep them just south of the Straits until I can get the *Truman* around from the Med. General, not much I can do for you until we get this political situation worked out with Saudi Arabia. You'll just have to hang tough," said McClintock.

"I like your plan, but what about the mines in the Straits of Hormuz?" asked General Philips.

"Let me worry about them," replied Taylor. I've got a few MK 105 minesweeping sleds and a minesweeper off the coast of Oman. We'll sweep the Straits until the *Washington* arrives and then send her through. There's been plenty of commercial shipping passing through the Straits every day and so far nothing's blown up. If the Straits are indeed mined as intelligence indicates, perhaps the mines haven't been activated yet. We'll just have to take our chances. Anything is better than keeping the carrier at risk," said Admiral Taylor.

"General, I'm afraid that leaves you without any air picture, but it can't be helped. The Saudi's will just have to fend for themselves," said McClintock.

"That doesn't give me the warm and fuzzies, but I agree with you. We don't have much choice," said General Philips.

The Malacan Straits

COMMANDER LEWIS WAS preparing to enter the water as two enlisted SEALs attached detonator cord to the last of the mines. They'd worked tirelessly for the past two hours switching between rest periods in the zodiac and time in the water. Even when he wasn't in the water supervising the work, Lewis kept in contact with his divers via a two-way data link operated by one of the men in the water. It was a simple device that allowed a diver to type out a message on a thigh mounted keyboard and read a response on an LED display. They had less than thirty minutes remaining before the work would be complete. The plan was to get clear the area in the zodiac and then detonate the mines.

Petty Officer Goldman was attaching the detonator cord to the shaped charges on the CAPTOR warhead when out of the corner of his eye he sensed a swift motion. Instinctively, he recoiled into a defensive position just as a diver with a spear gun fired at him. Goldman tried to twist out of the projectile's path but wasn't fast enough. All he succeeded in doing was turning enough to take the spear in the side instead of the stomach. The deadly razor sharp steel barb pierced his right side and completely penetrated his body and was now sticking out of his left side. He didn't have enough time to assimilate what was happening before the attacker finished the job by cutting his throat.

Lieutenant Commander Parsons was intently watching him make his connections and didn't see the attacking swimmers until they were upon him. Two Russian swimmers fired their spear guns at him scoring hits in the center of his chest. Blood erupted from the mortal wounds as he slowly drifted to the bottom. He summoned his last bit of ebbing strength and typed "Z1" on his keypad, a pre-designated code for "under attack".

Commander Lewis spit in his face mask as he prepared to roll backwards off of the side of the zodiac to rejoin his team. Lieutenant Bill Myers forcibly grabbed his arm and showed him the display.

"Get the gear! We're under attack!" shouted Lewis.

Without waiting for further clarification of the situation three angry SEALs grabbed the tools of their trade and plunged into the tepid water. Each had an explosive bang stick, a standard issue fighting knife, and a new weapon that had yet to be tested in combat.

The lethality of the new weapon was deceiving because of its harmless appearance. Shaped somewhat like a flashlight it was little more than a small tube that discharged a high velocity dart. The dart was armed when fired and exploded on impact.

Commander Lewis was in the lead as they followed the dive buoy's line to where his men had been working. The water was nearly pitch black which limited visibility to about two feet. The dive line was marked every ten feet with green chemlites which stretched eerily through the dark waters to the work site.

Ahead in the depths they saw the light rigged near the *CAPTOR* mine Goldman and Parsons had been working on. As they approached they saw shadows swimming through the light. The SEALs were still surrounded by darkness and thankfully, undetected by the enemy swimmers.

Lewis counted nine shadowy figures. "OK, outnumbered three to one. Could be worse." He gave the signal to follow him away from the dive line, directing his small team to float in the darkness. Instinctively, he knew what the Russians would do next. It was what he would have done in their place. They'd killed the divers in the water and now they were going to attack the men resting in the zodiac. Well, they were in for a big surprise. Lewis held his fist up in front of the facemask of the man next to him signaling for him to hold tight. The man passed the command down the chain. Lewis' three man team could monitor the enemy's progress up the dive line in spite of the dark water by watching the shadows pass by the green chemlites.

As the last Russian followed the diving buoy's line past the SEALs on their way to the zodiac Lewis motioned his men forward. He gave the water a ferocious kick with his fins and chased after the unsuspecting attackers. Each SEAL picked a man and overtook them one at a time, cutting their throats and leaving them sinking in the dark, blood clouded water as they chased after the next in line.

The SEAL's killed five men before the Russians knew what was happening. That made the odds five to three. As the swimmers approached the surface visibility increased to well over fifteen feet. A Russian in the rear of the column saw the death below him and grabbed the leg of the man in front of him. This was repeated three more times in less than two seconds. Before they could raise their spear guns and get off a shot two more Russians recieved a massive twelve gauge shotgun blast to the chests as Lewis and Myers expended their bang sticks.

One of the surviving Russians fired at Lewis, missing cleanly. Lewis fired back with his experimental *EX-3* underwater pistol and almost bit through his mouthpiece as he witnessed the weapon's effect on the swimmer. The man's chest erupted violently, expelling pieces of internal organs in all directions. The Russian commando was obscured from view by a cloud of gore. Lewis thought, "two to three!"

The remaining two Russians tried frantically to swim away but were too tired from their long swim to the SEAL work area to out swim the Americans. Lieutenant Myers scored a direct hit on the slowest retreating swimmer with his *EX-3* and followed up by slicing a deep gash across his throat. As Lewis swam after the last attacker he noticed Lieutenant Myers holding the dead man from behind, repeatedly plunging his knife into his neck.

THE LAST RUSSIAN STOPPED and faced his attackers. He held his spear gun out at arm's length and let it fall. Lewis thought he was going to surrender but soon understood what he wanted. The Russian pulled a knife out of his ankle sheath and motioned toward himself. "So, he wants to get personal," thought Lewis. "If that's the way he wants to die, it's OK with me!"

Lewis motioned for the other two SEALs to standoff as he dealt with the Russian. The man was smaller than he was - probably no more than six foot tall and one hundred seventy five pounds. In the water that didn't make a lot of difference. Speed meant more than physical size.

The defiant Russian closed the short distance between them and circled Lewis. He jabbed with his knife and Lewis parried, grabbing the knife hand with his free left hand and spinning around so that their backs were touching, and then drove his knife into the back of the Russian's thigh. Lewis was dealing death with all his heart. "Twist, pull up, twist, push down, and pull out. Release and reposition."

Blood obscured the view of the Russian's lower body as Lewis faced the enemy and closed for the kill. He was going to enjoy this. Why have mercy on someone who'd taken part in killing two of his men without even giving them a chance to defend themselves? He wanted desperately to make him pay, but it was not to be. His training took over and he backed off.

Placing his knife back in its sheath he held his hands up and pointed at the knife the Russian was holding. With Lieutenant Myers and the other SEAL covering with their *EX-3's*, Commander Lewis approached the enemy's now lowered knife and took it out of his hand. He couldn't get information out of a dead man, and after all, he owed it to the men who'd died under his command to find out who his attackers were and how they knew about his mission.

Twenty-five minutes later the surviving SEALs had detonated all of the *CAPTOR* mines and were boarding the USS *Houston*. Commander Bruster met them at the hatch with a concerned look on his face.

"What happened, Kevin?"

"We got ambushed," said Lewis. "They killed Parsons, Smith, and Goldman before we had a chance to help."

"Who are they?" asked Bruster.

"I don't know for sure, but I think they're Russians. Maybe this guy can tell us something," Lewis said.

Bruster said, "Who's he?" when he noticed the prisoner for the first time. The man had his hands tied behind his back with a plastic tie and was bleeding badly through a makeshift bandage on his thigh.

"Prisoner," said Lewis.

Commander Lewis noticed the CO staring at the wound and said, "It's not fatal, but you'll need to get him to sick bay. I need to make a call to SPECWAR and let them know what happened. I want to know how somebody found out we were here."

"My thoughts exactly. They had to have a lot of advance warning to coordinate the attack," said Bruster. "Ensign Mallory, assist Commander Lewis in making his call."

"Aye, Aye, Sir!" replied the Communications Officer.

14

DEEP WITHIN THE musty confines of the ancient Grand Mosque in Tehran the twelve ruling ayatollahs lounged around the remains of a tray of rice and roasted lamb. All were now sipping strong Indian tea and waiting for Ali Bakr Rafalgemii to emerge from his study.

Ali Bakr had come to power after Ayatollah Rafsengani had failed to return from a trip to visit his eldest daughter in France. The Ayatollah had quite unexpectedly died in his sleep from what his autopsy report dubiously determined to be natural causes. Most people in the know considered his death to be anything but natural. However, to express that thought aloud would ensure the offenders a sudden fatal illness of their own.

With great flourish, Ali Bakr parted the thick curtain that concealed the door to his private office and stepped into the room. A small man with skeletal features, he somehow seemed to project an image of a much larger person. His intense black eyes burned holes through whomever he looked upon. The aura of power surrounding him was almost magical. The assembled ayatollahs visibly stiffened when he appeared in the doorway.

"My dear friends, God is great. Today, he has revealed his divine pleasure to his humble guardian of the holy tombs and rightful heir to the Ka'bah." Ali Bakr moved ceremoniously to a small settee elevated on a slight platform. He liked to compensate for his small stature.

"You are all aware that we have moved over one hundred and fifty thousand of our brave soldiers to our northern border to liberate our Islamic brothers in Azerbaijan. I must now confess to you that I have no intention of ordering our young men to fight to free the half-breed Muslims in that filthy little insignificant territory. They deserve the chastening hand of God for deserting the true Islamic homeland of Iran!"

"May Ali Bakr live forever," interrupted the Minister of Interior, Ayatollah Mohammed Dekmejian. "Then to what purpose have we sent our fearless warriors to dwell in tents in the north?"

"Do not trouble your heart my dear friend. These young men will indeed fulfill the will of God in the very near future. Only, they will not fight against the Russians- they will fight with the Russians!"

The room immediately erupted into a loud chorus of protests. "With God as my witness," proclaimed one ayatollah, "I cannot consent to God's people joining hands with infidels. This is blasphemy!"

"Silence!" Ali Bakr snarled. "I don't need your consent or approval when God speaks to me. Hold your peace and I will reveal to you the hand of God in this matter!"

Twelve sets of eyes stared holes into the plush *Tabriz* silk tapestry under their feet.

"Many years ago when I was exiled in Brussels, a young Russian KGB agent and I worked together on a number of mutually beneficial projects. While he was indeed an infidel, he was an infidel that was of great use to God in accomplishing his will for his holy people."

Ali Bakr paused briefly and poured himself some tea. When he'd filled his cup and taken a drink he resumed his discourse.

"This young Russian was instrumental in recruiting many influential and wealthy western supporters for our struggle against the Shah. He found that many of the contacts that were sympathetic to his socialistic philosophy were also quite willing to help rid Iran of the greatest imperialist of all, Shah Reza. I even visited Moscow to meet one very important prospect and managed to win his loyalty to our holy struggle"

Just then a servant bowed and entered the room and silently approached Ali Bakr. He leaned over the frail cleric and whispered something in his ear. Without apology, Ali Bakr stood and left the room through the same curtain from which he'd entered.

Ayatollah Mohammed Dekmejian looked at the mullah who'd interrupted Ali Bakr and said, "Do you have a death wish, my foolish friend?"

"Please forgive my impertinence 'Hammed, but my heart burned when I thought of sending Islamic soldiers to fight side by side with infidels."

"It is not I that you need fear. I've watched many men die for less of an insult than you committed moments ago."

"Yes, you're right. I will beg his pardon this very hour when our meeting is concluded."

Dekmejian stood and faced the assembled ruling clerics. "While I know that many of you share the same emotions as our dear brother let me caution you to hold your peace and patiently wait for Ali Bakr to reveal what he has on his mind. He is a wise and holy man of God. He would not so foolishly risk his standing with the Revolutionary Guard by violating the writings of the Holy Quran. I assure you that we will all understand and agree with his reasons for undertaking such an unusual course of action."

"But what possible reason could he have in defiling our faith by making an alliance with Satan's children?" asked the man seated across from Dekmejian.

"I don't know, but I suggest you hold your tongue and wait until you hear Ali Bakr's explanation."

Dekmejian took his seat with the others and made small talk as they waited another twenty minutes for Ali Bakr to return. Just as they were beginning to wonder if the aged mullah had forgotten about them he reappeared.

"Please forgive me for neglecting you. Now, where was I? Oh, yes. I was telling you of the young Russian. As I was saying, we helped each other on several occasions. Unfortunately, his duties soon required his presence elsewhere.

"We have not seen each other since that time but we have kept abreast of each others activities. Not long ago, my old Russian acquaintance surprised me by sending an agent to see me. Since that time we have spoken numerous times through somewhat clandestine means. In fact, a courier just brought word from him a few moments ago. It was he I went to meet. The messenger delivered the final details of an arrangement I made with my old friend."

"May we ask, who is this Russian of whom you speak so highly?" asked Dekmejian.

"Perhaps you have heard of him. His name is Alexi Yanochev."

Manama, Bahrain

SARAH CRAWFORD COULDN'T believe her luck. She was actually sitting in her room at the *Mannai Plaza* in Bahrain. No one could accuse the U. S. Government of mistreating military personnel stationed in the Arabian Gulf. The *Mannai Plaza* was nothing less than a posh high-rise condominium, complete with cafeteria, hot tub, gymnasium, and game room.

Jake was going to have a cow when he found out she was here. Ambassador McClintock had finagled a set of temporary orders for her out of an old friend at Central Command. Sarah was assigned to the Naval Medical Clinic at the Administrative Support Unit. Americans had to be very careful not to call the ASU compound a "base" for obvious political reasons.

Sarah was sitting in her comfortable living room listening to the stereo when the telephone rang. "Sarah, this is Theo McClintock."

"Oh! Hi, sir!"

"It appears you had a safe flight. I hope you aren't too tired to go out tonight. I've arranged a little surprise party for you and Jake tonight at Ambassador O'Hare's residence."

"Great! What time should I be there?"

"Don't bother driving. I'll have my aide pick you up at 8:30 p.m. Take care. I'll see you then."

* * *

THE WHITE FORD Galaxy sedan Sammy was driving flew across the causeway separating Saudi Arabia and Bahrain at over 105 kilometers an hour. The alarm on the aging motor pool vehicle's governor was emitting a constant, irritating "DING-DING-DING". Jake and Sammy were willing to trade irritation for speed. They'd been in the desert training Saudi's for forty-three days straight and thoughts of spending a relaxing evening at a party with Ambassador McClintock completely dominated their weary minds.

"So, Jake, what do you suppose the ambassador meant when he cracked off about you needin' a good nurse tonight?"

"I don't have the slightest idea Sammy. Sometimes the old man is a strange duck. I suppose he was just commenting on how hard we've been working lately."

"I dunno boss. I was thinking more like he was hintin' he's gonna fix us up with a couple of nurses from ASU."

"No way! He may be strange, but he'd never do anything like that. He and Sarah are pretty tight and she'd kill him for a stunt like that."

"Ya never know. The desert sun does funny things to a man's mind," laughed Sammy.

"Not that funny," Jake said. "But I've got to admit, I wouldn't mind seeing one nurse in particular. I'm a little embarrassed to admit it, but I'm really starting to miss her."

"Man, have you got it bad. You're not even married and already you're hen pecked," said Sammy.

"Some day, my dear Sammy, you'll understand the advantages of being pecked by the right hen," Jake replied. "Better slow this crate down. We're coming up on the Bahraini check point."

"Sure thing," Sammy said as the slowed and entered the long line of cars waiting to pass through the three separate check stations. First, you had to show your causeway pass and military identification. This usually took thirty to forty minutes. The next line led to the vehicle inspection station. The drill at this stop was to get out of the car, let the Bahraini guard inspect your vehicle for contraband, and then wait for them to stamp your Causeway Pass that it was alright to proceed to the next station. At the last station you presented your pass for inspection. Depending upon time of day and day of the week, this process could take anywhere from one to three hours. Today it only took an hour and twenty minutes.

Clearing the first traffic circle on the island Sammy looked over at Jake and asked, "You think this Russian situation is going to escalate?"

"I don't know Sammy. It has all the signs of turning into something real serious. Mining international waters is an act of war. All the Russian subs off our coast have the people in Washington scared stiff. Scared people do stupid things. I'm watching to see what all this has to do with the Iranian build-up, if anything. Something doesn't figure, but I don't know enough to say what it is. Anyway, I doubt if it will involve us. We've got our work cut out for us for the next few months. This thing will probably be all over before we get back to the 'teams' in the states," Jake said.

15

HENSLEY FARGO WAS the Officer In Charge of the twenty man Blue Team forces defending the so-called command post. It wasn't really a command post. The casual observer would've mistaken the scene for a bunch of overweight, middle-aged hunters having a few beers. Sure, the funny looking toy-like guns and camouflage painted faces seemed out of place, but no one would've considered them a military force. To the men in the C.P., they were doing much more than having a few beers. They were, after all, defending their title as the *Allegheny Militia Annual Paint Ball War Game* champions.

Fargo had personally selected the site for the command post. It was the same one he'd used last year to win the competition. Fortunately, the rules dictated that the victor had the honor of choosing to defend or attack. That was an easy choice for him. To his way of thinking, if taking the defensive worked once it would work again.

TO THE FRONT of his position was 100 yards of open meadow with grass so short a grasshopper couldn't hide. A wide mountain stream cut a slash between the forest tree line and the meadow creating a perfect field of fire. His flanks were guarded by one of the densest brier thickets in West Virginia. Rabbits had a hard time navigating the tangled limbs and inch long thorns. There was no danger of a bunch of out of shape weekend militiamen attacking from that direction. To the rear of the CP was a sheer sandstone cliff rising one hundred twenty feet from the meadow floor. The cliff was slightly concave, making Fargo's position virtually impregnable.

All he had to do to clinch the title again this year was sit tight and keep a sharp eye out. The Red Team's suicide charge was sure to happen any moment now. He was going to decimate the attackers with twenty of the new *Tipman Pro-Lite* high powered paint ball rifles his team had purchased with tonight's victory in mind. He already had plans for how he was going to spend his share of the one thousand eight hundred dollars prize money. That was only ninety dollars each, but it was more than enough to put on a keg at the victory party and buy a fifth of *Chivas Regal* Scotch for a certain reporter at the *Greenbrier County News*. He couldn't wait to see the reaction of his archrival Terry O'Brian when he read the article that would appear in Sunday's edition of the paper.

LAUGHTER SIGNALED THIER closeness to the defending team's position. Terry O'Brian led his scraggly Red Team squad of wanna-be soldiers to within inches of the cliff's edge overlooking the Blue Team. They were almost comical crawling snake style on their over-sized bellies as they took up positions behind the Blue Team camp. Besides Terry, only one man had the appearance of a real soldier. He was O'Brian's new second in command.

O'Brian had a hard time waiting for the signal as he listened to

Fargo telling his men how they were going to kill the Red Team again this year. He wanted to stuff his fist down the fat man's big mouth. But he didn't. He wasn't going to mess this up by acting prematurely. Terry didn't care about the prize money one bit. All he wanted was to get even for all the grief the braggart Fargo had caused him over the past year. Sure, they were members of the same militia, but they'd developed a seething animosity toward each other over the years. Terry was a college graduate who retired from the Marine Corps in '98, and Hensley Fargo was an elementary school drop out coal miner who'd taken a bogus black lung disability. Fargo felt bad about his lack of education and looked for any opportunity to take it out on O'Brian.

Since last year's defeat Fargo's gloating had become merciless. Everyday he would drop by O'Brian's hardware store and publicly brag about his military genius and O'Brian's ineptitude. O'Brian had to endure endless stories about how the "poor dumb coal miner" had "showed a thang' or two" to the "college boy war hero". Well, all that was going to end soon. He had a secret weapon. His name was Billy Ray Johnston.

Billy Ray was a newcomer in town who'd just been discharged from the Green Berets. O'Brian had seen Billy Ray's pictures from the Gulf War and everything. Renting a small farmhouse on twenty acres just down the road from O'Brian, they quite naturally kept running into each other around town. Billy Ray was a real friendly sort of fella and went out of his way to befriend Terry. O'Brian figured it was because they had so much in common, considering their common military backgrounds and all. Anyway, they'd become fast friends in the two short weeks since Billy Ray had been in town.

One day while Billy Ray was visiting O'Brian's hardware store, Hensley Fargo swaggered in behind his enormous stomach and started into his usual tirade about his military prowess. After he left Terry filled his newfound friend in on the embarrassing details of last years poor showing in "The Games" as they were called by those in the know. Billy Ray offered his help and O'Brian was quick to accept.

Billy Ray's plan was simple, yet devious. O'Brian loved it. They got started right away. Every night the week prior to the games Terry, Billy Ray, and two others spent several hours practicing their repelling skills. Billy Ray was an expert and after several demonstrations he convinced the others that they could repel down the cliff without killing themselves. The rest of the week was spent in speed and control drills – getting down the cliff fast while maintaining control of their weapons. They worked tirelessly until they had it down.

A few yards to the right of the CP they built a concealed blind for a video camera, provided courtesy of Billy Ray Johnston. A remote control would activate the camera as O'Brian and his men descended upon Fargo's men.

The film was intended to be the *coup de gras*. Fargo was going to regret the day he was born. Not only was Terry going to utterly defeat his nemesis, he was going to get the whole thing on videotape and send copies to every bar and barber shop in the county. That way, everybody in Greenbrier County would see first hand how soundly he'd defeated Fargo. Finally, he'd get even for all the grief Fargo had put him through.

Terry and his men were now in position. They did a fairly good job of keeping quiet as they waited. There, he saw it! A green flare raced into the darkening sky from the distant tree line beyond the stream. As one man O'Brian's group jumped over the side of the cliff and dropped down upon the unsuspecting Blue Team. The rest of O'Brian's Red Team charged when they saw their leaders repelling down the cliff. Fargo's team was pelted with red paint balls from two directions. The surprise was complete.

Fargo had his head thrown back gulping a *Strohs* beer when he saw O'Brian dropping from the sky. Terry shot him in the neck – a large bloody welt appeared on the side of Fargo's neck. Those who had time to react and were unfortunate enough to turn around and face their attackers were shot at point blank range in the chest. Most were wearing green T-shirts with their cammies. Some were wearing the prescribed safety clothing. Regardless of their apparel, they'd all sport bruises and welts for the next few days.

One of O'Brian's men grabbed the video camera and filmed each defender in detail, making sure every hit was recorded for posterity. Every shocked expression, every whining excuse, and every whimper of the wounded was captured.

One piece of footage that proved especially gratifying to the Red Team was a close-up of a red paint ball exploding on Hensley Fargo's throat as he took a pull on his long neck beer bottle. You could even hear Fargo cursing O'Brian as he gasped for breath and fell to his knees. Terry fantasized about having a poster-sized freeze frame made to adorn a wall in his store.

Terry savored the thrill of the victory, the flood of relief, the sense of vindication, and the total humiliation of Fargo. It was such an intensely pleasurable experience he felt almost sinful. But Terry didn't feel the least bit sinful for his feelings. In fact, tonight's victory was about to culminate in the biggest celebration party in *Allegheny Militia* history.

Billy Ray Johnston walked over to Terry grinning like a monkey. "Hey buddy, way to go! You really kicked Fargo's butt!"

"Nah. I owe it all to you. Without your help Fargo would've beaten me again this year," Terry said as he gave Billy Ray a crushing bear hug.

"So, when's the party start?" asked Billy Ray.

"Soon as I can round everybody up and get off this mountain. I'll get some lights rigged up and we'll meet down at *Hawk's Nest State Park*."

"I've got a better idea," said Billy Ray. "Why don't we meet at my place. That way we don't have to worry about making too much noise and having the cops break up the party."

"That's a great idea. I'll pass the word, get the beer, and meet you there in an hour or so."

Salt Lake City, Utah

ELIZABETH ANDERSON'S HOUSE was an older two-bedroom home on the outskirts of Salt Lake City. The only difference between her house and all the others on her street was the address. She'd just finished a *Weight Watchers* dinner and was sitting in her *Lazy Boy* recliner watching Peter Jennings on the evening news. Since the death of her husband from cancer two years earlier she found herself spending more and more time in front of the "idiot box", as she called it. Perhaps it was due to loneliness or boredom. She didn't know or care.

The night's lead story was already over and Peter Jennings was babbling about some health issue when the phone rang.

"Mom, this is Mike. Sorry it's been so long since I last called," the voice said.

"Nonsense, Mike. I love hearing from you whenever you call. I know you're real busy with your important government job, so don't worry about me," his mother said almost too sweetly. "How are you son?"

"I'm fine, Mom. Look, I'm in a real hurry. I called to let you know I'm sending you a package to hold for me. If I don't call you next week, I'd like you to mail it to the following address..."

"Wait a minute. Let me get a pencil and paper...uh...OK, I'm ready."

Mrs. Anderson copied down the name and address. She reread the name again to herself and started to get a burning sensation in the pit of her stomach. "Mike, is everything OK? Why do you want me to hold a package for you?" she asked. "You've never done that before."

"Don't worry, Mom. It's just routine business. Look, I've gotta go for now. Love you," he said. The line went dead.

Greenbrier County, West Virginia

T HE VICTORY PARTY at Billy Ray's house was one to remember. They went through two kegs of beer, drinking and laughing 'til daybreak. When the sun finally came up Billy Ray whistled between his teeth to get everyone's attention. "Hey, soldiers. Let's get some pictures with some real guns. I've got some AR-15's in the house. Killers like us ought to be seen with some respectable firepower. Wait here, I'll be right back," Billy Ray shouted as he pretended to stagger into his cabin.

Moments later her returned with an armload of shiny new military style weapons. He had a MAC-10, an MP-5, and two AR-15's with collapsible stocks and flash suppressors. He handed out the weapons and said, "Over here. Let's lean against these blue barrels. Gotta look macho for the ladies."

Everyone thought that was a great idea. After Billy Ray took the pictures he said, "Hey, anybody want to do some target practice with these?" Everybody thought that was a great idea, too. They spent the next two hours shooting every stump and bottle in sight.

A few days after the victory celebration was over Terry took Billy Ray to the airport in Lewisburg. Terry was a member of the *Greenbrier County Air Force*, a small flying club composed of small aircraft owners who met once a month and talked about airplanes over a few beers. He'd joined the club for the same reason he'd joined the *Allegheny Militia*; he just plain liked people. Since his retirement, he'd joined the Kiwanis club, the militia, the *Moose Club*, the *Greenbrier Air Force*, and the volunteer fire department.

Although Terry had many interests, his one great love was flying. Talk to him for more than twenty minutes and the conversation would invariably turn to flying. Billy Ray had spent hours in the hardware store listening to Terry talk about the exhilaration of flying over his beloved mountains. It was only natural for him to ask Terry to take him for a ride. Terry was thrilled Billy Ray was willing to fly with him. Most of the men in the county didn't care much for aviation. They figured that if God meant for man to fly he'd have given them wings.

Terry was beaming as they approached his pride and joy, an aging *Piper Super Cub*.

"Billy Ray, meet Mildred."

"You mean your plane has a name?"

"Sure enough. I spend so much time with her; folks tease me about being married to her. I figured if I'm married to her she ought to have a name."

Terry led Billy Ray around Mildred, pointing out every feature, instrument, option, bolt, and nut. He recited the performance envelope and cruising range. Obviously, what everyone said about Terry and his airplane was true. He was in love with her.

"Nice aircraft. I used to fly one just like her when I was in the Army."

"No kidding. Was it yours? asked a bemused Terry. Privately, Terry didn't believe it for one second.

"No way. Not on Army pay. I joined a flying club run by a bunch of retired Army Rangers. I used to hang around the hangers at the airport admiring the aircraft. When they found out I was in the Green Berets, they sort of adopted me. Gave me free flying lessons and everything. After I got my license, they let me go flying anytime I wanted. All I had to do was buy the gas."

"Wow, what a deal!" exclaimed Terry. "How long has it been since you've been at the controls?"

"Oh, about two years. I logged my last flight hours a few days before leaving Fort Benning when I mustered out of the army."

"Well, maybe I can do something to help. How'd you like to go up with me? Maybe I'll let you fly Mildred," said Terry. He was enjoying this. He was going to have some fun at Billy Ray's expense. He couldn't wait until he put him at the controls. Nothing was more fun than to watch somebody panic the first time they flew. Terry was sure Billy Ray's stories were all a bunch of bull, "Let's go file a VFR flight plan and take her up," Terry said as he headed for the tower.

Twenty minutes later they were sitting at the end of the runway and Terry was requesting clearance for take off. "Tower, this is VC 36, requesting takeoff from 04 west."

"Roger 36. You are cleared for takeoff. Winds are 030 at 10 knots. Altimeter 30.15. Proceed standard departure to White Sulphur VOR. Report and proceed VFR. " Terry recognized the Greenbrier Valley Regional Airport tower voice as that of Becky Ranson, an old high school friend who'd been working at the airport for twenty years.

"This is VC 36...Wilco."

"Hey Terry, lets go look at that big hotel in White Sulphur Springs. I've wanted to see her since I got here. I hear she's a beauty,"

"You mean the *Greenbrier?*" asked Terry.

"Yeah. I've heard a lot about it. Sure would be nice to get a bird's eye view."

"Sure, why not. It's been a while since I've been over that ways."

Twenty minutes later, as the small *Piper Cub* approached the VOR at White Sulphur Springs, Terry said, "OK, hot shot. Let's see how good your flying lessons were. Slide over here and take the controls."

"Great. I was wondering when you'd ask," replied Billy Ray. They quickly exchanged seats without so much as a ripple in the aircraft's heading or altitude. Once Billy Ray was at the controls it was Terry who panicked. Billy Ray did a nose over and headed for the ground. He pulled up seconds before impact and flew at tree top level.

"What on earth do you think you're doing! Pull up, pull up!" Terry screamed.

"Relax, Terry. I'm gonna show you how the Green Berets fly."

"Not in my aircraft you're not!"

"Too late, pal. I've got the stick. Don't worry, I know what I'm doing. I'm not going to get us killed or hurt your precious airplane. Just sit back and enjoy the ride."

Terry O'Brian was white as a ghost. Every drop of blood had drained from his face and seemed to be frozen in his throat. He was hyperventilating and gripping the seat so hard he tore the vinyl.

Billy Ray laughed maniacally as he barely cleared a ridgeline. He descended even lower as the trees gave way to an open field. Less than a thousand yards ahead lay Interstate 64. Just beyond the highway he could see the stark white columns of the stately *Greenbrier Resort*.

"You can't go over there at this altitude," screeched Terry. "You'll kill somebody."

"Oh don't be a prude. I doubt anyone will even notice us. We'll be over the next ridge before anyone even knows we've been there." Billy Ray was wrong. A tall man with a military looking haircut just happened to be video taping nothing in particular when the *Piper Super Cub* crossed I-64, center field in his lens.

A NUMBER OF GUESTS saw the aircraft approaching at the same instant a small group of well-to-do tourists broke into pandemonium. A lady in a pink dress and pearls screamed and then fainted. Dozens of people sitting on the verandah hit the deck, skinning their elbows and knees on the concrete, as a hotel security man copied down the aircraft's number off the fuselage.

The man with the military haircut expertly taped the entire scene. Soon, this videotape and another like it would become indelibly etched in the minds of the American public. Every television on the planet would run the footage over and over for days. Newspapers and radio talk shows would ask how such a tragic event could happen after such a clear warning as this.

Terry sat frozen beside the lunatic pilot. The whole terrifying ordeal seemed to be playing out in slow motion and he was helpless to stop it. He started to protest, but some inner voice told him he was better off keeping quiet.

Billy Ray was saying something. His voice had lost the familiar Appalachian drawl it once had. "Hey Terry, you still with me partner?"

"Yeah. Get out of my seat. I'm taking this plane back to the airport,'" responded Terry.

"Don't think so Champ. Think I'll keep the controls a while longer."

"I swear, when we get on the ground I'm gonna kick your teeth down your throat," swore Terry. "What kind of idiot are you? We're gonna have the FAA and the State Police waiting for us when we get back to Lewisburg."

"Afraid we're not going back to Lewisburg." Before Terry could respond, Billy Ray reached behind his back and pulled out a 9mm Browning. Without warning he gave Terry a wicked backhand smashing the butt of the pistol against Terry's left temple and opened a bloody three-inch gash. Terry went out like a light.

"No use giving you a chance to try and play the hero," Billy Ray said to his unconscious passenger. "Then I'd have to kill you and that would ruin everything. I need you healthy if the plan is going to work."

After flying around aimlessly for twenty minutes as instructed, Billy Ray made a perfect landing on a small strip of grass that lay beside the New River. He taxied toward the nearby trees and came to a stop under a camouflage net which made the plane invisible from the air. Wasting no time, he climbed out of the cockpit and walked over to a waiting *Dodge Ram* 4 X 4. The driver was a tall man with a military looking haircut.

"Welcome home, Mike, or should I call you Billy Ray?" asked the driver.

"No sir! If I hear Billy Ray one more time I'm going to puke."

"It appeared from my vantage point that everything went as planned. Any problems?"

"**N**O SIR. NO problems at all. Did things go OK on the ground?" asked Special Agent Mike Anderson.

"Indeed they did, but no time to waste. Sedate your passenger and load up. We're supposed to debrief the DCI at the safe house in less than an hour."

Andy Renfro was the senior field agent working the operation. There were only four men who knew the entire plan. Special Agent Mike Anderson was the forth man. Soon, there would be only three men who knew the entire plan — Andy Renfro, Director of the CIA General Marshall Freeman, and Donald Braxton, the Vice President of the United States.

16

ERLINE FRAZIER WAS wearing the smile she reserved for when things were going her way. As the Press Secretary for a President facing a tough reelection campaign she wanted today to be perfect. After surveying her handiwork for the forth time, she felt confident she'd done all she could do. The Vice President had personally selected the *Greenbrier Resort* in White Sulphur Springs, West Virginia as the site for today's speech. It was a great decision. She couldn't have done better herself. This was the perfect place to kick off the President's reelection bid.

The podium with the *Seal of the President of the United States* was positioned strategically so that the breathtaking West Virginia foothills served as a television camera backdrop. Hundreds of white folding chairs were set up on the well-manicured lawn in pristine ranks; soon to be filled by local townspeople and visiting school children. The free BBQ after the speech would ensure all the seats were filled.

A few lucky children would get their pictures taken with the President and their teacher, thus ensuring their families would have lots of pleasant memories of him on Election Day. It wouldn't hurt him in his bid to secure the endorsement of the National Educators Association either.

She'd worked hard to ensure that the television cameras would convey just the right visual message. The American flags and bunting, the country setting, and the carefully scripted speech would reinforce President Carpenter's campaign theme - A President in touch with the American people.

When President Carpenter faced the cameras the American people would see a very Presidential and important international peacemaker. As he explained his sweeping initiatives to reestablish peaceful relations with Russia and diffuse the deteriorating situation in Azerbaijan the voters would hopefully see that they were better off with a man like Christopher Baines Carpenter in office.

Her only frustration was in having to work with the most paranoid and draconian Secret Service Detail Chief on the federal payroll. He was quickly becoming a royal pain. He'd placed Secret Service agents everywhere. Perhaps the viewing public wouldn't notice all of the serious looking people in sunglasses wearing their inconspicuous ear pieces, but they couldn't miss over a dozen uniformed state and local law enforcement officers positioned inside the perimeter of the television camera's field of view. Something had to be done. All of her work would be in vain if people got the idea that the President was unreachable. How could he be in touch with the American people if they couldn't get to him because of all the security?

Ross Bostich was a thirty-year veteran of presidential security. He joined the Secret Service fifteen years after Lee Harvey Oswald had assassinated President Kennedy and learned the ropes from those who'd felt deep personal shame and guilt over allowing the President to be shot and killed while under their protection. Special Agent Bostich was committed to making sure nothing like that ever happened on his watch. He'd leave no stone unturned to prepare for this assignment. To say that he was prepared was an understatement of epic proportions. He'd ordered the usual checks on the locals who were members of extremist groups or had voiced complaints against the government. Nothing substantive had turned up.

His advance party had interviewed the local law enforcement agencies and compiled a list of troublemakers. None were considered dangerous, but all the same, they wouldn't be allowed to attend the President's speech.

All of the guests not on the VIP list would be required to pass through a metal detector prior to taking their seats. Another routine precaution he'd just completed was sweeping the entire area for explosives with a team of bomb squad canines. He also had several highly secret "black" anti-terrorism devices on hand to help him eliminate any surprises. Counter-sniper teams were on the roof of the resort as well as that of the adjacent cottages that surrounded the main building.

The Greenbrier County Sheriff had informed him of an incident where some local guy had buzzed the hotel in a "bug smasher" as he called it. In actuality, it was a small, two seat *Piper Cub*. The Sheriff had investigated a complaint from the hotel management and been unable to locate the owner of the aircraft.

An employee had copied down the airplane's ID number and called the airport in Lewisberg to complain. Lewisberg was thirty miles away, but it was the closest regional airport to White Sulphur Springs. The Airport Manager at Greenbrier Valley Regional Airport in turn had run the number through the FAA. He'd no sooner obtained the name of the owner than his own operations manager reported the same aircraft to be overdue by twelve hours.

The Airport Manager really didn't have many options. He initiated a missing aircraft report with the FAA and notified the Greenbrier County Sheriff. Since the pilot was a resident of Beckley, they in turn passed the report to the local police. The sheriff's shift supervisor sent a patrol car by Terry O'Brian's house to see if he'd landed elsewhere and managed to make it home. He hadn't.

Now, O'Brian and his plane had been missing for over forty-eight hours. O'Brian's friends said they were sure he'd suffered a stroke or a heart attack while airborne and crashed into a ravine somewhere. The police thought perhaps he'd been intoxicated and lost control. Perhaps his aircraft had suffered some type of catastrophic mechanical failure. The sheriff told Bostich that the prospects of finding Terry O'Brian alive were not very promising.

To Special Agent Bostich's way of thinking this was a loose end, and he didn't like loose ends. An unaccounted for aircraft and pilot who'd overflown the same hotel the President was scheduled to speak at was too much of a coincidence for his liking.

Several witnesses to the incident at the *Greenbrier* said the airplane seemed to appear out of nowhere flying low and fast. Could this have been some sort of a practice run for a suicide bombing?

Terry O'Brian seemed to be a stable individual according to all accounts from people that the Secret Service had interviewed. He owned a hardware store, was a retired Marine Corps officer, and wasn't known to cause any trouble.

On the other hand, he was a member of the *Allegheny Militia*, whatever that was. The FBI didn't have anything on this particular group, but they didn't have anything on the *Michigan Militia* either, at least not until after two of its members blew-up the Alfred B. Meyer Federal Building in Oklahoma City.

Bostich wasn't going to take any chances. He'd already placed a team of men on the roof of the hotel with shoulder fired Stinger anti-aircraft missiles. If this O'Brian character was planning to make an attempt on the President's life he was going to be in for quite a surprise. Any aircraft flying a threat profile would be knocked out of the sky long before it could get close enough to cause any harm to anyone under his protection.

Sure, he'd broadcast a warning over the Guard Frequency. He'd already filed a Notice to Airmen (NOTAM), making the airspace over the *Greenbrier* off limits. His rules of engagement had already been approved and rehearsed. One warning over Guard was all any aircraft would get if it closed within two thousand yards and had a constant bearing and decreasing range. The missile team had an acronym for this CBDR. It meant that an aircraft was headed straight for you on a collision course.

Bostich brought the whole "package" with him. The "package" was a series of preplanned defense kits designed to protect against any conceivable threat to the President. They'd recently added a portable M-8 alarm system to detect a chemical agent attack. Soon after the *Shiniri Kyo* attack in the Tokyo subway the Secret Service had procured the kits just to make sure they were ready for everything.

Erline Frazier didn't like Ross Bostich and she didn't care who knew it. She liked to be thought of as a no-nonsense, hard charging, rising star and she didn't care if she had to ride roughshod over people to garnish her reputation. Ross Bostich could prove to be another opportunity to show how tough she was.

"Hey Bostich, why don't you just mount a few machine guns on the podium? Would that make you happy?" she said acidly.

"Thanks for the suggestion, Ma'am. If I think it's warranted in the future it's nice to know I have your approval." Bostich countered.

The Press Secretary gave him a look that was meant to let him know he was messing with the wrong person. "Don't get smart with me mister, or I'll have you replaced," she said a little too loudly.

Everyone within earshot stopped what they were doing to watch Erline Frazier vent on another unsuspecting man. Much to everyone's amusement, Bostich proved to be far too smart to be baited by the President's pretty young appointee.

"Sorry if I offended you, ma'am. I'm just a humble public servant trying to do my job. Now, if you'll excuse me, duty calls." With that he turned and walked away. As he disappeared around the corner it looked as if he was laughing.

Erline Frazier was fuming. Oh well, the President was speaking in just a few more hours and this would soon be just another job well done. Then she would be sure to drop a memo to the Director of the Secret Service and complain about how difficult it was to work with Special Agent Bostich. Bostich didn't know it but he'd just ended his career. She was going to make it her mission in life! In the future people would remember what she'd done to Bostich and jump when she gave orders. Little did she know that both of their careers would end in less than five hours.

Tehran, Iran

AYATOLLAH RAFALGEMII NOW had the complete attention of the assembled high clerics. "I know you are all wondering why I would defile our holy warriors by ordering them to fight on the side of imperialist Russia. However, I beg your patience while I explain. I promise, you will all understand very shortly how Allah will use Satan to destroy the greatest Satan of all."

"Are we going to make war with America?" asked Ayatollah Dekmejian.

"No, my friend. Allah has seen fit to use America to help us defeat an even greater enemy of God."

"Who is a greater enemy of Allah than the United States?" asked the Defense Minister.

"My friends, we are finally going to destroy our ancient enemy Israel!" Rafalgemii answered as he leapt to his feet.

His words were met with initial silence before the stunnedroom broke into a din of competing voices as the ruling council members all began to speak at once.

"How will we defeat Israel?" asked one.

"What about the United States?" shouted another.

"WHAT WILL PREVENT Israel from using their nuclear arsenal against us?" asked the Defense Minister.

Ali Bakr raised his hands and said, "Please, please, hold your questions and I will answer them one at a time. Allah is good. Infidels cannot defeat his purpose. All of the devices Satan has used to strangle our people and prevent us from assuming our rightful role in ruling the Islamic peoples of the world will very soon be swept away in a single stroke of God's great hand.

"Alexi Yanochev has pledged to provide our army with modern weapons of war. We will provide Russia with oil and manpower. Russia is already taking steps to ensure they have air superiority over the Arabian Peninsula and we are using our three *Kilo* submarines and control of strategic choke points to keep America and her allies from entering the Persian Gulf."

"Ali Bakr, do you think we can defeat the Americans in a war?" asked Ayatollah Dekmejian.

"As I mentioned before, that will not be necessary. We are about to undertake the greatest military campaign in our history.

"Turkey is now under Islamic control. I have spoken with the new Prime Minister and he has pledged that he will deny America use of his country's airfields. Russia will use its overwhelming air power to capture all of the airfields the Americans would need to stage their fighters and bombers. We will reinforce their troops around the airfields and also seize the oil fields held by Iraq, Kuwait, and Saudi Arabia. By denying American aircraft carriers access to the Persian Gulf they will be forced to make limited attacks from far out in the Indian Ocean. They will be unable to exert sufficient force to do much more than annoy our troops. This is stage one of the campaign.

"Stage two is the invasion of Israel. Russia has agreed to provide us with twenty SS-20 theater nuclear missiles in exchange for our support in this operation. We will launch a preemptive nuclear strike against Israel and destroy much of their ability to retaliate. After our initial attack, Russia will begin a massive bombing campaign against Israeli cities and destroy the Jewish infrastructure and war machine. When our troops invade Israel, Russian fighters will engage their fighters and deny Israel the use of its air force."

"But what will prevent America from attacking us with her intercontinental ballistic nuclear missiles?" asked the Defense Minister.

"That is stage three," Ali Bakr Rafalgemii replied. "As we speak, an operation is underway that will ensure America does not resist our plans too vehemently. Their attacks will be very mild and soon stop altogether. You will find that before it is all over they are actually our allies and will help us take control of the entire region."

"But how can this be?" asked the Finance Minister.

"We must thank our old friend Saddam Hussein for giving us a way to hold America at bay in the short-term. We will capture American Embassy personnel and hold them prisoner in places the American military consider high value targets. We will use their own CNN to ensure that the whole world knows their welfare depends upon how the Americans respond.

The second part of stage three provides even more concrete assurance that they will not intervene. We are going to replace their President with an old friend of mine." Ali Bakr paused for effect. "Alexi Yanochev is not the only acquaintance I made while in exile."

Moscow

ALEXI YANOCHEV WAS enjoying a glass of his favorite vodka when the secure telephone on his desk rang.

"Yes! Who is it!" demanded Yanochev.

"This is Admiral Rybakov. Sorry to disturb you at this late hour, but I have urgent news."

"And what might that be, Admiral?"

"I have just learned that our troops were not successful in preventing the Americans from clearing our mines from the Malacan Straits!"

"What! You assured me you'd taken the necessary measures to stop them!

"I cannot explain how our *Spetsnaz* failed. They had the American SEALs outnumbered three to one. Regardless, the mines have been destroyed," said Admiral Rybakov.

"Then that means the two carrier battle groups in the Pacific will be able to get close enough to launch aircraft and intervene in the Arabian campaign. Admiral, we cannot allow that to happen! The entire operation depends upon keeping the American carriers out of the picture until we can remove President Carpenter. We can deal with the carrier in the Indian Ocean and the one in the Mediterranean, but we don't have enough aircraft to accomplish our mission and fight two more carrier air wings," said Yanochev.

"Then I recommend we attack them before they have a chance to sail out of range of our land based bombers on the Kola Peninsula. We have enough fighters to overwhelm the U.S. Air Force defenses in Japan. If we can keep the American fighters busy long enough to allow our bombers to surge past them we have an excellent chance of sinking both carriers. I am convinced we will be successful, especially since most of our missile submarines are within range as well," said Rybakov.

"Very well. I'll alert General Masavich and the forces in Azerbaijan. We will begin the Arabian bombing campaign once we hear that the carriers are under attack!

17

THE RHYTHMIC, GENTLE pitch and roll of the Pacific Ocean the USS *Carl Vinson* had enjoyed since she set sail had now been replaced by a violent shuddering and jerking that had no discernable pattern. The ship's navigator had reported a falling barometer for the past seven hours and the sea conditions had worsened with each report. Waves were breaking over the bow and sending giant columns of white water shooting skyward completely obliterating visibility.

Admiral Buck Thompson felt vulnerable as he paced the Flag Bridge nervously. He was normally the picture of professionalism in appearance but right now he could care less how he looked. Dressed in his work khakis and an navy blue pullover sweater, his salt and pepper graying hair looked like he'd combed it with a hand grenade. The howling wind on the bridge wing had whisked away his ball cap and blown his hair every which way. He'd forgotten to comb it when he came inside the skin of the ship.

SHORT, STANDING ONLY five feet five inches tall and a little on the heavy side, he hadn't earned his stars by impressing people with his physical prowess. His meteoric rise to flag rank was due solely to his incredible ability to grasp the essence of complex issues and take decisive corrective action.

A nagging sense of foreboding fought its way to his consciousness. He wasn't frightened by the weather conditions *per se*. He'd ridden out a number of typhoons in this twenty-six years at sea and today's weather was nothing by comparison.   His concerns were strictly tactical. His carrier was pitching and rolling too hard to launch or recover aircraft. The destroyers and frigates, "small boys" in navy-speak, were thrashing around so wildly that their sonars were leaving the water with each wave rendering them useless for submarine defense.

The rough seas effectively blinded the admiral's battle group. Unfortunately, the disadvantage was one-sided. Russian land based aircraft had clear skies and could pick his ships out of the raging seas without difficulty. After the news he'd received an hour ago this concerned him gravely.

The *Carl Vinson* Battle Group was less than three hundred miles off the Kamchatka Peninsula steaming in Anti-Submarine formation tracking thirty-three Russian submarines when the first report came in. National intelligence sensors had picked up large-scale activity at three bomber airfields in Russia. That was bad news and it couldn't have come at a worse time. His ships were out of position to provide air defense and the weather was limiting his ability to launch fighters to defend the battle group.

Immediately after receiving the FLASH-TOP SECRET message he'd ordered his forces redeployed into an Anti-Air Warfare formation. His escorts were heading toward AAW stations at best speed but it would take at least an hour for all the ships to get there - time they might not have.

The *Carl Vinson* and her escorts had been ordered to sea on short notice when the Russian submarine fleet surged to sea. Besides the USS *Carl Vinson*, the battle group was comprised of the USS *Cowpens*, an *Aegis* Cruiser out of San Diego, the USS *Stethem*, a Guided Missile Destroyer also out of San Diego, the Guided Missile Frigate USS *Crommelin* out of Pearl Harbor, and the Destroyers USS *David R. Ray* and *Paul F. Foster*, both out of Everett, Washington. The Oiler USS *Cimarron* was shuttling between the *Carl Vinson* Battle Group and the *Abraham Lincoln* Battle Group to the south which was commanded by Admiral Skip Warren.

In Admiral Thompson's opinion, all of his ships were good ships commanded by good, solid naval officers. "Not a weak link in the bunch," he thought. The only concern he had about the ships was that they'd onloaded weapons and assets with the prosecution of Russian submarines in mind. For instance, he had two squadrons of S-3 *Viking* ASW aircraft onboard the USS *Carl Vinson*. This meant that he'd been forced to leave a squadron of F/A-18's ashore. If he'd known he was going to be facing Russian bombers he would've deployed with F-18's instead of the S-3's. The F/A-18's were the best short-range fighter in the inventory.

He was ruminating upon these facts when a messenger from Flag Intel approached and handed him a clipboard with an orange **TOP SECRET** cover sheet. The admiral signed the receipt and dismissed the messenger.

The Battle Watch Officer, Lieutenant Commander Larry Wiggins, noticed the admiral's furrowed brow as he read the message and inquired, "Bad news, Admiral?"

"It's more than bad, Larry," Admiral Thompson said. "We've just received indications that the Russians have launched at least five regimental sized raids from the three airfields we've been monitoring."

"Do you think they're all coming our way?" Wiggins asked.

"I suppose Admiral Warren will get his fair share of the action.

Larry, order the battle group to General Quarters. Get the Warfare Commanders and the Commanding Officers on the Battle Group Command circuit. I need to speak to them in five minutes. In the meantime get on TACTERM and get me Third Fleet."

"YES, SIR!" REPLIED Wiggins as he spun around and trotted across the Flag Command Center to the red handset. Lieutenant Commander Wiggins was sweating in spite of the frigid air conditioning.

Five minutes later Admiral Thompson, surrounded by his senior staff, picked up the handset for the secure Battle Group Command Circuit satellite radio and pressed the transmit button. "Gentlemen, you have by now all read the message traffic and know the situation. I've just spoken with Third Fleet and briefed him on our readiness and our read of the situation. Regrettably, he informed me that we are on our own on this one and can't expect any help from the Air Force.

"What you do not know is that as we speak U.S. Air Force fighters deployed out of Japan are engaged with Russian fighters over the Sea of Okhotsk. They were overwhelmed by the number of fighters the Russians threw at them and have suffered heavy losses. They report that while they were engaged with the fighters approximately fifty *Backfire* and *Blackjack* Bombers broke through unscathed and are headed in our direction," Admiral Thompson paused and took a deep breath before continuing.

"Our position is less than optimal with the present sea state, but we're still in pretty good shape AAW wise. The weather has not affected our Missile Weapons Direction Systems aboard the cruisers. However, I expect the high winds to negate the effectiveness of our Chaff countermeasures.

"Due to the seriousness of the situation, I'm ordering our fighters to attempt to get into the air. The pilots are in their aircraft and we will begin the launch cycle immediately. The wind and sea state are well outside of the launch envelope, but we have no other option. I have relayed to AIRPAC via Admiral Sykes at Third Fleet my intentions and he concurs.

"Folks, this is what we get paid to do. We have superior weapons and we're better trained. The enemy will be determined and will attack fiercely, of that you can be sure, but I am confident we will prevail.

"Keep you sensor operators alert and rotate every radar you have at full power. I'm relatively sure the enemy subs in the area have relayed where we are and what our disposition is so there's no need to attempt to remain covert. Are there any questions?"

The men on the other end of the radio responded in turn, "No questions, sir."

"All right then, good luck and may God protect you and your men in the battle to come. It is an honor having you under my command," the admiral said. "Give my regards and prayers to your men."

On the flight deck of the USS *Carl Vinson*, F-14 *Tomcats* were on all three of the working catapults waiting for the ship to turn into the wind. One CAT had a mechanical failure and was unavailable.

Before she started her starboard turn to put the wind on the bow the carrier's deck had been gyrating and rolling thirty-five degrees one way and then snap rolling in the other direction. Every other wave was crashing over the bow. The ship was heeling sharply to starboard as the wave action worked in concert with centrifugal force to roll the *Vinson* in the direction of the turn.

The flight deck crew was bravely tending to tie-down chains, fuel lines, and equipment on the slick, wet, rolling deck. Under normal conditions their orders would have seemed suicidal, but not a man on deck wanted to be anywhere else. They all knew that the survival of the battle group, over five thousand men and women, rested in their hands.

As the ship completed her turn Airman Apprentice Mike Radey removed the tow bar from an NC-5 tractor. Without warning, the ship rolled violently to port and a huge wave came down the side spilling over onto the deck. Aviation Ordnanceman First Class Jerry Lowe was checking a *Phoenix Missile* cable under the port wing of the F-14 on the Number Three Catapult when he saw the wave coming and dove for the deck. Wrapping his arms around the port wheel of the F-14, he was submerged in the frigid water. The rushing water pulled at his body with a terrible force but he held on with strength that only those in mortal fear of death can muster. He was going to make it! That was when Mike Radey washed into him knocking his grip loose from the wheel. Both of them were carried over the side of the ship and vanished into the sea.

Lieutenant Pat Carson was the Catapult Officer on the number three CAT. He ducked under the oncoming wave and grabbed onto a stanchion. The catwalk bulkhead broke most of the force of the wave as it passed over his head. "Man, I could've been safe launching from the bubble," he thought. The bubble was a reinforced plexiglas enclosure near the catapults designed for launching aircraft in inclement weather, but he'd decided to join the others out in the weather so that the enlisted troops wouldn't think they were being called upon to do something officers were too good to do.

He looked up and saw Vixen 01, the F-14 on his Cat, still sitting where she was supposed to be. In weather like this aircraft are prone to slide out of position. The pilot was the squadron's commanding officer. Unfortunately, his plane's engines had been drowned by the surge of water down its intake. Great, now the plane will have to be towed off the CAT and another aircraft towed into positioned. That would take time. Time they didn't have.

The aircraft on CAT One and Two were luckier. They weren't damaged by the rogue wave. The Air Boss ordered their launch as soon as the next wave cleared the bow. The idea was to launch an aircraft each time the bow reached its lowest point and started to come up. Hopefully, by the time the catapult reached the end of its stroke and the plane reached the end of the carrier the bow would rise clear of the water. The timing would have to be absolutely perfect. The USS *Carl Vinson* was steadied on the launch heading. There was no time to waste!

The Catapult Officer was friends with most of the aircrews preparing to launch and he didn't like what he was being ordered to do. Admiral's orders or not this was just too dangerous. "Boss, this is crazy. The sea-state is way outside of the envelope. We're going to kill whoever we launch," Lieutenant Carson said to the Air Boss.

The Air Boss simply said, "Proceed with launch."

The pilot of Vixen 11 saluted Lieutenant Carson. Reluctantly, Carson circled two fingers in the air, checked for a thumbs up from the final checkers, and touched his fingers to the deck. When he lifted his fingers from the deck the Catapult Petty Officer depressed the button activating the CAT. Vixen 11 bolted down the deck. She was nearly clear of the bow when the ship snapped violently to starboard. Her right wing caught a wave and the plane cartwheeled out of control across the raging sea. There was no ejection.

The young Catapult Officer felt as if the wind had been knocked out of him, but he couldn't allow himself time to grieve the loss of the crew. Seconds were precious if they were going to meet the oncoming bombers before the enemy was within their weapons release range. He looked at the next aircraft and Vixen 09's pilot was saluting. Carson repeated the launch sequence.

Lieutenant Mike Faucette and his backseater Lieutenant Junior Grade Randy Porter were thrown back against their ejection seats by the force of the catapult. Lieutenant Faucette had the throttles in afterburner as they raced down the deck. He pulled gently back on the stick as the deck edge passed underneath of them and climbed steeply through four thousand feet. "Vixen 09 airborne," he reported.

Faucette pushed the throttles back to military power and headed toward the projected intercept point that his Radar Intercept Officer had entered into the system. Each aircrew had received rather unconventional orders. They were to proceed after take-off to engage the enemy at best speed. American fighters never went into combat without a wingman, but the admiral wasn't sure any aircraft would make it off the deck and he didn't want to delay a possible intercept waiting for a wingman that might never arrive.

Vixen 09 turned to heading 278 degrees and began searching the skies with her AWG-9 radar. Loaded with four *Phoenix* missiles and four *Sidewinders*, she was a potent threat to the Russian bombers by herself. She could launch the fire-and-forget *Phoenix* missiles from over sixty miles away and then close in on the heavy bombers with her remaining heat-seeking *Sidewinders*.

THREE MILES ASTERN of the USS *Carl Vinson* the Russian K-419 *Morzh*, an *Akula* class attack submarine, was at a depth of two hundred feet trailing the massive carrier. The boat's Commander, Captain Uri Bessmenny, was at the passive sonar display studying the lumbering CVN's acoustic signature. He would've preferred a fix from the periscope but the weather was too bad to get that close to the surface. He had to settle for the next best thing - a passive fix. A fire control computer determined range and bearing to the target by comparing the lines of bearing from the sub's towed array and hull mounted sonar.

This information was then routed to two separate computers. The first relayed the targeting information via underwater communications to two other *Akula* Class SSN's that were in company with the *Morzh*. The second computer translated the targeting information into a latitude and longitude and inserted the coordinates into a preformatted computer generated position report. A light flashed on the communications computer monitor as the operator uplinked the targeting information via a Super High Frequency (SHF) data link to a satellite in geosynchronous orbit over the Sea of Okhotsk. This was accomplished via a directional microsecond burst transmission from a trailed communication buoy that had no chance of being intercepted by the *Carl Vinson* Battle Group.

Seconds later the commanding officer of the K-119 *Voronezh*, an *Oscar* II class Guided Missile Submarine, was reading the targeting information two hundred miles to the north. A large grin spread across his face. "Comrades, it would appear that fate has smiled upon us at long last. The *Morzh* has assumed a trail position on the USS *Carl Vinson* undetected. She is now relaying continuous targeting information," he said triumphantly to his bridge team.

"Targeting data entered," the Fire Control Team Leader reported. Thirty SS-N-19 *Shipwreck* anti-ship missiles on the five *Oscar* II Class SSGN's patrolling the Sea of Okhotsk were programmed with targeting data on the USS *Carl Vinson*. Three hundred miles to the south bombardiers on twenty *Blackjack* bombers and twenty-five *Backfire* bombers received the downlink from the satellite at exactly the same instant. Six *Bear* bombers accompanied the *Blackjack* and *Backfire* bombers. The *Bears* had large airframes under each wing that were much larger than the AS-4 and AS-6 missiles that the *Backfires* and *Blackjacks* were carrying.

ADMIRAL THOMPSON HUNCHED over the most recent intelligence report. The speaker assigned to the Anti-Air Warfare circuit suddenly blared, "Jamming, Jamming, Jamming. Bearing 278 degrees. Broadband noise."

So this was it. The attack had begun. Admiral Thompson jumped out of his seat and ran to the Flag Naval Tactical Data System (NTDS) AAW console to see the jamming for himself. The large screen JOTS display wasn't much help at times like this because it didn't provide raw radar video. It only showed electronically generated symbology entered into the system by an NTDS operator once a firm track was established on a contact.

Another F-14, Vixen 04 attempted to take off from the pitching deck above. Admiral Thompson heard the loud thump of the catapult as it reached the end of its travel. Another circuit somewhere in the Command Center announced that the aircraft was in the water and the crew didn't eject. As the admiral reached the AAW NTDS console he saw what the operator was talking about. Forty-five degrees either side of 278 degrees was a white electronic snow storm.

USS *Cowpens* and the USS *Stethem* were equipped with the SPY-1 radar which was supposedly invulnerable to jamming. Surely, they'd be able to see through this mess and provide tracking data on the inbound bomber raid. So far, he'd received no reports of radar contact on the Russian aircraft.

Ninety miles to the west in Vixen 09 Lieutenant Faucette and Lieutenant J.G. Porter were running through their pre-engagement checklist. Porter was running a weapon check on his *Phoenix* missiles when the first contact came up on his scope at one hundred miles. Contacts began flooding the outer edge of his scope. The same contacts were appearing on the radarscope of the USS *Cowpens* as well. "Hey, Mike, radar contacts bearing 278 degrees. Composition looks like... one, two, three, ...uh, ... fifty-one! Speed six hundred knots at angels four three," reported Porter. "They must've sent everything that'll fly at us."

"Roger, I'll call it in," answered Faucette. "Bravo Whiskey, this is Vixen 09."

"Vixen 09, Bravo Whiskey...GO!"

"Whiskey, we have fifty-one inbound bogeys, angels four three at six hundred knots. They are on the deck and coming fast."

"Roger Vixen 01, *Cowpens* has them also. You have weapons free. I say again, weapons free!" ordered the AAW Commander.

"OK Randy, we have weapons free. Lock and load cowboy!" Lieutenant Faucette said over the aircraft's intercom.

"Roger that! Assigning missiles as we speak. Going computer launch," replied the RIO.

"Negative! We need to intercept targets before they reach their weapons release range. Launch when ready!" ordered Faucette.

"You're the boss, Mike. Four *Phoenix* armed, hot, and locked. Launching now, now, now! Missile One, away." Faucette and Porter felt nothing but heard a slight thud as the powerful missile dropped off the weapons pylon and sped away in a blinding flash. "Launching Missile Two. Now, now, now!"

Another missile dropped off and sped toward a *Blackjack* bomber. Vixen 09 launched the other two missiles in quick succession.

"Bravo Whiskey, Vixen 09, four *Fox* three's away. Taking tracks 232, 198, 230, and 227 respectively," reported Porter.

"Roger, Vixen 09. Continue to prosecute targets," ordered the Anti-Air Warfare Commander.

"Roger, BW, already on our way," replied Faucette. The backseater programmed the *Phoenix* but the *Sidewinders* belonged to the pilot.

Vixen 09 closed the gap with the Russian bombers in less than five minutes. The four *Phoenix* missiles arrived first and four bombers disintegrated. Radar operators onboard the American ships watched the rapidly decelerating pieces of debris fall into the water. Lieutenant J.G. Porter continued to relay course and speed recommendations to Lieutenant Faucette until they were in a trailing position one and a half miles behind the bomber formation. "I'm coming around for a tail shot now," he grunted as he loaded up the aircraft with "G's." "Tone, fox two away! Breaking right!"

"What about the follow-up shot?" asked a perplexed RIO.

"I've only got four *Sidewinders* and over forty bombers. I'm taking one shot at a time to make them count. If I need a second shot I'll take it!" The RIO responded with a double click of his intercom signaling his agreement.

Faucette snapped the stick to the right and came around behind another *Blackjack*. The entire formation was wildly executing evasive maneuvers trying to prevent Vixen 09 from getting a missile seeker head lock on their aircraft. It was an exercise in futility. The big bombers couldn't maneuver effectively while loaded down with the heavy AS-4 and AS-6 anti-ship missiles mounted under their wings.

"Splash one Rooskie!" shouted Porter as the first *Sidewinder* slammed into the big bomber and exploded. "BW. Vixen 09. Splash one," Porter said over the AAW circuit.

"Tone, Fox Two away!" Faucette said.

THE SECOND *SIDEWINDER* missile sped toward a doomed *Backfire* bomber. The missile flew up the starboard engine exhaust and exploded in a ball of flames. The pilot of the *Backfire* felt a bone-rattling explosion, but the bomber didn't come apart. Good! He still had a chance of survival. His engine fire alarms all came on at once and the cockpit and crew spaces began filling with smoke. He was loosing altitude rapidly. He tried the stick and the aileron foot pedals. Nothing. Great! He was on fire and had lost hydraulics and control of all flight surfaces.

Flying low in an attempt to evade the Battle Group's radars, he didn't have much altitude to work with. When the aircraft descended out of control below one hundred feet he command ejected the crew into the icy waters. They would all die of exposure within twenty minutes.

"SPLASH TWO, PORTER radioed, dispensing with call-ups on the AAW circuit.

"Tone, missile away," Lieutenant Faucette announced as he launched on a *Backfire*. The bomber ejected flares in a rapid stream attempting to decoy the missile's heat seeking guidance system away from its primary target. It didn't work. The *Sidewinder* flew under the starboard wing fuel tank and exploded. The *Backfire* exploded in a huge fireball, throwing large pieces of the airframe in all directions.

Faucette was intently focused on the attack and didn't think to take evasive maneuvers until it was too late. Vixen 09 flew through a large cloud of debris-laden smoke at the speed of sound. A piece of the stricken *Backfire's* engine compressor struck the F-14's canopy and it imploded on the aircrew. Faucette was dazed by the impact. The aircraft shuddered, thick in the grip of a stall.

Lieutenant J.G. Porter heard the impact and hunched forward to escape the fatal impact of the wind blast. The freezing cold felt like a million knives stabbing him all at once. Fortunately, he had no exposed skin or he would've suffered instant frostbite. Still, the cold was nearly debilitating. But the worst part was the incredible noise. Porter had never heard such a deafening roar in his life.

PORTER FORCIBLY WILLED himself to calm down. He'd wasted several valuable seconds screaming in absolute terror doing nothing to help the situation. People who didn't think at times like this usually died – he didn't want to die today.

Vixen 09 was nose up and bleeding airspeed fast as the violent shudder gripped the aircraft. They were in a stall and the pilot wasn't flying out of it!

"Mike! Snap out of it! You still with me?" shouted Porter. He could barely hear himself above the screaming wind and engine noise.

Faucette made no reply but after a terrifying thirty seconds the nose of the aircraft dropped and the airspeed picked up as the pilot flew the plane out of the stall. Quickly checking the controls and scanning the instruments, he determined Vixen 09 was in no immediate danger of falling out of the sky.

"Randy, you OK?" Faucette asked.

"Yeah, man. You had me scared. We OK?" Porter asked, referring to the condition of the aircraft.

"Yeah. The only thing we lost is our canopy. The windscreen is keeping most of the windblast off of me. I should be able to handle it. If we stay below ten thousand feet we shouldn't have too many problems. We'll have to keep our airspeed down but otherwise we should be OK."

"Good. Let's get out of here. I'll enter a navigation waypoint for homeplate," the RIO said.

"No way! I've got one *Sidewinder* left and I'm taking the shot!" the determined pilot said as he pushed the throttles forward and put the plane into a tail chase of the nearest bomber.

"I thought we were keeping our airspeed down!" Porter said sarcastically.

The noise was deafening and the wind was beating into his helmet visor and chest like giant pistons. He ignored the pain and closed on the last bomber in the formation. The Russians had climbed through several thousand feet. At first it didn't register on Faucette what was happening. When it did, he was flooded with an animalistic rage that erupted into burning fire, pulsing through every nerve ending in his body. The Russians were within missile launch range of the Battle Group and were climbing to launch altitude.

It took less than ninety seconds to get a tone in his headset indicating his last *Sidewinder* had a seeker lock on the target. "Tone, Fox two away! Vixen 09 Winchester." Faucette reported to the Battle Group, indicating they were out of missiles. The words were no sooner out of his mouth than the big AS-4 and AS-6 missiles began dropping off the pylons of the Russian bombers and racing toward the *Carl Vinson* Battle Group.

"VAMPIRE, VAMPIRE, VAMPIRE. Bearing 278 degrees. Raid count six!" the Anti-Air Warfare circuit announced.

"Missiles away," was the next announcement. The USS *Cowpens* ripple fired twelve vertical launch Standard Missiles as the inbound targets slowly descended on a direct slope toward the USS *Carl Vinson*.

"Cease Fire!" ordered Captain Jeremy Parker, the *Cowpen's* commanding officer and Battle Group Anti-Air Warfare Commander. "Target speed is five hundred knots and decreasing. Assess targets as decoys."

"Vampire, Vampire, Vampire. Bearing 017 degrees. Raid count 1,2,3...Break! New Vampires bearing 020 degrees and 023 degrees. Vampires assessed as SS-N-19 missiles. Raid count as follows: three stream raids of thirty." USS *Cowpens* ripple-fired seventy-two SM-2 missiles in less than two minutes. The intercepts were crossing targets but well within the envelope of the SM-2.

The USS *Stethem* was tucked in tight close to the USS *Carl Vinson*, and was assigned the mission of providing a missile umbrella for the carrier. She was monitoring the progress of the *Cowpen's* missile engagement and would fire on any "leakers" - enemy missiles that weren't destroyed by the first barrage from the cruiser. She was also waiting for the other shoe to drop from the inbound bombers. She didn't have to wait long.

"VAMPIRES, VAMPIRES, VAMPIRES! Bearing 278 degrees. Vampires are AS-4 and AS-6 missiles. Raid count seventy-one. I say again, raid count is seventy-one," said the AAW circuit operator.

Captain Parker watched as the Russian coordinated attack unfolded and knew the USS *Carl Vinson* was going to be hit. There were more missiles inbound than he could handle. The attack was happening so fast there would be no time to make wise decisions on which threat to attack first. He walked over to the radio and picked up the microphone. "All stations, this is AAWC. Go *Full Auto* on all air defenses. I say again, go *Full Auto* on all air defenses."

"Well, Gentlemen, at least it can't get any worse," observed the

AAWC to nobody in particular. He was very wrong.

"Inbound torpedo, bearing 180 degrees!" reported the sonar operator aboard the USS *Stethem*. "Range six thousand yards and closing."

Things began to happen fast as the *Carl Vinson* Battle Group began making erratic torpedo evasion maneuvers. The missiles fired at the decoys all scored direct hits. The SS-N-19 counter fire was not so fortunate. Five made it through and the USS *Stethem's* Weapons Direction System automatically fired ten SM-2 missiles to engage them. She then fired her remaining fifty missiles at the inbound AS-4 and AS-6 threat.

The USS *Cowpens* had eight SM-2 missiles remaining. They were auto-fired at the AS-4 and AS-6 missiles as well. The USS *Crommelin* was out of the picture as far as the SSN-19 missiles were concerned but she launched twelve SM-1 missiles at the AS-4 and AS-6 raid. Launching at the extreme edge of her missile engagement envelope and at crossing targets, there wasn't much hope she'd score many hits. The two destroyers were entirely out of the picture. They only carried NATO *Sea Sparrow Missiles* for self-defense.

Admiral Thompson heard the distinctive BRRRRP of the Close In Weapon System's 20 mm gattling gun as it fired on the surviving Russian missiles. The CIWS destroyed the first two but was overwhelmed by the number of enemy missiles and didn't have time to engage them all.

Admiral Thompson had just turned to ask the Battle Watch Officer to update the magazine status of the *Cowpens* and *Stethem* when he was violently propelled against the overhead by the force of the torpedo explosion. His battered body fell to the deck amid the smoking debris and arcing electrical equipment of what had seconds earlier been the Flag Tactical Command Center. Both of his legs were broken as was his spine. He could move his arms and head but nothing else seemed to work. He opened the one eye that would obey and vainly searched the room for signs of life. The only light came from small fires burning in the weapons and NTDS consoles.

The most frightening thing was not what he saw, but what he heard. Deep within the ship he heard metal tearing. Loud explosions rippled through the hull as the reactors were submerged in the rushing frigid seawater. But that was not to be the final insult. Te first of seven AS-4 missiles slammed into the side of the critically injured ship. A wall of flame swept toward the admiral's broken bod. His last thoughts were that he would go down in history as the admiral who'd lost the first carrier in battle since World War II.

CAPTAIN PARKER LOOKED out the port bridge wing window and watched as the USS *Carl Vinson* sank beneath the waves. It was nothing like he'd pictured in his mind. The mammoth ship leapt from the sea in a column of white water when the torpedo struck. When she landed the missiles struck - and she simply disappeared. No lingering slow roll, no bow protruding out of the water as she slid slowly backwards, just sudden impact and immediate death.

The USS *Stethem* caught three of the big missiles intended for the *Carl Vinson*. When the smoke from the explosion cleared, *Stethem* wasn't there.

WITH THE LOSS of the carrier, and with it Admiral Thompson, Captain Parker was now the Senior Naval Officer. It was up to him to protect and fight the remainder of the battle group. The Russians would suffer greatly at his hands for what they'd done. The battle group couldn't do anything about the bombers which were now retreating victoriously to their air bases but there were a number of Russian submarines within his grasp that would pay the debt in full. He still had his destroyers and helicopters.

TWO HUNDRED MILES to the west the crew of Vixen 09 was flying at "max range", a speed calculated to get as many miles as possible from their remaining fuel. There was not enough to make it to Japan but Lieutenant Faucette knew that every mile he flew closer to land made their chances of rescue better. He'd already radioed their situation to the Air Force AWACS Air Controller that had launched to support the fighter engagement over the Sea of Okhotsk. They'd coordinated with the Japanese Defense Force which had a destroyer in the area. The destroyer was already making best speed to intercept the coordinates where he and Larry would most likely have to eject. With any luck they would make it.

18

THE RADIO SPEAKER in the Flag Command Center next to the commander's chair aboard the USS *Abraham Lincoln* provided Admiral Warren and his staff with a play by play account of the unfolding tragedy befalling Admiral Buck Thompson and his battle group fifteen hundred miles north. Admiral Warren knew that on ships spread over five hundred square miles of ocean the officers and men of his battle group were listening to the engagement as they manned their respective battle stations. Fearing that they'd become distracted he decided to do something to focus their attention on the enemy that was bearing down upon them.

"All Stations, this is Admiral Warren. Patch this circuit into your 1MC announcing circuits. I want to address your crews." He waited three minutes for each crew to make the patch, then continued. "Folks, the *Carl Vinson* Battle Group has just fought a heroic battle against a coordinated Russian attack. They suffered heavy losses and I know that you are all saddened by the loss of life and ships.

"However, do not for one instant think that we will suffer the same fate. They had inclement weather which prevented the launch of aircraft and the prosecution of submarines. We do not. We have all of our fighters airborne waiting for the Russian bombers to show up. The *Vinson* Battle Group was in Anti-submarine Screening Formation. We are not. Our cruisers are deployed in an Anti-Air Warfare screen along the threat bearing. They were operating alone. We have two SSN's in direct support, two TACTASS ships providing targeting data on all submarines in the AOR, and a P-3 out of Kadena on station.

"We also have the USS *Kuwait City* in company. Her class of missile barge provides an incredible force multiplier and will ensure we have enough SAMs to take out anything that the Russians can throw at us. We've also been utilizing a convincing operational deception (OPDEC) program since last night's underway replenishment. It's unlikely the enemy has reliable targeting data on the *Lincoln*. Furthermore, we're not waiting to be attacked- we are going on the offensive as of now. Warren, out!"

With that, Admiral Warren issued several orders rapid fire. "Battle Watch Officer, give Alpha X-ray weapons free. Have them order the P-3 to attack the missile submarines and have the SSN's take out those *Akula's* that have been trailing us. Launch the S-3's for follow on attacks. All units activate active anti-torpedo countermeasures.

"Order all AAW ships to go full power on their air search radar's and go EMCON (emission control) on all other units. Fighters have weapons free at max range. Now, let's see how the Russians like it when they're on the receiving end."

LIEUTENANT MIKE RAWLINGS' heart was beating double-time. He'd run hundreds of simulated torpedo attacks in his short five-year career. He'd even practiced on real Russian submarines, but this was the first time he'd ever been tasked to drop live ordnance on real people. As TACCO on one of the Navy's newest P-3C Maritime Patrol Aircraft it was his job to coordinate the torpedo attack. "Pilot, TACCO. I have control," he announced. The pilot flipped a switch and allowed the computer to take over control of the aircraft. The TACCO inserted symbology on his computer screen indicating where he wanted the system to place buoys and weapons. The aircraft banked hard right and flew itself to the correct coordinates dropping sonobuoys where it was instructed. As Golden Eagle One Zero approached the torpedo drop point the computer generated a prompt on the TACCO's monitor instructing him to open the torpedo bay doors in the belly of the aircraft.

"Opening torpedo bay doors," said Rawlings. He flipped the switch on his upper right hand weapons console. Nothing happened! "Doors failed to open. Recycling switch." Nothing!

"Navigator. Get on the manual hydraulic pump and open the doors ASAP. Our target is going evasive!" ordered the TACCO.

The NAVCOM unsnapped his seat belt and knelt in the isle between his seat and the TACCO's station. Lifting up a small door in the aisle floor between the two positions, he extracted a small handle from its snaps, inserted it in the retainer, and pumped feverishly. The radar operator heard what was going on and came forward to help the NAVCOM on the pump. It took seven minutes to get the doors fully opened.

"All stations, TACCO. I have an indicator light for the doors. Standby for Torpedo drop." Rawlings used his finger to keep his place as he ran through the torpedo arming checklist in his tactical manual lying open on his workstation. His other hand flew over the switches and knobs on his weapons console in a well-practiced motion. "Torpedo armed!" he reported over the ICS. The aircraft shuddered violently as it flew through the low altitude turbulence, throwing the crew around in their seats.

"Buoy away! Torpedo away!" reported Rawlings. "Coming around for reattack."

"Torpedo lock," reported the sensor operator. "Torpedo motor operating at attack speed and sonar tracking. Loud explosion! I hear hull noises. Target destroyed!" shouted the sensor operator.

"Confirm. Next target bearing three two five degrees at twenty-five nautical miles," said Lieutenant Rawlings.

ABOARD THE *OSCAR* Class submarine *Osaka*, the captain allowed himself a small grin. The American P-3 was flying right into the missile trap he'd laid. The newest addition to his weapons inventory was coming in very handy indeed. His secret weapon was a pair of small surface to air missiles much like the American made *Stinger*. The difference was that these missiles were encapsulated in a torpedo tube launched buoy. The buoy made its way to the surface and launched the missiles when the noise level of an approaching aircraft crossed a predetermined threshold. This ensured that the target was within range and denied the aircraft any opportunity to evade the missiles. The missiles had proven extremely effective in secret tests, but this was the first time they were to be used in actual combat.

"A little closer and you will be mine," whispered the captain. He noticed that he was holding his breath - he forced himself to exhale. If the missiles didn't work he and his entire crew would die in the next few moments.

"Missiles away!" shouted the sonar operator. "The P-3 engine noises have stopped. Sir, we have destroyed the aircraft!'

"Very well. Come to cruise missile launch depth. It's time for us to kill the *Abraham Lincoln*!" said the Captain. "Fire Control, you have weapons free. Launch all SS-19's!"

USS *Abraham Lincoln* CVN-72

"VAMPIRE, VAMPIRE, VAMPIRE. Multiple vampires emerging from the water, bearing one three zero at one hundred sixty nautical miles. Missiles tracking toward USS *Willamette*. Golden Eagle One Zero has been destroyed. No beacon detected!" reported the *Aegis* radar operator aboard the USS *Cowpens*.

There was no time to grieve the loss of the P-3. "Auto Engage all targets," ordered the Tactical Action Officer. The order was answered by a shudder throughout the ship as two dozen SM-2 missiles leapt from their vertical launch silos, simultaneously launched in less than two minutes. The entire crew in the Combat Information Center watched their scopes as their SM-2's tracked toward the mammoth enemy missiles. The crew didn't have to wait long. With a mach seven closure rate the air battle was over in a matter of minutes. "Grand Slam. All targets destroyed," said the Air Warfare Commander. There was no sound or noticeable explosion as the Russian SS-19's were destroyed at a range of one hundred miles from the nearest American ship.

"Sir, taking *Oscar* submarine with Wolf flight of two," the Anti-Submarine Warfare Commander reported to Admiral Warren's staff. "S-3's time on top (TOT) in five minutes. Wolf 701 monitoring Golden Eagle's buoy pattern and has firm track on target."

TWO HUNDRED AND twenty feet beneath the surface of the Pacific Ocean, Commander Peter Fisher, commanding officer of the USS *Seawolf* SSN-21, was in a trailing position two hundred yards behind the lead Russian *Akula*. Equipped with the new torpedo launching system, the *Seawolf* held a distinct advantage over the Russian submarine. Most subs must flood their torpedo tubes and open torpedo tube doors before launching their weapons. The resultant acoustic noise is easily heard by any sensor in the water and lets others know a torpedo launch is in progress.

The new *Seawolf* system was a radical departure from conventional designs. The *Seawolf* weapons are launched by pneumatic pressure through a rupturable seal much like *Harpoon Missile* tubes on surface ships. Retractable outer doors protected the seals at depth and during normal operations. These doors retracted prior to taking a low-speed trailing station on an enemy sub. With the *Seawolf* torpedo system there would be no tell-tale warning a torpedo launch was imminent. The first sound the enemy would hear would be the torpedo roaring out of the tube and the torpedo motor lighting off.

"Fire Control, launch tubes one, two, three, and four!" ordered Commander Fisher.

Four MK. 60 Advanced Torpedoes erupted out of their launching tubes and raced toward the unsuspecting *Akula*. Commander Fisher ordered his submarine into a high speed turning dive and closed on the second *Akula*.

"Targets two and three are going evasive," reported the fire control target plotting team.

"Target two now bears one eight four at six thousand yards. Target three bears two three six sat nine thousand yards."

"Roger. Prepare all tubes for target two."

"Aye, Aye, sir. All tubes now ready. Targeting data entry complete on all torpedoes."

"Conn., come right, steer course three five five. Make your depth two hundred fifty feet," ordered the captain.

"Coming right, steady on course three five five. Making depth two hundred fifty feet. Passing course three zero five, depth four hundred feet."

Halfway through the *Seawolf's* tight combat turn the boat was violently pushed toward the bottom as the shaped charge warheads on all four of her torpedoes exploded through the hull of the *Akula*. As the pressure wave passed over the *Seawolf*, the shuddering subsided and she slowly regained steerage and steadied up on the ordered attack bearing.

"MK. 60's tracking target two. Seeker heads have acquired and locked on target," reported the sonar watch.

"Very Well."

Seconds later a series of hull rattling explosions were heard as the second *Akula* was struck by the monstrous MK. 60's from the USS *Shark* SSN-32.

THE PILOT OF the lead S-3 pushed the stick forward to make his attack run on the *Oscar*. The Russian submarine had a titanium hull and was nearly the length of a cruiser. He knew that he'd be very lucky to sink the sub with his two torpedoes. Hopefully, he and his wingman would be able to disable the monster long enough for another flight of S-3's to arrive and finish the job. "Torpedo's away! Clearing right," the pilot radioed to his wingman.

The latest modification to the Mk. 50 eliminated the torpedo seeker head interference that older torpedoes experienced. Now, a pilot had the luxury of dropping as many torpedoes as he could carry all at once if he so desired. These pilots were inclined to do just that.

THE CAPTAIN OF the *Oscar* braced himself behind the attack plot as his sub made a hard turn, discharged a pair of torpedos decoys, and dove for deep water. He wanted to put as much distance between him and the American torpedoes as possible. Perhaps he could go below the torpedoes operational depth and save his boat from harm.

The first two torpedoes were getting closer. He didn't need a headset to hear their high pitched sonar's getting louder and louder as they approached. "Torpedoes have acquired," reported the sonar operator.

"Two more torpedoes bearing three six zero. Seekers transitioning to attack mode. They have lock!" screeched the young sonarman.

"Hard left!" ordered the captain.

The first two torpedoes impacted the screws and severed them from their shaft. Water began pouring into the reduction gear compartment. The *Osaka* plunged deeper, driven by its forward momentum. The deeper she got the wider the split in the hull where the shaft penetrated the aft end of the boat became.

THE CAPTAIN RAN to the forward bulkhead, grabbed the microphone for the announcing system and shouted, "Deploy the distress beacon! Execute plan Zebra!" Plan Zebra was a code word ordering the crew to scuttle the submarine to keep it from falling into enemy hands. The next two American torpedoes saved him the trouble. They impacted the outer hull and penetrated into the forward weapons bay causing two of the *Osaka's* huge wake homing torpedoes to explode. The colossal submarine ceased to exist.

ADMIRAL WARREN PACED in front of the large screen display in the Flag Command Center aboard the USS *Abraham Lincoln*. He had two squadrons of F-14's airborne which were racing toward the inbound Russian bombers. The bombers weren't on the radarscopes yet, but he knew where they had to be. One of the wonders of modern warfare was that the command center on the carrier could see what the fighters had on their radars. This extended the radar coverage of the battle group to nearly a thousand miles. The lead F-14 was two hundred miles out when it made contact.

"Alpha Whiskey, this is Diamond Flight. I have bogeys at three six zero, angels two seven. Raid count forty-seven," blared the air warfare radio circuit speaker over Admiral Warren's head. "Do you have the track?"

"Roger Diamond. Firm track. Weapons free. Take all bogeys at max range," ordered the Air Warfare Commander aboard the cruiser.

ADMIRAL WARREN WATCHED as missile symbols started to pour off of the friendly fighters. The world's most sophisticated computer game was starting to unfold. Only this was no game. Each symbol on the large screen display represented human lives. In some cases, thousands of lives. He had to remind himself this was not a computer generated training exercise. In the next few minutes real people were going to die. Hopefully, they would be Russian people and not Americans.

THE NEATLY PACKED formation of enemy bombers suddenly began to break apart in all directions as the *Phoenix Missile* symbols closed upon them. Hostile air symbology began blinking out and disappearing off the scope as the American missiles rained down upon them. The *Phoenix Missile* salvos destroyed twenty-six of the bombers. The F-14's were beginning to close for the kill with their *Sidewinders* when Alpha Whiskey changed their plans.

"Diamond flight, this is AW. Break contact to the east at max speed. Taking remainder of raid with missiles."

"Wilco Whiskey, Diamond Flight, out."

"Cliff, tell Alpha Whiskey to give the majority of the action to the *Kuwait City*. We'll conserve the cruiser's missiles for any leakers," said Admiral Warren. The Group Operations Officer acknowledged the order and relayed it to Alpha Whiskey.

The large screen display now showed the last F-14 was clear of the missile engagement zone. Seconds later, missile symbols started streaming off of the *Kuwait City* as she ripple fired forty-two SM-2 block 7 missiles. The Navy's newest surface to air missiles climbed to one hundred and fifty thousand feet and rocketed toward their prey at mach 3.5. At this altitude and speed the Russian bombers would never see them coming.

The missiles performed as advertised. Two were assigned to each target but in every case the first missile destroyed the target and the second harmlessly self-destructed. The *Kuwait City* destroyed all the Russian bombers with its first salvo.

Admiral Warren picked up the Battle Group Command Circuit handset and addressed the warfare commanders. "Well done, gentlemen.Congratulate your crews for me. Unfortunately, I'm afraid we don't have time to celebrate. While we were busy with the Russian bombers, it seems that the Russian and Iranian air forces began a bombing campaign on the Arabian Peninsula. Troops and heavy armor are reportedly rolling into Saudi Arabia and Kuwait as we speak. We have orders to proceed at max speed to the Straits of Hormuz and provide air support to American bombers launching out of Diego Garcia.

"I am ordering the *Lincoln* and *Cowpens* to proceed to our new area of operations. The rest of the battle group will proceed at a twenty-five knot speed of advance. Warfare Commanders meet in the flag mess in three hours. Alpha Bravo...Out."

19

JAKE AND SAMMY strolled into the ambassador's official residence exactly seventy-five minutes late. Wearing tailor made summer white uniforms designed specifically to advertise their superb physical conditioning, they weren't surprised by the large number of ladies smiling in their direction as they slid through the crowd looking for Ambassador McClintock.

The party was already in full swing and the courtyard surrounding the magnificent oversized swimming pool was dangerously overcrowded. Get a few more drinks into people and somebody was going to end up in the pool.

No party in this part of the world would be complete without a gas-fired grill producing hundreds of delicious *swarmas* for the guests. Lined against the walls surrounding the courtyard were tables brimming with trays full of *samosas* and vegetables. Waiters hurried through the crowd with trays full of drinks trying desperately not to spill anything on the crowd of VIP's.

Colorful Japanese lanterns swung gently overhead in the balmy Gulf breeze as a Blues Band comprised of British expatriates played a fairly good rendition of B.B. King's "The Thrill Is Gone." American music was hard to find in Bahrain and these guys were outstanding.

Sammy liked B.B. King. "This gig might not be a waste of time after all," he said, hitching a thumb toward the band.

"Yeah, they're pretty good. You see the ambassador anywhere?" Jake asked.

"Not yet, but he's bound to be in this tightly packed mass of humanity somewhere."

"Jake, glad you could make it!" shouted Ambassador McClintock as he smacked Jake's back enthusiastically several times. "Good to see you too, Sammy. I trust our Saudi friends have been treating you well."

"Yes, sir; it's good seeing you, too. Sorry I haven't been in touch lately, but I've been in the boonies training Saudis for several weeks. Haven't been able to get to a phone," said Jake.

"Nonsense. No need to apologize. You're not paid to cater to an old goat like me. I'm just glad I could get a message to you and spring you from your duties long enough to get a little relaxation," said the ambassador.

"Can't say that I'm disappointed you called. It's been a while since I've had any time off. I'm looking forward to spending a few days in civilization," Jake said.

"Well, I think I know just the thing to make your stay more enjoyable."

"How's that?"

"It might be better if I showed you. Come with me young man. Sammy, feel free to tag along," McClintock said.

"Sure thing, sir. This sounds like fun," said Sammy.

McClintock led the two SEALs through the crowd toward the residence and opened a side door. "Have a seat, men."

"So, what's the big secret?" asked Sammy.

"Well, I think Jake will appreciate my surprise more than you, but I'm sure you'll like it as well," McClintock said as he turned and walked across the room to the double doors leading to the *Charge de Affairs'* private study. He theatrically threw open the doors and Sarah Crawford gracefully walked out wearing a stunning black sequin evening gown.

Jake was thunderstruck. "Sarah!" he shouted as he lunged to his feet and enveloped her in his arms. "I've missed you so much it hurts."

Sarah looked as if she was going to speak, but didn't. She must've decided to just hold on to Jake instead. Tears were threatening to ruin the moment. Jake gently pushed her away, one hand softly on each shoulder, and asked, "What are you doing here? I mean...how'd you get here?"

"Ambassador McClintock finagled me a set of orders to the clinic at the Administrative Support Unit. I'll be here for three months," said Sarah.

"Three months. I don't know what to say," said Jake. "Ambassador, thanks. I really mean it. This is great."

"Believe me Jake, the look on your face is thanks enough," said McClintock.

"Well, thanks again. I owe you big time."

"No, I owe you. Now, you youngsters get out of here and have some fun," McClintock barked; waving them toward the door. "Be sure to say hello to Admiral Taylor and his wife Tina. They're around here somewhere. They'd love to see you."

"Sure thing, Ambassador. Thanks again," said Jake.

Smiling from ear to ear, Jake threw an arm around Sarah and led her out the door. "Let's get some swarmas and then get out of here," Jake said to Sarah. "Sammy, hope you don't mind if we ditch you, but I'd hate to make you feel awkward."

"No sweat fellas, I know when I'm not wanted. I'll see ya when I see ya. Jake. You know where I'm staying. If I don't hear from you in forty-eight hours, I'll head back without you."

"Deal. Thanks," said Jake.

Jake led Sarah toward a table in the far corner hoping to get away from the crowd and get some food without having to stand in line. As they approached the *swarma* tray he noticed one of the white-coated servants open a gate in the back wall. When the waiter saw Jake looking at him his eyes widened in fear. Jake got that bad feeling that always seemed to warn him seconds before he was about to walk into a trap.

"Sarah, I think we better be on our way."

"But Jake, I thought we were going to eat first," said a puzzled Sarah.

"Don't ask questions. Just trust me. Something isn't right. I'm going to find the Captain of the Guard and have him take a look around outside. Go get your purse and meet me at the front gate," Jake ordered.

Sarah looked miffed as she turned and fought her way through the crowded courtyard to retrieve her things out of the study. Jake made it twenty feet around the backside of the pool and walked behind a short one-meter high stone planter when grenades started exploding in the courtyard. Instinctively, he took cover behind the stone wall. Shrapnel knocked holes in the stucco wall behind him while burning metal bounced harmlessly off of the stones protecting his body from the blast.

Jake carefully peered over the lifesaving planter and reeled back in horror at what he saw. Scores of guest lay sprawled dead and bleeding across the courtyard. Four black clad commandos had apparently entered through the open back gate while the grenades were exploding and were now walking through the carnage shooting anything that moved. The guests were being slaughtered like helpless sheep.

Jake's eyes narrowed in rage at the cowardice of those who would kill defenseless, innocent civilians. Men and women were shot in the back as they cowered in corners and ran for the doors. Jake was helpless to do anything. Less than forty seconds had elapsed since the first grenade exploded.

Jake caught motion out of the corner of his eye and went flat behind the protective planter. Two commandos were on the top of the wall a few feet away and jumped down to join the melee. "Good, they didn't see me," thought Jake.

The two attackers turned their weapons toward the center of the courtyard and fired a long stream into the quivering pile of the dead and dying. Jake sprang from his hiding place and broke one man's neck with a wicked rabbit chop. As the other turned to face him Jake deflected his machine gun with one hand and crushed his windpipe with the other. Before the second man fell Jake had both guns and a few extra clips and was diving for the safety of the planter.

His heroics caught the attention of the first four attackers and they unleashed a merciless fusillade of hot lead in his direction. Well, now it was their turn to take some heat. Jake held a machine gun over the top of the planter and emptied the clip in one long sweeping burst. He was lucky and hit one attacker in the head and another in the hip.

Outside the compound, Sammy was just emerging from behind some greenery after relieving himself. Instinctively, he slipped back behind the shrubbery as he saw a team of four men running along the outside wall toward the guard post with weapons drawn. Suddenly, the night erupted into a deafening blast of noise as grenades began exploding inside the residence courtyard he'd just left.

Sammy watched patiently as one of the men in black shot the corporal in the guard booth in the head. The poor guy didn't have any warning. He'd turned reflexively at the sound of the grenades and was shot in the back of the head before he knew what was happening. The attackers didn't even slow down. They ran full speed into the front gate and opened up with their weapons.

As soon as the four killers were inside Sammy dashed for the guard post, hit the panic button, and grabbed the guards Colt 45. Twelve miles away on the third floor of the American Embassy a United States Marine Diplomatic Security Team was jolted from the video they were watching. The team grabbed their weapons from the rapid reaction locker and hastily assembled around the platoon leader. The Sergeant of the Guard radioed the guard shack at the residence and got no answer. He ordered his men to their waiting Humvee and sped off into the night toward the Ambassador's Residence.

Sammy was now armed but terribly outgunned. He couldn't just sit around and let everyone get killed, but it would be suicide to try anything with all the bad guys packing automatic weapons. That was when he detected a change in the pattern of the gunfire. It sounded like somebody else had managed to get a gun and was shooting back. That had to be Jake. Great, now he could get inside while the big guy distracted the bad guys.

Sammy dove through the gate and rolled into a firing position. He punched off two quick shots into the back of the nearest commando and rolled to the right, ducking behind a cement flowerpot just as a hail of angry bullets destroyed the front side of the three-foot high work of art. He could see Jake firing from the other corner of the courtyard and immediately perceived that he and Jake had caused major problems for the party crashers. They had the attackers in a crossfire with no place to hide.

Sammy carefully peered around the side of the flowerpot and lined up another shot. Before he could shoot he saw a gun barrel emerge from the same residence door the ambassador had led him and Jake through earlier. He whirled around cowboy style and fired off a shot from the hip. His world exploded in a blinding flash of light as a bomb went off inside his head.

Jake looked across the courtyard and saw Sammy go down and a bad guy fall dead on top of him. He couldn't tell how badly Sammy was hurt, but he wasn't moving. Seeing Sammy made him think about Sarah. Where was Sarah? He hadn't seen her or the ambassador since all of this started. He didn't have to wait long to find out.

Sarah and the ambassador were led out the side door with two commandos using them as human shields. Jake didn't have much opportunity to try and get a shot at their captors; the other three commandos that were still alive kept him busy with a steady stream of fire. With no other place to hide, they took refuge behind piles of dead civilians.

The two holding Sarah and the ambassador dragged them toward the door. Sarah was being dragged from behind and was off ballance. She tripped over a dead body and fell backwards leaving the man who was holding her exposed. Jake tried to get a shot off but the other attackers pinned him down with machine gun fire, but not before he saw an attacker viciously strike Sarah in the face and drag her to her feet.

Jake's vision blurred as everything around him turned red. He was thrown into the pool as a grenade exploded a few yards away, peppering him with shrapnel ricocheting off the back wall. Jake fought his way to the surface to face his executioners but it was not to be. He saw the last man run out the front gate.

He dragged himself out of the pool and checked himself over. He had a few small holes in his right leg and arm, his ears and nose were bleeding, but there didn't seem to be any permanent damage. The shrapnel hadn't penetrated very deep. In fact, he could feel each piece under his skin. Standing unsteadily to his feet he stumbled to the front gate and carefully looked around the corner. Nothing. They were gone.

Back inside he heard a familiar groan. He turned and saw Sammy pushing a dead enemy soldier off of him. "Sammy, you aren't dead!" said Jake.

"Are you sure? It sure feels like I am," said Sammy.

"Let me take a look at you," said Jake. "Looks like a bullet took about an inch out of your skull. Good thing they didn't hit you somewhere important."

"Always knew a hard head would come in handy," said Sammy. "Anybody alive?"

"Good question. Let's take a look see," answered Jake.

They picked through the nightmarish scene one body at a time turning each person over to check for signs of life. A few people were still breathing but they were in a bad way. Most were dead. Admiral Taylor was among the severely wounded. At his side was his wife Tina. She was dead.

Jake saw five men he'd killed and walked over to each of them, checked to make sure they were dead, and went through their pockets looking for papers. To his surprise he discovered the attackers weren't Arabs. They were Caucasian.

"Hey, Jake. This one's alive," Sammy shouted as he turned over one of the commandos.

Jake ran over and grabbed the man by the front of his shirt and began slapping him viciously across the face. "Wake up! Wake up I said!"

The fallen soldier's eyes fluttered opened. He erupted into a stream of panic-stricken vulgarity. "He's a Russian!" Jake said. Jake pulled the Russian's knife out of his leg scabbard and showed it to him. The injured man's eyes flashed in fear and recognition.

"Hold it, Jake. The battle's over. We can't kill this guy now. We've got to hand him over to the CIA for debriefing," said Sammy.

"I'm going to do a little debriefing of my own. They have Sarah and the ambassador and I aim to find out where they're being taken," Jake said.

Jake slapped the soldier across the mouth and asked him in Russian, "Where have they taken the prisoners?" No response.

"If you don't tell me I'll kill you. Now, where have they taken the prisoners?" Still no response. The Russian glared at Jake and he knew that this line of questioning would get him nowhere. The young commando was not afraid to die.

"Make it easy on yourself, but I will get the answer from you." Without another word Jake sliced off his right kneecap. The soldier let out a blood-curdling scream as he tried to twist out of Sammy's grasp. Jake slapped him again.

"Now. One more time tough guy. Where did they take the prisoners?" This time he got a response. The Russian spit in his face.

"OK. We'll do this the hard way. Jake pushed the knife into the wounded commando's knee joint and twisted the blade. A sickening, grinding pop was heard and the soldier screamed again in agony.

Jake put his face against the face of the soldier and growled, "Now, as I was saying, where have they taken my friends. If you don't tell me, I swear, I'll dismember each major joint in your body one at a time. Do I make myself clear?"

"No more! No more! They have taken them to Kuwait City! Kuwait City!" cried the Russian.

"Where in Kuwait City?" No response. "I said, where in Kuwait City?" No response. Jake was ready to start on the other knee when he threw down the knife and sat back on his haunches.

"I was hoping you'd stop. I'm really uncomfortable with what you're doing pal," Sammy said. "I don't know how much more this guy can take."

"He's dead Sammy," Jake said. "Sorry you had to see that, but I don't intend to let them have Sarah without a fight," Jake said.

"I understand what you're going through, but I 'm not for what you just did. But, don't worry, I'll keep it between you and me. You'll just have to make peace with yourself," Sammy said.

Outside, two Humvees arrived with the Marine Diplomatic Security

Detail. They were locked and loaded and ready for trouble. They leapfrogged through the gate ready to provide each advancing team with covering fire if necessary. They saw immediately that they were too late. Only two lone souls were moving and they were wearing bloody white uniforms of U.S. naval officers.

Jake and Sammy stood amid the carnage with their hands in their pockets as if they were old friends watching birds in the park. They just stood there looking around as if nothing out of the ordinary had occurred. They watched as Sergeant Jorge Torres surveyed the scene and deployed his troops, some searching for survivors while others took up defensive positions. The first two marines to enter the residence discovered the American *Charge de Affairs* to Bahrain lying face down in the stairwell near the top landing. His feet were on the landing and his head was twisted cruelly to one side, obviously the result of a broken neck. Most of his skull had been blown away allowing almost eight pints of thick dark blood to run down the stairs and pool at the bottom.

THE MARINES WORKED their way through each room, finding several dead servants in the kitchen, but the rest of the house was empty. The lance corporal leading the search of the residence reported to Sergeant Torres who was now trying to determine from Jake and Sammy exactly what had transpired.

"Sergeant, the house is clear. Ambassador O'Hare is dead plus a few domestics. No sign of Ambassador McClintock inside," he reported.

"Good job, Marine. Commander Gregory here tells me that Ambassador McClintock was taken captive by the attackers. Get the Communications Watch at the embassy on the radio," barked Torres.

"Don't you have any officers that can help with the situation, Sergeant?" asked Sammy.

"We did, sir. Four of them. But they're all over there by the pool. They were on the guest list tonight," replied Torres.

"Sorry, Sergeant; I didn't know," said Sammy.

"No problem, sir," replied Torres. "We better get you two to a Corpsman and have him checkout your wounds."

"We'll get ourselves to the Doc's, you just do what you can here," ordered Jake. "I'll call the Communications Watch and give him what he needs for his OPREP message from my car phone."

"Roger that, sir. I'll leave you to it. Now, if you'll excuse me, I need to get to work," said Sergeant Torres as he saluted, spun on his heels, and trotted off toward the residence.

"We don't have a car phone," said Sammy.

"I know, but I didn't want Torres trying to keep us hanging around while he gathered information to send off in his reports. We've got to get hold of Colonel Talib and get some help rescuing Sarah and the ambassador," said Jake.

"How do you figure to do that? We're in Bahrain, remember?" asked Sammy.

"Easy, I'll call him on his cell phone. He never goes anywhere without it," said Jake. "I'll use the phone in the ambassador's secretary's office."

Jake punched in the numbers slowly. His eyesight was still a little blurry from the concussion and he was having trouble hearing out of one ear. It sounded like people were talking in a tunnel. Jake figured this would pass.

"Yes, Talib here!" answered Colonel Talib.

"Colonel, this is Jake. I've got some trouble and I need your help," said Jake.

"Sorry Jake, we've got trouble of our own. Our country is under air attack and we have indications that enemy armor has just crossed our border with Iraq and Kuwait. I'm in our command center at Jabel Ali and can't talk. We're trying to figure out what to make of the situation, but tell you what, I'll send someone to pick you up. Where are you?"

asked Colonel Talib.

"We are at the Ambassador's Residence outside of Manama. There's been an attack and the Bahrani *Charge de Affairs* and a lot of innocent civilians are dead," said Jake.

"OK, can you get to Naval Piers at Mina Sulman?"

"Shouldn't be a problem," replied Jake.

"I'll have a patrol boat pick you up in two hours. I'd send a car but I doubt King Fahd Causeway will survive the first wave of bombers. By the way, keep your head down. It looks like you're going to get some of the Russian bombers at your location," said Talib.

"Roger that. See you in a few. Thanks, Colonel," said Jake.

Jake and Sammy walked out of the compound and crossed the parking lot and walked to their white Ford Galaxy sedan. They started the engine and squealed out of the gravel parking lot and headed toward the waterfront. They hadn't gotten far when a blacked out Manama began to light up the night as thousand pound bombs rained down upon the city. Bombs were falling everywhere, but judging by the intensity of explosions to the east and north, the main targets appeared to be Sheik Isa Air Base and the Mina Sulman Piers.

"GREAT, LOOKS LIKE we're going to have a little trouble making it to our pick-up by land — too dangerous with all the bombs falling on the naval base. Feel like hitching a ride with a local fisherman?" said Jake.

"Why not. It is getting rather hot. Might as well hit the beach and see what kind of transportation we can turn up," said Sammy.

Jake hauled the wheel hard left and jumped the curb on Al Fateh Highway, driving the car onto the beach. He drove close to the water where the sand was hardest and made it three miles before the car got stuck in the sand. They were within sight of the Grand Mosque. Several shallow bottom boats were beached on the shore, their owners standing in a large cluster pointing and gesturing toward the explosions at Mina Sulman.

Jake approached the group and spoke to them in their native tongue, "Friends, we have important business with the Bahrani Defense Forces at Mina Sulman. I'll give this car to anyone willing to take me and my friend to the naval basin in their boat," Jake panted. Though the shrapnel wounds weren't life threatening, he'd lost a lot of blood and He was fading fast. .

"Ench-Alla, I will help you. This way, please. I am Hammed. Please, this way," said an anxious fisherman.

"Thank you, friend. Here are the keys to your new car. God is great," said Jake.

Once they were aboard the boat they headed straight for the naval base at its top speed of seven knots. Fortunately, they didn't have far to go - just around the point of land that A.S.U. sat upon and then turn starboard into Mina Sulman.

Rounding the bend, they slowed their engine as two U.S. Navy Fast Boats came screaming out of the dark to intercept them. The Navy boats illuminated the little fishing boat with a powerful spotlight, blinding Jake's party. They came alongside without asking permission or giving any warning. A serious looking petty officer with an M-16A1 jumped onboard with a Bahrani Navy enlisted man. The Bahrani sailor spoke to the fisherman. "What are you doing here? We are under attack. Are you crazy! We don't have time to entertain the curious," he said.

"No, I am on important business. My passengers are with the U.S. Navy," said Hammed.

"Is that so?" the Bahrani sailor asked in English.

"Afraid so," said Jake. "Perhaps the uniform should've been your first indication! I'm Lieutenant Commander Gregory and this is Lieutenant Black of Navy Special Forces. We have an important rendezvous at the naval basin and this gentleman was kind enough to provide transportation."

"Commander, how can I be of assistance?" asked the American Petty Officer First Class.

"Can you give us a lift to the piers?" asked Jake.

"Yes, sir; but it's a little dangerous. We've been taking a pretty bad pounding from the bombers," said the Petty Officer.

"We'll take our chances. We can't miss our appointment."

"Can I have someone see to your leg, sir? It looks like it's bleeding badly." said the Petty Officer.

"You can do whatever you like on the way, but let's get moving. Thanks Hammed," Jake said as he climbed aboard the heavily armed Fast Boat.

The Navy patrol craft sped off into the darkness and had the SEALs at the pier in under five minutes. They were dropped off at the boat ramp next to the Bahrani Naval Command Center. They got out and walked casually up the ramp and took a seat behind a cement traffic barricade.

The bombs were no longer falling. The attack lasted a little less than forty-five minutes and probably consisted of three or four sorties of thirty or forty aircraft each. Most of the bombs fell on the base communications complex, the ships alongside the piers, and the fuel depot. The runway at Sheik Isa Air base had been totally destroyed by two thousand-pound bombs. Most of the hangars and maintenance facilities were destroyed as well.

Apparently, the strategy behind the attack was to take Bahrain out of the picture as an option for basing American aircraft or shipping. Regardless of the enemy's intention, judging by the devastation at Mina Sulman, Bahrain was out of the fight for the foreseeable future.

"So, Jake; how's the leg?" asked Sammy.

"Hurts."

"Thought so. You want me to hustle up some medical help?"

"No. I'll be OK 'til I get to Jabel Ali. I'll let you change the field dressings when Talib's men pick us up."

"It's your life boss. I'm here if you need me," said Sammy, more concerned than he was acting. The SEALs were accustomed to pushing their bodies to the edge physically and could absorb enormous punishment and still go on. A few pieces of metal under the skin weren't going to stop Lieutenant Commander Jake Gregory when he had a mission to complete.

Jake and Sammy didn't have very long to wait before a Saudi fast patrol boat pulled up beside the pier. He recognized one of the men onboard as the wily martial arts specialist he'd encountered his first day in Saudi.

"Good to see you my friend," said the Saudi. "Much has happened since you left yesterday. The Russians and Iranians conducted a coordinated bombing campaign against all Saudi military installations. Our air base and command center in Riyadh has been destroyed. The underground command bunkers are intact but little else survived. The runways are severely cratered and we expect it to be months before they can be repaired. It's the same all across the Kingdom. "

"Did your air force inflict many casualties on the enemy?" asked Jake.

"Unfortunately, our AWACS were not airborne at the time of the attack. Our ground radar stations unexplainably went silent fifteen minutes before the first bombs began falling on Jabel Ali. Russian *Spetsnaz* most likely destroyed them. We managed to get a few ready alert fighters off of the ground before the enemy bombers reached the airfield in Riyadh, but the Russians shot them down before they had a chance to inflict any casualties," explained the veteran Saudi commando.

"The Iranians joined the follow on bombing sorties and attacked from across the Gulf. From the reports we received in the Command Center, Oman, U.A.E., and Kuwait all suffered the same fate as Saudi

Arabia and Bahrain. It would appear that we are in a bad position."

"What about ground forces? Have the Russians or Iranians invaded on the ground?" asked Sammy.

"We're not sure if they have crossed into Saudi Arabia, but we did receive one report from our embassy in Kuwait that they were under attack."

"What are Colonel Talib's plans?" asked Jake.

"He's evacuating from the command center in Jabel Ali and taking our Special Forces underground. We will go behind enemy lines and give them something to do while our generals fall back to KKMC and organize some sort of defense of our country."

"OK, let's get underway and get things rolling. Do you have a secure radio?" Jake asked the Saudi.

"Yes, it's next to the helmsman."

"See if you can patch me through to any U.S. Navy circuit. I've got to let my higher ups know my whereabouts and what has transpired with Ambassador McClintock. The Russians are supposedly taking him somewhere in Kuwait," said Jake.

"Perhaps we will be able to help in that respect. We have many friends in Kuwait. Russians are easy to spot in this part of the world. I will pass along to our Kuwaiti cousins to be watching for Ambassador McClintock. McClintock has been a friend and is well respected among our people."

"Thanks, I can use all the help I can get," said Jake. "I'm going to need every break I can get to find them."

"Commander Gregory, we have the U.S. Navy on the Coordination Circuit," said an English speaking Saudi sailor.

"Thanks," Jake said. "This is Lieutenant Commander Gregory, who am I speaking with?"

"This is CENTCOM Forward Staff Watch Officer. If you have traffic, expedite. The net is jammed...Over," said the SWO.

"Roger, this is Lieutenant Commander Gregory on special assignment with the SEALs. I have OPREP III FLASH traffic... Over."

"Standing bye to copy, sir...Over."

"Under Secretary of State for Middle Eastern Affairs Theodore McClintock was captured by Russian *Spetsnaz* at 2140 Zulu at the Official Residence of *Charge de Affairs* O'Hare in Bahrain. Also captured was Lieutenant Commander Sarah Crawford. O'Hare has been killed. Break. How copy so far?" asked Jake.

"Copy all...Continue." Responded the Staff Watch Officer.

"Roger. Russian *Spetsnaz* soldier revealed that hostages are being taken to Kuwait City, location unknown. Lieutenant Samuel Black and myself are in pursuit and intend to infiltrate Kuwait City which is now under Russian and Iranian control. We will locate Secretary McClintock and observe until we receive further instructions. Will contact Central Command with more details as they develop. How copy, over?

"Copy all. Wait...Out."

"Negative. Will contact you later. Lieutenant Commander Gregory...Out."

"That's going to tick them off," said Sammy.

"Tough. I'm not going to give them a chance to get in my way. Next time I talk to them I'll be in Kuwait City," said Jake.

NINETY MINUTES LATER they were pulling alongside the ruins of the pier at Jabel Ali. Colonel Talib jumped aboard as soon as the first line was on a ballard.

"Jake, Sammy, good to see you are alive. Many of our American friends in the Kingdom are not so fortunate," said Talib.

"How's that?" asked Sammy.

"I'm afraid many Americans perished trying to get their aircraft into the battle. Regrettably, they did not have ample warning and were killed by the falling bombs," said Talib.

"How much time do you think we have before we hear from the Russian and Iranian troops?" asked Jake.

"I'm afraid they are already here. Our soldiers are engaged with Russian paratroopers as we speak. We haven't much time, so please, come with me. I'll have someone look after your wounds while I coordinate the evacuation of my troops. Of course, I assume you will be joining me," said Colonel Talib.

"For the time being. But I intend to go after McClintock and Sarah as soon as I can get what I need. Do you think you can help me get to Kuwait City?" asked Jake.

"In due time, my friend, in due time."

"Jake, let's find a satellite radio? If we can get hold of Commander Lewis he'll get us what we need for our insertion without giving us any grief," offered Sammy.

"That's not a bad idea. He'll help without getting in the way. He'd do the same thing we're doing if he were here. "Colonel Talib, can you set us up with the right radio gear," asked Jake.

"That shouldn't be too hard," the colonel replied.

20

THINGS WERE GOING better than planned for General Masavich. His force landed at Kuwait's commercial airport without opposition. A steady stream of transports brought in sixteen hundred tanks and support equipment in twenty-four hours. It was amazing how quickly you could move an army when the invasion forces were pre-staged.

Russian paratroopers were already engaging Saudi troops at Jabel Ali and on the outskirts of Riyadh. Other paratroopers had captured the oil fields in southern Iraq. The bombing campaign had already shut down all of the GCC airfields in Oman, Bahrain, Saudi Arabia, and the U.A.E., and Russian fighters had control of the skies.

Russian armor was proceeding unhindered across the Kuwaiti border into Saudi Arabia, followed closely by three hundred thousand Iranian troops. The Saudi Army was in full retreat and trying to regroup in the dessert south of Riyadh. The Royal Saudi Air Force stationed at

King Khalid Military City (KKMC) and Riyadh had never gotten off of the ground. Russian and Iranian fighters bombers had overwhelmed their airfield and destroyed hundreds of aircraft parked in neat rows on the tarmac.

With the American AWACS grounded because of political differences, the Saudi's had to rely on their ground-based radars for early warning. Saudi technology was no match for the Russians. First came the jammers, followed immediately by vicious anti-radiation missile attacks on the ground based radar sites. The Saudi's lost all of their transmitters in the first twenty minutes of the invasion. They were now at the complete mercy of the Russian and Iranian bombers, and mercy was in short supply.

Saudi Arabia

DESPITE APPEARANCES, KING Abdullah was not giving up, nor were his armed forces as anemic as General Masavich thought them to be. King Abdullah was a student of history. He'd learned a great deal from the Russian enemy he was now facing. Like the Russian strategy of World War II the king planned to use the vast expanse of his country to swallow the enemy. He was willing to concede control of the northern portion of his country while he stretched his enemy's supply lines to the breaking point.

Let them expend their bombs on the northern cities and military installations. He'd fight the enemy on his own terms. Let them chase phantoms in the dessert and burn up their petrol driving tanks through empty sand. This would buy him time to reach his secret stronghold and rebuild his retreating forces into a credible fighting force.

Actually, he'd planned for just such an eventuality. It was no coincidence that he was falling back to the south of Riyadh. He'd spent billions of dollars building secret underground bunkers, fuel reserves, and shelters for his troops. Early on he'd learned the American concept of pre-positioning supplies and weapons.

King Abdullah remembered well how vulnerable his country was when Iraq invaded Kuwait in the early 90's. He'd vowed then to never allow that to happen again. The Americans thought him to be completely dependent upon them to defend the Kingdom, a perception he'd worked very hard to achieve. It was difficult, but his Air Force swallowed their pride and pretended to be woefully incompetent around the Americans. The whole world would soon discover that things were not as they seemed!

He had a formidable surface to air missile arsenal hidden in the desert to repel the enemy bombers when they came, and he knew they would come. The Russians smelled blood and perceived the Saudi withdrawal as weakness. Yes, he would allow the Russians and simple-minded Iranians to arrogantly pursue his retreating forces until he had them exactly where he wanted them. Then his retreating army would turn and fight.

They would be reinforced by troops and equipment the Russians knew nothing about. The godless Russians and traitorous Iranians who dared defile the holy land of the prophets would find out about laser targeting systems and fiber optic computer controlled engagement management systems. Perhaps he was a simple nomad, but he knew how to spend his defense budget.

Even now, fighters and bombers were on their way from reserve airfields deep to the south. They would land on reinforced fiberglass Marshall matting and taxi to hangars that from above appeared to be nothing more than large sand dunes. This far out in the dessert not even the most inquisitive Russian spy satellites took pictures. Without mile long concrete runways there was nothing to see anyway. Yes, let the infidels come. Allah would soon exact his vengeance upon the enemies of God.

GENERAL MASAVICH WAS proud of his troops. The Russian advisors he'd placed with the Iranian Revolutionary Army were turning the rag tag third world soldiers into a fierce fighting force. The Iranians had courage and zeal in abundance - they just didn't have much training in modern warfare. What they lacked in knowledge was more than made up for by their overwhelming numbers and enthusiasm.

Masavich was sure that together the Russians and Iranians were unstoppable. Russian technology, advanced weaponry, and superior warfighting doctrine, coupled with the Iranian supply of manpower and fuel, made them the most powerful war machine in modern history.

General Masavich was beaming as he reported the progress of the invasion to his president over the secure satellite radio in his command vehicle. "Comrade Yanochev, I am honored to report that the invasion is ahead of schedule. Our losses have been minimal and the enemy is in full retreat. Our paratroopers have landed and captured the northern section of Riyadh. Our tanks are approaching the city as we speak and are nearly within range to bring their canon to bear on the Saudi's that are resisting our soldiers. I will have Riyadh before the sun rises in the morning."

"Excellent, General. The *Rodina* is indebted to your brilliant leadership. Do you still project sixty days to complete your occupation?" asked Yanochev.

"No, sir. We met with no resistance in Kuwait. Their leadership and armed forces crossed the Saudi border ahead of our invasion and joined the Saudi retreat. I left a few advisors with the Iranians to occupy the capital until we consolidate control after the invasion is completed. Our heavy bombers destroyed the airfields in Oman, U.A.E., and Bahrain. They are now unable to resist or provide assistance to the Americans if they should choose to intervene. I expect them to surrender within the next two weeks once they learn what has happened to their Saudi neighbors.

"I will have half of Saudi Arabia under our control by sunup. I expect to overtake the retreating Saudi's within the next forty-eight hours, at which time I will annihilate them completely. I will use that as an object lesson to force King Abdullah to surrender. Once Saudi Arabia falls the rest of the puppet governments in the region will follow suit. I'm confident we can have the entire operation wrapped up within the next ten days," said General Masavich.

"You seem very sure of yourself, comrade," said Alexi. "What of the Americans. Are you just as confident that they will not delay your success?

"President Yanochev, you have my word of honor that I will give to you the Arabian Peninsula within the next two weeks. The Americans are out of the picture. Your operation against the American President will buy us enough time. It would take President Carpenter another two weeks to get enough forces in theater to stop us and we both know he won't be around that long. It's too late for them to do anything now anyway. The Iranians have successfully sealed off the Persian Gulf. Their missile batteries at Bandar Abbas and on the Tumb Islands will keep the American carriers at bay and keep their fighter/bombers out of range. Comrade, we have won. It's just a matter of time before we obtain King Abdullah's official surrender."

TWENTY-FOUR HOURS later, the aging King Abdullah was personally in the command center watching the Russians and Iranians pursuing his troops into the trap. He was now thankful for his long-standing relationship with the Americans. Although the Americans had offended the Arabic pride and had been shut out of the Gulf region for the past few months, they were still providing an invaluable service during this present conflict. President Carpenter was doing what he could to help even though his carriers and air force couldn't get involved directly. The U.S. military had numerous support services working in his behalf of which the Russians were unaware. These services just might allow him to defeat the invaders without direct American intervention.

AN AMERICAN *PREDATOR* unmanned spy plane was aloft providing a live video feed to a large screen monitor in front of the King. The remotely piloted aircraft was flown by a pilot sitting at a console in Diego Garcia via a satellite data link. The small airframe of the *Predator* was powered by a nearly silent turbo jet engine that enabled it to stay over the target for twelve hours at a time. Stealth technology and the aircraft's high altitude ensured it was undetectable by radar or the human eye.

Unknown to the onrushing enemy King Abdullah and the Americans were watching their every move. The Russian order of battle was filmed and analyzed, their deployment scrutinized, and their precise location known to within one meter. They knew the location of every single command vehicle controlling the invading army.

To make matters worse for the Russians, an ELINT satellite was in geo-synchronous orbit over the Saudi desert collecting electronic information and providing targeting data to the Americans, which was quickly placed on the JOTS III display in the Saudi Command Center. King Abdullah's commanding general had everything he needed to strike a deathblow to the approaching enemy forces once they were within range. He was in a position to cut off the head of the Russian bear once and for all.

GENERAL MASAVICH GOT out of his BTR-60 tracked command vehicle and strode confidently up to the assembled commanders. The group came to attention as he approached. "Comrades, in a few moments we will launch what I expect to be the final attack of our victorious invasion of the Arabian Peninsula. Now that we have overtaken the enemy I want to make sure you understand my orders completely. You are to destroy every tank, kill every soldier, and destroy everything that comes within range of your guns. There will be no mercy. We must make further resistance so undesirable that King Abdullah surrenders immediately. Do you have any questions?"

THERE WERE NONE. "Very well, our bombers will commence their attack momentarily. Then, we will advance and destroy what remains," said General Masavich. The General turned and walked back to his command vehicle and closed the door behind him. Sixteen hundred tanks fired up their engines and waited for the order to move out.

As if on cue, the Russian and Iranian troops heard the roar of jet bombers passing overhead. The sky was filled with over two hundred various types of Russian aircraft. *Blackjacks, Backfires, Bears,* and *Badgers* filled the night sky. General Masavich had been promised more but their losses had been greater than expected during the attacks on the American carrier groups in the Western Pacific. Still, the scene was inspiring. He thought it was reminiscent of the air raids of World War II.

The Russian Air Force Commander saw no need to bother with the usual tactics of high speed, low-altitude, multi-axis attack, because the enemy was for all practical purposes defenseless. Neither did he see the need to provide the bombers with fighter coverage because the Saudi Air Force had been totally destroyed in the opening hours of the invasion. Besides, the Saudis had retreated so deeply into the interior of the vast wasteland that they were too far away for the fighters to accompany the bombers all the way to the target.

General Masavich agreed. He wasn't interested in surprising what was left of the Saudi army. He wanted to instill fear in their hearts and let them see their death approaching. Masavich was to get his wish. The Saudis most certainly would see the much-feared Russian bombers coming, but it was not to have the effect Masavich hoped.

DEEP WITHIN THE Saudi command center King Abdullah watched impassively as the bombers approached. He gave a nearly imperceptible nod to his commanding general and seventy-five F-16 fighters rolled out of their bunkers and leapt into the night sky with their afterburners burning brightly like comets across the darkness. They closed upon the unsuspecting Russian bombers at the speed of sound.

"Radar contact straight ahead," shouted the Russian flight leader's radar operator. "I have multiple fast movers rising off the desert floor."

"That's impossible!" shouted the flight leader. There are no fighters in this area. We destroyed them all on the ground. Check your equipment."

"The equipment is operating correctly. I now have over seventy unidentified contacts on constant bearing with decreasing range. Sir, we are under attack!" shouted the frightened radar operator.

EIGHTY MILES AWAY seventy-five Saudi fighters each salvoed two American made AIM-120 *Advance Medium Range Anti-Air Missiles* (AMRAAM). The weapons climbed above one hundred thousand feet and streaked toward their designated target. The missiles were fire-and-forget. Once they locked onto their target they would follow their seeker heads all the way to their assigned aircraft and blow up seconds before impact sending a cone of metal rods into the oncoming bombers. Over twenty pounds of high grade explosives sent the rods cutting through metal airframes, hydraulic lines, fuel tanks, human flesh, and bombs.

The Russian bombers jettisoned their bombs and tried desperately to outmaneuver the diving missiles. Explosions lit the night sky and scores of hapless Russian pilots lost their final battle. Miraculously, a few dozen aircraft survived and turned east in an attempt to flee across the Persian Gulf and land in Iran.

"Flight Leader, the fighters are disengaging and flying away from us. We are saved!" a jubilant radar operator reported.

"Do not be so sure. We aren't safe yet. Execute low level evasion. Fly as low as you can and try to avoid their targeting radars," ordered the flight leader.

"But we have not detected any enemy radars. How can they shoot us down without targeting radars?" inquired another pilot.

"I suspect they may have advanced targeting systems such as laser designators. If that is the case we are indeed going to be lucky to survive!" said the wizened flight leader.

Cheers erupted in the Saudi Command Center. Shouting airmen and soldiers jumped up and down congratulating each other for turning back the attackers. The commanding general grinned and called the Air Combat Officer to his side. "Order our fighters to the marshalling point. Get them out of the Missile Engagement Zone (MEZ) as quickly as possible. As soon as they are clear engage the fleeing attackers with our surface to air missiles."

King Abdullah's air commander had predicted that the Russians would try to escape to Iran after the attack because that was where the closest friendly airfields were located. He had a little surprise for the retreating enemy.

One hundred miles to the east several dozen truck mounted missile rails elevated to the launch position. The mobile surface to air missile system's laser designators were powered up and in standby mode. It was now time to spring his trap!

King Abdullah clenched his fist tight and slammed it onto the arm of his chair. "Destroy them all! Let the infidels feel the rage of Allah." The laser designators began a conical scan of the skies holding two dozen low flying Russian bombers. The doomed bombers were quickly detected and targeting data fed into the Saudi missile directors. Great plumes of fire blossomed and went out in the blink of an eye as the surface to air missiles raced off of the launchers and hurried to meet their prey.

"Visual contact on multiple inbound missiles!" yelled the lead pilot. In the confusion he yanked his stick hard to the left in a classic SAM maneuver hoping to turn away from the missile so tightly that it couldn't follow him through the turn. Before he had time to correct his mistake he flew into the ground and exploded in a ferocious fireball.

The other bombers could do little more than jink their aircraft from side to side in hopes that miraculously, their particular aircraft had not been targeted. The diving missiles made adjustments for every evasive maneuver the pilots attempted. One hundred and eighty seconds after the missiles were launched the Russian bombers were burning wrecks on the lonely desert floor. Silence spread like cholera through the armored command vehicles leading the Russian tanks toward the Saudi defenders. The only sound heard throughout the fast moving mechanized vehicles were the cries of desperate pilots calling out visual sightings of inbound missiles over the radio as they tried to outfly their remorseless pursuers.

The commanders listened in utter shock as the last of their bombers were destroyed. This was a devastating defeat for the invading forces. Without the help of the Russian air force the occupation of the Middle East was in jeopardy. Russia had committed almost every bomber that could fly to the invasion. They were now effectively without an air force and could no longer maintain air superiority in the region.

If anything happened to the arrangement President Yanochev had with the soon-to-be American president to stay out of the conflict there would be no chance to win. Unless the Iranian Air Force entered the fray in force victory would now take months if not years to obtain.

Masavich cringed at the thought of putting the success of the invasion in the hands of the Iranians. He knew he didn't have much time. If he didn't end things very soon there was a remote possibility that the Americans would have the time to fight through the Straits of Hormuz and then clear a path through the mine field still blocking the Suez.

The entire operation was designed to happen so fast that President Carpenter wouldn't have time to get his powerful Navy carrier fleets within striking distance or repair and stage a defense from the damaged airfields in the Gulf. All of that was now falling apart. His only chance was to smash the Saudi command center and force King Abdullah to surrender immediately.

Masavich was beside himself with rage. "How long until we are in range to engage the Saudi armor?" he demanded of his regimental commander.

"WE CAN BEGIN our bombardment in fifteen minutes. We have the Saudis outgunned and can begin our bombardment well outside the range of their tanks and artillery," he replied.

"Very well. After we are within range order all commanders to dig fighting positions. We will begin the bombardment after we are dug in. I don't want anymore surprises. I'm going to try and order another air attack on the Saudis before we overrun their position. This time we will let the Iranians keep their fighters busy while the bombers are attacking. We've lost enough assets."

The regimental commander asked, "Don't you mean people and not assets?" General Masavich didn't bother to reply.

The Iranians were only too happy to help. They promised several squadrons of fighters to escort the next attack into Saudi Arabia. They'd been preparing for this very thing for decades and had amassed an impressive air order of battle. Most of their aircraft were older versions of the MIG sold by the thousand after the breakup of the Soviet Union. They were sold so cheap that a country could buy ten MIGs for the price of one American F-16. What the Iranian Air Force lacked in sophistication they made up for in sheer numbers. They had over five hundred fighters and bombers to commit to the attack that were all within tactical range of the Saudi position. The next attack would begin in six hours.

Communication security within the Russian forces was exceptional. The problem with the Desert Bear Coalition was that the Iranians didn't have the sophisticated encryption equipment and computer generated key lists their allies possessed. Whenever the Russians desired to have secure conversations with the Iranians they had to rely on an earlier version cryptological device that they'd sold the Iranians years earlier. Unbeknownst to them, the Americans had obtained a copy of the "black boxes" from undercover agents earlier in the year and had reverse engineered several for their team of highly trained code breakers. With the assistance of NSA and a very special computer program they'd broken the code and could circumvent the daily changing key materials. American intelligence personnel were now able to listen to the secret communications between the Iranian and Russian high command as it transpired.

National Security Agency
Fort Meade, Maryland

THE SENIOR NSA cryptologist immediately relayed the context of the interception up the chain of command. The Commander, Middle East Forces, passed the information to the Saudis.

Saudi Arabia

KING ABDULLAH LISTENED to the speaker above his seat intently as the report was coming in. The Royal Saudi Army Chief of Staff, General Hammed Saif, held up a hand motioning those around him to be silent so that he and the king could hear the report more clearly.

"Hammed, are we able to counter the new attack plans?" asked the king.

"As long as our troops and equipment stay in their shelters we should survive. The Russians don't have enough of the type ordnance required to penetrate our bunkers. We'll be able to destroy scores of the Iranian MIGs. They don't have onboard countermeasures to defeat our missile. Once we shoot down the fighters the bombers will be easy prey. So, yes, I am confident we will hold up well against the air attack," said the chief of staff.

"Hammed, this is not the time to speak guardedly. There is more, is there not?" asked the king.

"Yes, if the Russians use the air attack to cover the advance of their armor, we are lost. We have two batteries of 155mm howitzers and eight hundred M-1 main battle tanks. In a simple tank battle we might have a slight chance of repelling the Russian T-72's, but we will not prevail if they approach under the air umbrella. Their tanks would be upon us before we could bring our armor out of the bunkers."

"Yes, but the pictures from the *Predator* indicates that the Russians have entrenched their tanks in defensive positions. What makes you think they will attack simultaneously?" asked the king.

"That is what I would do, that is all. Perhaps I am being overly pessimistic," said the general.

"Is there nothing we can do if they attack?"

"They have us vastly outnumbered, but we have one advantage they do not know about."

"What is that?" asked King Abdullah.

"We can use the *Predator* to identify their command vehicles. Perhaps, if we concentrate our efforts on their command structure the rest of their forces will be unable to continue the attack," said General Saif.

"Yes! I remember studying the Russian Command and Control structure when I attended the Army War College in America," said the king. "They demand blind obedience and punish their commanders for personal initiative. General, your plan makes sense. How do you suggest we attack their commanders?"

"Well, we know the location of their command tracks. I suggest we bring out our M-1's and 155's to their prepared defensive positions and open fire on the Russian command vehicles before the Iranian air attack begins. We can use the *Predator* to adjust fire and provide battle damage assessment. When we see that we have destroyed one vehicle we will shift fire to the next. We will systematically destroy every vehicle that has more than one antennae."

"Won't that expose our tanks and artillery?" asked the king.

"Yes, I fully expect the Russians to begin counter-battery fire with their tanks and artillery the moment we begin our counter attack. We will also be vulnerable to their bombers, but the Iranian bombers will have to be very accurate and score direct hits to destroy our tanks in their firing pits. We will put up our fighters to make it more difficult for them to target our ground forces. Who knows, perhaps our F-16's will sweep the attackers from the sky," said General Saif. "The largest threat is from the massive firepower of the Russian armor. They have radar units that will track our incoming shells. They'll be able to provide accurate counter-battery fire. However, I suggest we coordinate our artillery fire with our attack aircraft. If God be for us, we may be able to destroy their leadership before they can do us any serious damage."

"General, your plan is authorized. Commence your attack when you are ready. May God be with you!"

GENERAL MASAVICH WAS perched in the cupola of his BTR-60 watching the tracks around him finish the task of digging in. The engineers were using their bulldozers to scrape gashes in the dessert floor and pile the rocky soil in berms around the trench-works. Tanks and personnel carriers rolled into each position as soon as they were ready. These positions would serve them well when they began their artillery barrage. Doubtlessly, the Saudis still had the ability to return counter-battery fire. His tanks would fire from their protective defensive positions while the bombers attacked the Saudis. When the bombers left the target area he'd conduct a classic frontal assault on the Saudis. He dropped down into the BTR to radio Alexi Yanochev just as the first Saudi shell exploded next to his position.

THE BLAST THREW him against the driver's seat cutting a gash in his forehead. Masavich reflexively put his hand on the spot that was causing all the pain. When he took his hand away it was covered in blood. The driver pushed him back into his seat and placed a field dressing over the cut. He was too weak and disoriented to resist. He tried to get up and make his way to the radio but the inside of the BTR began to spin. His vision blurred and darkness spread from the corners of his eyes until it appeared he was looking through a tight cone. He fell to the floor of the command track. The driver tried to rouse him but failed. He was unconscious.

Outside Masavich's vehicle artillery shells began relentlessly raining down upon the Russian armor. The regimental commander ordered his tanks and artillery to open fire. The Russian guns roared to life. The first several salvos were simply fired in the general direction of the enemy. After a few moments the stunned tank commanders regained their wits and began receiving reports from their company counterbattery radars. The battle was now joined in earnest as they zeroed in on the guns firing at them.

Masavich's staff called for an armored ambulance and opened the back door to the General's command vehicle and dragged him out the back and into the waiting ambulance. The medics strapped him onto a gurney and sped off to the rear to escape the merciless barrage. They'd traveled no more than one hundred meters when a HEAT round (High Explosive Anti-Tank) scored a direct hit on the command track Masavich had just exited. The BTR-60 erupted into a fireball that shot fifty feet into the air. Masavich's minor head wound had saved his life.

The regimental commander wasn't so lucky. Two artillery rounds struck his track simultaneously. Targeted by an entire battery of Saudi 155mm artillery, he was dead three minutes into the attack.

Russian company commanders began going off the air one after another as the Saudi artillery continued to shift fire from one command vehicle to the next. General Masavich's operations officer was the first to recognize what was happening but was at a loss as to how the Saudis knew where the command vehicles were located. "Somehow, they can see us!" he shouted over the command net. "Search for helicopters or aircraft. They must have something airborne!"

A Russian radar operator tasked to provide targeting for a cluster of ZSU-23-4's saw a momentary blip on his radarscope - then nothing. Unable to reestablish contact, he ordered his gun crews to open fire in the direction of the momentary contact. Anything was better than doing nothing. The four barrel 23mm gun emplacements positioned in a star around the radar truck began firing blindly into the night sky. They fired until they emptied their ready magazines. They didn't know what they were firing at or if they were hitting anything, but at least they were doing something.

"THE VIDEO LINK is down! *Predator* has been hit!" reported the pilot operating the *Predator*.

"Roger that. I'll report the casualty to CENTCOM," intoned the civilian shift supervisor. "God help the Saudis now!"

"WHAT HAPPENED TO the picture?" asked King Abdullah. I don't know. The *Predator* must've been hit by anti-aircraft fire," replied General Saif.

"So, what do we do now?"

"I'm going to order our bombers to attack immediately. We've plotted the location of their commanders. We'll continue the artillery barrage as our bombers approach, but we'll need to cease fire while the aircraft are making their attacks to prevent them from being struck by our own artillery," replied General Saif.

"Very well. What are our losses so far?"

"Reports are incomplete but it appears we've suffered very few casualties. Our defensive positions have proven to be effective. We've lost fewer than ten tanks and three artillery pieces," Saif said.

GENERAL PETER TOMANICH, the Russian Chief of Staff, assumed command while General Masavich was disabled. A former tanker himself, he was the senior officer now that the regimental commander had been killed. He noticed that soon after the ZSU battery had opened fire the Saudi artillery fire began to disperse. Once he understood the Saudi intention to primarily target his command vehicles, and figuring that the Saudis had lost their targeting platform, he decided to make their job more difficult. "All commanders, reposition to alternate fighting positions!" he ordered.

The tankers didn't have to be told twice. Word had spread over the regimental command net that they were the primary focus of the attack.

They were more than willing to expose their tanks and BTRs long enough to move to new positions. Hopefully, the moves would confuse the Saudi artillery and they would bombard empty positions.

The Russian commanders began a coordinated repositioning. They didn't want to expose their senior personnel all at once. Half way through the maneuver the Saudi artillery stopped. The chief of staff waited a few moments then raised his hatch to take a look. Burning tanks and personnel carriers lit the moonless night in all directions. There were at least three hundred vehicles on fire. He stood on his seat and started to climb out of his vehicle to relieve himself when the ZSU's came to life. He dropped back down into the steel safety of his BTR-60 and slammed the hatch shut. He heard a jet scream overhead followed by a loud explosion. Secondary explosions followed quickly, indicating that another Russian tank had been destroyed.

WHAT WAS LEFT of the Royal Saudi Air Force came screaming in over the Russian position one hundred feet off the deck, protected from being detected by the Russian anti-aircraft radars by standoff jammers. The Russians were spread over a three mile arc and were several thousand meters deep. With only two bombs each the Saudi F-16's had to make each one count. They were greatly assisted by the fact that all of their ordnance was laser-guided munitions. Seventy-five winged emissaries of death spread over the Russian tanks like a swarm of angry hornets unleashing their deadly stings upon the helpless Russian armor.

The Russians fought back bravely, firing their ZSU's and shoulder launched antiaircraft missiles blindly into the night skies. In General Masavich's haste to overtake the fleeing Saudi armor he'd left most of his support elements behind in Riyadh thinking they were unnecessary and would needlessly slow him down. Fortunately, after the massacre of the first wave of Russian bombers, he'd reversed his ill-conceived desire for haste and had the foresight to dig defensive positions for his tanks. That last minute decision was all that saved his troops from total destruction.

The Saudi fighter-bombers were unerring in their delivery of death. They carried one hundred and fifty bombs on the mission and destroyed one hundred and four tanks. It was over minutes after it started. The pilots flew to their designated targets, released their bombs, and raced off into the waiting safety of the dark desert night sky. Not a single Saudi jet was destroyed.

THE RUSSIAN CHIEF of Staff listened dejectedly as the battle damage assessment reports began flowing in. A few hours earlier he'd been on a great adventure pursuing a beaten enemy with sixteen hundred T-72 tanks. Over four hundred of his tanks were now burning ferociously and lighting up the darkness. Great plumes of fire shot into the sky as ammunition and fuel exploded. The Chief of Staff watched several tanks blow apart before his eyes. That was all the urging he needed to make his decision. He had to get his tanks out of danger until he could figure out what to do.

KING ABDULLAH SAT before the microphone of the high powered AM station that was designed to give instructions to the general populace in times of emergencies. His address would be beamed via a narrow beam SHF signal to a geosynchronous satellite over Central Saudi Arabia and then downlinked to repeater stations all over the country, which would in turn transmit the address on an AM frequency.

The Russians had destroyed all of the military and commercial transmitting stations thinking that would deny the Saudis the ability to keep their people informed about the progress of the war. They were mistaken.

King Abdullah took a deep breath and keyed the microphone, "To the faithful of the Kingdom, guardians of the holy shrines, greetings in the name of Allah. God is faithful. Today, the godless Russian infidels, with the assistance of our traitorous Iranian brothers, viciously attacked the Royal Army of Saudi Arabia. Although we were outnumbered ten to one, we inflicted heavy casualties upon the enemies of God. I am pleased to announce that by the mercies of God our enemies have retreated. We destroyed all of their attacking bombers and hundreds of their tanks. We are now strong enough to resist further attacks. Very soon we will begin offensive operations to drive the invaders from the holy ground of Islam. I regret that I cannot say more at this time but time is of the essence and I must return to the war. May God be with you as you help us repel our enemies from our homeland."

GENERAL TOMANICH CALLED Moscow with a disturbing situation report. "Comrade Yanochev, General Masavich has been gravely wounded and I have assumed command. The Saudi's have destroyed hundreds of our tanks and I have fallen back ten kilometers to regroup. Our bombers were completely annihilated before they could inflict any damage upon the Saudi stronghold. I am afraid we have failed. I will await reinforcements from Riyadh and reattack at our first opportunity."

Yanochev jumped to his feet and screamed into the microphone, "You will do no such thing! Reattack at once! I will divert our entire air force as soon as I can get them in theater, but in the meantime, I expect you to attack with your remaining forces!"

"Sir, what about the Saudi Air Force? We have no aircover. We will be defenseless if they launch an attack."

"Silence! I will not tolerate cowardice! You will proceed with the attack at once! We have sixteen hundred of the most feared tanks in the entire world at our disposal. We will prevail and be remembered as heroes of the Motherland."

Alexi slammed down the radio handset and cursed Masavich's incompetence before Tomanich had a chance to remind him that they now had fewer than twelve hundred tanks remaining. He had entrusted Masavich with the most crucial part of the invasion and he had failed. Worse yet, the American Navy had neutralized the minefield in the Malacan Straits and the *Lincoln* Battle Group had joined the *Truman* and *Washington* Battle Groups just south of the Straits of Hormuz. It was time to call Braxton and get things moving on his side of the equation.

GENERAL TOMANICH CALLED his staff together and briefed them on President Yanochev's latest orders. "Comrades, we have been beaten back on our first two attempts to take the Saudi position. I'm afraid we badly underestimated their resolve and capabilities. We must not repeat our mistakes. We will proceed according to doctrine from this point forward. Our next attack will be from two directions and we will take no chances. Our artillery will provide anti-aircraft suppression in conjunction with our ZSU's. All commanders will ensure that their commands are screened by smoke when they attack. We will attack at full speed and we will not stop until the defenders have been crushed! I estimate it will take four hours to reposition. The attack will commence in four hours and thirty minutes!"

21

CHARLOTTE JENKINS SAT on the front row with her third grade class from Meadow Bridge Elementary School. This was her second year teaching and she loved her job. Third grade children were so impressionable and fun to be around. Teaching was all she ever wanted to do. Unlike a lot of her friends who seemed dissatisfied with how things turned out after college she was living her dreams and felt blessed to be alive. And now she was here, sitting on the front row with her class, getting ready to hear the President of the United States speak.

Looking around the crowd she saw several of her colleagues from around the county milling about and soaking in what for them was an historic event. Everyone around the county enjoyed a simple life and it wasn't often that someone got to hear a President speak in person, much less meet one. The entire faculty from her school andmost of the student body were here. She recognized several mayors and a few state legislators.

Governor Phelps was going to be on the platform next to the President. What a day! "Good thing I brought my camera," she thought.

"Charlotte? Charlotte Jenkins, is that you?" asked a well-dressed man in his early thirties.

"Yes, but I'm afraid you have me at a disadvantage."

"I'm John Randolph. I lived right down the street from you when you lived in Charleston. I used to cut you grass. You mean you don't remember me?" he said with a mock hurt look.

"John, for heaven's sake. You've grown up!" she said excitedly. "Last time I saw you I was eleven and you were, what, eighteen?

"Yeah, eighteen. Talking about growing up, you look wonderful. I wouldn't have recognized you if your principal hadn't pointed you out. I heard from my station manager that you and your class were going to be here," said John. "The AP wire service released the names of the locals who were getting VIP treatment and you and your class were on the list."

"Station Manager?"

"Yes. I'm the news anchor for Channel Eight out of Charleston. After your family moved I went off to USC and majored in journalism. I was hired by Channel Eight a few months ago," said John. "They sent me up here to cover the President's speech. We've been told the President is going to announce some type of bold initiative to get this Russian problem under control. It's also been leaked that he's going to announce his candidacy for the next election."

"No kidding? Well, there's no surprise there. I think he has been doing a wonderful job," Charlotte said.

"Well, better get back to my camera team," John said.

"John, it's really good to see you. You think maybe we could get together sometime and talk about old times?" Charlotte cooed as she tilted her head coyly to one side.

"Charlotte, I'd love too. Here's my card. Call me tonight and we'll set something up," he replied.

"OK, sure. Thanks, I'll talk to you later. Bye!"

"Good-bye Charlotte. I'll make sure we get a good shot of you and your class. Be sure to watch the news tonight because you're going to be on it," he said as he backed away into the crowd and disappeared.

What a day this was turning out to be. The future was really looking up. First, she was selected to sit on the front row by the President's press secretary, and now, a possible relationship with John Randolph. If nothing else came of their meeting at least she was going to be on the evening news. That would make her parents so proud.

TWENTY-FIVE MILES AWAY, two men in coveralls worked feverishly connecting the last of two stainless steel canisters to a manifold mounted behind the pilot's seat of Terry O'Brian's *Piper Super Cub*. Tubes ran from the manifold to a series of spray nozzles running the length of both wings. The canisters were pressurized and equipped with electrical solenoid valves wired to a toggle switch in the cockpit. Each canister contained a chemical that, when mixed in the manifold, would become a toxin one hundred times more lethal than Sarin, the most deadly nerve agent known by the public to exist.

This particular nerve agent was a genetically altered pesticide developed by chemists at Union Carbide. The military called it VX-6. The toxin was made from chemicals not known to be used in chemical weapons. Therefore, it wasn't monitored by watchdog groups or included in the Chemical Weapons Ban Treaty signed by the President's predecessor.

Their work completed, the two men put away their tools and climbed out of the aircraft.

"OK Mike, it's done. Shouldn't be any leaks when you hit the switch," said the taller of the two.

"At least you'd better hope not. Know what I mean, good buddy?" joked the other man. "Hate to think you might get a taste of your own medicine."

Special Agent Mike Anderson was waiting for them at the tail of the aircraft with a silenced 9mm pistol.

"Sorry Guys, I'm afraid we can't allow any loose ends.".

He shot them both in the chest and then calmly stood over the fallen mechanics and shot them in the forehead just for good measure. One at a time he loaded their lifeless bodies into the cab of the Dodge Ram 4X4. He put one behind the wheel and the other on the passenger side, latched their seat belts, started the engine, and rolled down the windows. Putting the truck in gear, he steered it toward the riverbank and watched as it went over the bank and into the water. He waited to make sure the truck sank and then walked back to the aircraft. Now, it was time to do the real dirty work.

"Come on Terry, time to take "Mildred" for a little spin," he said as he guided a heavily drugged Terry O'Brian into the passenger seat of the *Super Cub*. Agent Anderson had been instructed to take O'Brian along for a couple of reasons. First, the DCI wanted to make sure Terry didn't escape. Second, if anything went wrong and the aircraft crashed, O'Brian's body had to be in the wreckage to make the cover story plausible.

The little airplane taxied out from under the camouflage netting and onto a narrow dirt road that ran along the bank of the New River. Anderson gunned the engine and bounced down the long neglected road picking up speed until he felt the wheels begin to leave the ground. Pulling back on the yoke he climbed to one hundred feet and pointed the aircraft toward the *Greenbrier Resort*. With ninety knots of airspeed it'd take him just under twenty minutes to reach his target.

The Greenbrier

Special Agent Ross Bostich made one last round of the *Greenbrier* just to make sure everyone was in their proper place. Stopping at the counter-sniper position on the cottage roof to the rear of where the President would be speaking he looked out over the gathering crowd.

"Everything look OK to you boss?" asked Special Agent Mike Carey. Mike was the spotter for this particular counter-sniper team and the junior agent assigned to the Presidential Security Detail.

"Yeah, I guess so," replied Bostich.

"You don't sound convinced, Ross. What's up?" asked Terry Bose. Terry was the best marksmen of the three teams assigned and a longtime friend of Ross Bostich.

"I don't know, Terry. I've got the usual security package in place plus a lot of extras and still I feel like I'm missing something. I can't put my finger on it, but for some reason I've got this nagging feeling I've missed something obvious," Bostich said.

"I don't know, Ross. Looks to me like we've got every contingency covered. We've planned for bombs, suicide aircraft, and shooters. What else is there?" Bose asked.

"Beats me. Let's just pray I'm getting superstitious in my old age," Bostich laughed. "Keep a sharp eye out. I'm going to mosey over to the *Stinger* Team on the hotel roof. I'll call you when I get there."

"No problem. Talk to you in a few minutes," replied Bose.

ERLINE FRAZIER WAS high on adrenaline. She was standing next to President as he waited for the signal to make his entrance. All her hard work was about to pay off. She'd done her homework and planned every detail of this event. Nothing could happen now to steal the recognition for her resourcefulness and intellect that she so richly deserved. She let her mind race ahead a few hours to the flight back to Washington and imagined the praise the President would lavish upon her. She was about to make her entrance upon the national stage.

GOVERNOR PHELPS WAS already at the lectern making a flowery introduction. As the Marine Corp Band played the first bars of "Hail to the Chief" the President stepped through the side door located directly behind the platform and mounted the steps. He waved vigorously to the cheering crowd as he walked toward the front rail by the dais. Spending several moments walking back and forth waving, pointing to recognize people in the crowd and flashing the victory sign, he strode purposefully to the podium and stood looking out over the admiring throngs of supporters and party faithful.

"MY FELLOW AMERICANS, I stand before you today as the President of the greatest nation ever to grace the pages of history. For over two centuries we've stood for freedom and prosperity and have been a beacon to the oppressed peoples of the world. Regretfully, once again the dark clouds of aggression are beginning to gather on the horizon and our great nation is being called upon to take the lead in standing up to those who would deny the poor and helpless the freedom to chose their own way of life.

"As your President, I represent you and your commitment to freedom and peace for those who seek the same basic rights and privileges that the American way of life represents. Throughout history some have sought to take advantage of those who are weak and vulnerable. As you would personally come to the defense of a victim of violent crime we as a nation are morally bound to defend those who cannot defend themselves. We must rally around the peace loving peoples of all nationalities, regardless of their race, religion, or economic standing in the world community..."

The President was in full stride. Ross Bostich always admired President Carpenter, even though he was a member of the opposing party. President Carpenter was a sincere man who put his country first, and didn't spend too much time playing politics. Sure, he did what he had to do to get reelected but he was an honest, hard working man. That counted for a lot in his book.

Bostich reached the rooftop *Stinger* Team a little out of breath. The roof was accessible only through a service hatch and eighteen feet of ladder work that went straight up. After the brisk walk through the expansive hotel he was more than a little winded. "Man, I'm getting too old for this," he thought.

"Hey people, everything squared away up here?" asked Bostich.

"Sure. No need for you to climb up here with us. Why didn't you just call us on the radio?" asked Sam Nelson, the team leader.

"No particular reason, Sam. I just wanted to do something to work off some of my nervousness. Anything interesting going on?" asked Bostich.

Nelson's eyes were glued to a set of high-powered binoculars as he scanned the horizon. "Nothing out of the ordinary. We've had a few news helicopters flying around right outside of the restricted airspace. They're all on the list. Nothing else of note," he reported.

"OK. I think I'll hang out here for a few moments and catch my breath," said Bostich.

"Sure, why not. Old timers like you have to be careful with their heart," joked Nelson.

JOHN RANDOLPH STOOD beside the technical director in the Mobile Eight News Van as the camera crews filmed the President's speech. Channel Eight was the largest and most prestigious television station in West Virginia and they were making sure they provided the people of the state the best coverage of this historic event possible. History was being made today and they were going to get it all on film. They had three cameras and four reporters committed to the task.

"Hey Pete, let's have camera three get some film of the mountains for some background scenes. The whole country will be watching this speech. We might as well let them see how beautiful this part of America is," Randolph said.

"Sure thing. I've also got a camera on that new girlfriend of yours. That ought to give us some good human interest shots," replied Pete Tracy, the technical director.

"Thanks Pete. I owe you."

"Hey, what's this!" Pete said. "Camera Three has an airplane coming this way just above the trees. Man, I didn't think you were allowed to fly that low."

"Let me see. Put it on the monitor," John barked.

"As you wish, Captain," Pete said with a salute. "Anything else you desire?" he said sarcastically.

"Shut up Pete, and get the Secret Service on the line! Don't take that camera off the aircraft. We might be filming an attack on the President!"

ROSS BOSTICH WAS leaning on the ornate banister that ran around the roof when the call came in. In one well-practiced motion the *Stinger* Team swung in the general direction of the report as the spotter searched the horizon for the tiny aircraft.

"Got him!" the excited missile crewman reported.

Sam Nelson picked up the VHF radio and depressed the transmit button. "Unidentified aircraft bearing 085 degrees magnetic from the *Greenbrier Resort Hotel*, this is the United States Secret Service on Guard. You are flying into restricted airspace. Alter course immediately, Over."

After ten seconds he retransmitted his warning with more urgency. "Unidentified aircraft, this is the Secret Service on Guard. You are entering a restricted airspace. Alter course to the north immediately or you will be fired upon, Over."

"Range two thousand seven hundred yards and closing," reported the spotter as he read off the numbers from his laser range finder that was built into his binoculars.

"OK Sam, batteries released at two thousand yards. I'll alert the team. Call out when the plane gets within two thousand yards and we'll get the President to safety. This place has a bomb shelter left over from the cold war days," said Bostich.

As he turned and ran for the roof access hatch Special Agent Bostich went with his gut feeling and called the security detail that was on the platform with the President. "Team Two, this is Bostich, get the President to the shelter. Aircraft threat at two thousand yards and closing."

SPECIAL AGENT GARY King was standing ten feet from the President and didn't waste any time. He ran up to the President and threw a kevlar overcoat around his shoulders and pulled him away from the microphone and herded him toward the back steps. "Come with me, sir. No time to explain!"

Two other agents reached into their overcoats and pulled out Uzi's and backed away from the platform nervously scanning the crowd as they guarded the retreating President.

"See anything?" asked a tall dark haired agent in his mid thirties.

"Not a thing. Maybe it's just a false alarm," said his partner without lowering his gun.

ERLINE FRAZIER SAW the unfolding scenario and ran out the side door yelling, "What are you doing? Every family in America is going to see you idiots make a fool of the President on the evening news. Let him go!"

A Secret Service Agent pushed her to the ground as another whisked the President down the back steps and attempted to cover the twenty-five yards to the side door and safety. A CNN camera crew filmed the scene unfolding behind the speaker's platform and was broadcasting it live all over the world.

The crowd was on its feet as panic began to erupt in the guest seating area. Governor Phelps walked to the microphone and said, "No need to worry. Everything is under control. This is just a routine safety precaution." He wasn't fooling anybody.

SPECIAL AGENT NELSON put his hand on the shoulder of the agent with the *Stinger* Missile. The missile was trained on the incoming aircraft as the agent operating the weapon reported, "I have tone. Missile locked on target."

"Range two thous two hundred yards," reported the spotter.

"On my command, standby to fire!" ordered Nelson.

"Range two thousand one hundred yards. Aircraft turned and now on a parallel course and climbing!" reported the spotter.

"Roger. Maintain missile lock. Aircraft has not closed to within our engagement zone," Nelson said as calmly as possible. He was just beginning to breathe easier when the M-8 alarm system erupted with a squealing high-pitched tone.

Special Agent Sam Nelson looked at the anonometer and checked the wind direction. Bad news. The wind was blowing in their direction. Ashen faced, he realized too late what was happening. The nerve agent would be upon them in seconds. "Fire! All teams fire when ready!" He barely got the words out of his mouth before he fell to the ground clutching his throat.

The missile teams pulled the triggers on their tube launchers in unison. Two long, thin missiles streaked out of the tubes, only to tumble out of control as the launch teams fell to the ground convulsing uncontrollably, voiding their bowels and bladders.

Panic filled Special Agent Nelson as he tried unsuccessfully to make himself breathe. No matter how hard he concentrated his lungs wouldn't respond. He vomited into his throat. Unable to clear his airway the bile ran down his air pipe and into his lungs. He was drowning in his own vomit. One hidden blessing of VX-6 was that it killed in less than sixty seconds.

A television camera mounted on the roof of the *Greenbrier* recorded the effects of the nerve agent as it swept through the crowd felling its victims in what looked like a wave of death. Panic-stricken victims were screaming and running in every direction trying to evade the advancing death, but their efforts were futile. The advancing invisible cloud of death cut them down in rows showing no mercy to men, women, young or old. All in its path were subjected to the cruel and horrifying death designed for the enemies of America.

But this was no battlefield. Pete Tracy from Channel Eight had a camera filming the reaction of Charlotte Jenkins' third grade class to the President's speech when the nerve agent struck. The world watched in horror as the stampeding crowd pushed and shoved and threatened to trample her young charges. The camera caught the determined set of her jaw as she tried to gather her children to her side. The film continued to roll in spite of the now dead camera crew as Charlotte Jenkins's gruesome death was recorded for posterity as she clutched two young girls with her last bit of strength.

Mercifully, the children went quickly, but Charlotte lingered on for several seconds before a national television audience. Perhaps it was due to a strong will to survive, perhaps it was because she was fighting to save her children, whatever the reason, her struggle for life was captured in full color. The horrible scene would inflame a raging lust for the blood of those responsible for this atrocious act and arouse a righteous demand for vengeance from the American people.

The CNN camera trained on the President filmed the most defining record of the attack. Christopher Baines Carpenter died obscured from the view of the cameras quite by accident. Two Secret Service Agents were literally pulling him at a fast trot toward the shelter of the hotel when the lead agent succumbed to the fast moving VX-6 vapor and fell to his knees. The President and the agent pushing from behind fell headlong over the downed agent and sprawled across the sidewalk with the President tangled underneath the trailing Secret Service agent. The silent eye of the CNN camera watched reverently as the three tangled bodies choked and convulsed for a few seconds and then grew still as death took them in its hungry arms.

22

SPECIAL AGENT ANDY Renfro switched off the engine of his rented white Ford sedan and let the car coast the last twenty yards into the stand of poplar trees. He parked far enough off the dirt road leading to Terry O'Brian's house to ensure that the car wouldn't' be seen by anyone driving down the county road a short distance away.

Terry's house sat atop a clearing on a hillside and had a commanding view of the small scenic valley. The land between the house and the road was heavily forested with pines, poplars, and sycamores. Terry spent many evenings sitting on his porch drinking coffee and waving at the occasional car that drove down the lonely two-lane blacktop. More often than not Terry saw more deer than he did cars. Renfro knew this because he'd spent many hours watching the house through his binoculars from behind the very trees he was now parked.

Renfro was being careful not to be seen. He wasn't worried about O'Brian. He knew Mike Anderson had him under control elsewhere. No, his only concern was keeping nosy neighbors from seeing a strange car at O'Brian's house and telling the police. The success of everything he was about to do depended upon ensuring that the FBI and the State Police thought O'Brian was the last person to be in the house.

It was almost sunset as Renfro crept through the lengthening shadows and worked his way around to the back door. It would've been better to wait until dark for the break-in but he didn't have the time to waste. This was to be the first operation in what was to be a very busy night.

Renfro couldn't believe his luck. The back door was unlocked. Obviously, this country bumpkin wasn't big on personal security. Entering through the kitchen he went straight to the master bedroom. Renfro didn't think master was an appropriate term for the tiny, nondescript bedroom O'Brian slept in. He stood in the doorway and surveyed the room. Locating the closet, he twisted the old-fashioned glass doorknob and opened the door.

Renfro unzipped the nylon bag he was carrying and extracted a set of old combat boots that he'd removed from this same closet a few weeks earlier. He'd also taken a few strands of hair from O'Brian's brush in the bathroom and a pair of gloves from a box in the bottom of the closet.

He placed the boots among the neat ranks of shoes standing at parade rest in the closet and put the bloodied gloves back in the box beside the shoes. O'Brian's military training was evident by looking at the neat arrangement of the closet contents. All of his shoes were carefully arranged with the heels touching the wall and their highly polished toes pointing out.

Renfro took a wicked looking Kabar knife out of the bag and hid it among the neatly folded trousers on the shelf above the hanging clothes.

He chuckled as he took out two grenades and hid them next to the knife. The media would go nuts when they learned he had grenades.

The last item he took out of his bag was a photograph of the *Allegheny Militia* holding the automatic weapons at Billy Ray's victory party. He placed the photo on the nightstand next to O'Brian's antique cherry wood poster bed. He stared at the picture for several moments. This would be the clincher. Mike Anderson had come up with the idea. He thought it would add to the anti-militia frenzy to have a photo showing the "militia nuts" holding machine guns. To make sure the media made the connection, he'd included the blue barrels in the picture - the same blue barrels he'd stolen from the chemical storage facility in South Charleston.

The job complete, Renfro examined his work one last time. Satisfied that everything looked natural he left the house and walked to his car. He had to hurry. He still needed to anonymously deliver a few videos.

He punched a number into his cellular phone and waited for someone to pick up. A brusque male voice answered, "Yeah!"

"I'm clear. Make the call," said Renfro. The man on the other end hung up without acknowledging. The FBI, United States Secret Service, and the West Virginia State Police were on their way to O'Brian's house in a matter of minutes. The news of what they discovered at his house would be public knowledge as the sun rose over the eastern seaboard.

As he drove onto the two-lane with his headlights off despite the darkening twilight he allowed himself a mischievous grin. He was making history and pulling off one of the greatest cover-ups of all time. Terry O'Brian's notoriety would eclipse even that of Lee Harvey Oswald. Like the Kennedy assassination, there'd be no loose ends to point a finger at any of the conspirators. There was too much at stake. He was on his way now to take care of the last loose end.

Moscow

THE TELEPHONE RANG in the darkened room next to Alexi Yanochev's bed. His eyes opened immediately. He was expecting this call. Normally, he didn't receive calls in his residence, but this one was special. "Yes."

"Alexi, this is Donald," the voice said in English. "It's done. We can now proceed with our plan. I am to be sworn in as President in just a few moments."

"Excellent. This news doesn't come a moment too soon. Our entire operation is in jeopardy. General Freeman has reported to our people that your navy is preparing to launch an airstrike to assist the Saudis. Their unexpected stiff resistance has already stalled our armored units and our Air Force has been virtually wiped out. We need time to regroup! If you do not prevent the attack we may suffer sufficient casualties to make it impossible for us to continue the occupation," said Alexi.

"I assure you, my first order of business as President will be to call off the attack. I'll address my nation within the hour right after I'm sworn in. Watch your television and you'll hear me explain why we are withdrawing our troops. I'll call you again tomorrow." With that, the line went dead and Alexi rolled over and went back to sleep.

West Virginia

SPECIAL AGENT MIKE Anderson broke off a branch from a rhododendron bush next to the river. He walked backwards swishing the lush greenery back and forth across the tire tracks that cut through the low standing weeds along the bank. The 4X4 tires had left two obvious impressions in the soft earth on their way to the river smashing weeds and making a trail anybody could follow. All Anderson hoped to accomplish was to keep the local police from finding the bodies until they'd killed O'Brian.

He was relatively sure that would happen within the next hour or so. The injection he'd given O'Brian would wear off soon. Terry would initially be disoriented but he'd be alert enough to discover the 9mm lying next to him on the cot. It was the same gun that Anderson had used to kill the two men who'd connected the spray rig. When the police found their bodies in the shallow waters of the New River with bullets in them from the gun O'Brian was found with they'd pin those murders on him as well.

Hopefully, O'Brian would stumble outside of the cabin holding the gun and be killed by the FBI Hostage Rescue Team (HRT) or the local police, whichever arrived first. If that failed it would be a simple task to have him killed in jail. How he died really depended upon what he did when the police arrived. It was likely that he'd get himself killed right away. After all, the last conscious thought he had was Billy Ray commandeering his airplane and hitting him over the head. That ought to be enough to make him pick up the gun and wave it around.

Now it was time to make sure O'Brian received a warm reception when he awoke. Anderson flipped open his cellular phone and dialed 911.

"911," the operator said.

"The person who killed the President of the United States is hiding at the following location." Anderson read the latitude and longitude off of his hand-held global positioning system (GPS) receiver's display. "He is barricaded in a cabin by the river and is armed and dangerous. The aircraft used in the attack is in a field next to the cabin."

"Sir, may I have your name?" asked the operator. The line went dead.

Anderson put the phone back in his pocket and started walking toward the cabin. As he stepped onto the front porch he caught movement out of the corner of his eye. He could just make out a cloud of dust rising over the trees in the dusk. A car was approaching just around the bend in the dirt road. A white Ford sedan appeared seconds later ahead of the dust cloud.

"Company's coming," he said aloud. Anderson instinctively reached for the holster in the small of his back and unsnapped the restraining strap. Positioning himself in the middle of the dirt road he waited for his uninvited guest to arrive. Anderson ran a host of options through his head and decided that whoever it was would not leave alive.

Anderson relaxed when he recognized the car as the one he'd rented a few days earlier. The car rolled to a stop a few feet from where he was standing and Special Agent Andy Renfro stepped out from behind the wheel.

"Hi boss. Wasn't expecting you. I thought I was supposed to hike out and meet you at the hard road," said Anderson.

"Plan's changed. Nothing personal, but the DCI wanted me to make sure we rolled up the operation without any loose ends," said Renfro.

"Nothing to worry about. It's done. The mechanics are already in the river with the 4X4 and I've taken care of O'Brian. He's out cold. Should wake up about the time the state police show up."

"I want to see," demanded Renfro.

"Sure. Follow me."

Anderson turned and walked toward the cabin. Renfro followed several paces behind, silently withdrawing a revolver taken from Terry O'Brian's house, and pointed it at Anderson's back.

"Hey, Mike," said Renfro.

Anderson looked back over his shoulder and saw the gun. Throwing himself to the ground he grasped for his own weapon, but he was too slow. Renfro fired four shots into his body before he hit the ground.

"Sorry, Mike. The Director said no loose ends and that includes you." Special Agent Mike Anderson didn't hear the explanation. He was already dead.

INSIDE THE CABIN Terry O'Brian was lying on a cot in the corner with his eyes closed. His mind was in a tailspin. Facts and images were whirling through his brain in quick succession without any pretense of order. Caught somewhere between sleep and semi-consciousness, he wasn't sure if his thoughts were dreams or reality. He tried to speak and move but his body wasn't taking orders.

Reality was lost in a jumble of disjointed images spinning through his head. He was on a roller coaster. No! He was screaming in terror as his plane plunged to the ground. His head was throbbing and pain was beginning to register through the mist that held his thoughts hostage. Still, he couldn't focus.

Crashing! He was crashing. He heard a loud explosion in his head. They were so loud and so real. Somewhere in the deep recesses of his mind a coherent thought sprung to the forefront. Those weren't explosions. They were gunshots and they were real. Terry's eyes flew open and he bolted upright on the cot.

Special Agent Renfro picked that precise moment to open the door and walk into the cabin. He paused for a moment to adjust to the total darkness of the interior. The cabin had only one window and it was tightly shuttered.

Terry saw the gun in Renfro's hand and his mind no longer had any problems commanding his body. Instinct took over and he rolled off the cot onto the floor. As he did so he felt the distinctive shape of a pistol against his rib cage. He grabbed the gun and pointed it at the shape standing in the doorway.

The man in the doorway snapped off several shots in his direction and Terry heard himself let out a low grunt. The next thing he heard surprised him. It was the roar of the gun he was holding.

Terry emptied his gun into the intruder and saw him go down. O'Brian tried to stand but his legs wouldn't respond. There was a hard deep burning pain in his left leg. Looking down he saw the bloody mess that was his leg. "Stop the bleeding. Can't do anything if I bleed to death. The shooter is down and not moving. I've got time." Terry's Marine training was coming back to help him.

He tore off a piece of the sheet from the cot and stuffed it into the hole in his leg. There was a hole in the front but no exit wound. "Good thing nobody uses a .45 anymore," he thought. Terry used his teeth to tear off a longer strip of sheet and secured the makeshift bandage in place.

Terry dragged himself across the wooden planking to the still figure lying in a pool of blood by the doorway. He didn't need to feel for a pulse to see if he was dead. One side of his skull was missing and he had three bloody holes in his chest. "Nice shooting," Terry thought. He didn't waste any time feeling remorse for killing this stranger. The man was responsible for his own death. When you draw a gun on a man you have to accept the consequences of your actions.

Terry rifled through the dead man's pockets and relieved him of his car keys. Car keys meant a car was nearby. In the dead man's inside jacket pocket he found a leather carrying case with an official looking identification card. It read, "Special Agent Andy Renfro, Central Intelligence Agency." Terry's heart sank. He'd just killed a CIA agent. What was the CIA doing here? Was Billy Ray with the Agency as well? Why had Billy Ray hit him with the gun? Why had the CIA agent shot at him? Terry's thoughts were disturbed by the distant sound of an approaching helicopter.

Terry picked up the agent's gun and used the door frame to pull himself to his feet. A bolt of searing pain shot through his body and exploded in his head. His eyes momentarily lost focus as his nervous system struggled to absorb the punishment. He closed the door behind him and hobbled outside. Looking to the east he saw red aircraft warning lights blinking faintly as the tiny shape of a black helicopter approached from the distance.

Running for the car he stumbled over something in the lawn. It was Billy Ray and he was dead. Terry relieved the dead man of his gun and ID card; they might come in handy later. He forced himself back to his feet and made his way as quickly as his injured leg would allow him to the Ford parked next to the cabin. Sweat covered his forehead and ran down into his eyes as he fumbled with the keys and inserted the proper one into the ignition.

The engine started on the first try. Terry threw the automatic transmission into gear and raced down the dirt road in the opposite direction of the helicopter. Next to him on the front seat a portable police scanner came to life.

"HRT has cabin in site. There's an adult male lying next to the front door. He appears to be dead. No other activity in the yard. Be advised, white Ford sedan headed your way at high speed. I have both of your units in sight. Ford is approximately two miles from your position. Vehicle has no place to turn off. Suggest you intercept," said a strange voice. "They must have night vision goggles if they can see all that," thought Terry.

"Roger, State Police copies. We'll set up a roadblock and wait for him to come to us."

"Roger. I'll drop off the team and investigate the cabin. If we don't have any problems I'll swing over and cover you from the air. HRT out."

THE H-60 SIDE slipped to the earth parallel to the cabin and eight black clad men in body armor jumped out and took up defensive positions in a small semi-circle with their automatic weapons pointed at the cabin. The helo immediately lifted off and hovered over the cabin with a sniper in the doorway and a crewman shined a spotlight on the cabin door. From his vantage point the sniper had a clear field of fire over the entire area.

Two men on the ground jumped up with their MP-5's extended to the limit of their straps. They ran to the porch and crouched on either side of the door. A two-man team rifle team covered the shuttered window.

A second set of men ran to the porch with a small battering ram, stopped, swung back, and slammed the blunt end into the plank door. The doorframe shattered sending the thick plank door crashing inward. They tossed two flash-bang grenades into the cabin, followed seconds later by a second team of FBI agents with machine guns at the ready.

Nothing was moving in the cabin. "We have one dead inside the cabin. We're clear."

S O, THE POLICE are setting up a roadblock for me," thought Terry. The steep Appalachian foothills were on his left and the New River was on his right. The water was higher than normal and racing downstream producing stage four rapids. He could abandon the vehicle and try to escape over the hills, but with his bad leg he wouldn't make it very far. That left only two options: surrender or the New River. Surrender wasn't an acceptable option.

Terry jerked the wheel to the right and careened across the short distance between the dirt road and the water's edge. He slammed on the brakes and brought the car to a stop with the front wheels in the water. As he opened the door and started to get out he saw a newspaper illuminated by the dome light lying on the passenger side floor. His face was on the front page.

Grabbing the paper he quickly scanned the headlines. They read, "Local man chief suspect in assassination of the President." Terry couldn't believe his eyes. As he quickly read the first few paragraphs things started falling into perspective. He was beginning to understand that he'd been Billy Ray's pawn. His plane had been used to kill the President along with hundreds of innocent people. The newspaper had several articles about the slain school children. He had to get away and think this thing through. What was he going to do? How could he get a chance to explain what had happened?

Taking off his Rugby shirt he carefully tied off the sleeves and made a knot closing off the neck hole and eased himself into the near freezing mountain water. Terry took a few moments to soak his shirt in the slow moving water near the bank. He held the waist opening above his head and violently jerked the shirt to the water's surface, trapping a large pocket of air in the shirt. As long as the shirt stayed wet it would serve quite well as a makeshift life preserver. He side stroked toward the fast moving water near the center of the river and let the current take him downstream.

Years before, Terry had spent two days white water rafting and kayaking down the Kern River in California and the guide's instructions came flooding back to him. "Keep your feet out in front if you fall into the water. Don't try to stand up. Use your legs to break the impact when you see submerged rocks in your path. Adopt a California lounge chair position," he said. The reason most people drown in fast moving rapids is that they get their feet caught in the rocks below them and the water pushes them over face down. The force of the river holds them underwater and they drown.

Terry's strength was deserting him rapidly. The makeshift life preserver helped keep his head above water but he was taking a terrible beating from the pounding water and collisions with the rocks. He was propelled over a particularly large rock and took a nasty spill as he fell four feet and was buried under a wave. Terry lost control of his body and was rolled over and over in the turbulent undercurrent. He tried to get his head above water but he kept getting pushed to the bottom. He was almost out of air when he saw a boulder directly in front of him. He jammed his good leg stiffly against the rock and let the force of the water crashing against his back pole-vault him to the surface.

Terry surfaced in time to see his worst nightmare a few yards ahead. A tree was partially submerged and the current was flowing through its thick branches. If he was pushed against the tree he would be helplessly entrapped and drown. Terry swam with every once of his fleeting strength to the center of the river and narrowly missed the "strainer" that threatened to drown him.

Somehow the wounded former Marine made it around the tree but the exertion took its toll. Terry re-inflated the shirt and gasped for air. He let the water carry him downstream and tried to conserve energy. The cold water and constant physical exertion were enough to sap the strength out of a man in the best of health, but for Terry with his wounded leg, it was enough to kill him.

Terry estimated he had less than ten minutes to live unless he got out of the water. His conclusion was confirmed when he saw the horizon disappear a short distance ahead in the dim moonlight. That meant the river fell away vertically. There was no way to tell if it was a four-foot drop or a forty-foot waterfall. He had to get out of the river right now or he was going to die.

Terry scouted the riverbank for a convenient place to get out. The water had carved the riverbank out of sheer sandstone and granite. Flat land was at least twenty feet up a steep cliff-like embankment. Regardless of how small his chance of successfully climbing out in his present condition was he had to give it a try. He couldn't wait for a better place. He wouldn't survive long enough.

Mustering his last energy reserves he managed to swim near the bank. He could hear the roar of the river as water crashed onto rocks below the waterfall ahead. He frantically clawed at the rocky embankment as it raced by. He ripped out several fingernails as he desperately tried to get a handhold.

Then he saw it. A tree had lost its roots in some long forgotten storm and fallen over the bank into the river. From the looks of the tree it'd been dead for years. A few large, decaying branches lay beside the massive trunk. It reminded Terry of the skeletal remains of some long dead dinosaur.

Terry threw both arms around the tree trunk as he sped by. It was angled such that he could lay against it in a semi-standing position once he was out of the water. There was no time to rest. The State Police would long since have tired of waiting for him to arrive at the roadblock. They were no doubt standing around his abandoned vehicle summoning the helicopter to help search the river for their suspect. His suspicions were confirmed by the beating of distant rotor blades.

ABOARD THE HELICOPTER Special Agent Jon Perez scanned the river with a thermal imaging scope. Conventional binoculars wouldn't be much help trying to locate a bobbing head or floating body in the turbulent waters at night. His best chance to find the President's killer was by his thermal image. The specially designed thermal scope he was using for the search could find O'Brian even if he was dead and his body trapped underwater. As long as there was a temperature difference between him and the water the scope would detect him.

The State Police were bringing in small planes to search both sides of the river and were offering dogs to track O'Brian if he tried to escape through the hills. All of these assets were a waste of time as far as he was concerned. Nobody could survive the rapids. O'Brian's body would most likely wash up against the bank several miles downstream where the river slowed and made a sharp turn.

The FBI's file on O'Brian was growing rapidly. Less than an hour after the attack they had the registration of the aircraft used in the attack. The film footage of the attack showed the numbers clearly. After confirming it belonged to Terry O'Brian the pieces began to fall into place rapidly. They had his military records couriered to Quantico and discovered that he was a retired Marine Corps officer. That meant he was a dangerous character. They'd also learned of his membership in the *Appalachian Militia*, a connection the news media made after receiving a video from an anonymous source. It showed a camouflage clad O'Brian on some type of military exercise with a group of other men. The press was currently pontificating upon the militia angle across the national airwaves.

There was no doubt in anyone's mind that O'Brian had conspired to kill the President. The search of his house had turned up incontrovertible evidence. Several plastic barrels were found in his shed that matched the ones taken from the army storage depot in South Charleston. Tests were underway to confirm that they had once contained the binary chemicals used to kill the President. A fully loaded assault rifle was found in his closet of the type and caliber used to kill the storage depot guards. A blood stained knife found in his closet was being tested to see if it was used to kill one of the other guards. Hair fibers taken from his hairbrush were of the same color as found on the floor next to the dead guards. Numerous pieces of hard evidence left little doubt that they were after the right suspect.

The other players in the conspiracy hadn't been identified yet, but it was likely they were the corpses found in the cabin. His own crew had discovered the 4X4 in the river just moments before. That had cost them twenty minutes of search time for O'Brian, but it couldn't be avoided. The two bodies in the vehicle had no identification but they both had large bullet holes in their backs. From the looks of things O'Brian killed them all. He was no doubt making sure there were no witnesses to his involvement.

"O'BRIAN MUST BE pretty good with a gun," Perez thought. Two of the dead men were armed. One had been shot in the back and one had died in a shoot out in the cabin. Although they hadn't found the dead men's guns the evidence suggested a gun battle. There was blood pooled in one corner - probably O'Brian's. A trail of blood was smeared from the corner to the corpse. Obviously, O'Brian had been wounded in the firefight, killed the other man, dragged himself over to the body, and searched his pockets. The dead men had no identification and their holsters were empty. That led them to believe O'Brian must have taken what he wanted. The other dead man was shot in the back, presumably by O'Brian.

SOMEHOW, TERRY FOUND a hidden reserve of strength and made it out of the water and up the fallen tree trunk. The tree's roots had caused a fissure in the sandstone ledge above the river. A large slab of solid rock had been pulled forward as the roots were pulled out of the ground, creating an overhang of sorts. Terry rolled back under the rock and passed out as a helicopter passed overhead.

AS THE MOON illuminated the normally tranquil mountain scenery, the cabin by the river turned into an armed camp. The FBI, the United States Secret Service, the West Virginia State Police, and a contingent of the National Guard had shown up in force to gather evidence and search for O'Brian. The National Guard was offering a squadron of ancient H-1 *Hueys* to help in the search. The FBI gratefully accepted their offer. The State Police set up roadblocks on all major highways in the county and distributed pictures of O'Brian to every truck stop and rest area throughout the state. If O'Brian survived the river, which was doubtful, he would be found tomorrow.

23

JAKE AND SAMMY slipped silently over the side of the dhow into the tepid, still waters. Jake's eyes were a cold picture of death as he surfaced and got his bearings. There would be no mercy for those who stood in his way this night. The people who'd kidnapped Sarah had unwittingly sealed the fate of many who would die without knowing why. Their death would come suddenly and with much violence. There would be no fair fight, no warning, simply death. Sure, Jake's official mission was to rescue Secretary McClintock, but the Russian Colonel had made tonight's mission personal when he took Sarah.

The Saudi's had been informed through the Kuwaiti underground that Ambassador McClintock had been spotted at the Kuwait Center of Fine Arts. The Russians had taken over the building and were using it for some type of command center. As were most large buildings in Kuwait it had been built by the British. The plans were procured from the architects that designed the building and forwarded through diplomatic channels. Colonel Talib had been provided a copy which he in turn had used to brief Jake and Sammy via radio. A hard copy would be handed to him when he made contact with the Kuwaiti underground. Jake wasn't clear on when that would be but had enough experience to know that they would find him.

Commander Lewis had indeed come through when Jake called him from Jebal Ali several days earlier and had arranged the airdrop of the supplies Jake had requested. Jake and Sammy were each now equipped with a silenced Uzi submachine gun, a 9mm Berreta pistol, a crossbow with a dozen bolts, hand grenades, a fighting knife, a garrote, and a large amount of explosives. Sammy had the secure SHF satellite radio strapped snugly to his back in a watertight pouch.

The night was eerily quiet as they entered the water. Jake would've preferred the seas to be a bit rougher to conceal their approach but he'd have to accept the cards he was dealt. At least there was no moon.

The insertion plan was simple. They were to swim the channel buoy line and use them as cover whenever possible. Without a set of air tanks they'd have to rely upon their own wits to avoid detection. If things went well that wouldn't be too much of a problem. The enemy wasn't expecting them and an awful lot could be accomplished through sheer boldness when surprise was on your side.

The dhow that Colonel Talib had provided for the insertion dropped them off 4,000 yards from the entrance to the channel and continued on a course parallel to the shoreline. The guards on the piers weren't suspicious because the boat didn't appear to be entering the channel. As far as they could tell it was one of scores of local merchants that plied the waters nightly.

Jake and Sammy swam for ninety minutes without speaking. Covering half of the distance to the shore swimming freestyle they were now precisely one mile from their chosen landing site according to the hand held global positioning system receiver Sammy carried. All was going according to plan. Now that they were within visual range of the shoreline they slowed their pace in order to minimize their wake. They were a little ahead of schedule so they could afford to be more careful.

Jake reviewed the insertion plan in his mind as he swam. They were to approach a damaged stubby pier that had been neglected since it was partially destroyed during the Gulf War over a decade ago. A half-submerged tugboat would conceal them as they climbed out of the water and made their way toward a nearby warehouse. From there they'd stick to the shadows as they made their way out of the port facility. They hoped to steal a car to carry them to the western end of town where McClintock and Sarah were being held. Then the fun would start. The plan was simple, gutsy, and plausible. Jake spoke fluent Arabic, the enemy was not alerted, the night was dark, and they were determined to succeed.

Suddenly, a spotlight leapt out of the darkness and cut a path across the water less than thirty yards ahead of them. They were midway between two buoys with no place to hide. A powerful engine roared to life. The sound was unmistakably that of a *Boghammer* Patrol Boat. Jake realized it was an enemy patrol drifting in the darkness waiting to ambush intruders.

Silently Jake and Sammy slipped beneath the surface and swam feverishly for the nearest buoy hoping to put something between them and the fast approaching *Boghammer*. They heard the patrol boat approaching and knew they didn't stand a chance. All it would take would be one concussion grenade dropped into the water and they would both be dead. Worse still, Sarah would never be rescued.

The *Boghammer* passed overhead and opened their position. "Maybe they didn't see us," Jake thought. At least he hoped they hadn't. His lungs were on fire from lack of oxygen as he and Sammy swam underwater with all their might toward the buoy. He had no choice but to risk a quick breath. He looked over at Sammy and saw that he had the same idea.

They stopped swimming and allowed their natural buoyancy to carry them slowly to the surface. All they had to do was let their heads break the surface undetected, take a quick breath, and go back under. The buoy they were trying to reach was now only twenty yards away.

Their noses barely cleared the surface and they inhaled great gulps of the life giving air. As they did, the Boghammer swung around and opened up with a heavy caliber machine gun. Bullets were piercing the water all around them and the boat was mercilessly closing the gap.

Jake and Sammy miraculously managed to reach the far side of the buoy unharmed. With practiced speed they surfaced, unslung their Uzi's, and prepared to return fire. Seconds before Jake and Sammy unleashed a deadly fusillade at the Iranian patrol it unexpectantly cut its engine and stopped firing.

The crew began talking and gesturing wildly as the searchlight swept back and forth over the area where Jake and Sammy had surfaced just a few short moments before. After what seemed like an eternity the patrol appeared to be satisfied and started their engine and calmly motored off toward the channel entrance.

"You speak Arabic. What was that all about?" a breathless Sammy whispered.

"They were speaking Farsi, you bonehead. They're Iranian, remember!" Jake teased.

"Oh, yeah. Anyway, what was that all about?

"I don't know. The best I could make out, one of the guards thought he saw something and he opened up. They must have orders to shoot first and ask questions later," Jake replied.

"Yeah, well, that was a little close for me, partner," Sammy said.

"Put a lid on it, Junior. We've got work to do."

It took another forty minutes to swim the last mile. Both of them could swim the distance in a fraction of the time under normal conditions but they were going slow to avoid detection. Swimming the last 25 yards underwater, they surfaced beside the sunken tug with their Uzi's at the ready.

THE PIER WAS deserted. The nearest guards were a little less than 200 yards away smoking foul smelling European cigarettes. They were casually standing beside a truck conversing and paying only occasional attention to what was going on around them. "Good sign," thought Jake.

He signaled Sammy and they silently pulled themselves up onto the pier. Lying flat in the shadows of the tugboat's superstructure, they were less than fifteen yards from the nearest warehouse. They'd be totally exposed to view as they crossed the road separating them from the safety of the warehouse shadows.

"I'll go first. Cover me," Jake ordered.

After checking to make sure the guards weren't looking Jake slowly rose and crept across the road. Once he was safely in the shadows he motioned for Sammy to join him. Sammy checked the guards and started to get up. Just as he was about to make his dash across the street the guards threw down their cigarettes and began walking toward him. Sammy was lying in plain view with nothing between him and the guards but a shadow, and that would soon evaporate as they got closer. A few more steps and they'd be sure to see him.

Jake saw the guards as they approached Sammy. He couldn't just hide and watch them shoot him. Yet, if he fired on the guards the rescue mission would be a failure. There'd be no way he could complete the mission. Perhaps there was a way he could help Sammy and save the mission.

"Help me. Please, somebody help me," Jake moaned in Arabic.

The guards froze in their tracks and raised their rifles. They didn't speak the language, but they knew enough Arabic to know some crazy local had wondered into a restricted area. Well, they'd take care of the stinking Kuwaiti. No God fearing Iranian soldier would miss an opportunity to punish those who had corrupted the true faith by pandering to infidels.

"Help me, I'm hurt," Jake moaned again.

THE GUARDS POINTED their rifles in the direction of the sound and walked into the alleyway between two buildings where the voice seemed to be coming from. Jake could read their minds. They were no doubt thinking their boring late night watch might end on an enjoyable note after all. Their smiles said it all. They'd relish smashing a Kuwaiti's head with the butts of their rifles.

Jake unsheathed his fighting knife and prepared to spring upon his prey. He peered around the corner of the empty oil barrel he was hiding behind and watched them approach. The tactical situation wasn't good. The guards were showing more common sense than he'd hoped. They were split up and cautiously walking 15 feet apart. Oh well, it was too late to back out now. He'd just have to take out the nearest man and hope for the best with the other one.

Jake let the first guard pass his position. The second man was not so fortunate. As soon as he was past the oil barrel which obscured him from view, Jake leapt upon him from behind and plunged his knife into his throat just above the collarbone at the base of the neck. The knife's downward angle carried it into the man's heart and severed an artery. The guard was dead before he hit the ground.

The second guard saw movement out of the corner of his eye and reacted with lightning speed and took aim at the middle of Jake's chest. Jake looked up in time to see the guard pointing his rifle at him. Before the guard could fire an 18- inch aluminum alloy bolt from Sammy's crossbow entered his forehead and dropped him like a slaughtered cow.

Sammy ran toward Jake with an impish grin on his face with his crossbow hanging carelessly from his right hand. "Couldn't let you have all the fun," Sammy said.

"Thanks, Sammy. I mean it. That one was close. I owe you one!"

"No sweat, Jake. I gave up keeping score a long time ago," Sammy said. He looked at the dead guards lying in the sandy alleyway. There were large pools of thick blood around both dead men. "We better clean up this mess and hide the bodies or we'll have a lot more company than we want for the rest of the night."

"OK, let's stuff them in some of these empty barrels and kick sand over the mess. That's the best we can do. It's time to get moving," Jake said.

After completing their gruesome task, Jake and Sammy made their way slowly out of the port facility. Keeping to the shadows they made relatively good time. Several blocks into town they found a truck parked on a dark side street. Sammy deftly jimmied the door and hot-wired the ignition. The truck started immediately and they drove away without arrousing any of the locals. Jake pulled out their map of Kuwait City and gave Sammy directions to the building where McClintock and Sarah were reportedly being held.

Although there were few vehicles moving at this time of night Jake felt reasonably sure he could reach his destination without serious challenge. Both of them had changed into traditional white thobes and Jake's dark complexion ensured he could pass for a Kuwaiti from a distance. If they were stopped they'd just have to shoot their way out.

THE KUWAITI CENTER of Fine Arts was a sprawling three story complex on the outskirts of town. As with most public buildings, the Kuwaitis had built an elaborate bunker system under the building to protect their citizens from Iraqi air attacks. Had the Kuwaiti leadership not fled their country and abandoned their people at the first sign of trouble they would've found it ironic that these same bunkers were now serving as the secret command center for Colonel Boris Illyn Solsteniski of the Russian *Spetsnaz*.

Colonel Solsteniski was the grandson of a highly decorated Red Army General who defended Stalingrad during the Nazi invasion in World War II. Colonel Solsteniski's name had earned him a commission, but his iron will, intellect, and raw physical prowess had earned him a spot in the *Spetsnaz*. A natural born leader and a consummate warrior, he enjoyed a meteoric rise to the rank of colonel. He was somewhat of a legend among the career soldiers in the former Red Army.

He was sent to Kuwait to oversee and ensure the safe delivery of twenty SS-20 mobile intercontinental nuclear missiles Russia was transferring to the Iranians. That mission was now complete and the missiles were safely secured at a secret compound in another country built specifically for that purpose. Colonel Solsteniski wasn't satisfied to simply sit around and nursemaid a few missiles, even if they were nuclear. That was why he'd relentlessly pressured the general staff to let him come back to Kuwait and lead the mission to capture the American Ambassador to Bahrain. It was unfortunate the ambassador had gotten himself killed during the attack. That could have caused Colonel Solsteniski's career a great deal of harm had it not been for a stroke of blind luck. Who could've known that the American Undersecretary of State for Middle Eastern Affairs would be visiting the Ambassador's Residence the very night of the attack.

The colonel had taken the girl on the spur of the moment. It was one of the few unprofessional decisions he'd ever made. Every ounce of logic and training screamed that it was the wrong thing to do, but he couldn't help himself. The girl captivated his thoughts and seemed to draw him to her. He didn't understand why at the time but he decided to take her with him. Besides the obvious value of having such a beautiful woman nearby, she would also prove to be a powerful psychological weapon as a human shield. Americans were squeamish about endangering women.

As Colonel Solsteniski turned these thoughts over in his mind, little did he know that on a nearby rooftop Jake and Sammy were peering down at the front entrance to the building in which he was now sitting. Their perch provided an ideal position from which to watch the Fine Arts Center and get acquainted with the building's security. They could easily record when the sentries changed the watch, what time the Russian staffs arrived and departed, and generally, observe all who came and went. Jake was grateful they'd found such a good place to watch and wait. There were three heavy-duty air conditioning units on the roof, each with a screening enclosure two meters high that completely surrounded the unit. Jake and Sammy made themselves at home behind the unit closest to the where Sarah and Ambassador McClintock were being held.

Sammy set up the SHF radio and called the Central Command Special Warfare Node in Tampa. "CENTCOM, this is Blackbird...Over."

"Blackbird, CENTCOM...Go ahead."

"Blackbird reporting in position. Coordinates brown four three, red two seven...Over," said Sammy.

"Roger. Copy all. Will relay position to local contact," said the CENTCOM radio operator, a post-executive officer Navy SEAL. "You are directed to remain covert and await further orders. Report every four hours. CENTCOM...Out."

"Well, might as well get some shut eye, Sammy. You take the first watch. Wake me before first light."

"Gee, thanks boss," shot Sammy. "Let me stay up all night while your dream about Sarah."

"Rank doth have its privileges young man," Jake said as he pulled his hat over his face and fell asleep.

Sammy crawled to the parapet and focused his attention on the Fine

Arts Center. It would be light in a few hours. Then their job of watching the building would become grueling. The sun would be merciless as it beat down upon them. They'd have to work out some type of routine to keep cool.

Sammy heard groaning coming from behind the screening enclosure they were calling home. He crawled over to see what was going on and found Jake thrashing back and forth, talking in his sleep. Just as Sammy approached Jake he bolted upright and pulled out his pistol, swinging it wildly in all directions as if hunting for some ghostly tormentor.

"Hey, you OK?" asked Sammy.

JAKE STARED BLANKLY for a few moments before he seemed to find himself. "Yeah, sure; I'm fine."

"Jake, what's up with you? You've been having a lot of nightmares lately. I haven't said anything, but you've been waking up almost every night. Something's bugging you and I think I have a right to know."

"It's nothing. Forget it. Aren't you supposed to be watching the Arts Center?" Jake said.

"Just trying to help. Anyway, it's your watch, boss man," Sammy said as he handed Jake the binoculars and curled up where Jake had been sleeping.

The first thing Jake did after relieving Sammy was call CENTCOM. After the usual call-up procedures, he found himself talking to Lieutenant General Joseph Fuller's Chief of Staff.

"Blackbird, this is Colonel Jackson. There's been a change of plans. The rescue mission for Secretary McClintock is on hold! You are to remain in position and continue reporting until further notice."

"No disrespect sir, but you must have holes in your head! I can't stay on this roof forever. Besides, they might move McClintock at any moment. You need to get some help in here ASAP!" said Jake.

"Sorry, Commander. There've been some developments stateside that preclude conducting an insertion."

"Colonel, look, I'm in a pretty bad spot here and I don't have a lot of time for small talk, so why don't you just tell me what's going on!" demanded Jake.

"Look, I've been where you are, so don't get smart. But you're right, I do owe you an explanation. President Carpenter was assassinated a few hours ago. President Braxton has ordered all offensive operations in the Persian Gulf AOR cancelled. I'm afraid there's nothing we can do. We have the plans ready and we are continuing to try and persuade the President to change his mind. In the meantime, I need for you to keep your cool and do your job!"

"Roger, sir; I'll hold my position as long as possible. I may have to find a better hidey-hole. I'll keep you informed. Blackbird, out."

Jake sat down with his back to the parapet. This wasn't good. He and Sammy weren't equipped for a prolonged observation of the Arts Center. They had enough water for perhaps two more days. They had enough MRE's for two days after that. He'd have to go and scrounge some more water before daybreak. "Well, might as well let Sammy get a few hours sleep before I set out to find supplies."

24

PRESIDENT DONALD BRAXTON came straight from the Oval Office where he was sworn in a few hours earlier and stood in the hallway behind the pressroom waiting to be introducted. This was to be his first address to the people of the country as the President of the United States. The newly appointed press secretary motioned him forward. "OK, Mr. President. It's time." Braxton strode through the doorway and waved to the reporters crowding the tiny room.

A hush fell over the room and all eyes were riveted upon the man behind the Presidential Seal. The veteran reporters in the room noted that President Braxton looked older than normal this evening. They would go easy on him tonight because he had to be suffering from the sudden shock of losing such a close friend. He cleared his throat and wiped a tear from his eye before speaking.

"Good evening. The entire world is reeling from the vicious and cowardly massacre that occurred in the West Virginia foothills earlier this afternoon. An unspeakable atrocity was played out on live television as someone attacked at the heart of this great nation. We are all saddened that President Carpenter perished in the attack and our entire country grieves his loss together.

"I can now tell you that we have identified our prime suspect. A deranged member of an obscure paramilitary group called the *Allegheny Militia* assassinated President Carpenter for reasons only he knows. We identified the aircraft used in the attack and determined that a man named Terry O'Brian was the owner. He is a retired Marine Corps Officer and highly trained in all aspects of warfare. The photograph you are now being handed was found during a search of his residence earlier today.

"The other men in the photo that you see holding automatic rifles are fellow members of the *Allegheny Militia*. We are trying to determine at this time whether they were involved in the assassination. Of particular note are the blue barrels in the background. These barrels are of the type and size used to store chemicals stolen from the army storage facility several weeks ago. The stolen chemicals are a powerful chemical nerve gas called VX-6. Those exposed to the nerve agent experience immediate death. The FBI crime lab is running tests on residue collected from the victims but we are relatively confident the stolen chemicals were used in the massacre.

"Within an hour of the assassination the FBI received a tip as to the whereabouts of our prime suspect. O'Brian was hiding out in a cabin in the West Virginia hills near the *Greenbrier Resort* where he landed his aircraft. We came very close to capturing him but he killed two federal agents and managed to escape.

"We have a massive manhunt underway and are closing in on him. I assure you that we will find this man and prosecute him to the fullest extent of the law. I have instructed the Attorney General to ensure a speedy trial and to seek the death penalty. The heartless execution of hundreds of innocent men, women, and children in an attack upon the Presidency is unfathomable regardless of political views or perceived injustices one may have suffered. How a person could inflict such grief upon so many to achieve a political aim is beyond the imagination. This crime must not go unpunished!" The President paused and looked resolutely into the camera.

"Like you, I'm struggling to come to grips with this devastating, senseless act of inhumane cruelty. But come to grips we must. As a nation we must bind up our wounds and continue dutifully in our quest to ensure the peace and well being of our peoples. We must not let grief, or our sense of outrage, prevent us from focusing upon that which is larger than any one individual. That one thing is the preservation of the freedoms guaranteed by our constitution that so many brave men and women have sacrificed their lives to preserve.

"We must be strong and courageously take our minds off of our grief. We must focus upon events that threaten to draw our nation into a course of action that would jeopardize the welfare of every man, woman, and child in America.

"Recently, America responded to a perceived threat to our country by deploying our armed forces to regions surrounding the Persian Gulf. Unfortunately, our actions were perceived as provocative and threatening by parties involved in the conflict. Our ill-concieved military response provoked the attack upon our fleet. America was never the target of the Russian deployment of nuclear submarines in the Pacific Ocean. It was never our intention to become an aggressor on either side of the regional dispute involving Russia, Iran, and the Gulf Coalition forces.

"President Carpenter ordered our ships to sea to protect America from a nuclear attack by Russia. A series of misunderstandings resulted in the Russians attacking two of our navy's battle groups. Many

American and Russian lives were lost in the conflict. Again, we misunderstood the Russian intentions and I believe they misunderstood ours.

"I know all true Americans were outraged when they learned of the loss of so many servicemen aboard the ships in the carrier battle groups that were attacked. I have experienced much of the same anxiety so many others felt as we watched our country being propelled toward certain war.

"I am happy to be able to put your minds at ease. I spoke to Russian President Alexi Yanochev moments before this press conference and he assured me that he does not wish to pursue hostilities with the United States. We both agreed that a series of misunderstandings had driven our two countries to the brink of nuclear war. We cannot allow this to happen.

Therefore, President Yanochev is ordering all of his nuclear submarines back into port. I am reciprocating by pulling back our carriers from the Persian Gulf and standing down all planned offensive operations. I am ordering our troops to step back and give peace a chance.

"It will take strength and resolve to pursue peace in the future. America cannot allow herself to be drawn into every regional conflict around the globe. There are just too many international disagreements and we don't have the resources to involve ourselves in all of them. I believe it is in our best interest to exercise restraint and not order America's men and women to jeopardize their lives by engaging in battles that we have no legitimate right to fight. We have no vital strategic interest in the outcome of the difficulties between those engaging in hostilities in the Persian Gulf. We can purchase oil from whoever is in control once they settle their dispute.

"Therefore, I will do all within my power as your President to keep all Americans safe and keep America out of the war. For all practical purposes the war is over and the situation has been defused.

"In closing, I believe it is appropriate for America to come together as a family to help the unfortunate people who suffered such unspeakable losses in the massacre at the *Greenbrier*. Loved ones where violently snatched away from them and they must be experiencing agonizing grief.

"I want to lead the nation in easing their pain and I hope all of you will join me in a prayer for the families of those who perished on the lawn of the *Greenbrier Resort*. Let us join in their sorrow and extend to them our hearts as well as our help.

"I am setting up a fund for the surviving family members to ensure that their children receive a proper education and that all of their families are fed while they come to grips with their loss and make the necessary financial adjustments. I am personally donating one million dollars to show my commitment. I am asking all Americans to look deep within their hearts and consider what they can do to help. Let's all pull together as a family and do what we can to care for our own.

"I know many of you have questions but there is much to do and I must get back to work. I'll have my press secretary answer your questions. Thank you." The President turned and left the room as reporters shouted questions at his back.

General Marshall Freeman was waiting for him in the hallway. "Mr. President, may I have a word with you?

"Why, of course General."

When they were out of earshot of the Secret Service Presidential Protection Detail he grabbed the President's elbow and gave it a tight squeeze. "Sir, we have an unforeseen problem in Kuwait."

"What are you talking about, General? Kuwait is already under our control."

"I was just briefed by the Defense Department that they have two SEALs in a building across the street from the Fine Arts Center. They are providing intelligence to Central Command," said Freeman.

"So, what's the big deal? Surely you don't think two SEALs can hurt our operation."

"Not if they just sit and watch but one of them has a reputation for doing things on his own. To make matters worse that navy nurse the Russian kidnapped is his fiancé. They've been ordered to sit tight and do nothing but I don't think we can trust them to do that. It goes against their egotistical view of themselves. You know those hero types. They think they have to save the world, rescue the damsel in distress, and all that baloney."

"So, tell me General, if we know where they are why don't the Russians know where they are?"

"I understand, sir. I just wanted to make sure you were aware of the situation before I started getting Americans killed," said the general.

"General, you don't get it. Soon there won't be an America, much less Americans. The world has outlived its need for petty nationalistic loyalties. We're only a few weeks from lying all of that aside and giving the world a chance to flourish under more enlightened leadership. Now, be a good general and go do what you do best."

"I'll see to it immediately," said General Freeman.

Kuwait

Jake woke Sammy at zero three thirty. "Hey, bud, get up! Sleep is for the dead."

"What's up?" asked Sammy.

"There's been a change of plans. We'll be here a while longer," said Jake. He quickly briefed Sammy about his conversation with the CENTCOM Chief of Staff and their need to gather more supplies. Jake outlined his plan to Sammy and left immediately to scout the perimeter of the Fine Arts Center and left Sammy on the roof with the binoculars to continue the surviellance of the Fine Arts Center.

He made his way down the steps of the abandoned office building and exited through a back door that opened into a deserted alleyway. He laid on his stomach and stole a quick glance both ways down the alley. Empty.

He was crossed the street and cautiously walked down the predawn street keeping to the darkest shadows. He was three blocks away when a frantic Sammy called him on the radio. "Jake! Troops are pouring out of the Arts Center and coming my way. Hide! I'll do what I can on my end to hold them off," said Sammy.

Jake felt the heat pulsing through his veins as he always did just before the killing started. "Sit tight, buddy. I'm on my way." Jake ran toward Sammy's perch as fast as his feet would carry him with his Pausa rifle bouncing wildly against his back. Jake unshouldered the massive .50 caliber and readied it for action as he ran. He bounded around the corner just in time to see two dozen Russian commandos enter the building that he and Sammy had been using as an observation post.

Jake skidded to a halt and retreated back around the corner of the alley he'd just exited. Throwing himself onto the ground he snapped the bipod into position to steady the barrel. He was too late. All of the Russians were already in the building. There was no way he could go in after them and hope to survive long enough to help Sammy. He'd just have to wait for them to come out. He knew Sammy had a surprise waiting for them at the top of the stairs leading to the roof. He'd supervised the installation of the explosives himself. Maybe that would make them reconsider.

He didn't have to wait long for something to happen. A terrific explosion signaled that the first soldier had tried to open the door to the roof. Jake held his breath hoping for the best. Seconds later a series of explosions erupted as the Russians tossed grenades onto the roof preceding their charge through the shattered doorway. He heard automatic weapons fire - all of it Russian.

Suddenly, the ground shook with an earsplitting explosion as the entire top story of the building erupted into a confused concert of fire and concrete. When the dust settled there was nothing left of the roof or the top story. Sammy must've detonated every piece of ordnance they brought with them. Jake had enough combat experience to know that there would be no survivors.

SAMMY WAS DEAD. He'd lost a few friends in combat before but somehow this time was different. He'd liked Sammy from the moment they first met. He appreciated his sense of humor and found him to be a kindred spirit. Sammy was always making jokes about everything, even when things were going badly. Their special bond had helped them to grow closer than brothers over the past several months. Now he was gone. Jake sat against the wall with his .50 caliber between his knees so grief stricken he couldn't make himself move. The sound of voices in the street caught his attention.

Troops were pouring out of the Fine Arts Center. They started searching the surrounding buildings. Jake figured they were more than likely looking for him. He picked up his weapon and trotted off to find a safe hiding place. Without a radio or supplies he wasn't going to be much help to CENTCOM. It was time now to concentrate on living long enough to fight again another day.

Saudi Arabian Desert

KING ABDULLAH WAS pleased with how well his troops had performed. He was now reaping the benefits of years of training and smart military procurement decisions. After the death of his father King Fahd he'd dedicated himself to transforming his armed forces into a world class fighting force. The past few days proved that he'd been successful.

King Abdullah wasn't like many of his Arabic neighbors. He wasn't interested in showing off how big his army was or gaining the respect of other governments. His only concern was building a military structure that could defend his country, and the way he saw it, it was better if others didn't know his full capabilities. Hopefully the enemy would underestimate his ability and make a tactical mistake. That was precisely what the Russians had done. But all of that was history. His biggest concern right now was the next engagement.

His *Special Forces* were preparing a few surprises for the advancing Russian armor columns. They'd been plaguing the rear of the columns with anti-tank rockets picking them off one at a time. The Russians turned to fight and found nothing but empty desert. Colonel Talib's men were exploiting the one advantage they had - centuries of experience at living in the desert.

The Americans taught him a great deal about fighting tanks when he attended the Army War College in Kansas. Years earlier when he was the Crown Prince his father sent him to study war in American. He'd been a quick study and developed a love for the science of modern warfare. Unlike his father, he'd taken a personal interest in defending the Kingdom, refusing to try and hire others to do his fighting.

The plan for the final defense of their stronghold outside KKMC was his brainchild and he couldn't wait to see the drama unfold. Strange how a man could be looking forward to a fight that would determine if his country would survive or cease to exist - but he was. He was looking death in the face and feeling more alive than ever before.

One thing his country possessed in abundance was petroleum. He'd learned the value of petroleum as a weapon by researching American air-fuel bombs. He'd watched an American Defense Department film demonstrating the destructive power of vaporized fuel. His scientist had modified the American concept slightly and buried thousands of large fuel bladders around his secret command center. Each one of them had the destructive power of a tactical nuclear weapon and could incinerate anything within one hundred meters.

The fuel bladders ringed the secret command center at a distance of two kilometers. If the enemy penetrated the first ring of defense he had another surprise awaiting them. Hundreds of troops equipped with American-made Dragon anti-tank missiles would be waiting in reinforced firing positions that were connected by a labyrinth of trenches. He still had eight hundred tanks and an equal number of artillery pieces, plus seventy-five fighter/bombers. Considering the heavy Russian losses from the first two attacks, his chances of victory were fairly good. So, yes, let the much-touted Russian war machine attack his feeble, third world army. They just might learn a lesson or two about warfare themselves!

GENERAL TOMANICH'S TANKS were in position awaiting his word to attack. They were divided into two attacking forces with a third waiting in reserve. He was directing the battle from the reserve force. His artillery and tanks had been bombarding the Saudi position for the past hour. He was waiting for word from the air force that they were ready to commence their bombing. When he received word, he'd cease his artillery barrage and order his tanks forward under cover of the air attack - standard military doctrine.

"General, the bombers are ready to begin their attack," the Operations Officer reported.

"Very well; order the tanks forward!"

THE SAUDI PILOTS SAT in reinforced hangers with their engines running. Even if the enemy bombers reached them they didn't expect them to cause much damage. Without laser-guided munitions or cruise missiles the Russian bombardment would have little effect on the Saudi aircraft hangers. Their bombs would harmlessly explode on top of several meters of steel reinforced concrete.

As soon as the artillery stopped the pilots pushed their throttles forward, rolled out of the hangers, and leapt into the sky to meet the enemy. The Saudis had the predominately Iranian fighters and bombers outclassed in both aircraft and pilot skill. The Iranians escorted four hundred bombers with over five hundred fighters. It was the largest single air attack in over fifty years.

The Saudi pilots attacked the Iranians with an initial volley of *AMRAAMs*, filling the skies with a deadly army of angry missiles. Each Saudi pilot fired four missiles and then closed for close-range *Sidewinder* attacks. At seven miles the Saudis fired their second volley, this time with the heat-seeking *Sidewinder Missiles*. Twenty-five minutes after the air battle began five hundred Iranian aircraft had been destroyed. The remaining Iranian bombers jettisoned their bombs and retreated for the safety of the Arabian Gulf. Unfortunately, a dozen Saudi pilots had been overwhelmed by incoming missiles and were destroyed.

The crushing defeat of the combined Russian and Iranian air attack stunned General Tomanich. The massive air raid had failed to deliver a single bomb on the Saudis. It appeared he would have to do this the old fashioned way, with the steel of Russian tanks!

KING ABDULLAH WATCHED the large screen tactical display as the Russian tanks approached. He didn't want to spring his trap too soon. Patience... patience...just a little closer, he thought. When fifty percent of the Russian armor was deep within the fuel bladder fields King Abdullah jumped out of his command chair and shouted, "NOW! Detonate the fuel bombs!"

The ensuing explosion rocked the underground command center. The returning victorious pilots reported seeing numerous fiery mushroom clouds rising hundreds of feet into the air. King Abdullah had to refrain himself from joining the triumphant cheering sweeping through the command center.

THE REPORTS THAT began streaming in were more terrible than he'd imagined possible. Nearly one thousand tanks had simply vanished in the massive explosions. General Tomanich thought the Saudi's had used nuclear weapons on his men. The devastating defeat took all of the fight out of him. "Commanders, order your troops to retreat. We cannot drive our tanks into the jaws of a nuclear attack."

General Tomanich thought about how he was going to break the latest news to higher command and decided it was not something he was going to do. Let someone else die at the hands of Yanochev's thugs. He pulled his pistol from its holster and fired a single round into his right temple.

25

TERRY AWOKE SUDDENLY and found himslef shivering uncontrollably. His left leg was throbbing and sending lightening bolts of searing pain into his hip. Rolling out from under the overhang he tried to stand. A pained gasp erupted from deep inside and he fell to the ground. His leg was badly swollen and felt like a hot branding iron had been surgically implanted from thigh to hip. Fortunately, the bleeding had stopped.

Terry looked around and spotted a dried branch a few feet away that looked like it would make a good walking stick. He picked it up and used both hands to pull himself erect. Gingerly, he tried to put some weight on the injured leg – no good. It hurt too badly. He'd just have to use the stick for a leg and do the best he could. Slowly, he started out through the dense, wooded foothills.

There was no moon as he struggled up and down the darkened hills.

He walked on ignoring the intense pain in his leg. It didn't matter that he wasn't walking on the bad leg, it throbbed anyway. He no longer had the strength to keep his foot in the air so it was more or less bouncing along behind the walking stick. Each time it touched the ground pain shot up the leg and exploded in his head.

Somewhere deep inside an intense will to survive welled up within his breast. He was no longer afraid of being captured. The more he hurt the more he focused on making sure he survived to tell his side of the story and make sure the real killers were captured. Fear was replaced by anger. How dare someone disrupt his peaceful retirement and drag him into this nightmare.

A plan began to emerge from the confusion. Somehow, he would get in touch with his old friend John Denton at the *Charleston Gazette* and tell his story. Terry had no illusions about his chances of survival if the authorities found him first. They thought he'd killed a couple government agents, the President of the United States, and worst of all, he was being blamed for the deaths of hundreds of men, women, and children that were attending the President's speech. He'd most likely be shot on site. If that happened the world would never know the identity of the true killers. He couldn't let that happen.

Terry pushed himself forward despite the growing pain in his leg. He felt his resolve melting away with each step he took. He'd pushed himself beyond the limits of his adrenaline and willpower and was rapidly reaching what he knew to be the end of his ability to resist.

His mind began to wander and he realized that he was experiencing the onset of a mild delirium. Shortly before dawn he saw a light from what looked like a lantern in the woods ahead. He tried to quicken his pace as he went toward it but tripped over something in the darkness and fell to the ground with a crash. A loud siren shattered the pre-dawn stillness.

JEREMIAH LEWIS HAD worked through the night tending his moonshine still. He didn't drink the stuff himself but since being laid off from the coal mines several years before he hadn't been able to find work. Granted, it didn't take a lot of cash to live in this part of the country, but you had to have some money. Moonshine was an easy source of tax-free money. It wasn't quite as lucrative as the drug trade, but Lewis couldn't bring himself to sell drugs. He'd seen what they did to a lot of his friends, so, he made moonshine.

This night's labors yielded several gallons of the clear, high-powered alcohol. He'd already filled the glass gallon jars he'd brought for the occasion and was loading them two at a time and packing them into crates in the back of his truck.

A lot of people thought moonshining was a thing of the past but they were wrong. Jeremiah had established a thriving business. He was one of the largest suppliers of moonshine in Greenbrier County. That meant he was careful.

He wasn't a killer by any means, but he carried an AR-15 assault rifle just to make sure people knew he was serious. He also took a number of other precautions against being caught or robbed by other moonshiners. One of his more imaginative ideas was placing several trip wire activated sirens around his still on a one hundred-yard perimeter. Jeremiah didn't think anyone could sneak up on him without setting one off. He hoped the defenses would prevent him from getting put into a situation where he'd have to shoot somebody.

Lewis was almost finished loading his truck when something tripped one of his sirens. He grabbed his rifle and ran for cover behind a stand of pines. He was torn between sneaking quietly off through the woods and checking on his still in a few days or hanging around to see what set off the alarm. The siren was set to deactivate after thirty seconds. Lewis cocked his ear to one side and listened for several minutes after it went silent. Hearing no movement in the forest around his camp he figured an animal must've activated the trip wire, but you could never be too careful. He silently worked his way around to where the siren was that had sounded. It took him over thirty minutes.

Terry O'Brian lay sprawled face down across the path leading to his campsite. Lewis kicked him with his toe and waited. No movement. He bent down and turned the intruder over and felt for a pulse. He was still alive. The stranger looked like death warmed over; -haggard, bruised and unconscious, - but he was alive. A bloody bandage was tied around his leg. "Well partner, can't leave you out here like this. You're probably gonna die anyway, but I guess I gotta do what I can to help," Lewis said to the unconscious O'Brian.

Lewis put down his rifle and grabbed O'Brian by one arm and threw him over his shoulder in a fireman's carry. He carried him back to the still and loaded him into the back of the truck next to the moonshine.

TERRY OPENED HIS eyes and saw a large man in blue jeans and a tee shirt staring at him over the end of large caliber handgun. The cabin behind the stranger looked like something out of a Daniel Boone story. There were three log walls built against the sheer rock face of a hillside. The cabin's interior was lit by a kerosene lantern which revealed a dirt floored room with a single small table, one chair, no windows, and shelves from floor to ceiling stocked with neat rows of canned goods. Besides the cot he was occupying there were no other furnishings.

"Where am I and who are you?" Terry asked.

"You're in my cabin and my name isn't important. I brought you here after I found you passed out in the woods the other night," said Lewis.

"The other night? How long have I been here?"

"Two days. You were in pretty bad shape, especially that leg of yours. I had to dig out the bullet and sew it up," said Lewis.

"You did what?" Terry said as he grabbed his leg. It felt much better and the swelling was almost gone. It was still black and blue but now that the bullet was out most of the throbbing pain had subsided.

"Don't worry, Mister. I've fixed up gunshot wounds before. Out here you either take care of stuff like this yourself our die."

"Yeah, well, I'll probably die from an infection. I hope you knew what you were doing," said Terry.

"I don't think you have to worry too much about infection," said Lewis with a sly grin. "I doused your leg and my hunting knife with some of my famous elixir. The stuff will kill any microscopic varmints Mother Nature can come up with. You and your leg are gonna be fine."

"Well, thanks for all the help. If you'll just lower that cannon I'll be on my way," said Terry. His head began to spin as he tried to stand up.

Lewis pushed him back down with the barrel of the gun and said, "Not so fast. I know who you are and you aren't going anywhere just yet!"

"What do you mean?" asked Terry. Lewis replied by tossing a newspaper on Terry's lap. Terry silently flipped through the paper's pages. The front page held two stories about the President's assassination. One column was devoted to chronicling the dead and recounting the viciousness of the attack. The other story ran several pages and described the efforts to find the prime suspect. Several pictures of Terry holding guns or standing by his airplane adorned four pages. Terry recognized the photographs. They were taken from his home.

"Look, none of this is true. I didn't kill anybody."

"Mister, if half of what that paper says is true I oughta blow your head off and save the government the trouble. Only reason I ain't killed ya already is that I found some interesting things in your pockets, and that got me to thinking. After I read you were active in the *Appalachian Militia*, I remembered what all of them "one worlders" did to the patriots at Waco and Ruby Ridge. When I found the two CIA agent's ID's in your pocket it started to make sense. I figured that maybe they're trying to frame another true patriot and use the press to make everybody think some wild-eyed, dangerous, crazy militiaman killed the President, when in fact they did it themselves."

"You may be right about that. Is that why you didn't turn me over to the authorities when you found me?" asked Terry.

"Partly, but it's mostly because of the line of work I'm in. Think about it. I couldn't very well tell the cops I found you when you set off an alarm near my moonshine still, could I?"

"I guess not," admitted Terry. "So, where does that leave us?"

"That depends on what you tell me. If I think your story makes sense maybe I'll help. If not, maybe I'll just get even for all those dead kids and put a bullet between your eyes," Lewis said. "So, I suggest you start talking."

Terry told Lewis everything that had happened starting with Billy Ray offering to help him with the annual paintball wargames. Lewis listened intently stopping Terry occasionally to ask questions. When Terry finished, Lewis holstered his gun and said, "OK, I'll help. What's your plan?"

"I can't hide out forever and I realize that eventually the FBI will track me down. The only chance I have of getting out of this alive is to make my story public before I turn myself in. Once I tell the news media what I know there won't be any advantage in killing me. You can be sure that there are people looking for me who will kill me on sight. The only way they can keep their involvement in the President's assassination secret is by making sure that I'm dead. If they find you with me they'll kill you too."

"Hey, I'm in. Don't worry about me 'cause I can take care of myself," said Lewis. "Nobody said the war against the Commies in our government was going to be easy. I'm happy to have something I can do to fight back."

"OK, it's your funeral. Can you get me to Charleston without running into a roadblock?"

"That shouldn't be too hard. My truck is set up for running the back roads. Most of the roads I know don't even show up on a map. Might take a couple of extra hours but I'm pretty sure we can do it," said Lewis.

"OK, but before we start, if I'm going to trust my life to you I don't think it's too much for you to tell me your name," said Terry.

Lewis' face split into a toothy grin. "Jeremiah Lewis at your service."

"OK, Jeremiah, but before we leave do you have anything to eat? I haven't eaten in days and I'm starved," said Terry.

Lewis laughed. "No sweat. I'll fix you some chili. While you eat I'll load a few things on the truck. We'll get started right after dark. I like to drive the mountains with the lights off. Makes it harder for some nosy cop to accidentally spot me," said Lewis.

Terry rolled his eyes and prayed he would survive the trip.

THREE HOURS AFTER sunset Lewis and O'Brian crossed over the Gauley Mountain and saw the lights of the Kanawha Valley spread before them. Charleston lay twenty miles ahead. So far they hadn't seen another human being as they travelled the back roads. All that was going to change. There was no way to avoid driving down old route 60 through the small towns that lay between themselves and Charleston.

Up until now the darkness and late hour had been their friend. Now those same two factors made them stand out like an Eskimo in Miami. On weeknights there were few vehicles on the road at this time of night. If they ran into a roadblock they would surely be noticed if they tried to turn around or take a turn off. All they could do now was drive within the speed limit and pray that nobody important took notice of them.

Terry started to doze off despite the seriousness of the situation. His body had been through so much that he was starting to shut down no matter how hard he tried to stay awake. Lewis elbowed him hard in the ribs.

"Wake up, O'Brian. Cars are stopping up ahead and there ain't no stop light. I think we got a roadblock," said Lewis.

"What are you going to do?"

"Well, I'm sure fire not going to give up without a fight. I've got four wheel drive and they don't. We'll see if they can follow me."

SAM DAWSON OF the West Virginia State Police shined his flashlight in the window of a maroon Dodge *Caravan* and asked the driver for her license and registration. He leaned in the window and shined his light around and saw two little girls asleep in their car seats.

"THANK YOU MA'AM. Sorry for the inconvenience," he said to the slightly annoyed women at the wheel. As he motioned for the next car in line to roll down their window he saw a battered old pick up truck cut across the median a couple hundreds yards down the road. It jump the curb on the opposite side and drove down the embankment to the access road running parallel to the highway. Trooper Dawson pressed the button on the microphone clipped to his left chest shirt pocket as he ran to his cruiser. "Dispatch, this is unit fifty-one. I have a dark colored pick up evading roadblock at post 12A. Late model Chevy or Ford. I am in pursuit. Suspect travelling east down access road.

"Roger five one...Break...All units in the vicinity of post 12A, officer in pursuit of late model Chevy or Ford pick-up truck. Request assistance," said the dispatcher.

"Dispatch, this is Air One. ETA to post 12A is five minutes."

LEWIS SAW A red traffic light ahead and floored the accelerator. He hit the intersection at ninety miles and hour and turned onto the northbound lane on two wheels. Several crates of moonshine flew out of the back of the truck and disintegrated on the pavement. Trooper Dawson's cruiser smashed through the debris and closed the distance.

Dawson hit his siren and spoke into the loudspeaker. "This is the

State Police. Pull over."

Lewis pulled a .44 magnum handgun out from under the seat and handed it to Terry.

"Look, I'm not going to shoot a policeman," said Terry.

"Didn't think you would," said Lewis. "Just thought it might come in handy after I let you out."

"How do you plan to do that? This guys right on our tail," said Terry.

"Just watch and see." Lewis slammed on his brakes with both feet bringing his truck to a screeching stop in the middle of the road. Lewis had a steel bumper that was welded to railway ties running longitudinally under his frame. On the back of the bumper was an extended trailer hitch. Lewis didn't have any brake lights so Trooper Dawson didn't see him stop until it was too late.

Dawson locked up his brakes and skidded the last ten yards before he slammed into the back of the Lewis' pickup truck. The rusty old truck's hitch punctured the cruiser's radiator and the steel bumper destroyed the entire front end of the cruiser. Lewis accelerated leaving Patrolman Dawson and his cruiser sitting in the middle of the street.

"How was that?" Lewis asked, grinning from ear to ear.

"You're incredible. That's all I've got to say," said Terry.

"OK, better find a good spot to let you out. The cops will have reinforcements here before long. It's now or never good buddy. Good luck!" Lewis drove off the road behind a deserted gas station and came to a stop. "Been a pleasure. Good luck and God bless," he said, taking Terry's hand and shaking it manfully.

"Thanks for everything, Jeremiah," said O'Brian. Terry opened the door and limped off into the darkness. Lewis peeled out from behind the gas station and sped off down the dark road.

Terry watched Lewis drive away from behind a tree on the hillside. Soon after his truck faded out of view a police helicopter flew overhead and followed the road in the same direction Lewis was travelling. No matter how many tricks Lewis had up his sleeve he couldn't outrun a helicopter. They'd catch him soon and that meant they might start looking for him in the area depending upon what kind of story Lewis came up with.

Lewis pushed the old Chevy truck to the limits. The engine was wound as tight as a clock and the temperature gauge climbed into the red zone. The old engine could hold its own climbing hills and operating at the relatively slow speeds while in four wheel drive, but it was too much to ask it to sustain ninety miles an hour for such a long time.

White steam started streaming out from under the hood. Lewis was contemplating his next move when a helicopter suddenly flew over his truck at rooftop level. The chopper turned and shined a spotlight into his eyes temporarily blinding him. Lewis stopped his truck and got out. He laid spread eagle face down on the pavement and waited for the police to come and get him..

Moments later an officer with a shotgun ran up and stood over him. "Stay down! Don't move!" he shouted. Lewis didn't move.

"OK! OK! You caught me. Should've known better than to try and sneak moonshine into your county," said Lewis. "Good luck, Terry," Lewis muttered under his breath.

SEVERAL MILES AWAY Terry sat behind a poplar tree at the edge of a heavily wooded hillside and contemplated what to do next. With his picture plastered all over the front page of every newspaper in the world and shown on the evening news every night, he couldn't very well call a taxi and have it take him to the *Charleston Gazette*. He'd be recognized immediately and arrested. Neither was he in any condition to spend anymore time on the run. One way or another he had to get to Denton and do it fast. He was running out of time and energy.

Well, if he couldn't get to Denton, he'd have Denton come to him.

Fortunately, he still had some change in his pocket. He remembered seeing a 7-11 convenience store as it whizzed by his window while he was being chased by the state police about half a mile down the road. They always had pay phones. He started walking through the woods parallel to the road.

Terry approached the back of the store and peered around the corner toward the parking lot. Good, it was empty. He saw the pay phones near the other corner of the building. Terry cautiously walked around the side of the building and picked up the receiver and placed it in the crook of his neck. He reached down for the phone book. The black plastic cover hanging on the short chain was empty. No phonebook! There was no dial tone either. Terry slammed the phone back onto the cradle. Great! Now what! There was only one thing he could do. He was running out of time.

Terry brushed his hands through his hair and stood up as straight as he could and walked through the double glass doors into the store. The lone clerk was stocking cigarettes behind the counter. "Excuse me. Could you let me borrow your phone? The pay phone outside is broken," said Terry.

The clerk looked up and smiled. "Sure thing," he said. "Man, you look like you got run over by a Mac truck. What happened?" asked the clerk.

"I had a little accident just up the road," Terry lied.

The clerk seemed satisfied. He reached under the counter and pulled out a black phone and set it on the counter and then walked over to the coffee station and busied himself loading coffee filters with fresh coffee. Terry thanked him from across the room and dialed directory assistance. He spoke softly as he requested the number for John Denton making sure the clerk couldn't hear him. Fortunately, Terry remembered Denton's middle initial and there was only one John F. Denton.

It was after midnight so he was relatively sure Denton would be home. Denton picked up the phone on the third ring. "Hello."

"John. This is Terry."

"Terry who?"

"The one you've been writing about at work," said Terry.

Denton was immediately awake. "Yeah, Terry. What can I do for you?"

"Actually, I'm going to do something for you. Can you meet me right away?"

"Sure. Where are you?" asked Denton.

"I'm at a 7-11 in Belle. How long will it take for you to get here?"

"About thirty minutes."

"Great. I'll be waiting." Terry read the address backwards off the glass over the door and hung up the phone. When he hung up he saw the clerk was staring at him. Terry stared back. The clerk's mouth dropped open as he suddenly recognized the man standing in his store. Terry saw the change in expression and knew he was in trouble. He pulled the .44 magnum out of the back of his belt and pointed it at the clerk's chest.

"Let's not do anything hasty, fella," said Terry. "Sorry, but I'm going to have to ask you to take off the pretty green smock you're wearing."

The clerk nervously complied without protest. "Now, if you'll be so kind as to step into that little office of yours over there," Terry said as he motioned with the barrel of the biggest gun the clerk had ever seen.

Terry looked around in the office to make sure there was nothing in the room that the clerk could use to fight back or call for help with. "OK, give me your keys," Terry demanded. The clerk hesitated. Terry cocked the pistol and the clerk decided to hand them over without further delay.

"Look friend, I need to wait for somebody and I can't allow you to call the police until I'm gone. I'm going to lock you in here and wait behind your counter until my friend arrives. You won't get hurt as long as you keep quiet and don't give me any trouble. I'm not going to rob you or anything like that. Trust me, this isn't the time to play the hero. I've come too far and there is too much at stake for you to act like John Wayne. This will all be over for you real soon. Do you understand me?"

"Yes, sir!" said the frightened twenty-two year old clerk.

Terry fumbled with the keys until he found the one that fit the office. He backed out of the room and locked the clerk inside and then looked around the small store to make sure nobody had seen him. Satisfied that he was alone, he put on the clerk's smock and stood behind the counter. Anybody passing by would think everything was normal.

Terry settled in for the wait. After twenty-five minutes had passed Terry thought about the surveillance cameras. "Well, they have good pictures of me, but I can make sure they don't see who picks me up," he thought to himself.

Grabbing a one-quart can of tomato juice off a shelf, Terry methodically went to each security camera, stood on a chair, and beat the camera into pieces. Just to make sure they were out of commission he cut the power cords with his pocketknife sending sparks flying. The breaker must have blown after he cut the cord on the first camera because it was the only one that arced and sparked.

Denton slowed his new *Cadillac El Dorado* and pulled into the 7-11's parking lot.

The store was empty with the exception of the lone clerk behind the counter. He switched off the ignition and looked around the vacant parking lot. Perhaps O'Brian was hiding nearby and was waiting for him to arrive.

The clerk came outside and walked directly up to his car. It was O'Brian. "Good to see you, Terry," said Denton.

"Yeah. Thanks for coming. Mind if I get in?" asked Terry.

"Sure, it's unlocked."

Terry walked around and got in the passenger side. "Let's get out of here," Terry demanded.

"Right," said Denton as he pulled out of the lot and headed toward Charleston.

"John, sorry to get you out of bed at this hour, but I really need your help."

"What do you need? I'm all ears," said Denton.

"Well, for starters I don't want you to get me arrested at the roadblock up ahead!"

"Not to worry. There wasn't any roadblock when I came through. I did hear on my scanner that a State Police cruiser had crashed up the road a bit after a high speed chase trying to catch a moonshiner."

"That would be Jeremiah. Did you hear if he got away?" asked O'Brian.

"Sounded like they had him in custody. Is he a friend of yours?"

"Yeah, sorta. He found me in the woods and patched up my leg, but that's another story. Let me get right to the point and tell you why I called you. I need your help."

"Terry, I've got to honest. I came out here because I'm your friend, but I'm not sure I want to get mixed up in all of this. Some really serious people are looking for you. I'll wind up in jail if I help you," said Denton.

"Not if you do what I have in mind. I want you to help me surrender, but first, I want to give you the scoop of your life. I'm going to tell you who really killed the President."

"Why would you do that?" asked Denton.

"Because my only chance of surviving is to make public what I know. The CIA is trying to kill me to keep me from telling my side of the story. Once I go public they won't be able to kill me without being implicated."

"OK. What do you have in mind?"

"First, I want you to take me to a really good lawyer. Then I'll let you have first crack at my story. I want you to arrange for Channel Eight in Charleston to broadcast a live interview with me. I want the cameras to be rolling when I surrender to the State Police. Think you can handle all of that?" asked O'Brian.

"Sounds doable. There's a tape player in the backseat. Grab it and start talking."

26

NIKKI MAKOROV SAT alone in her simple two-room Jerusalem apartment watching television. It was her sole modern extravagance. She was content with a no frills existence to which her choice of living conditions loudly testified. A kitchenette graced one wall of a combination dinning room and living room. A door separated the living room from a bedroom barely large enough to handle her single bed and three-drawer dresser. Since the death of her husband eight years earlier she'd adopted a Spartan lifestyle similar to that of her youth. In spite of her meager furnishings her sporadic visitors left her home thinking it was much larger. Perhaps it was her charm and grace that deceived them.

Life had been good to her since those early days in Russia. Her work with the Mossad in the late sixties caught the attention of a dashing young Zionist leader. They married after a short whirlwind romance, as was so prevalent in Israel shortly after the Yom Kippur War. God had for some reason chosen to make their marriage childless. Yet, there were many blessings for which she was thankful. Her ambitious young husband was elected to the Israeli Parliament and served his fledgling country faithfully until his untimely death in a car bomb assassination.

After the loss of her husband, she found no solace in her elegant surroundings and chose instead the simple way of life she had known as a child. Somehow, it made her feel real and alive to live closer to the way the average Jewish person lived. Besides, she hated the pretentiousness of the political elite she had been surrounded by for the past forty years.

She chuckled out loud as she thought how quickly things change. Just a few short years ago she was jetting all over the world with her husband, working late nights collecting intelligence for her country, and living every day on the edge. Now here she sat with nothing better to do than watch television in the early afternoon.

Bored with the simpleminded programming, she changed the channel to CNN. Old habits died hard. CNN had played such a large part in her life as a source of intelligence and current events in America for so long that she often found herself watching it for hours a day even though it no longer had any relevance to her existence.

She got up out of her chair and walked to the kitchen for a glass of water. The running tap water partially obscured the sound of the television but she thought she heard the pretty new anchorwoman say, "We are going to break to a live feed from WCHS Channel Eight in Charleston, West Virginia. The man accused of killing the President of the United States is giving a news conference."

Nikki sat her glass down and hurried back to her seat. A Special News Bulletin streamer scrolled across the bottom of her screen. "We now are going live to the news conference in its entirety," said the anchorwoman.

John Denton looked steadfastly into the camera and said, "Good morning. I am here this morning with Terry O'Brian, the accused assassin of the President of the United States. With me is Jonathan Barksdale, Mr. O'Brian's attorney. Early this morning Mr. O'Brian contacted me and asked me to assist him in surrendering to the authorities. Mr. Barksdale and I have contacted the FBI and the State Police and have arranged Mr. O'Brian's surrender as requested.

"That isn't the reason we called a news conference at 7:00 a.m. After contacting the proper authorities I called several of my journalistic colleagues and asked them to help me bring to the American people a message I believe has a good deal of credibility. I wouldn't have been a party to this news conference if I didn't believe there was an element of truth to the story you are about to hear. At this time, I am turning the microphone over to Terry O'Brian."

Denton passed the handheld microphone to O'Brian. Little attempt had been made to make Terry presentable to the worldwide viewing audience. Perhaps his battered condition would lend credibility to his story.

"Let me begin by saying, I did not kill the President and all those people at the *Greenbrier*. I know that's what you'd expect me to say even if I was guilty. But if you'll listen to me for just a few moments, I think I can give you enough proof to show you who the real killers are. When you hear me out, you'll know why there are many that would kill me on sight to keep me from making my story public. That's why I contacted Mr. Denton."

Terry started with meeting Billy Ray a few months earlier. He recounted how Billy Ray had helped with the annual war games, he explained that he wasn't a member of a radical militia group, and how Billy Ray had hosted the party at his house after the victory and staged the picture with the automatic rifles. He explained how he had invited Billy Ray to go flying with him and how Billy Ray had hijacked his airplane and overflown the *Greenbrier*. Terry told the world how he was drugged and kept in a cabin in the mountains. He concluded his story with the CIA agent trying to kill him in the cabin, finding Billy Ray dead on the front lawn, and how he made his escape.

"I don't really expect most of you listening to me to believe this seemingly outlandish story. I only hope that somebody out there in the right position will hear what I'm saying and ask the right questions. Perhaps somebody in the FBI or elsewhere in our government will hear enough to know that what I am saying is true. I have no way to prove that what I've told you is true. My only piece of corroborating evidence is this," Terry said as he pulled out Mike Anderson and Andy Renfro's CIA identification and badges.

"Take a good look at these. I found this man lying on the front lawn. I knew him as Billy Ray Johnson. That wasn't his real name. He was a CIA agent. I don't know who killed him but I'm pretty sure it was this man," he said indicating Renfro's ID.

"I did kill CIA agent Andrew Renfro in self-defense. He was trying to kill me. Ask yourself, what was he doing at that particular cabin in the mountains of West Virginia? The CIA has no jurisdiction in an assassination. He wouldn't have been assigned to search for me or to apprehend me. I submit to you that he was part of the conspiracy to assassinate the President of the United States. I believe he orchestrated the efforts to frame me and had come to kill me to make sure I couldn't generate any questions about the cover story.

"I would ask the American people only one thing, please examine the evidence before you believe everything you're being told. If I wind up dead, ask yourself why. I'm turning myself in to the proper authorities and intend to cooperate fully and truthfully with their investigation. If I am killed by a modern day Jack Ruby you'll know that what I've told you this morning is the truth. Thank you."

NIKKI TURNED OFF the television and stared into space for several minutes deep in thought. Of course, now it all makes sense. The pieces didn't fall into place until O'Brian had shown the CIA identifications. Others wouldn't figure it out. They weren't as close to the situation as she was. There were probably five people still living who had the information to make the connection, but they most likely had long forgotten the event. Nikki would never forget. How could she? It was an event that had changed her life forever!

Salt Lake City

NINE TIME ZONES away another widow watched the same news conference. She really didn't care all that much about politics but the deaths of all those children had broken her heart. She glared at O'Brian with hatred as he spoke, not believing a single word. She was about to turn off the television and fix herself some breakfast when O'Brian produced two CIA identification badges.

She had to blink hard to make sure she was seeing what she thought she saw. The TV close-up of the CIA identification badges almost stopped her heart. The one on the right was her son! What was it O'Brian had said? He called himself Billy Ray and he was dead on the front lawn.

A strange sense of calm swept over her as she got up out of her chair and walked over to the closet. She took her time putting on her coat and in taking the box down from the shelf over the closet. She replayed in her mind her son's last phone call as she picked up the keys and went outside to the car. She had a mission.

Her son had tried to warn her he was in danger before he died. Mike had given his life for whatever was in this box. She was going to make sure he didn't die in vain. Her son's last words kept playing over and over in her shock-ridden mind, "If anything happens to me, or you don't hear from me in the next few weeks, mail the box to the address I told you!" That's just what she was going to do!

Charleston, West Virginia

THE RED LIGHT on the camera blinked out signifying they were off the air. Terry turned to Jonathan Barksdale and said simply, "OK, Let's do it." Barksdale pulled out his cellular phone and called the FBI agent he'd spoken to earlier in the morning and told him where they were. Terry and Barksdale made small talk for the twenty minutes it took the FBI to arrive.

ON THE OUTSKIRTS of Washington, DC a furious Marshall Freeman drove like a madman toward the White House. How did he ever get talked into being a part of this crazy scheme to rule the world? The two dead CIA agents would soon be traced to his doorstep. Once congressional investigators got on his trail it would just be a matter of time before his involvement became apparent. Braxton had better protect him or he was going to bring the whole thing down around his ears.

Freeman showed his pass to the Uniformed Secret Service and was escorted to the anteroom outside the Oval Office to await his audience with the President. Thirty minutes later Garrison Parker, the Chief of Staff, entered the room and said, "Marshall, what are you doing here? I don't have you on the President's schedule today. Is there something I can do for you?" The Chief of Staff guarded the President's time like a trained attack dog.

"I'm not on the schedule but the President will see me and he will see me right now!"

"Calm down, General. You know that's not how things are done around here."

While they were talking a side door opened and the President stuck his head into the room and said, "That's OK Garrison, I'm expecting the General." Freeman smirked an "I told you so" at Parker and pushed past him following President Braxton into the Oval Office.

General Freeman walked toward the small settee but Braxton stopped him and said, "Don't get too comfortable, General. You won't be here that long. You should be elsewhere working out what you are going to do about the mess you made."

"I made!' yelled Freeman. A Secret Service agent stuck his head in the door. "Is everything all right, Mr. President?" he asked.

"Thank you for your diligence, Agent Demming. Yes, everything is all right. Please close the door after yourself," the President said, dismissing him with a wave of the hand.

In a hushed voice Freeman continued, "My mess? This was your idea. I've kept my part of the bargain and I expect you to keep yours. I need a little protection here!"

"General, I'm afraid I can't do much to help. If I get involved in covering for you and your agency it would implicate me and draw too much attention to what I'm doing. I'm too close to pulling this off to jeopardize everything just to make you feel safe!"

"I'm not going to sit idly by and allow you to throw me to the dogs, you worthless scum!" shouted the general.

Outside the Oval Office Agent Demming's hand went to his weapon as he pressed his ear against the door. He called the uniformed agent monitoring the video camera watching the Oval Office. "John, I've got a bad feeling about General Freeman. Does everything look kosher to you?"

"Yeah. Nothing out of order in there. Freeman is standing in front of the President's desk. He looks upset, but he's not acting in a threatening manner. I think it's under control. Relax."

"Take it easy," said the President. "I'm not hanging you out to dry. Time is on our side. By the time anyone discovers your involvement it will be too late. Pretty soon people will have more pressing things on their minds than what two of your agents had to do with an assassination."

"Look, I need to get out of the country. I don't trust you or anybody else right now. I've done my part. Now I want you to give me what's coming to me and get me out of here until all of this is over," demanded Freeman.

The vein above Braxton's finely tailored silk collar began to bulge as his face flushed bright red. "You gutless moron! Don't tell me what I'm going to do. You're in no position to demand that I do anything. I can make you disappear, you worthless insect!" he hissed.

Freeman leapt across the highly polished cherrywood desk and hit Braxton over the head with the expensive marble paperweight adorning the right corner. The President went down hard, blood gushing out of a deep gash in his forehead. Freeman grabbed Braxton onehanded by the front of his shirt and yanked him upright as he raised the heavy paperweight to strike him again.

Agent Demming burst through the door at that precise moment with his pistol drawn. Seeing the bloody President and Freeman with the upraised weapon, he fired three shots into the general's torso. Freeman was propelled against the curtains behind the desk. He stood there momentarily with a puzzled look and then slowly slid to the floor as death seized his lifeless body.

"Are you OK, Mr. President?" asked Demming as he helped the President to his feet.

"Yes, I'm fine. Thanks to you, I think I'm going to be just fine," said Braxton. The President wasn't referring to his health. Braxton smiled and thought, "Freeman was the last living person who knew of my involvement in the assassination of President Carpenter. Things are looking up indeed!"

CONGRESSMAN HANK MASSEY was busy reviewing his notes for an upcoming news conference in which he was going to criticize President Braxton for deserting historic American allies in the Persian Gulf. His secretary brought in a package addressed to him and laid it on his desk. She had learned not to talk to the Congressman when he was deep in thought. Massey had a short temper and wasn't particularly kind when interrupted.

He worked without looking at the package for another hour. Finally, he noticed the notebook sized box and used an exacto knife to cut the tape sealing the package. The first thing he saw was a picture of President Braxton, General Marshall Freeman, and two unidentified men. Next, he removed a note that caused his fingers to burn. The words jumped off the page and grabbed him by the throat making it hard to breathe.

"SINCE YOU ARE reading this letter, I am dead. The men you see in the picture killed President Carpenter and the people at the *Greenbrier Resort*. I'm sure you recognize President Braxton and General Freeman. The other two people pictured are Special Agent Andy Renfro of the CIA and myself, Special Agent Mike Anderson. This picture was taken from a video surveillance camera at the White House. Included in this package is a tape recording of a meeting I attended with Braxton, Freeman, and Renfro, in which we reviewed our plans to kill the President. I'm not aware of Braxton's reasons for killing President Carpenter, but my immediate superior Andy Renfroindicated that DCI Freeman implied it was tied to some type of aspiration to form a New World Order. You will also find included a detailed documentation of my involvement,the details of how we obtained the binary chemicals used in the attack, and notes I made of conversations with Director Feeman.

In summary, President Carpenter's assassination was conceived and carried out upon orders from President Braxton and Director Freeman.

May God forgive me for my involvement,

Mike Anderson

CONGRESSMAN MASSEY'S HANDS were shaking as he dialed the direct number for his old college friend, Richard Greeley, Director of the Federal Bureau of Investigations. "Rich, can you drop what you're doing and come over to my office immediately?"

"Can't do it. I'm up to my ears in the Carpenter assassination."

"God help us man, but I have in my hand a detailed report on the assassination written by the killer himself," said Massey.

"I'm on my way."

The following day Richard Greeley spoke to a select group of senior congressmen and senators from both parties in a congressional conference room. The evidence Hank Massey handed over was quickly verified for authenticity and the veracity of the claims made by Agent Anderson seemed to be supported by corroborating evidence. General Freeman's death in the Oval Office went a long way to dispel any doubts Braxton's cronies may have had.

Greeley was nearing the end of his presentation when an assistant silently crept to the side of the Chairman of the House Foreign Relations Committee. Congressman Terrance Sattis cleared his throat and interrupted Director Greeley. "Gentlemen, I have just received an intelligence report from the government of Israel. I have in my hand a picture taken by an agent in the Mossad, dated September 23, 1968. It's a picture of three men we all know by name outside a tavern in Moscow. The men are President Donald Braxton, President Alexi Yanochev, and the Grand Ayatollah of Iran, Ali bakr Rafalgemii.

"Perhaps this sheds light upon Braxton's reasons for killing his predecessor. If he is indeed conspiring with the other men in this picture we are in deep trouble. Even if we expose Braxton for what he is and take the necessary steps to save the Persian Gulf from Yanochev, the American people's confidence in our government will be irreparablydamaged."

"What are you suggesting, Congressman?" asked Massey.

"There is another option that will save the people from having to know how close they came to losing their country," said Sattis. He spent the next twenty minutes explaining what he had in mind. Everyone agreed with his plan.

After a private meeting with the Director of the United States Secret Service, Hank Massey and Richard Greeley prevailed upon the President's Chief of Staff to get them in to see the President. Braxton stood up and walked around his desk when they walked in. He greeted them warmly shaking their hands vigorously.

"So, I understand you have information about the assassination. Let's hear it," said Braxton.

Richard Greeley did the speaking. He laid out the evidence he had and creatively filled in a few blank spots. He could tell from the President's face that he was correct. When they were through Hank Massey stood in front of the desk and said in a quiet, low voice, "Donald, you have two choices. I can hold a press conference and tell the world what I know or you can do the right thing. I'll wait to hear from you."

As the two turned to leave Director Greeley reached out and placed his hand on Braxton's shoulder. "I hope you'll do the right thing." Greeley laid a 9mm *Browning* on the corner of the President's desk. Congressman Massey and Director Greeley walked quietly to the door. The Director of the Secret Service met them outside and sadly shook his head. This was the best way.

BRAXTON SAT FOR several hours in the growing darkness of the Oval Office. He'd come so close. He tried to analyze what it was he was feeling. Remorse? No, that wasn't it. Sadness? That wasn't it either. It was something deeper than that. Shame. That was it. Not for killing the President or snuffing out the lives of hundreds of innocent people, but rather, for failing to free the world of the parasitic, capitalist, industrialized scourge that would eventually destroy nature itself. He let out a deep breath. In one quick motion he swept up the pistol, stuck it in his mouth, and pulled the trigger.

THE PHONE RANG in Congressman Massey's office. It was the Director of the Secret Service. "It's over, Mr. President. The Presidential Security Detail is on its way. We need you at the White House right away."

Mr. President! It hadn't sunk in yet. Hank Massey sat back in his chair and put his feet up on his desk. I'm the President of the United States! A satisfied smile crossed his face as he thought about the opportunities that lay before him. A twinge of guilt quickly passed as he had a fleeting thought that perhaps he should feel some sense of remorse that the former President of the United States had taken his own life. But, in classic Massey form, he didn't waste any emotional energy on things he couldn't change. His revelry was broken as aides began rushing into the room intent upon preparing the new President to ascend to the highest office in the land.

Asmara, Eritrea

THE ERITREAN EARLY morning blackness engulfed ten C-141 aircraft as they sat single-file with their engines running. The smell of salt from the nearby Red Sea was overpowered by the heavy odor of jet exhaust. Powerful turbines shrieked a familiar chorus to those accustomed to working a military flight line, shattering the tranquility of the normally idle runway.

Isaiah Durante', the small, pro-western African country's President, granted President Massey permission to use Eritrea's only military airfield capable of handling the massive American aircraft three hours after Massey was sworn in as President. Hank Massey wasted no time giving Secretary McClintock's rescue mission the go ahead after Donald Braxton was found dead in the Oval Office. It was his first official act as President of the United States.

THE JOINT CHIEFS of Staff had disobeyed a direct order from the former President by not shelving the rescue plan as Braxton had commanded. Holding onto a glimmer of hope that they could change his mind, they continued planning the mission and had placed all participants on a twelve hour alert. Now, twenty-four hours after President Massey had taken office, the main elements of the rescue forces were on the runway awaiting orders to launch the mission. They didn't have long to wait.

"Flight Leader, this is General Phillips. I just got off of the horn with the JCS Chairman. He wanted me to relay that the President has given the green light to your mission and that he personally led a prayer asking for Divine protection for you and your men. Go with God, Colonel. You are cleared for take-off."

All ten of the special operations C-141's from the 13th Air Squadron were off the deck and over the Red Sea in twelve minutes. These highly secret aircraft, capable of high-speed intercontinental flight, were designed to covertly penetrate a hostile coastline at low altitude. General Phillips personally requested the SPECOPS 141's because of their advanced navigation and electronic countermeasures systems and because they were heavily armored, a feature he was sure they would need on this mission.

Onboard, 600 Army Rangers of the 1st Battalion, 504th Parachute Infantry Regiment out of Fort Bragg, North Carolina, were bristling with confidence. Too many times the political powers that be had sent them into harms way without the proper tools to do the job. They always cited philosophical idioms like "a measured response", or "right sized force structure" to keep them from using the firepower they needed to get the job done right. Nobody that had ever put his or her life on the line believed in terms like that.

That wasn't the story this time. The Rangers were augmented with five *Apache* Attack Helicopters from the 1st Squadron 17th Air Calvary

Regiment. Behind the C-141 carrying the *Apaches* was an aircraft loaded with Surface to Air Missile Systems from the 3rd Battalion 4th Air Defense Artillery Regiment. Another aircraft carried four M119 105mm howitzers from the 319th Airborne Field Artillery Regiment. All were part of the mighty 82nd Airborne. The part of the mission the Rangers liked the most was the fact that three of the specially equipped C-141's were each carrying five of the new M8A1 light tanks and an armored personnel carrier. The high speed and maneuverability of the fifteen M8A1's with their turret mounted 105mm main gun made each tank a force multiplier. They were ideally suited for decimating any enemy armor or infantry defensive positions that might be encountered. They were confident they could take on anything the Russians or Iranians had to throw at them and walk away the winners.

The rescue mission was designed to hit the enemy fast and hard and then get out of Dodge before the enemy had a chance to regroup and mount a counteroffensive. With that in mind the Joint Chiefs of Staff had selected Colonel Mike Danson, a former commander of the elite Delta Force, to command.

Colonel Danson was the embodiment of what you'd see if you closed your eyes and tried to imagine what an elite commando colonel looked like. With broad shoulders and rugged features he stood ramrod straight and spoke in crisp, efficient sentences. His hair was cut severely short - Ranger style, with just a hint of jet-black hair down the center of his head. Everything about him was strictly business.

Danson designed the mission himself and was confident of success. The only part of his plan that the brass didn't like was leaving all of the high priced M8's and other support equipment behind. His plan was to shoot and scoot. He planned to blast his way in, grab the hostages, egress Kuwait City, load everybody on the C-17 *Globemasters* that would come in behind the assault force, blow up all of his equipment, and fly to safety. It was a good plan, but was very expensive.

The White House authorized the mission thinking that the political gains resulting from such a daring military rescue in the heart of enemy territory far outweighed the price of any lost hardware. The American public needed some good news. Colonel Danson's job was to give them that news.

"Landing Zone coming up, Colonel. We've started our approach," said Mission Commander, Lieutenant Colonel Jeff Scott, over the intercom.

"Thanks, Jeff. Anything on ESM?" asked Danson.

"No, sir; the E-3 reports all quiet. The nearest active enemy radar site is three five zero degrees at forty-three miles. Insufficient power to get a return off of us."

"OK, soon as you open the ramp we'll be out of your hair. Thanks for the ride," said Danson, drawing upon his trademark propensity for understatement.

The Rangers were thrown forward in their seats as the big aircraft touched down on the hard-packed desert. There was no need for Marshall matting or runways. The ground was hard as rock. Most people picture the Arabian desert as mountainous sand dunes for hundreds of miles in all directions, but that isn't completely accurate. Much of the desert is flat and rocky. Fortunately, this particular section of desert was flat and smooth, resembling the Bonneville Salt Flats in America more than the Hollywood version of the Kuwalti desert.

Equipment was disgorged from the massive cargo bays onto the desert floor in a practiced, continuous stream. The troops worked feverishly and completed the offload in twenty-five minutes, shaving three minutes off of the rehearsal time.

"Good job men. Mount up and let's go do our stuff. We'll rendezvous at the target in forty-five minutes. I'll meet you in the hot zone," said Colonel Danson.

The *Apache* attack helicopters lifted off in formation and circled low overhead to cover the C-141's as they took off. Half of the aircraft turned west and headed back to Eritrea. Three others carried paratroopers and headed for Kuwait City. The M-8's formed and ring around the mobile air defense batteries and began the short drive to their target.

So far everything was going according to plan. The enemy hadn't detected their low-level insertion. That was going to change very soon. The Rangers in the C-141's were going to jump at fifteen hundred feet over the Fine Arts Center. The pilots would stay on the deck until they got word the anti-aircraft batteries were in place and the tanks and artillery began their barrage. The *Apache's* would sweep the streets ahead of the landing zone and prevent any troops from approaching while the paratroopers made their descent. Once the 600 Rangers were on the ground they would attack the Fine Art Center, rescue the Undersecretary of State and the Navy nurse, load them aboard the ambulance, and race away to the waiting C-17's.

Straits of Hormuz

HUNDREDS OF MILES to the south Admiral Warren's Battle Group was sitting off the tip of the Straits of Hormuz. News cameras from the media pool were set up on the missile ships and the carrier's bridge wings and flight deck to record the event. "Stand clear of missile decks for missile launch." Two minutes later two destroyers and two cruisers under Admiral Warren's command unleashed a deadly salvo of ninety *Tomahawk* missiles.

A CNN reporter stuck a microphone in the admiral's face. "Admiral, now that you've launched the missiles can you tell our viewers where they're headed?"

"I'm not at liberty to identify the exact target, but I can say that our missiles are headed for Kuwait. We're planning a coordinated time on top of the target at twenty-one thirty. The *Tomahawks* are our first strike against those who are attempting to deny the free people of Kuwait and the Saudi Arabian Peninsula their freedom. However, the Russians have more to worry about than just our *Tomahawks*," said Admiral Warren.

"Does that mean other forces are involved in this attack?" asked the reporter.

"Yes, it does. But like I said, I'm not at liberty to provide any more details at this time other than to say that American forces are attacking a wide variety of targets. The Pentagon will release more information in a few hours. Now, if you'll excuse me, I have a war to fight."

Once the camera was turned off Admiral Warren said, "Of course you know we won't transmit your digital film until after the *Tomahawks* arrive on target and our aircraft are out of danger."

"Roger, sir; that's the usual arrangement," replied the reporter.

"I'll try to let you get it to your people a few minutes after your cameras in Kuwait report the missiles have arrived."

"Thanks, sir; I understand. I don't want to endanger any of our troops any more than you do," said the reporter.

Kuwait

FIVE APACHES ARRIVED on target six minutes ahead of the column of M-8's and anti-aircraft batteries. The lead chopper, piloted by the flight leader Major Jack Myers, reported the missile impacts to Colonel Danson. The rescue team was counting upon the confusion caused by the *Tomahawk* attack and the heavy jamming from the Navy EA-6B's to screen their approach long enough to reach their objective. Once they were there there was little the enemy could do to stop them. They'd rescue the undersecretary and the nurse at all cost.

"Flight leader, this is Danson. Commence your attack!" The *Apaches* reacted immediately and unleashed a blistering rocket attack on the Russian tank park four blocks from the Fine Arts Center. The M-8's arrived at the Arts Center as the first Russian tanks tasted American firepower.

THE C-141'S WITH the paratroopers popped up to altitude behind the Arts Center just long enough for the Rangers to exit the aircraft and then did a nose over and headed for the deck. They appeared on the Russian radarscopes for ten seconds before the scopes became an unreadable white snowstorm. The Navy EA-6B's identified the enemy transmitters, matched their frequencies and sent an overpowering identical signal back to the radar site, effectively blinding them. Although the radars could no longer direct weapons toward the American aircraft the fact that they were being jammed stirred the sleeping Russian military organization into action. Alarm klaxons began sounding all over Kuwait City as the lights came on in barracks's and armories.

The Russians were completely blindsided by the attack. The first reports of damage came from the tank park. Three tanks reported they'd escaped the hellish carnage unleashed by the American tank killing helicopters. Initial reports indicated that the rest of the armor had been destroyed.

The troop barracks were not fairing any better. One by one the dilapidated one-story structures began erupting into hungry infernos killing everyone inside. The *Tomahawk* missiles claimed the lives of four thousand Russian soldiers in less than five minutes.

The lead American M-8 barreled through the Arts Center's perimeter fence and blasted a hole in the back wall. Stopping a few yards inside the fence it covered a platoon of Rangers as they entered the building in force. The other tanks and troops formed a protective ring in the street in front of the Center.

COLONEL SOLSTENISKI WAS at his desk going over the *Night Orders* he was issuing to his SS-20 crews operating out of Ethiopia. The Iranians had struck a deal with the new Ethiopian Islamic government to let them build a military installation on the site of the former American Consulate. Both countries thought it would be a fitting insult to the Americans once they discovered its new usage.

The Iranians in turn had decided it would be the perfect place to hide their new nuclear arsenal. If the Americans discovered that Russia had delivered nuclear missiles to them they wouldn't think to monitor Ethiopia with their spy satellites. That would give them plenty of time to learn from their Russian teachers how to operate the missile launching and targeting systems.

COLONEL BORIS SOLSTENISKI was tasked to command the Russian advisors that were helping the Iranians. It was proving to be a difficult process. Especially difficult was trying to command troops on a different continent. After his successful raid on the American Ambassador's residence in Bahrain the high command had refused to let him rejoin his troops. Some idiot up the chain of command thought he was more useful babysitting his prisoners. So, here he was, writing his *Night Orders* from several thousand miles away.

He'd been reviewing the message from his second in command concerning the missile-targeting list when he was knocked to the floor by the overpressure of an explosion somewhere in the building. He picked himself up off of the floor and stumbled into the hallway just as the first American soldier dove through the breach into the hallway. The soldier rolled to the right and fired a three round burst from his M-16 in the colonel's direction. Solsteniski felt two rounds zip past his head and another tear through his shoulder. Someone grabbed him from behind and pulled him to safety around the corner of the hallway.

The Russians were offering fierce resistance. A small gaggle of commandos with automatic weapons were holding the intersections to the basement hallway. The long passageway that ran the entire length of the building was intersected in several places on both sides by perpendicular hallways. The Russians were at every intersection firing down the main passage at the slowly advancing Americans.

THE TOP STORIES were cleared in a matter of minutes. Apparently, all of the Russians were concentrated in the basement. A search of the cleared floors failed to turn up Undersecretary McClintock or the Navy nurse. That meant they were either in the basement or they'd been moved. Danson hoped they hadn't been moved.

Unlike some commanders Danson was a front line leader. He was in the building with his men so that he could see first hand what was going on. This was where the action was so this was where he was. It was as simple as that. The tank commander or *Apache* pilots would let him know if he was needed outside.

"OK, I'm tired of fooling with these guys. Let's end this!" Colonel Danson yelled to no one in particular. "Major, I want grenades. Toss the grenades and follow them up the hallway. The Russian high command won't give us enough time to let this drag on," he said to his executive officer.

The XO passed the instruction to the squad leaders via their tactical headsets mounted inside their kevlar helmets. A dozen grenades bounced down the center hallway and exploded in a ragged, earsplitting staccato. The building filled with a smoky cloud as the cordite from the explosives quickly spread through the passageway. Several Russians staggered into the field of fire and were cut down by a solid wall of automatic weapons fire.

The Rangers charged up the hallway seconds after the explosions behind a withering stream of machine gun fire. They leapfrogged from one cross-passage to the next, throwing several grenades down each one and killing scores of enemy soldiers. The mutilated bodies where sprayed with bullets just to make sure they didn't cause anymore trouble.

It was over in minutes. A grayish cordite cloud hung from the ceiling and assaulted the nostrils of the Rangers as they moved from door to door clearing the floor. Colonel Danson walked outside to check the situation with the Russians. There was no counterattack yet but he knew that was only a temporary convenience. The Russians would be coming in force in a matter of minutes. Time to find the hostages and beat feet back to the waiting *Globemasters*.

Two M-8's were guarding the right flank of the rescue force. Several Rangers and the crews to the tanks were standing beside the vehicles serving as a trip wire in case the Americans were attacked from their direction. Gunners were standing in their cupolas with guns at the ready. They were listening to the speaker tied into the tactical radio and monitoring the progress of the troops in the Fine Arts Center, glad that they weren't getting shot at. Their luck suddenly changed. The M-8 closest to the Fine Arts Center erupted into a ball of flames killing the crew instantly. Machine gun fire raked the other M-8, ricocheting harmlessly off of the armor but killing the gunner. The American's that weren't killed or wounded dove under the tracked vehicle and returned fire. They were pinned down but managed to locate where the enemy fire was coming from. A sergeant loaded a grenade into the launcher on his M-16 and raised his head to try and take out the enemy antitank fire team. A hail of machine gun bullets impacted his chest and head before he could pull the trigger.

Two privates held their rifles over their head and emptied their magazines in the general direction of the enemy. The Russians raked their position again, kicking up dirt and impacting the M-8 they were hiding under. They were about to get away from the M-8, expecting it to be the next target, when they heard several shots that sounded like an

American fifty caliber. The Russian machine gun fell silent.

LIEUTENANT COMMANDER JAKE Gregory came trotting out of the shadows behind where the Russian anti-tank fire team had been hiding. "Hold your fire! I'm one of the good guys," he yelled.

Jake walked up to the Rangers and said, "SEAL Team Five, take me to your leader."

"COLONEL, THERE'S SOMEBODY that wants to talk to you. Some Navy SEAL took out an enemy anti-tank team that had us pinned down, then asked to speak with you. He's been observing the Fine Arts Center for a few days," said a young platoon sergeant. He motioned to a man standing a few yards away leaning against the covering M-8.

"Good evening, sir; I'm Lieutenant Commander Jake Gregory. Been hanging around for a few days watching the building. I'm a friend of Secretary McClintock and Lieutenant Commander Crawford. Have you found them yet?"

"No. I've got men searching the building room by room. We've got to find them in the next few minutes or we're leaving without them. It's going to get hot around here real soon once the Russians figure what we are up to," said Colonel Danson.

"Mind if I help look?" asked Jake.

"No, not at all. Have at it," said Danson.

Jake reported to the captain in charge of the search teams to find out what rooms still needed to be searched. Once he was up to speed on the progress of the search he set out to help find Sarah. The first room he entered contained a desk that had been knocked over and papers spread haphazardly all over the floor. He was about to check the next room when something on one of the papers caught his eye. Cyrillic's spelled out the words "Top Secret". Jake reached down and picked it up.

With his excellent command of the Russian language it didn't take him long to see that he was holding a targeting list in his hand. Before he had time to read further he heard a voice in the hallway. "In here! We found them!"

Jake stuffed a handful of papers in his flak jacket and sprinted down the hallway following the shouting voice to a small equipment room three doors away. The captain entered the room at his heels.

When Jake burst into the room he found a soldier kneeling next to Sarah and Ambassador McClintock. They were chained to a large electrical cable that ran a few feet off of the floor supplying a massive breaker box. The cold concrete floor had a drain in the middle of the room that evidently didn't work very well. Standing water was backed up all the way from the drain to where Sarah and the ambassador were sitting.

Sarah burst into tears when she saw Jake come in the door. "Jake! Thank God it's you! I was so scared. I thought they killed you. I saw them shooting at you when they dragged me away."

Ambassador McClintock watched in silence as Jake ran to her and took her in this arms. Jake said nothing about her battered appearance. Her right eye was swollen shut and her lip was split. Her black evening dress was in shreds and barely covered her trembling body, "It's OK now. I'm here. I won't let anything happen to you. Can you walk? We've got to get you out of here," said Jake.

"I don't know. We've been chained like this for two weeks," said Sarah.

The ambassador spread his hands as far apart as possible while a soldier used a pair of bolt cutters to free him from his bonds. When he was free, he said, "We've been locked in here in the dark most of the time. They didn't even allow us the dignity of going to the restroom. They just opened the door and sprayed us down with a hose once a day. I'm surprised we weren't electrocuted. We've had very little to eat or drink. They fed us once every two days and gave us two bottles of water per day. I'm afraid we aren't going to be much help if we have to make a run for it."

Suddenly, the sound of heavy artillery and automatic weapons fire assaulted their ears. The young Ranger captain standing next to Jake grabbed his arm and said, "Sir, we've got to get moving. The Russians have mounted a counterattack. We're running out of time."

The soldier with the bolt cutters freed Sarah. Jake picked her up and whisked her down the hallway toward the waiting armored personnel carrier that served as an ambulance. Sarah threw her arms around his neck and clung to him tightly. Another soldier threw the ambassador over his shoulder in a fireman's carry and jogged after them.

Colonel Danson was waiting by the armoured ambulance when they exited the building. "Let's move it people! Get the hostages on the ambulance, and I mean now! I can't hold the Russians off much longer."

Jake lifted Sarah through the rear hatch of the ambulance and a strong looking medic strapped her to a cot. "Jake, don't leave me!" cried Sarah.

Jake tried to close his ears to her screams as he closed the hatch and approached the colonel. "What can I do to help?

INSIDE THE FINE Arts Center a pile of dead men began to move. Colonel Solsteniski pushed aside the bodies of the men that had pulled him to safety. They were riddled with bullets. Solsteniski didn't know how it had happened. The last thing he remembered was being pulled around the corner and feeling an explosion behind him. He tried to stand - a searing pain in his shoulder reminded him that he'd been shot.

He heard the raging battle in the street outside and decided that it was best for him if he just sat down and waited for reinforcements to arrive. Besides, he was in no condition to do anything to help.

FIVE *APACHE* ATTACK helicopters flew low overhead and joined the battle unfolding in the streets in front of the Fine Arts Center. Jake and the colonel ran around the corner of the building to see what was going on, with the commander's APC following at their heels.

When Jake and Danson rounded the corner they ran into the middle of a raging artillery duel between the American M-8's and small 105 battery and the much superior Russian mortars and heavy artillery. The Russians had them outgunned in both number and caliber of ordnance.

Jake heard a growing whistle and was knocked off his feet by an explosion behind him. Blood was streaming into his eyes when he managed to get to his feet. "That was close. Must've been a heavy mortar!" he said to Colonel Danson.

Jake turned when he didn't receive a reply. Colonel Danson was sitting upright with his legs folded underneath of him and his back against his APC. Thick gore ran down the front of his flak jacket emanating from the spot his head once occupied. Jake wasted no time climbing aboard the APC as it joined the rear of the small column of M-8's and APC's retreating from the artillery fire.

MAJOR JOHNNY WARD assumed command when he learned of Danson's death. The hostages were already well away from the action and the *Globemasters* were making their approach to the pick-up point. Now it was time to get the troops out of harm's way. "All units, fall back to Point Bravo!"

The M-8A1's began falling back, covering the retreating APC's and firing from their aft facing turrets as they withdrew. The M119 *Howitzers* joined them and laid down as much counterbattery fire as the four cannons could sustain, but it was no match for the overwhelming Russian force building a short distance away. The Russian heavy mortars weren't much of a factor, but when the heavy artillery began falling among the retreating tanks Major Ward knew he was in for the fight of his life.

THE C-17 GLOBEMASTERS had touched down at Point Bravo thirty minutes earlier a few miles out of town. Colonel Danson called ahead and ordered the drivers to come and get his troops as soon as their tracks hit the deck. The loadmasters quickly unloaded their cargo of armored personnel carriers and watched them race off into the darkness.

RUSSIAN TROOPS SUPPORTED by heavy artillery were pushing hard at the retreating Americans. Major Ward was no longer trying to engage the enemy. All he wanted to do was get his command back to the pick-up point and get them in the air. After that, it was up to the Air Force to keep his men alive.

28

MAJOR MYERS AND his *Apache* helicopters were wreaking havoc upon the Russian armament. They'd already destroyed two dozen pieces of artillery and two of the tanks that had escaped the tank park. He was beginning to think things were going to go his way when he saw two thin, white trails of smoke heading for his wingman.

"Hammer Two, break right. Incoming!"

It was too late. His wingman exploded in a ball of flames nearly engulfing his own aircraft in the flames and debris. He pulled his eyes off of his now dead wingman and quickly scanned in all directions. The skies were filled with tracers from a dozen ZSU's, but that wasn't what got his attention. Missiles were streaking toward all of his remaining helicopters. The other aircrews were already taking evasive maneuvers but one by one he saw them explode and crash violently into the buildings surrounding the battle below.

EXPERIENCE OR LUCK, he wasn't quite sure which, helped him to evade a pair of shoulder launched missiles that had been tracking him. He'd been so busy destroying enemy artillery that he'd led his men into a hastily constructed enemy missile trap. Judging from the number of missiles in the air the Russians must've issued SA-7's to several dozen missile fire teams.

Major Myers reported the loss of his aircraft to Major Ward and was ordered to cover the retreating APC's. He was more than happy to comply and get out of the heart of the anti-aircraft fire.

COLONEL SOLSTENISKI WAS sitting with his back to the wall looking at his dead soldiers when a young Russian enlisted man stuck his head in the room. "Hey, we've got a live one in here." A medic rushed over to him and gingerly examined his shoulder. "You should be fine, sir. Looks like a flesh wound. The bullet dug a gash across your shoulder. I don't think it broke the collarbone or did any serious damage."

"Then help me to my feet and get out of my way!" demanded the colonel.

"Just a minute. I have to disinfect the wound and put on some bandages," said the medic.

"Well, then you'll have to do it as we walk!" Solsteniski got to his feet and walked out into the hallway. The building was a mess – wires hanging from the ceiling, cement and cinderblocks littering the once clean tile floor, the obvious result of the hand-grenades.

"Does the whole building look like this?" the colonel asked.

"No, sir. The upper levels were barely damaged at all."

"Good, find whoever is in charge of your party and have them take me upstairs. Then find me a phone or a radio. I have to report what's happened here." The medic found the captain in charge of the troops who'd retaken the Fine Arts Center.

"Colonel, I've had my men reconnect a telephone line to the building. It's not a secure line but it's all we can do for now. We should be able to resupply you with secure radios by this time tomorrow," reported the captain.

"Very well. Am I the only survivor?"

"You were the only one in the building. However, a few of your men have reported in since we arrived. They were on errands when the attack occurred and were spared."

"Have them report to me at once!" he demanded.

JAKE'S APC ROLLED up to the waiting *Globemaster* and dropped the back hatch. He followed a dozen soldiers as they scrambled out and ran up the C-17's cargo ramp. Two aircraft had already departed by the time he arrived. He'd been assured that Sarah's was the first to leave. At least she and McClintock were safe.

Jake felt a twinge of guilt as he buckled himself into his canvas seat. He'd never left the middle of a battle before, but this wasn't his fight. The Rangers were in command and he had to get back to Eritrea and see how Sarah was doing. The first rounds of Russian artillery began falling as his aircraft cleared the deck.

MAJOR WARD STOOD in the cupola of the rear M-8 as it raced to safety. The APC's had completed their pick-up of all of the troops and were well ahead of the M-8's. The Russians were now too far away for he M-8's to return fire with any accuracy. The best he could do was to place his tanks between the troop carriers and the advancing Russians.

While the Americans could no longer direct effective fire at the enemy, the Russians were not at the same disadvantage. They'd managed to get an observation helicopter airborne which was now providing amazingly accurate targeting to the heavy Russian artillery. Major Ward watched helplessly as huge mounds of earth flew skyward all around his tracks. So far, none of the tanks or APC's had been hit, but that was purely through the mercies of Lady Luck.

He thought that he'd been amazingly calm under the heavy enemy barrage. That confidence ended when he arrived at the pick up point. One of the *Globemasters* had been hit and was burning fiercely. That meant somebody wouldn't be going home and he knew who that somebody had to be. How could he order others to stay behind if he was too cowardly to do the same?

He didn't consciously determine what he was going to do. It more or less slowly became apparent that he wasn't going to surrender. A line he'd read in a book about the Spartans came into mind, "*Come home victorious carrying my shield, or in defeat dead upon my shield.*"

Major Ward called his remaining company commanders together and broke the obvious news to them. "Looks like some of us won't be making the trip home with the rest of you. I need forty volunteers willing to buy the rest some time. I'm not ordering anyone to stay behind but we all know we can't all fit onto the remaining aircraft. If some of the volunteers can fight the M-8's that would be helpful." The tank crews volunteered without hesitation as did the M119 anti-aircraft batteries.

Major Myers circled overhead and came to the same conclusion as Major Ward. He turned his *Apache* toward the enemy and made his final attack run. A convoy of trucks carrying Russian troops was closing in on the *Globemasters*. He pushed the helo's nose over and fired his remaining 20mm canon rounds. The two trucks in the lead burst into flames as the hot magnesium projectiles ruptured their fuel tanks. The third truck was instantly incinerated when it was struck by two tons of *Apache* helicopter.

There was no high ground and no naturally defensible terrain available so Major Ward decided to defend an arc of real estate a few hundred yards away behind the last aircraft. The M-8's, M119 Howitzers, and anti-aircraft batteries chose their positions as carefully as possible under the circumstances, dispersing their units to make the enemies job as difficult as possible. The anti-aircraft batteries weren't really designed for ground targets, but ordnance was ordnance. A small missile could really ruin a tank or BMP's day.

Unbeknownst to Major Ward, a small helicopter on the horizon was using enhanced optics to watch his tracks as they hastily took defensive positions. The Russian pilot called his fire team leader and reported the coordinates, waiting well out of range of the anti-aircraft batteries.

Major Ward hoped he had the courage to fight to the death. He'd run the possibility through his mind several times late at night and he thought he could do it. But the way he had pictured it just wasn't in the cards. Ward snapped out of his thoughts when the sporadic artillery fire stopped. He knew he didn't have long. At least the last *Globemaster* had lifted off!

THE RUSSIANS TOOK their time assembling their artillery batteries. They wanted to get it right. As far as the major commanding the counterattack was concerned he was in no hurry to send his troops to their deaths in a frontal assault on the Americans. He could kill them just as effectively from a distance. The enemy was in an exposed position and lightly armored. Yes, he should be able to dispatch the Americans in short order.

MAJOR WARD GRIPPED the cupola tightly as the first round impacted behind his tank. He dropped down inside the vehicle and closed the hatch. A blinding flash of heat and light burned into his eyes a fraction of a second before his flesh was torn from his body. As the last *Globemaster* flew out of sight the stranded rag tag American defenders met their deaths bravely under a merciless Russian artillery barrage.

Moscow

ALEXI YANOCHEV PACED nervously across the plush red carpet behind his ornate desk. His forehead glistened with the dewy perspiration reserved for the seriously frightened. As he desperately tried to think of a way to save his life the irony of the situation momentarily cluttered his mind.

He couldn't remember a time he'd not been plotting and scheming to sit in this very office. Now that he was here it was likely to be the cause of his death. The power that resided in this room, surrounded by czarist era furnishings and rich in Russian history, had early on captured his desires. It dawned on him that, perhaps, the focus of his lifelong ambition had been nothing more than the bait used by fate to draw him to his death.

It had all fallen apart so quickly. First, the Saudis had overcome staggering odds and repelled his invading armor. The final tank assault had failed miserably. Then the most devastating blow of all - Braxton had been discovered. At least he died with honor and refused to die at the hands of his enemies. Then, the Americans had embarrassed all of Russia by brazenly charging into Kuwait and rescuing the hostages. It looked to the world as if his troops couldn't do anything right. Worse still, many in Russia were getting the same idea.

To make matters worse, Ayatollah Rafelgemmii wasn't returning his calls. What was that all about? Was he cutting his loses and bailing out of the agreement? After his staggering loses in the attack on the Saudis perhaps he wasn't looking forward to taking on the American carrier battle groups assembling in the Straits of Hormuz. How could he blame him. Even Admiral Rybakov had refused to use his submarines to attack the carriers sitting just outside the Gulf, claiming the American defenses were impregnable. Alexi had to admit that he wasn't in a position to help the Iranians. Most of his aircraft had been destroyed.

Now, Deputy Defense Minister Sergi Valshenko was downstairs conspiring with the very leaders who earlier had been his most vocal supporters. How tragic that the smallest men with the smallest minds could seriously threaten the true intellectual giants. Petty little weasels like Valshenko always followed in the shadows of history's really great men looking for opportunities to supplant them.

Yanochev knew the risks when he undertook such a courageous and innovative course of action. Russian history was replete with stories of great men who failed and then disappeared. Russians only followed successful visionaries. They killed the rest.

The plan appeared in his mind as if dropped there from above. All was not lost. He still had one card left to play. He would show the world that he was not to be written off quite yet. But first, he must buy himself time to show the men downstairs that victory was within reach. He walked back to his chair and keyed the intercom, "Colonel, tell Comrade Valshenko and his friends I will join them shortly in the reception room." As Yanochev's personal attaché scurried off to do his bidding, Alexi called the commander of his personal security force.

"General, I have Minister Valshenko and a number of his cohorts in the main reception room. Arrest them. Take them someplace comfortable and treat them with respect until I tell you differently. Make sure no one sees them leaving the building."

Alexi knew that he couldn't hold them for very long. Those loyal to them would soon have him assassinated and free their friends, but this would buy him a day or two. A few days were all he would need to take decisive action and show everyone he was still able to deliver what he had promised.

THE ENLISTED *SPETSNAZ* in charge of the security detail carefully shook Colonel Solsteniski out of his death-like sleep. "Colonel, wake up, sir. You have an important telephone call from Moscow. It is President Yanochev himself!"

Colonel Solsteniski had fallen asleep in his chair after hours of searching through the lower level to assess the damage. He ran down the short hallway with the soldier who'd awakened him and picked up the handset of the one working telephone in the building.

Solsteniski had never seen Alexi Yanochev in person much less personally spoken with him. He'd met General Masovich several times and even eaten dinner with him, but this was much different. Two enlisted men stood wide-eyed looking at the telephone as if it would bite them. "Get out!" Solsteniski ordered.

The colonel put the phone to his ear and tried to sound as if he had been awake and dutifully serving his country. "Yes, sir. Colonel Solsteniski here."

"Colonel, we don't have time for small talk. I have a mission for you of the utmost importance. It will be a chance for you to redeem yourself."

Yanochev's words cut him to the heart. So, the President had taken a personal interest in his failure to guard the hostages. And what was this offer of redemption? "I am at your service. What can I do for you?" asked Colonel Solsteniski as contritely as possible.

"I am going to give you the short version of your mission. Our forces are on the verge of defeat at the hands of the Saudis. The Americans are very close to entering the war with enough forces to cause the total collapse of our initiative. If that happens we are both dead men. Do you understand what I am saying?" asked Yanochev.

"Yes sir. What is it you'd like for me to do?"

"I'm ordering a military transport to pick you up tonight at the Kuwaiti airport and fly you to Ethiopia. Once there, you will program the SS-20's to attack the following targets: Two of the missiles will destroy the Saudi forces at Ali Bakr waddi. One missile each will be assigned to Riyadh, Dhahran, and King Khalid Military Center. The majority of the others will destroy targets in Israel. That should make our Iranian friends happy and help them to be patient until I can supply them with missiles to replace the ones we use. One missile will be reserved for an airburst over the American carrier fleet near the Straits of Hormuz. The targeting data will be awaiting you upon your arrival in Ethiopia. Do you think you can handle this mission competently?"

"Yes, sir; I will not fail!"

The next call Yanochev made was to the commander of his strategic missile forces. "General Blyuker, things are going poorly in the Arabian Campaign. The Americans are preparing to intervene and I want to send a message that will make them reconsider. Order our nuclear forces to their highest state of readiness. I promised I'd use our nuclear weapons if anyone tried to interfere with our plans and I want to give the Americans reason to believe I'm serious."

"But sir, won't the Americans consider your moves as provocative? We could cause them to retaliate with a pre-emptive nuclear attack of their own. I urge you to reconsider," said General Blyuker.

"Nonsense! The Americans wouldn't dare launch an attack. We've done the same thing hundreds of times in the past and they did nothing but complain."

"Yes, sir, but this time is different. We're in the middle of a conflict that we are in jeopardy of losing. They'll likely confuse what we're doing. They'll think we are preparing to use our missiles to win a victory that we couldn't achieve through conventional means," said Blyuker.

"General, I don't have time to argue foreign policy with you. Order our nuclear forces to prepare to attack! The Americans must know that I'm ready to strike if necessary," said Yanochev.

TWO BLOCKS FROM the Fine Arts Center a teenage boy held his hands tightly over his earphones. The boy's father was a wealthy first cousin of the royal family who had a position in the upper levels of the country's oil ministry. Twenty years earlier, the boy's father had been negotiating a military sale of petroleum with the Soviets in Moscow where he met and married a beautiful Russian woman. The young woman jumped at the chance to leave the harsh conditions of Russia and live in a palatial home complete with servants and swimming pool. But she soon found that all the money in the world couldn't help fill the void she created when she left her homeland. To preserve a little bit of her culture she taught all of her children her native tongue. The boy's command of the Russian language was what had finally convinced the Kuwaiti underground to risk allowing him to help.

He'd been listening to the wiretap on the Fine Art Center's telephones every night since the Russians had overrun his country. None of the older men wanted to listen to the Russians in the middle of the night. After all, nothing ever happened this late. That's why they'd put him on the headset. He was to wake somebody up if something important happened.

He sat alone behind the thin curtain in the little coffee shop trying to stay awake as he listened to nothing but routine dribble. But tonight was different. He felt his pulse rising as the words burned into his ears. All of the hours he'd spent listening to static now seemed worthwhile. The older men would be glad they'd let him be part of the Kuwaiti underground resistance.

JAKE AWOKE WITH a start and realized an Air Force sergeant was shaking him. "Wake up, sir; we're about to land."

It took a few moments for Jake to clear his head. The last thing he remembered was getting onboard the C-17, taking off, and artillery shells exploding all around the aircraft. Then, a few minutes later when he knew they were safe, he remembered leaning against the bulkhead and looking around the interior of the aircraft. Sitting in the open cargo bay, the engine noise made it impossible to hear anybody talking without being plugged into the intercom, which he wasn't. So, like everybody else around him he was left to his thoughts in the dim red interior lighting.

He didn't remember going to sleep but it must've happened. He felt the aircraft descending rapidly and saw everyone else sitting up straight getting ready for landing. When the fog of sleep cleared his first thought was that he had to find Sarah!

The aircrew opened the passenger door and rigged the ladder. Jake was the first man off of the airplane. He ran across the tarmac to the makeshift American Flight Operations Center and burst through the double doors. He stopped the first officer he saw and asked, "Where did they take Secretary McClintock and Commander Crawford?"

"I'm really not sure. I suppose they're in the visitors lounge down the hall. We've turned that into a temporary hospital. Those who's injuries aren't life threatening are in there. The more serious cases are already loaded on a Medevac flight which takes off in fifteen minutes. I'm really not up on how bad either of the VIP's were injured. They could be either place."

Jake ran back out the double doors and raced to the visitor's lounge. Sarah was on a cot near the back wall. McClintock wasn't in the room. He'd have to find him later. Right now all he could think about was Sarah.

"Sarah!" Jake called softly as he approached her bed.

Her head turned in his direction and the brightest green eyes he'd ever seen opened. More accurately, one eye opened. The other was swollen shut — an ugly black and blue bruise covering the right side of her face.

"Jake!" she sobbed as she sat up and embraced him. Jake felt the tangled IV lines against his shoulder as she hugged him and cried. A cold rage began to burn deep inside, but that would have to wait. First he'd make sure Sarah was OK then he'd find a way to even the score with the person responsible for hurting her.

"Are you OK? You had me so worried," blurted Jake.

"I'll be fine. The doctors say I'm dehydrated. We had very little to eat or drink the whole time."

"Did they hurt you?"

"Let's not talk about that right now. I just want to hold you!" Sarah said as she hugged him tightly and wept softly against his shoulder.

Jake had all the answer he needed. The torn dress and the cuts and bruises on her face told it all. His imagination filled in the blanks. Somebody was going to pay for hurting her.

After a few minutes Sarah pulled away and looked Jake in the eyes. "I thought it was all over for me," she said. "I was so scared. That first night was awful. The Russian colonel who kidnapped me from the party came for me. He tore off my dress and forced himself on me. He tried to rape me Jake! Ambassador McClintock was chained a few feet away and kicked him in the face. That took his mind off of me, but the colonel gave the ambassador an awful beating. He was so brave."

"Shhhh. Don't try to talk." Jake sat and held her until she fell asleep thirty minutes later. "The sedatives must be doing their job," thought Jake. He left the room and went out into the hall. He leaned against the wall and let out a deep breath and tried to get himself together. When Jake closed his eyes the Russian colonel's face appeared in his mind's eye.

Sarah had suffered so much. He'd let her down - allowed something bad to happen to her while she was under his protection. Jake was whipping himself for letting her down when he heard a familiar voice emanating from the room straight across from him. It was Theodore McClintock.

Jake opened the door and found Ambassador McClintock talking with General Bull Phillips. The ambassador informed Jake that General Philips had flown to Eritrea to meet with him. McClintock looked much better now than he did a few hours earlier. Obviously, he hadn't been injured all that badly. "Jake, thank God you're alright. It seems I owe my life to you, again. Without your quick work when we were abducted nobody would've known where we were," said McClintock.

"No, I want to thank you. Sarah told me how you tried to look out for her while you were being held hostage. Are you hurt?"

"Got a few broken ribs, but I'll be fine. I'm more worried about Sarah than myself. How is she doing?" asked a visibly concerned McClintock.

"Physically, I think she's going to be OK. I'm not a shrink, so I'm not really sure about what this whole ordeal will do to her head," said Jake.

"Sarah's a strong woman, Jake. She'll bounce back, I'm sure."

"I hope you're right. Look, I want you to know I'll never forget what you did to help her when that Russian attacked her," said Jake.

McClintock was silent for a few moments as the two men stood and stared at each other, overwhelmed and deeply moved by each other's courage and sacrifice. "Jake, I think you have a right to know what the general just told me." Turning to Phillips, he said, "General, explain the latest developments to Commander Gregory."

"Sure, I guess it's OK to tell him. While you were airborne we got a report from the Kuwaiti underground that Yanochev is planning to use nukes against several targets – one of them is our battle group in the Straits of Hormuz. The other targets are in Saudi Arabia and Israel."

"How'd they find all this out?" asked Jake.

"Seems the Kuwaitis had a wiretap on the Fine Arts Center. Yanochev called a colonel there and told him to fly to Ethiopia and prepare the missiles for launch. Our only problem is that we don't know where in Ethiopia," said General Phillips.

"Maybe these will help," Jake said, pulling the forgotten papers out of his shirt.

"What are those?" asked McClintock.

"Some papers I found on the floor in the Arts Center," said Jake. He quickly scanned the papers and let out a soft whistle between his teeth. "Ambassador, you're never gonna believe this. The Iranians have converted the old American Consulate into a missile facility. The Russians are training them how to use the missiles. Seems they have twenty SS-20's, and your colonel, a guy named Solsteniski, is the man in charge of the technical advisors."

The White House

PRESIDENT MASSEY LISTENED intently as each member of the Carpenter cabinet briefed him on the hottest topics concerning their departments. President Braxton hadn't had time to appoint replacements for any of them, so they were now briefing their third president in four weeks. He'd have to make a lot of changes later and place people from his team on the Cabinet, but that could wait. The Secretary of Energy was giving his spiel about the need for more solar power when a serious looking Navy Captain entered the room and knelt beside the Secretary of Defense and whispered something in his ear.

"Mr. President, I've just been informed that Russia has gone on nuclear alert. That means they could launch their missiles without further warning!" said Secretary Hartman. "We need to meet with the National Security Team ASAP!"

The White House Situation Room

"MR. PRESIDENT, OUR nation is in grave danger," declared Franklin Samuelson, the National Security Advisor.

"I concur," said General Joseph Gore, the Chairman of the Joint Chiefs of Staff. "This latest move with their nukes makes me really nervous. If we hadn't intercepted the message from Yanochev about nuking the regional targets with their SS-20's in Ethiopia, I wouldn't be so concerned. But now that they've made the decision to cross the nuclear threshold I believe it's reasonable to assume they may escalate the conflict and use their ICBM's against us."

"What's the CIA read of the situation?" President Massey asked Geoffrey Travis, the acting DCI.

"I'm afraid we concur with Defense and NSA. Yanochev's psychological profile indicates that he'll do anything to hold onto power. Our interpretation of the overhead intelligence and the increased communications between their strategic rocket forces and the Kremlin leaves us little choice but to conclude that they're serious about attacking," said Travis.

"OK, where's that leave us? What're our options? Anybody?" asked the President.

The Situation Room was quiet for several moments as the people in the room stared at the tabletop considering the consequences of the only option available.

Finally, the President answered his own question. "People, I don't think we have any choice but to strike first. Anyone disagree?"

One by one everyone nodded agreement. "OK then, what's the plan?" the President asked.

The JCS Chairman cleared his throat, and said, "Well, sir, the way I see it we have to make a choice. We can launch an overwhelming strike with our nuclear triad. If we choose that option, we guarantee a nuclear response from Russia. They'll detect our missiles and launch a counterstrike. The strong point of this option is that we'll limit their response to one salvo.

"Our second choice is to covertly launch our B-2's, attempt an undetected penetration of the Russian coastline and hit their command and control centers before they have a chance to order the attack. We'd follow up immediately with an ICBM attack on their missile silos."

"Mr. President, I may be out of my element on this one, but I think there may be one more option we haven't considered," offered Margaret Clark, the Secretary of State.

"I'm all ears, Margaret. Please, go on," said the President.

"It's my understanding that the thing that's driving us to the nuclear option is the Russian intention to use their SS-20's in Ethiopia. If we remove that threat, we remove any advantage nuclear weapons play in the Arabian Campaign," Clark said.

"How do you figure that?" asked the Secretary of Defense.

"Well, it's simple really, Yanochev's whole reason for crossing the nuclear threshold is to win the victory in Saudi Arabia. If we deny him that outcome he'll have no reason to risk the destruction of his whole country. He's got to know he can't win an all-out nuclear war!" Clark insisted.

"She may have a point, Mr. President," offered the JCS Chairman. "Perhaps we could scale back our first strike and only go after the nukes in Ethiopia. Since that SEAL provided us with the location of the missiles we may have another option. If we destroy the SS-20's before Yanochev uses them we can wait and see what the Russians do. We can order our ballistic submarines to conduct the first ICBM strike if it comes to that. That'll reduce the Russian's response time and limit their second strike capability."

"Thank you for your support, General, but I think I have a way to remove Russia's nuclear threat without having to resort to using nukes ourselves," said Clark.

"How's that?" asked the President.

"Well, I've met the SEAL that provided us with the location of the missiles. If you'll remember, he's been to the consulate before. He's the guy who rescued Ambassador McClintock from the rebels. General Gore, couldn't you send him back into Ethiopia and have him destroy the missiles?" asked Clark

"Madame Secretary, I don't think you know what you're asking. In the first place, we don't have enough Special Forces in the area to pull off a mission like this. Secondly, if we had a team in place, there wouldn't be anytime to rehearse. Thirdly, even if we had the people and the time to rehearse the mission, the odds against success would be astronomical. I don't think it's plausible," said General Gore.

"Wait a minute, General," said the President. "She may be on to something. I'm willing to give anything a shot that'll keep us from resorting to nukes. Besides, I've met this guy she's talking about. He might be able to pull it off single handedly. He knows the lay of the land and he's one tough hombre."

"Mr. President," interrupted Secretary of Defense Roger Hartley, "if we send in a SEAL, the best he'd be able to do is disable the missiles. Then the Ethiopians would have a large amount of fissionable material and maybe even enough of the missiles would survive to reverse engineer missiles and warheads of their own."

"The SECDEF has a point, sir," said General Gore. "If the SS-20's aren't incinerated completely we risk adding another country to the list of nuclear capable nations. However, there is one outside chance. If we can generate a low yield nuclear explosion when we destroy them that would solve all our problems."

"Is that possible?" asked the President.

"I figure we have about a fifty-fifty chance if the explosives are placed on the missile warheads," said General Gore.

"What happens if the explosion doesn't result in a nuclear yield?" asked Massey.

"I guess we do it the old fashioned way," said Gore. "We'll have the B-2's inbound. If the explosives don't produce a nuclear explosion we'll drop a tactical nuke and incinerate half the city."

"But what about Commander Gregory? If he destroys the missiles without setting off a nuclear explosion how will he get out before you bomb the consulate?" asked Secretary Clark.

"He won't, ma'am," said General Gore.

After several seconds of silence, the President looked around the table and said, "OK, I like it! Let's go with Margaret's plan. General, make the calls!" ordered Massey.

Asmara, Eritrea

FOUR HOURS LATER Jake was sitting by Sarah's bed gently holding her hand while she slept. A somber General Phillips entered the room. "Jake, can I speak to you outside for a moment?"

The two men walked outside and stood on the sidewalk near the busy street that was bustling with military traffic. "Jake, I just received orders for us. Seems the President is really worried about the nukes in Ethiopia. He's ordered a preemptive nuclear strike."

"Isn't that a bit drastic? There's got to be some other way to take them out without risking a nuclear war with Russia."

"That's where you come in. The Joint Chiefs have convinced him to hold off the attack until midnight tomorrow night, provided we can get a team into Ethiopia and destroy the nukes. He's proceeding with the strike plans and the bombers will take off as scheduled. They will not be cancelled unless they receive confirmation the SS-20's have been destroyed."

"So, do you have a team ready to go?" asked Jake.

"Unfortunately, no. We don't have enough time to get the people here and rehearse the mission," General Philips said.

"So then what do you want from me?" asked Jake.

"Secretary McClintock told me you know your way around the old

American Consulate pretty well. You made it in once so there's a good chance you could make it in again."

"You don't mean alone, do you?" Jake said.

"I don't see any other way. We don't have time to get you any help," said Phillips. "Look Jake, I wouldn't be asking you if I could think of any other way. I agree with you, a preemptive nuclear strike poses too great a risk of starting a full-blown nuclear exchange between our two countries."

"OK. What else aren't you telling me?"

General Phillips grinned, "You're as smart as they told me. OK, here's more bad news. The President would only agree to wait if we could assure him the nuclear warheads would be completely destroyed."

"What's that supposed to mean?"

"He means they have to be destroyed by a nuclear explosion. We can't allow nuclear technology to fall into Iranian or Ethiopian hands. If we simply blow up the rockets the warheads can be reused or reverse engineered."

"Are you asking me to carry in a nuclear warhead to do the job?" asked an incredulous Jake.

"No, here's the plan..."

29

EXHAUSTION RACKED JAKE'S superbly conditioned body as he struggled against the pounding surf to pull his heavy rucksack ashore. The USS *Salt Lake City* had dropped him offshore an hour ago and the mile and a half swim had been anything but routine. The drag of the explosives and weapons he had in the bag made swimming in the heavy swells nearly impossible. Jake's success was entirely the result of his uncommon upper body strength and exceptional skill in the water. Most of the men on his SEAL team would've drowned on this mission.

Blackness shrouded the beach as a high cloud cover obscured the stars and lonely crescent moon. Jake dragged his gear clear of the waterline and collapsed in the moist sand. He lay exposed on the cold windswept beach for several moments desperately trying to marshal enough strength to move. His arms and legs were screaming in pain and refusing to obey his commands, rebelling only after having been pushed by Jake's iron will to keep working long after they should have failed him.

A T LAST, HIS limbs responded long enough to carry him over the sand berm and into a tiny patch of scrub bushes. Fatigue rushed over him once again like a black wave and carried him into oblivion. Jake lay beneath the protective shadows and branches of the scrub bushes and slept the sleep of the dead. The sun was signaling it's imminent arrival by painting the morning horizon with a faint splash of orange when Jake's eyes finally opened.

His thoughts were still foggy from the previous night's grueling ordeal as he cautiously raised his head and took his first look at his surroundings. Failing to detect any immediate threat to his safety, he reached into the front pocket of his rucksack and pulled out an energy bar. Unwrapping his breakfast with his teeth and one hand Jake chewed the specially formulated concoction with relish. He could feel strength pulsing back into his muscles as he leisurely got to his hands and knees and opened his bag.

Jake quickly checked the action of his *Pausa* and slung it over his shoulder, inspected his explosives, and resealed the bag. He didn't change out of his wet suit even though he had a dry uniform packed with his gear. He couldn't imagine doing what he was about to do without the comforting protection of the thick neoprene between him and his surroundings.

The task completed, he gathered his gear and set out for his next objective with practiced silence. There was no need to consult a map for he had long ago memorized the landmarks leading to his target. With one minor difference he would follow the same path to the American Consulate that he had on his first trip to Ethiopia. Whereas before, he was to observe the consulate from outside the compound, on this mission he'd enter the recently rebuilt facility, blow up the nuclear missiles, and egress the vicinity undetected. All in a day's work. At least that was the plan.

Jake found what he was looking for after only thirty minutes. The manhole cover was partially obscured by sand and weeds, but it was right where he remembered. He pried the lid off and jerked back in disgust as the fumes from the cities decrepit sewage system assaulted his nostrils. This was the part of the mission that he dreaded the most.

The sewage system's design was relatively simple, but it had served the residents well enough until the pumping stations had been destroyed during the revolution. Seawater had been pumped through a maze of thirty-six inch cement pipes to carry the waste into the ocean. The wealthier residents and businesses fortunate enough to have indoor plumbing were connected to the larger pipe via smaller feeder lines. The old government hadn't had the resources to make the necessary repairs before they were toppled and the new government wasn't overly concerned about the creature comforts of the citizenry.

Jake didn't really care about the politics of the issue. He was just glad that the system was no longer operational and would lead him to his destination undetected. This was how he had approached the consulate previously and it was still the only way he could think of to do it on this trip. This time however, he would exit the sewer from a manhole in the driveway behind what was once the ambassador's residence.

Well, there was no use putting off the inevitable. Jake pulled his infrared goggles out of his rucksack, dropped his gear into the sewer and wiggled himself into the cramped pipe. After he pulled the heavy manhole cover back into place he adjusted the straps on his goggles, donned a respirator to protect him from the deadly methane gas fumes, and began the long journey to the consulate, pulling his bag behind him.

The respirator protected him from the repulsive odor of the human waste encrusting the walls of the pipe but there was no way to avoid crawling through the slimy, partially dried mess that was still standing inches thick in the bottom of the pipe. By the time he reached his destination he would be covered in the foul smelling slime. This was a major concern for more reasons than personal hygiene. It would be impossible to remain covert once he exited the sewer if his smell alerted people to his presence.

Therefore, he'd brought along a towel and a number of large, odorless chemical towelettes designed to neutralize the odor and dissolve any grime sticking to his face and hands. He'd leave his soiled wet suit in the sewer and change into his black tactical suit. The system had served him well before and there was no reason to think it wouldn't work equally well again.

Jake consulted his watch. Things were proceeding according to schedule. He still had several hours of daylight remaining before it would be safe to climb out of his hiding place in the sewer and it would take him less than an hour to make it to the consulate. Plenty of time. He had every turn and fork in the piping system memorized. If he happened to get confused, he had scraped marks in the walls of the pipes on his last trip that would help him find his way.

He had another hour of work and then he'd rest beneath the manhole cover until dark and then complete his mission. Jake was relatively sure he could destroy the missiles and avert a nuclear war with Russia. What he was unclear about were his chances of getting out of the compound alive. Well, it wouldn't help matters to dwell on things he couldn't change. He crawled forward toward his objective.

Onward he crawled. Jake scanned the dim red world as viewed through his infrared goggles and felt he was safe from harm. The way he figured it since he was several feet below the city and hidden from view there was little that could go wrong to prevent him from reaching his objective. He was mistaken.

In the distance he heard a faint noise. The sound grew louder and reminded Jake of something akin to a large flock of swallows chirping as they darted across the sky. Fear welled up inside of him as the noise increased to a near deafening scream of confused squealing. He tried to escape the onrushing sound but his rucksack jammed in the narrow pipe and prevented him from backing up. A few feet ahead there was a fork in the pipe. Perhaps he could make it to the fork and escape whatever was rushing toward him generating the horrific din.

They rounded the bend in the pipe in a whirling, tangled frenzy. Hundreds of rats descended upon Jake in a shrieking rampage. They were everywhere. Jake swatted at them to no avail. The confined space in the pipe gave him no room to strike them with any power. The rats engulfed him. He could feel them on every part of his body. Overcome with panic, a primal scream erupted out of Jake's mouth. There was nothing he could do but cover his head and hope for the best.

It ended as quickly as it had started. The main body of rats, finding the pipe that Jake occupied blocked, took the other fork and disappeared into the darkness. In the melee with the rats, Jake lost his infrared goggles and was now surrounded by thick darkness. With his heart racing as he tried to regain his composure he groped with both hands like a blind man until he found where they had fallen.

Thankfully, none of his equipment was damaged. His goggles and respirator were still in good shape and the rucksack was intact. Jake looked at his hands and found they were covered with scratches from the rat claws. His face felt as if must be in the same shape. Not good. With all the bacteria generated by what he was crawling through he was sure he was doomed to die of some terrible infection or disease. He found a few packets of Betadine in his first aid kit and cleaned himself the best that he could. He remembered what his instructors at BUD's had told him, "Gregory, nobody said it was going to be easy. The only easy day was yesterday!"

He started crawling forward. He would finish the mission and destroy the nuclear missiles. At least his death would count for something. He would play the cards he was dealt and, who knows, maybe even live to tell about it.

This was it. His mini GPS confirmed he was inside the consulate walls. Jake climbed slowly up the ladder leading to the manhole behind the ruins of the ambassador's residence and pressed his ear to the holes in the cover. He could hear a faint conversation in Russian. Good! His intelligence had been correct. The Russians were indeed on site and in charge of the Iranians assigned to guard the missiles.

JAKE CLIMBED BACK down the ladder and began the task of cleaning the slime off of his body. When he was sure he was clean, he changed into a skintight black uniform, donned a flak vest, and snapped his combat webbing over the vest.

Carefully, he began loading the various pockets and snap rings with equipment and weapons. Hand grenades, detonator timer, combat knife, and spare clips for his 9mm Beretta and Uzi; all of these were secured into their designated positions. Jake memorized where they were all located and could find each item instinctively.

But the most important piece of equipment he carried was the tiny satellite beacon that would signal mission accomplished. It was no larger than a deck of playing cards, yet, after midnight tonight it was the only thing that could stop a pre-emptive nuclear strike by President Massey against the Russians, Iranians, and the soil upon which he was standing. If a satellite miles above the earth did not receive a coded message from the beacon he now held gingerly in his hands the President would have no choice but to guarantee the Russians couldn't launch their missiles by dropping nuclear bombs on the compound. He placed the beacon in a thigh pocket on his right leg.

Lastly, he picked up his trusty .50 caliber sniper rifle and lovingly began cleaning the weapon. This was the same rifle he'd used to kill the N.I.P.P.L.E. soldiers attacking the American Consulate on his first trip to Ethiopia. The weapon was the one thing he knew he could count upon to work. He trusted it to do the job. After he was satisfied the *Pausa* was clean and well oiled he attached a huge infrared scope.

Jake ran down a mental checklist of what he'd need for tonight's mission. Everything was ready. There were several hours to kill before it got dark and he knew he'd need his strength. Perhaps he could get a few hours sleep without being awakened by "the dream." He leaned back against the ladder at the bottom of the shaft and quickly fell asleep.

HUNDREDS OF MILES away on the secluded island of Diego Garcia the last two B-2 bombers lifted off. Like the others that had launched a few hours earlier, they were each loaded with two ten-kiloton thermonuclear bombs. There were two flights of two aircraft each. Their mission was to conduct a coordinated time-on-top nuclear strike against the former American Consulate in Ethiopia. The Joint Chiefs of Staff assured the President that the bombers would have little trouble penetrating Ethiopia's air defenses. The President knew enough about their technology to know that they had no chance of detecting the sophisticated front line stealth bombers of America's nuclear strike force.

The world would be aghast that the United States used nuclear weapons first. America had stated hundreds of times that they'd never do such an unthinkable thing. Just a few short days before President Massey would've agreed. Now, he was convinced that was the only prudent course of action. He only hoped that others would understand his reasoning when he made everything he knew public. All he could do now was pray that the SEAL in Ethiopia would be successful. If not, he was going to have a hard time sleeping knowing that he'd killed a courageous American soldier along with thousands of other innocents. There was no other way.

J AKE'S WATCH VIBRATED against his wrist at 2215 hours rousing
him out of his haunting nightmare. It was the same dream every night.
He was standing on the roof of the armory in the American Consulate.
An Ethiopian soldier was raising his rifle and squeezing the trigger.
Bullets erupted from the soldier's barrel in a blinding flash and tore into
Jake's flesh. Strangely, he could see the bullets leaving the gun barrel and
coming at him. He was helpless before the onrushing emissaries of death
and simply stood frozen in place as they penetrated his body. The surreal
scene was repeated over and over.

Panic welled up within him as he fought his way out of the grasp of
the region that holds people hostage between sleep and being fully
awake. As always, the shakes began. Jake tried to drive the image out of
his mind as he sat up with a start. Try as he may to focus upon the
mission and what he needed to do next, the dark foreboding of
impending death clung to his consciousness like a wet towel over the face
of a sleeping man.

Jake wasn't afraid of dying in the dream. It was more like he was
dying for nothing. Sacrificing his life for something that really didn't
matter. That was it! After months of suffering through the stupid dream
he finally understood what it meant!

A few minutes later the tremors subsided. Jake swept the sweat off of
his face and through sheer determination forced his mind into
submission. "No time to psychoanalyze myself." He'd already tried that
and it didn't do anything to stop "the dream."

He slung his gear and weapons over his shoulder and climbed to the
top of the ladder. Stopping briefly, he pressed his ear to the manhole
cover. Satisfied that all was clear he used his head and right shoulder to
heave the heavy manhole cover out of the way. Sand rained down upon
him as the cover gave way. Jake slid it to one side and scanned the
darkness for any sign of movement. He was out of the hole and crouched
in the darkness beside the ruins of the consulate in a flash.

Satellite imagery indicated that the SS-20 missiles were being stored in a series of covered bunkers less than a hundred yards from where he was hiding. The missile bunkers were three sided with reinforced concrete and steel roofs. Arranged in a semi-circle, they were constructed not only to protect the missiles from air attack, but also to make it possible to drive the missile launchers to their pre-surveyed launch sites, elevate the launch rails, and fire the missiles in as little time as possible.

The Pentagon had drawn the arcs indicating the effective range of the SS-20's and what they found wasn't good news. They could strike any target in Africa, the Middle East, or southern Europe. Yanochev's threat was not to be taken lightly. The missiles had to be destroyed and Jake fully understood the stakes if he failed.

JAKE MADE A dash for the front corner of the consulate and threw himself on the ground and peered carefully around the corner of the building. He scanned the complex with his binoculars and found that the missile bunkers were well guarded and lit up like a night game at Dodger Stadium. There were six men. Two Russian soldiers were in a machine gun equipped all terrain vehicle, obviously supervising two teams of roving sentries.

Jake would have no room for error if he were to take out the sentries, place explosives on the missile warheads, make his escape, and get back to the beach before the explosives created a low yield nuclear detonation of the SS-20 missiles. The meteorologists had convinced him to stay in hiding until 2215 local time because a high cloud cover was forecast to obscure the moon by that time. Total darkness was critical to the success of his plan. The downside to waiting for the skies to darken was that it severely limited the amount of time he had to execute his mission. He had to do it all in the two hours before midnight, after which time the bombers would make their attack.

He could almost feel the B-2's approaching. Sure, he had a little time rolled into the timetable just in case there was a minor delay, but that didn't do much to console him. He wanted get as far away from the compound as he could as quickly as possible. He trusted the Air Force pilots, but the thought of a plane carrying a nuclear bomb with orders to drop it where he was standing if they didn't receive a certain signal, didn't make him feel very safe. Lots of things could go wrong. Perhaps the beacon wouldn't work right.

What made him feel more exposed was having to depend upon an unknown American sympathizer to have a vehicle waiting for him a block away. Especially since his get-away car wasn't going to wait past the designated time thirty minutes from now. Oh well, no plan was without risk.

"OK, buddy, it's now or never," Jake told himself. He stood up, took aim at the man manning the machine gun in the back of the technical vehicle, and began increasing pressure on the trigger of the *Pausa*.

SUDDENLY, THE COMPOUND broke into pandemonium. Russian troops came pouring out of the barracks herding a large group of Iranian soldiers before them. Jake shouldered his weapon and scanned the compound. The Russians were rounding up all of the Iranian soldiers and the Iranians weren't very pleased about it. Jake heard a shot and saw an Iranian fall to the ground clutching his chest. He must've been moving too slow. Several Russian soldiers surrounded the Iranians and guarded them with machine guns.

Now that the Russians had the majority of the Iranians sitting in a big gaggle in the middle of the compound they began searching the place building by building looking for anyone they might have missed.

Jake turned on his heel and ran back to the manhole he'd just climbed out of. This wasn't good! He had to think. There was no way he could blow up the nukes with all those Russians running around with guns.

COLONEL SOLSTENISKI STRODE into the middle of the compound with his second in command at his heels. "Major, as soon as we have all of the Iranians under control come and get me. I'll be in my quarters."

"Yes, sir; I already have the technicians programming the missiles with the new targets. We should be ready to launch in fifty minutes," said the Russian major.

"Very well. I want to check the readouts to ensure there are no mistakes," said Solsteniski.

JAKE STOOD ON the ladder with his ear pressed to the manhole. He'd already wasted close to an hour. If he was going to live to see tomorrow he had to get moving. The smart thing for him to do would be to retreat through the sewer and let the B-2's take out the target. But he couldn't do that. He'd come to prevent a nuclear war and he had to try and see it through.

Jake climbed out of the manhole and ran back to the corner of the consulate he'd used to scan the compound almost an hour earlier. Things were relatively calm. The Iranians were sleeping on the ground with a few Russian guards watching over them. The technical vehicle was covering the prisoners with a machine gun. Jake could see a large group of Russians near where the missiles were staged.

Somewhere off the coast of Ethiopia

"FIFTEEN MINUTES TO bomb release point. Come right to new heading three four two degrees. Next waypoint, three minutes," intoned the Weapons Systems Officer (WSO). He pressed a button on his communication console sending an updated position report to an overhead satellite which was instantaneously relayed to the Strategic Air

Command's headquarters. The B-2's updated position appeared on the large screen display in the White House Situation Room seconds later.

"Beginning weapon arming checklist..." The WSO began reading the step by step process from the laminated checklist on his kneeboard. Each crewman responded with "Check" when they completed their assignment.

The old American Consulate, Ethiopia

DASHING FROM ONE shadow to the next, Jake made his way to the spot he'd memorized from photographs he'd been shown aboard the USS *Salt Lake City*. The electrical transformer was hidden behind an overgrown shrub along the back wall of the compound. It supplied all the electrical power for the compound. There was also an emergency generator in a small shed thirty yards away that fed critical lighting circuits throughout the complex. Besides this, the only other threats to Jake's mission were two gas powered light carts in a fenced in area serving as the motor pool.

Jake planted C-4 with timers on both the transformer and the shed housing the generator. He didn't waste time trying to gain access to the shed, he was relying upon the C-4 to take out the shed and the generator in one fell swoop. The timers were set to detonate the explosives in three minutes.

Jake took cover behind a parked truck and waited for the show to start. He energized the infrared scope on his *Pauser* .50 caliber rifle and counted down the seconds. The luminescent dial on his ancient dive watch inched slowly toward the mark. KABOOOM! The shock waves were still rolling past him as he rolled to his right, steadied the rifle on its bipod, and took aim at the Russians in the ATV.

CRACK! CRACK! Two unfortunate soldiers were propelled backwards out of the open cab by the force of the large caliber projectiles. Jake swung his scope to where he'd last seen the other sentries. His rifle bucked twice more in a well-practiced killing rhythm. Without waiting to see the effect of his shots he searched for the last two targets. They were still crouching where they had taken cover when the explosions rocked them off their feet. Both were hit center chest and never knew what killed them.

The Iranians heard the explosions and awoke with a start. They didn't wait for the Russians to regain control of their prisoners. They scattered in all directions, hidden from their captors by the total darkness.

Jake was up and running before the sound of his last shot faded. Guided by his infared goggles he ran straight toward the now darkened missile bunkers. Jumping across the dead guards on his way he pulled the explosives from his combat rigging and activated the timers as he ran. He slapped the C-4 on the warheads at a trot, slowing only long enough to make sure the explosives were attached to the right spot and the timers were running down.

Rounding the corner to the last bunker two figures came out of nowhere and collided with him. In the pitch darkness they hadn't seen him, and they in turn had been hidden from Jake's view by his goggles' limited field of vision. Jake was knocked to the ground and winded, his goggles knocked askew. Gasping to regain his breath he forced himself to his feet and pulled his goggles back into place. Instinct took over as his left hand pulled his Beretta out of the waist holster. He fired two shots across his waist into the prone, writhing bodies of the two figures, striking them both in the middle of the back. They stopped moving.

Jake reached the last bunker and attached the explosives right on schedule. His next targets were the two gas powered light carts. The success of his plan depended upon keeping the complex in darkness until the explosives destroyed the SS-20 warheads and set off the low yield nuclear explosion.

Running toward the improvised motor pool, Jake threw a number of small, timed charges randomly behind buildings and shrubs. He hoped a couple of explosions going off every few minutes would keep the enemy confused and away from the missiles until the detonator timers ran out of numbers.

Jake tossed a hand grenade over the motor pool fence and kept on running. Seconds later, WOOOMPF! The light carts were no longer a problem. A smile spread across his face as he made his way to the back wall. All he had to do was blow a hole in the wall, run one block to the waiting vehicle, and drive to the beach and get picked up by the *Salt Lake City*.

He stooped at the base of the back wall and dropped the satchel containing the last of the explosives. He reached into the bag and pulled out the small C-4 charge. In a few short moments he would be free of the compound. Perhaps "the dream" wasn't a harbinger of death after all. Ever since the nightmares had started in the hospital so long ago Jake had been sure they were an omen prophesying his imminent death. Now, he wasn't so sure. If he could make it out of this alive he could survive anything.

"Please put down your weapon and turn around, Commander!" ordered a voice behind him. "You have been quite busy tonight. I didn't think it proper to let you leave without saying good-bye," mocked the voice.

Jake did as he was ordered and dropping his *Pausa* .50 caliber rifle and 9mm pistol. He turned slowly toward the voice with his hands in the air. The voice behind the night vision goggles belonged to Colonel Boris Solsteniski. Jake felt rage building in his chest as a picture of the colonel beating Sarah in the face raced through his head.

"I have savored thoughts of a moment such as this for a very long time. You have caused me very much embarrassment," said Solsteniski.

"You've caused me a little grief yourself, Colonel. Tell you what, I'm willing to let bygones be bygones if you are. What do you say we kiss and make up and go our separate ways?" sneered Jake.

"Sorry, that's not the way I've pictured it," said the Russian. "I see this ending with you dead and me standing here with an empty pistol in my hand."

"Can't blame me for trying. But before you shoot do me a favor, would you?"

"And what might that be, Commander Jake Gregory?"

"If it wouldn't be too much trouble, could you tell me the time?"

Colonel Solsteniski snorted contemptuously and said, "Why is the time so important to a man about to die?"

"Oh, I don't know, I just wanted to know how much longer you had to live, that's all."

"Good-bye, Commander!" snarled the colonel.

The colonel leveled his pistol at Jake's chest. As he pulled the trigger an Iranian soldier blindly running for his life crashed into the colonel's back, sending him sprawling to the ground. The bullet whizzed by Jake's ear missing him by a few inches. Jake dove on the colonel and grabbed his gun hand, applying a wicked wrist-lock. The colonel's hand involuntarily released its grip on the weapon. Jake grabbed for the pistol but the colonel delivered a hard knee to his rib cage, knocking the breath out of him momentarily. The colonel jumped to his feet and kicked the pistol away.

Jake sprang to his feet still trying to catch his breath. He managed a ragged breath and threw up his left arm, blocking a roundhouse from the colonel. Solsteniski didn't give Jake time to recover before he charged and butted him with his forehead, breaking Jake's nose. Jake reeled back, his night vision goggles knocked askew and his head spinning.

The Russian took advantage of the opening and delivered a roundhouse kick to Jake's chest, knocking him to the ground again. He kicked him again, this time in the ribs and tried to follow up by stomping his head. Jake rolled into the colonel and grabbed his legs, taking him to the ground. Jake, finding that he could see several feet in the thick darkness, threw off his goggles and pulled himself on top of the Russian.

The two commandos held onto each other tightly grappling for position, each man trying to get an advantage. They rolled on the ground several times as each man struggled to get a hand free to strike a blow, but to no avail.

As they fought for their lives, Jake snarled, "I might have let you live if you hadn't hit the girl. Say, goodbye, colonel!" Jake bit the colonel's nose with all his might, severing it in the middle. The Russian screamed and let go of Jake, reaching involuntarily for the searing pain in the middle of his face. Jake slammed his fist onto the top of the colonel's goggles, fracturing both eye sockets. The colonel sagged and relaxed.

Jake was in a blood rage, intent on killing the colonel as quickly as possible. He looked around for a weapon to finish the job and spotted the colonel's pistol lying nearby. How fitting! He'd kill the colonel with his own weapon.

He started for the gun but the colonel was on his back before he could take a step. The Russian tried to apply a naked strangle hold, but Jake grabbed his wrist before he could lock it with the other hand. He clamped onto the Russian's wrist with his left hand and twisted out from under the arm around his neck. Facing his enemy and still holding onto the colonel's wrist with his left hand, Jake threw a right into the colonel's rib cage with all of his strength. The colonel's legs buckled momentarily from the force of the blow.

Jake followed up immediately with a knee to the inside of Solsteniski's right knee, ensuring the colonel didn't regain his balance. As the Russian started to fall Jake pivoted, pulled the Russian's left arm over his shoulder in an elbow lock and pulled down forcefully. Jake heard a sickening, tearing sound, immediately preceded the colonel's agonizing scream as the bone broke.

Jake held onto the Russian's wrist, slipped under the outstretched broken limb, and twisted the arm another forty degrees as his enemy fell to the ground. He was rewarded by another agonizing scream from the colonel. "It's a little tougher when you pick a fight with a man, isn't it!" Jake shouted at Solsteniski.

The Russian tried to get to his feet. Jake waited just long enough for him to get half-erect before he kicked him viciously in the face. He followed him to the ground landing on his chest with one knee in the sternum. Jake heard another crack as the sternum gave way under his weight. The Russian was out of the fight but Jake wasn't going to let him off that easy, not after what he'd done to Sarah. Jake ripped off his opponent's night vision goggles and pummeled the Russian with his fists until Solsteniski's face was unrecognizable.

The thought of the approaching B-2's finally forced its way through Jake's anger. The colonel was unconscious and would soon be vaporized with the rest of the compound. "Time to stop beating on him and get to the beach," thought Jake.

Rising to his feet, he walked to the back wall once again. Bending over, he picked up the plastic explosive he'd dropped when Solsteniski had surprised him and stuck it to the base of the wall. He pressed the detonator into the soft block of explosives, picked up his weapons, and backed away from his work. Just as he was about to depress the remote detonator he heard the unmistakable sound of a semi-automatic pistol's slide being thrown back to manually insert a round into the chamber.

Jake closed his eyes and heard the gunshot a second later. What he didn't feel was the bullet. Opening his eyes, he saw Colonel Solsteniski lying on his back in a growing pool of blood, his night vision goggles in one hand and a pistol in the other with vacant eyes that could no longer see staring at the night sky. Jake was grappling to understand what had just happened when he heard a familiar voice from just beyond the Russian's corpse.

"Hey boss, are we going to stand here all night, or are we going to get out of here before we learn to glow in the dark?" joked Sammy.

"Sammy, you're dead. I saw the Russians blow off the top off of the building myself."

"Nah. I did that myself just before I roped off the backside. Figured I make 'em think I blew myself up or something. I had to lay low for a few days before I could contact the Kuwaiti underground. By that time, I'd missed my ride out. But listen pal, if we don't get a move on we're all going to be toast. Get my drift?"

"Enough said! Do you have a ride or are we walking to the beach?" asked Jake.

"Would I come to a party without a designated driver? Sure I have wheels. I met up with your driver and borrowed his keys. Follow me to our coach, sire!"

Jake blew a hole in the wall and they ran to their waiting Nissan sedan. Jake got behind the wheel started the engine. Sammy hopped in and had no sooner closed the door than Jake jammed it into gear and floored the accelerator. He was quickly careening through the darkened city streets at over seventy miles an hour. It was too late to worry about drawing attention to themselves. If somebody got in their way they'd just have to ram their way through and run for the beach. There was no time to be covert.

"I don't know if you've been briefed about what's about to happen, but I rigged a bunch of nukes to go off in a few minutes. We've got to get some distance between us and the nukes in a hurry," said Jake.

"Yeah, I heard. Just do your stuff and get us back to the beach. I don't relish the thought of being turned into a human marshmallow over a nuclear campfire."

"Me neither! By the way, where did you come from? I mean, how did you get here and how did you find me?" asked Jake.

"Nothing to it, really. After I got left behind when you flew off with the ambassador, I joined up with the Kuwaiti underground. They put me in touch with Colonel Talib. He helped me get in touch with Commander Lewis on our Joint Special Warfare circuit. Commander Lewis gave me the brief about what you were up to and ordered me to stay put until they could come get me. I convinced him to let me try and help. He agreed and Colonel Talib had one of his C-130's drop me a few miles down the road. I've been here for a few hours waiting for you to show up."

"Look, Sammy, I don't know how to thank you. You really saved my bacon back there."

"Don't mention it, Jake. I just hope we don't get nuclear sunburn before we leave this garden spot. How much time do we have left?"

"Five minutes." Jake didn't have to say more. They both knew they didn't have enough time to get far enough away. Even if they made the beach the force of the explosion would still kill them. The fireball from an SS-20 would incinerate everything within a mile of the blast if a full yield detonation occurred. That was unlikely, but a low yield detonation was going to take place on several of the missiles. There were too many missiles with C-4 on their warheads for some of them not to go nuclear when they exploded.

FOUR B-2 STEALTH bombers crossed the Ethiopian coastline one hundred miles to the south. They'd be on target in a matter of minutes. Their bomb release points were in ninety miles, a little over five minutes flight time. If the satellite signal from the SEAL wasn't received soon America would be dropping nuclear bombs on an enemy for the first time in over sixty years.

"Bomb release point in five minutes," reported the mission commander over the encrypted radio circuit. The radio transmission from the B-2's was being monitored at the National Military Command Center and in the White House Situation Room. The men and women assembled in both rooms waited in silence for the next transmission, which would most likely signal the start of World War III.

At exactly one minute after midnight Jake and Sammy careened onto the beach and drove the truck into the water. A blinding flash illuminated the sky behind them followed immediately by a small mushroom cloud rising into the glowing sky. They dove under water just as the remains of the nuclear shock wave passed over the beach.

Surfacing after a few seconds, they both began laughing uncontrollably. "We're alive! Hey! We didn't die!" shouted Sammy.

"So I see. Let's not hang around to celebrate. I imagine there are a lot of upset Ethiopians around that might not be so glad we made it."

"Aren't you supposed to let somebody know the missiles are destroyed?" asked Sammy.

"Won't be necessary. The bombers are close enough to see the mushroom," said Jake.

The two SEAL's swam toward their rendezvous point happy to be alive but not understanding how it was possible. They had no way of knowing that Colonel Solsteniski's second in command had organized a team with flashlights to examine the SS-20 missiles. They found the C-4 and successfully disarmed all but one missile. That missile exploded and produced a one-kiloton nuclear explosion. The resultant destruction wasn't anything near what the Pentagon had planned, but it was enough to vaporize the former American Consulate and all of the SS-20 missiles.

TWO B-2 BOMBERS were preparing to release their bombs when the specially designed visors on their helmets went black. They were designed to do this to protect their aircrew's eyes from the flash of a nuclear explosion. The visors opened to reveal a mushroom cloud rising from their target area. The lead pilot ordered his flight to return to base and made an authenticated voice call scrubbing the mission of the other flight of bombers.

IN WASHINGTON, DC, cheers erupted in the NMCC and the White House Situation Room. Secretary of State Margaret Clark exhaled loudly and exchanged high fives with the Secretary of Defense. "That was close!" she said.

"Margaret, it doesn't get any closer."

Epilogue

SARAH STOOD IN the pouring rain at Andrews Air Force Base on the outskirts of Washington, DC, waiting for someone to open the passenger door to the C-141 that had just landed. After a brief stay at the Army hospital in Germany to checkout her injuries, she'd been released and flown back to the states to resume her duties at Balboa Naval Hospital in San Diego. The day after she arrived in San Diego she received word from Commander Lewis letting her know that Jake's mission was over and that he'd be flying straight to Washington. Another President wanted to meet the man she loved.

Months earlier she'd wondered if she could spend the rest of her life with a man who killed people for a living. She'd wondered if he'd be able to turn off the violence when they were together, or if he'd make a good father. Could she handle letting him go on missions not knowing if he'd return? She'd asked herself numerous times how he could expect her to live under those conditions.

THE PAST FEW weeks had answered all of her questions. She realized she'd lived a sheltered life — naïve was closer to the truth. After witnessing the massacre in Bahrain and surviving the ordeal in Kuwait she understood that what Jake did needed to be done and that Jake was good at it. No, he was the best! She owed her life to him. She was beginning to realize that Jake made a difference. Without people like him too many others would suffer and die at the hands of cruel — no, evil, men.

Living each moment not knowing if it would be her last helped her understand why she wanted to live. Sarah spent a lot of time in Kuwait thinking about what was important to her. Being a nurse brought her a lot of personal satisfaction – helping the helpless and all that, but her thoughts kept going back to Jake. She wanted to live to be with him – to have a family – to be his wife. Nothing else really mattered.

JAKE STEPPED OFF the plane fully rested and dressed in a crisp set of desert cammies. He'd slept through the night without the nightmare for the first time in months. He felt more alive than he had since before his first trip to Ethiopia. The old confidence was back and he'd lost the nagging sense of foreboding that had plagued him for months.

Somewhere over the Atlantic it dawned upon him that what he did made a difference. The sacrifices he made kept people like Sarah alive, and that meant something. Preventing a nuclear war had to go in the good column, too. Yes, sometimes things didn't turn out the way he hoped and good men died in losing causes. But in the grander scheme of things, the world was a safer place because of people like him.

As he stepped onto the tarmac he heard a familiar voice screaming his name above the noise of the busy runway. He turned and saw Sarah running for him. Dropping his overnight bag in a puddle in the nick of time, he caught her as she threw herself around him and gave him a crushing hug. She wasn't acting very dignified, but he didn't mind. To his way of thinking worse things could happen to a man than having a beautiful woman stuck to you like a rag in a windstorm.

"WELCOME HOME, SAILOR!" said Sarah as she planted a long pent-up kiss on him.

They were both soaked to the skin before either said another word, content to simply hold each other in silence. They didn't need to talk. What they felt in their hearts passed freely between them, unhindered by the blowing rain or the good-natured comments from the Rangers filing past them.

Sarah finally let go and put both hands on Jake's broad shoulders. "Yes, Jake!"

Jake looked at her puzzled, and said, "Huh?" Great, he thought, the first thing I say to the woman I love is "Huh."

Sarah didn't mind at all. She flashed him a killer smile and said, "A long time ago you asked me to marry you. I've had a lot of time to think recently, and I can't imagine spending another day without you in my life. If you still want me, yes, I'll marry you."

Jake was thunderstruck. Somehow, he thought that after what Sarah had been through she'd want to be as far away from people like him as possible. He'd been nothing but trouble for her. She wouldn't have been taken captive if she hadn't come to see him. She wouldn't have suffered at the hands of the Russian colonel, wouldn't have seen the slaughter in Bahrain, and wouldn't have the burden of knowing that so many Americans had been killed rescuing her. She had to live with that on her conscience for the rest of her life, and that really grieved him.

"Sarah, I love you more than life itself. I'm sorry for all that I've put you through. I don't understand why you love me but, if you'll have me, there's nothing in the world I want more than to marry you."

"Let's get in out of the rain," said Sarah.

Suddenly, it occurred to Jake that he was forgetting something, "Wait, I don't have the ring! I left it with my stuff in San Diego!"

"The ring can wait. I've got what I want," Sarah said, wrapping her arm around his waist as they walked to the waiting rental car.

Things were not going as well for Alexi Yanochev. Shortly after General Tomavich's crushing defeat at the hands of the Saudi's the acting Army Chief of Staff, General Vladimir Tribuk, sent a cryptic message to the general in charge of the Russian garrison in Moscow. Twenty-four hours later tanks had the Kremlin surrounded. Careful not to repeat the mistakes of the early nineties, General Tribuk confiscated the camera equipment from the international television and news correspondents as they arrived to document the event. He wanted what he was about to do to be carried out as quietly as possible and far from the prying eyes of the rest of the world.

General Tribuk sent a simple message to those holed up in the former seat of the mighty Soviet Empire, "Deliver the body of Alexi Yanochev within twenty-four hours or I will seize the building and kill everyone inside." He realized he was being a bit melodramatic, but those protecting Yanochev would believe him, of that he was sure. The history of the Motherland provided ample testimony to convince any skeptics.

His press release was already prepared. It read simply, "The free democratic people of Russia have prevailed and restored President Boris Chelstenov to his rightful position as President." General Tribuk was content to let President Chelstenov handle the foreign press once he arrived back in the country. That was a mater for the politicians. Let them lie to the world.

A YATOLLAH RAFALGEMII AND Minister of Interior Ayatollah Dekmejian met privately with the Iranian Revolutionary Guard Commanding General. The Grand Ayatollah leaned forward in his chair and directed his gaze at the nervous general. The way the invasion was going, he wasn't sure if the Ayatollah was going to have him executed or give him new orders from the Revolutionary Council.

"General, things have not been going well in the Kingdom," he said, referring to Saudi Arabia. "Do you think there is any possibility that we can prevail? Please, be candid."

"V ERY WELL, I will tell you what you already know, and if I die, I die. The Russians have been defeated. They have lost control of the skies over Saudi Arabia and King Abdullah has decimated their armor. Unfortunately, we lost many of our own fighters and bombers in the failed attack on the King. We have also lost over thirty thousand soldiers that were supporting the Russian armored units," said the general.

"Ali Bakr, I am concerned with the growing American presence south of the Straits of Hormuz. They have more than enough firepower to inflict great destruction upon our people and possibly destroy most of our military infrastructure," said Ayatollah Dekmejian.

"General, do you think we have sufficient force to resist the Americans without the aide of the Russians?" asked Ayatollah Rafalgemii.

"Our forces on the Tumb Islands would be destroyed quickly by their carrier based aircraft as well as most of our *Silkworm* missile installations. Perhaps our three *Kilo* submarines could destroy one carrier, but they would still have overwhelming firepower. They could fly bombers from Diego Garcia.

"It would not take them long to establish a foothold in the U.A.E.

or Oman from which to launch sustained airstrikes against our country. I estimate that they could destroy our ability to conduct offensive operations within two weeks. Without the control of the skies we were promised by the Russians, we have very little chance of victory," said the general.

"How would you suggest that we extract ourselves from this untenable position?" said Ayatollah Rafalgemii.

"I recommend that we stand down our *Silkworm* missile sites and evacuate the Tumb Islands. Have our *Kilo* submarines return to port. The Americans will understand the meaning of those moves. That should be sufficient until you can diffuse the situation through diplomatic channels," said the general.

"Thank you, General. You have provided the Revolutionary Council with much needed insight. You have permission to do as you have suggested. Also, order our ground troops to come home. Let's save our brave warriors for the next opportunity to strike at the heart of our enemies!"

Greenbrier County, West Virginia

TERRY O'BRIAN WAS released from custody at noon the day following his televised statement. He fought his way through the cameras and microphones and hailed a cab and had it drop him at Chuck Yeager Regional Airport. He chartered an airplane and flew home.

The next day an army of reporters descended upon his hillside home. He was about to call the county sheriff and have them thrown off his property when he saw the sheriff's cruiser pull into his driveway.

"Hey, Terry. Good to see ya got things straightened out. I never believed what they said about you," the sheriff said.

"Thanks, John. What brings you out this way?" asked Terry.

"Well, this here fella wanted to talk to ya. He's from Washington, DC. Figured you might want to speak to him," the sheriff said. "He's got something for you from the President."

The man who'd accompanied the sheriff onto Terry's porch smiled and extended his hand. "Hello, Mr. O'Brian. My name is Martin Bateman. I'm with the President's press office. Sir, the President of the United States requests the honor of your presence to apologize for your unfair treatment at the hands of the United States government. President Massey hopes you will accept his invitation to conduct a joint news conference in the Rose Garden."

"Thanks. Tell him I'll come." Terry closed the door in their face and sat in his favorite recliner. It had been a long week.